Castelle

The Tumultuous Life of James 'Ned' Kelly

Kerri Reeks

Castelle: The Tumultuous Life of James 'Ned' Kelly
© Kerri Reeks 2025

ISBN: 9781923289857 (Paperback)

Cover Design: Clark & Mackay
Format and Typeset: Clark & Mackay
Published by Kerri Reeks and Clark & Mackay

Proudly printed by Clark & Mackay

Disclaimer

CASTELLE IS A WORK of complete fiction. The storyline and characters are entirely invented, drawn from a mix of sources including accounts from people I have met in my travels, the imaginations of contributors (including my own), and publicly available material.

Every effort has been made to avoid offending or marginalising individuals or groups, or to include language or innuendo intended to affront. That said, the characters tend to speak and act for themselves — and at times, they express views or behaviours that may reflect social intolerance, racism, insensitivity, or political incorrectness. These portrayals are not endorsed by the author but are presented in the interest of character realism and narrative authenticity.

All names, characters, places, and incidents are fictitious. Any resemblance to real persons, living or deceased, or actual events or locations is purely coincidental.

While certain real-world institutions, agencies, and public offices are mentioned, the individuals depicted in relation to them are entirely fictional. The views and opinions expressed are those of the characters and do not reflect those of the author.

Acknowledgements

WRITING CASTELLE HAS BEEN a true adventure — one shaped by countless hours of research, collaboration with my domestic and international colleagues, and sheer perseverance. This journey would not have been possible without the support, inspiration, and guidance of many contributors, to whom I offer my sincere thanks.

While the storyline is a work of complete fiction — dramatized and at times fuelled by an overactive imagination — it is interwoven with strands of verifiable fact. The plot and characters are entirely invented, but the sequence of events draws from a broad array of sources, including my own travels, libraries, news articles, Google/social media and other publicly available materials.

Castelle continues the journey of James 'Ned' Kelly, first introduced in my earlier book *Cage of War*, a story inspired by the Vietnam War. Over the years, I've had the privilege of meeting and working with a wide variety of individuals across the globe. Many of their stories — some shared, others experienced firsthand — have influenced and helped shape the fictional world of *Castelle*.

To those who again offered their life experiences, wisdom, and invaluable feedback during the creation of this book, I extend my gratitude. Your contributions have helped sculpt the narrative into its final form. I am also profoundly thankful to all who offered encouragement, insight, or even a well-timed nudge, your support has kept me going.

Special thanks go to those who helped with research, story development, factual review, and the final editing process—you know who you are. A heartfelt nod to my gorgeous one, Angela, for her unwavering support, as well as Karen, Michael, and the fabulous team at Clark and Mackay, whose editorial guidance kept me on course.

Lastly, to you — the reader — thank you for stepping into the world of *Castelle*. I hope this story resonates with you in meaningful and lasting ways.

Chapter 1

NOUADHIBOU, NORTH WEST MAURITANIA, West Africa – I'm currently managing and evaluating the installation and trial of a quite complex, sophisticated Italian designed over-the-horizon Surface Wave Radar (or SWR) system. Our focus is mostly along uninhabited areas just off the coast of the countries of Western Sahara (Westra for short) and Mauritania, both countries in West Africa. The purpose of our attention – to identify and monitor the current invasion of international illegal fisheries, raping and pillaging the natural fishery resources of both countries. I have a gut feeling that there are other agendas at play. However, our team has kept these thoughts to ourselves, at least for the time being. We've just completed a month of initial trials, with all of the installation crews having now departed back to Australia.

I've just about concluded the final departure preparations before also exiting from our company warehouse. As I stroll back into my office from loading my truck, our local secretary Halima calls out to tell me she's transferring a call from our Operations Manager Ben Johnson. Odd. I look at my watch, 11 a.m. Friday. I'm a bit taken aback to be hearing from him actually. Ben drove off earlier in the morning with the Westra Environment Minister in his official vehicle entourage. Driving to Laayoune, the capital of Western Sahara, the country further to the North of Nouadhibou.

To be frank, it had all been a bit peculiar. Nah… a whole lot of it, really. Ben and I had earlier planned to drive to Laayoune together to finalise some other business. However, the Environment Minister, Mahmood Ould Sayed, who's working with us, or who's actually just watching us work, seemed to have a bee up himself in an absolute rush to depart – early. He practically demanded Ben accompany him to discuss future work scopes. It had almost seemed like a rather bizarre friendly kidnapping of sorts. I thought so, anyway. I know, it's a bit of a stretch with the kidnapping thoughts, except it'd just been so out of the ordinary, it actually did feel like it.

We'd suffered our fair share of equally unusual events since we'd been working in West Africa. These occurrences were mostly during operations in Westra, although we'd been subjected to similar interruptions in Mauritania as well. All minor, nothing dramatic, certainly nothing to set us off track or to overly alarm us. Basic things, like missing, damaged or stolen equipment, abnormal intense radio interference with the radar, frequent phone calls with the callers screaming indecipherably and then hanging up, local contractors and equipment not turning up when required or not at all. Those sorts of things, except a suspiciously high amount of them. So, due to those 'unusual' issues regularly occurring, we put some minor precautions in place. I pick up the phone to take Ben's call with some trepidation, with these thoughts pulsing around in the back of my mind as I answer the phone.

"Hey, how're you going, young fella? Trust all is well?" Ben asks jovially, quickly, which in itself is a dead giveaway for the grumpy old Australian-Canadian. He's never happy. Bells jingle, nerves rattle a bit and a few chains clang away in my brain, just a tad. He'd claimed the urgent necessity to use a latrine during their trip, so they stopped at a wayside shanty store, a 'hanout', a remote desert makeshift shop, to use their basic squat version. Strange – as he simply hated this variety of commode at the best of times. He'd apparently also paid the owner of the 'hanout' a small fortune to borrow the guy's mobile phone to call me to talk about a couple of things. This bothers me more so, as he has his own mobile and satellite phone, he can easily have called me with.

He speaks rapidly. "Glad I got you before you left. Hey, listen, I've been thinking about the electronic bistatic radar blind zone we talked about earlier. I think we'll have to rejig the modelling on it urgently, maybe relocate the focus on it as soon as possible. Can you look into it for me? We can discuss it further when we catch up in Laayoune. Gotta go, bud. I'll leave you with that to work on. Hey, say g'day to your brother for me when you see him next. Don't forget to be safe, old mate. Try to be just a little bit kind to yourself OK, see ya."

He'd spoken so fast that I didn't get a word in before he abruptly hung up. Although it's not like I'd wanted to get any in really. I'd already heard all I needed, or didn't want to hear, to tip me well and truly over the edge.

My senses are intensely jarred. In immediate high alert, I'm trying to coexist in my mind now with an elevated degree of stress and uneasiness, way more so than before I took the call. Portions of his message are undoubtedly part of the precautions we'd put in place beforehand. It's part of a prearranged code we'd developed to forewarn each other after the earlier questionable occurrences had distracted our attention. Except this specific 'blind zone' code is at the very top of the threat range, meaning 'relocate, get out urgently, as soon as possible, be blind... to others'. We hadn't been discussing the blind zone, ever. I'd have no idea what it is if I fell over it, as it's not our radar. We're only the gatekeeper contractors supervising the installation and monitoring the process and risks associated to the early trial phases. We know nothing behind the science of the radar.

What's far more concerning for me is though... I don't have a brother!

The reference to 'be safe and be kind to yourself' is a direct indication to ensure that whatever I plan to do, I do it myself. Don't get others to do it for me or to help me. It also hinted at securing whatever data I can get my hands on. The other 'tell' in his message is that he's glad to have 'got me before I left'. Rightly or wrongly, I take it to maybe mean 'do not enter Westra'. Something significant has happened for him to raise this level of concern with me.

I'm now in an extreme impasse. My rented 4WD truck is fuelled, nearly packed, ready to depart for Laayoune with my Westra government-supplied driver cum security guard. This is the same 4WD I'd been planning to travel to Laayoune with Ben earlier on. So, I have to quickly kick around what my options might be. Do I maybe drive to the Mauritanian capital Nouakchott myself instead, which is about 7 hours' drive on a good day, about 500 klicks, no big deal? Or do I maybe fly out of Nouadhibou to anywhere the next flight will take me to? I'd like to think I'm relatively safe in the context of harm here at the moment because I'm still in Mauritania. However, going by Ben's call, the minute I go over the border into Westra, it might all possibly change in the blink of an eye, as it seems to have for him.

As I regard the grey, turbulent Nouadhibou sea and small whitecaps in the Baie du Lévrier out of my office window, it begins to rain. This in itself is highly unusual, as it's a rare occurrence, although a very welcome one in this region. Gazing at the rain rivulets trickling down my window, I'm also reminded that Nouadhibou is home to the largest ship graveyard in the world. Has been for decades. Likely many more to come. This is no overstatement. Achieved wholly and solely on outrageous levels of graft and corruption of the local community, businessmen and politicians, apparently. Nonetheless, it's seemingly working well for some involved, as I'd seen literally hundreds of rusted and rotted vessels of all sizes and in various forms of decay or unseaworthiness – sinking, sunk or just rotting away – out in the bay.

As my concerns gather pace, I make a decision. Just as a precaution I suppose, I ring a local travel agent I know, S'mara Travex, at the airport. I managed to secure the only flight out still available today to Nouakchott later in the afternoon. The flight is at 2.30 pm, 3 hours away, if I still require it then. I next call our regular place where we stay in Nouakchott, Hotel Tfeïla, also just in case I need it later. Nouakchott isn't really where I want to be; although, considering my current circumstances, it's possibly safer than where I am. I'd have preferred France or somewhere in Spain or perhaps Tunisia. Anyway, its way less dangerous than going into Westra, it seems.

Time to now figure out a way to stall the not-so-subtle pressure building from my driver, Samir, to depart for Laayoune as soon as possible. Primarily so we can arrive before dark. He's a scary and careless driver in the daylight. I'd planned to not drive with him at night unless absolutely necessary. I call him on the handheld radio to explain there is some unexpected research that is essential to be completed for Ben and the minister, and it'd take me an hour or so to complete, I suggest. Then we'd drop the research package off at the airport on the way out to Laayoune. He doesn't sound pleased about the change in plans. In fact, he displays a somewhat belligerent attitude to the change. I have to shut him down quickly before he has a chance to build any momentum with it.

"Samir, your job is not to challenge my decisions or those of Ben or the minister. On the contrary, it is to safely drive me when or where as required. I'd be grateful for your support in remembering this, inshallah." I say this quietly, no anger in my tone as I release the transmit button. The intent of my message is crystal clear to comprehend, or so I'd like to think, anyway.

Samir reluctantly acknowledges, clicking off the radio abruptly. Pissed off is my guess. I want to call my wife Carla back home in Australia. However, I feel my anxiety might easily come across over the phone. I'll do it later when I know where I'm going. My thoughts are bouncing all over the place as I gather the last of the high-level confidential files from the filing cabinets not packed earlier. The next task, thanks to Ben's encouragement, is to remove the hard drives from the company computers. I have no real idea how to achieve this. Nevertheless I'm pretty resourceful sometimes, if nothing else.

Samir calls me back on the radio almost straight away. "Mister James sir, I no speak to Mr Oumar in minister's car, on radio or satellite phone. I very gravely concerned," pronouncing both James and concerned as 'Jam–es' and 'concern–ed', a quirk of language I find uniquely charismatic to the desert people.

"OK, I'll get back to you in a minute," I say as I click off. As for the no contact with Mr Oumar, Samir is not half as bloody concerned as I am, that's for sure. Christ. I try to contact Ben myself on his own satellite phone. It doesn't ring at all, let alone ring out. Something technically ominous has happened to his phone. Back to the hard drives, getting them out of the computers is a little more difficult than I'd anticipated or hoped for, barely completing it in time before Samir knocks on my door, calling out my name urgently. I finish putting the back onto the last computer then call him in.

"No car, Mr Jam–es," he says, visibly alarmed. I'm not entirely sure what he means. However, I share his alarm all the same.

"Our car, do you mean?" I ask earnestly.

"No." Samir replies simply, staring at me blankly.

No what? I urge with my look and expression. "What do you mean, Samir? Whose car are you talking about?" It hits me just as I finish the question about which car. "Do you mean Mr Ben and the minister's car?"

"Yes," Samir replies again simply, still staring at me with his blank look, sort of lost for what to say next.

"What do you mean, Samir? Please explain." I ask, a little impatiently now, frustrated at the single word answers that told me nothing really, except to keep asking more bloody questions.

"I have contact in Dakhla. He check–ed. Cannot find. Cannot call. Both car missing." Samir is clearly agitated. I don't really know why he is, but I'm way past becoming the same.

"So Samir, your contact, he has checked where? Why has he checked? How does he know the minister's car is missing? Is the escort car also missing?" This is all getting too bizarre for me, way too slow. "Please Samir, explain, *sarie*." Quickly, I demand, in Arabic, a hint of irritation added.

"We have *himayatan*… check-a-point in Dakhla, to quiet check-ed minister car movement, and escort, for safety. I call my friend to check—ed. He say no car to Dakhla. Cannot call both car. Now looking Dakhla to Nouadhibou. Is bad, Mr Jam—es. Is very bad, *sayi jiddaan*", he emphasises with his arms outstretched.

I can smell the sweat and tension oozing out of his skin, combined with his normal everyday rank body odour. Maybe just a little bit of fear now added to the mix as well. Not a good combination for my nostrils, regardless. *Himayatan…* I think this means protection or safety or something along those lines in Arabic. I figure *sayi jiddaan* to mean very, very bloody bad. What the hell is going on here? Why did Samir have a 'quiet' safety checkpoint in Dakhla? Did someone have the minister under surveillance? Why, I wonder? Was he being threatened? Is he a threat? Why'd he almost demand Ben travel with him? Is Ben maybe the surveillance target… Nah, surely not. I suggest to Samir he go back to his radio and keep trying to make contact with his colleagues, local police or any medical facilities en route. Meanwhile, I'll contact my people to see what we can put together. He gruffly agrees, then leaves, literally dragging his arse out the door.

Time to share my concerns with Sergio Perez, or Serge. He's the Managing Director from Marinetti Electronics in Melbourne, Australia, who owns the radar. It's now 11.30 a.m. Nouadhibou time, so about 9.30 p.m.-ish in Melbourne, unfortunately, though, on a Friday night. Probably going to be hard to find. I call his mobile first. Not surprisingly, there is no answer. He hates them and hardly ever answers at the best of times. I leave a message. Then, as an off chance, I try his office number, which remarkably does answer.

'Serge.' Is the usual one-word gruff response.

"James here, Serge. Glad I got hold of you. I thought you might be out on the town, mate?" I comment cheerfully, trying to tone down my anxiety.

"Good to hear from you, Ned. No partying tonight. I'm packing up my gear to come over and see you guys in Laayoune in a day or so. What's up?" He queries nonchalantly, a smile in his voice.

I'm stunned to hear he's coming to see us in Laayoune. I knew nothing about this. "When was this arranged, Serge? I'd no idea you're coming over?" I attempt to sound as indifferent as possible, not wanting to alarm him… yet. Or myself any further. I think my effort works, although a mild intensity of dread is leisurely creeping around my thoughts, advancing down into the pit of my stomach.

"Yeah, Ben called earlier today. He was with the Moroccan Environment Minister, what's his name again?" he queries impatiently.

"Mahmood Ould Sayed. I think he's Western Saharan, not Moroccan."

"OK, thanks. I have a hell of a time remembering those double-barrel Arab names. Anyway, Ben said the minister wants to urgently discuss an extension to our contract. Except, he wants me in-country with him to kick around the finer details with the minister. Didn't he tell you about it? I thought you guys are together?" Low-level alarm now crawling into his voice.

"No, no, he hadn't said anything to me about you coming over. He left earlier this morning with Ould Sayed and his entourage. We'd intended to leave a bit later together, except the minister was keen for Ben to go with him this morning. Anyway, Serge, listen up, mate, I've just had the strangest call from Ben not so long ago."

As I watch the increasingly rough seas battering the foreshore, along with the now harsh rain pounding at my office window and an accompanying angry wind howling its lungs out, I describe to Serge the odd call I'd shared with Ben. It felt almost like an out-of-body occurrence for me, as eerie as the call itself.

"Really? You sure? This is what he said?" Serge almost challenges my recollection, a bit taken aback, no longer a smile in his voice. Any smile in my voice has been missing for quite a while.

"Awkwardly, it's not where it all ends, though, Serge. Now Ben and Ould Sayed seem to be missing, as well as their escort." I relay the recent discussions with Samir, their failure to arrive in Dakhla and the inability to communicate with them on any of the numerous communication devices they have with them. What follows is hollow silence for a minor eternity. Yeah, yeah, I know… an improbably contradictory term. It's how it felt to me, anyway.

"*Fanculo*… sorry, that's an 'oh dear' to you. What in the name of Jesus Christ is going on?" he says almost angrily. Not at me, I don't think. Definitely no smile in the voice, though. "Why was Ben in the car with the minister, again? I thought it was planned for you two to go together in the rental truck?"

"Yeah, like I said, it had been the plan. Except after those unusual radar trials we ran yesterday into last night, for some reason, the minister got all hyped up this morning. He almost demanded to leave early and for Ben to accompany him. We both thought it a bit curious. He is the client, after all, I suppose, so we didn't think to challenge him on it. Maybe we should have?" I say, almost absently.

"What unusual trials were run yesterday or into last night, Ned? I wasn't aware of any additional runs being conducted… or considered. Who authorised them, do you know?" Serge queries, intense irritation building now, no silkiness in the voice, lots of exasperation seeping in.

"I don't know. I'd been busy packing up the other test equipment, then the minister came in saying he has a request from his Ministry… or a Ministry, or someone. Anyway, it was for some additional tests before he left to go to Laayoune. Something about the perfect sea surface along with high-quality atmospheric conditions. They apparently wanted to test the over-the-horizon capabilities, beyond the current 200 kilometres for all the previous tests, within the Westra Exclusive Economic Zone (or EEZ). That's all I heard; I went back to the packing room afterwards." It all sounds very iffy to me now, in the saying of it, after what appears to be happening with Ben and the minister.

"What the hell… What? Our contract, though… Jesus, Ned, our bloody contract prohibits us from testing beyond the 200k's of the EEZ. Who the hell sanctioned this? Do you know? Any idea?" I hear all this being uttered in an increasingly loud, irate Italian voice. No patience in it, no subtleness, all ugly invective.

I have to think fast. My guess is this is now turning into a borderline diplomatic issue, well above my pay, interest or enthusiasm grade. "Bloody hell, Serge, think about it. Who within the Environment Ministry – or whatever other ministry – could possibly have the level of clout necessary to actually order a minister of his own government department to conduct such an activity? Especially one that infringes on the covenants of the test contract between Marinetti as well as both the Mauritanian and Western Saharan governments?" I query bluntly. "Seriously, who the hell?"

"Good point. I predict it's not someone in either of the governments, that's for sure, if in fact it is the case. It'd be too difficult to hide such a decision, as all parties get to review each run of data and associated documents, including approvals. Unless, by some means, the data from those runs doesn't actually get to the primary file room. Do you know what the results of those runs are from yesterday or last night, Ned? Have they been sent off?"

"No, I haven't seen them. Ben's looking after all those elements. I wouldn't know what those results represented if I fell over them. Apart from that, we don't have access to the detailed data, anyway. As you know, we don't have the software here to interpret the data coming back in, anyway. We see it live, but then it gets analysed by you guys back in Oz, right? Or is it all done in Laayoune?" I query, a bit shocked by the many complications or fragments of information unfolding at the moment, along with how much I don't know.

I add. "The data from last night should have already been routinely auto-transmitted to the data point backup receiver in your Melbourne File Room, via satellite this morning, mate… wouldn't it?" I query, no longer sure what, if anything, is going according to plan.

"I know the minister left with a backup file of the data this morning, so I know it's been in our file storage here at least," I utter absently. "You know, though, Ben mentioned something to the minister last night. I took it as just a throwaway line. Something about an unusual sort of electrostatic interference they'd experienced during the test, something along those lines. I wasn't paying much attention at the time, to be honest. Does this make any technical sense to you?"

"Not really. He might be referring to some sort of atmospheric interference. It can be common at times, although it doesn't really have any technical impact, or it shouldn't. Did you have any lightning around last night, maybe? Anyway, I'm not aware of receiving anything yesterday or this morning. I always get an electronic heads-up when the system is activated or deactivated so that I can go interrogate the data interpretations. We've received nothing since yesterday morning during the last sea surface condition run."

Serge is silent for a moment. I'm guessing he's running the potential impediments associated with the unauthorised runs around in his head.

"Some really disturbing events going on here, Ned. In all honesty, I'm not entirely sure what our next step should be, or can be, at this early stage. Do we contact our nearest consulate about Ben being missing? If we do, then what the hell do we say? We can't really confirm those guys are missing yet, as they may have been in an accident or their communications are in a black spot or whatever. It's too early in this situation to ramp everybody else up either, don't you think? What are your thoughts? FUCK!" Serge bellows at the end of the phone. I pull it quickly away from resonating in my ear.

"Yeah, I know, I know, what to do now is a bit problematic," I reply, voicing my thoughts out loud. "As you know, we have a Crisis Plan in place here Serge, only none of the current scenarios we're facing today match our threat matrix in the Plan. Except to do something, anything, just to keep us moving forward. So, do I now stay in Nouadhibou until I can contact Ben, or at least until I can find out where he is? Or do I still leave, but for somewhere else, like right now, to flee any potential escalation of this current situation? Particularly if it's maybe aimed at me next?" I urge impatiently, looking at the office door as I speak, half expecting someone to come charging in to arrest me as we talk, God only knows for what bizarre reason. Smarten up, Kelly. Bury the paranoia.

"Whoa, wait a minute there, how did the minister get his backup file? Where was this data coming from, Ned?" Serge queries, interrupting my thoughts and input.

"From here, from off our spatial data server. It holds all of the data as it comes in from the tests. It just doesn't give us the full interpretive report. He downloaded the info he wanted onto a hard drive, or something looking like one. Why?" I'm now becoming very concerned, in particular with the unauthorised tests and no backup arriving in Australia as required. Then we have Ben, along with the minister, now potentially missing, the list just goes on. WTF. Settle yourself now, Kelly.

"Can you do a download as well on an external drive and then send it to me directly via the satellite feed? I'll be able to interrogate the data to hopefully determine what occurred during those unofficial runs yesterday." Serge asks this so fast that I almost miss what it is he wants me to do. Then it sinks in… sort of. I'm now thinking something about those rogue runs yesterday is the catalyst behind whatever seems to be going on with Ben.

"Well, I probably could have; except I've taken the hard drives out of both computers now, on Ben's suggestion. I gotta tell ya, though, I really had no bloody idea what I was doing when trying to get them out, so I'm unlikely to know how to put them back in. Happy to give it a whirl if you can guide me? I'm not good with things technical like this. I'm a fast learner, though, probably just not as fast as might help right now," I say. "Hang on, are you suggesting something about those unofficial runs yesterday is the cause of our current worries?" I challenge, impatiently.

"No… yes… Jeez, I don't know, mate, maybe. I'm buggered if I know what I'm thinking at the moment, to be honest. This whole situation seems to have become a bit cross-threaded ever since those unofficial runs yesterday. So I'm thinking they've discovered something outside of the EEZ they shouldn't have. Now everybody's ducking for cover. Or maybe nothing is happening and we've got hold of the wrong end of a very shitty stick on this. My gut is telling me to tread with extreme caution here all the same," Serge says, voice filled with concern.

"Let me check with Samir to see if he's heard anything back or if he's been able to contact the guys. Hang on the line, Serge, I'll be back in a minute," I say as I call Samir up on the handheld radio. On the second attempt, I become a bit anxious. By my third attempt with no answer, I've rapidly moved past the concerned phase. I'm well and truly into 'WTF' stage now.

"Another potential issue, Serge. I can't get hold of my driver Samir on the radio. Whole thing is starting to get just a little bit too weird for my liking, mate. I want you to stay on the line while I go out to the warehouse to see if I can find him," I suggest, hearing the tempo of the rain increasing as I say it, looking at the dark overcast sky and lightning outside my office window.

"Yeah, I figured as much. I heard the anxiety in your voice while you called him. I'll stay on the line. I'll also try to contact my government liaison in Laayoune with the Westra Environment Ministry guys. Hey Ned,… if we lose contact with each other or you feel you're under any sort of threat, revert to PQE right away, got it? Plan Quebec Echo. And no screwing around, got it?" Serge says with a raised voice, almost yelling it at me.

"Yeah, yeah, got it, got it. Be back in a jiffy," I reply, not as confidently as I'd like to sound. PQE, Plan Quick Exit. In other words, get the hell outta dodge urgently. Go directly to the Oasean Hotel in Cansado, one of the oldest hotels in Nouadhibou, one where we have many friends. Do not pass go. Do not collect $200. Screw this up, and you go straight to jail… or hell.

I contemplate the undesirable, although potential necessity for PQE as I walk out of the office foyer into the darkened back area of the warehouse onto the workshop floor, calling out for Samir as I slowly enter. Not at all sure what I might find, although I'm not expecting to have no reply at all. I stand in the darker back shadow of the powerful workshop floodlights, looking around, listening, letting my eyes adjust, only hearing the rain pelt down heavily. I then notice Samir standing out in the semi-daylight, next to our 4WD under the outside awning, protected from the winds and the thunderous downpour. He's smoking a cigarette, talking to another two swarthy-looking Arab… gentlemen. One with a badly damaged face, maybe a severe war injury or car accident – that level of damage. Both wearing light-coloured djellabas and Fez headdresses, the traditional dress of some in the region. I assume Samir has not heard my radio calls, so I'm about to walk over to him to ask how he'd gotten on with contacting Ben. Something held me back, though. Some intense gut impulse not to go out there. Maybe it's because I can see the radio sitting on the bonnet of the 4WD, right next to Samir, next to his AK-47.

I decide to call him again on the radio while I'm still hidden by the dark back shadow of the floodlights. I hear the faint, scratchy, hollow call reaching out to Samir from the radio on the bonnet. He initially ignored it. On my second call, he and his colleagues look over at the radio, almost in annoyance at its intrusion. Only he makes no move to answer it. Now this bothers me in so many ways, except not as much as the next move from Samir's busted-up buddy. He pulls a short-barrelled machine pistol out from under his djellaba, points it at the radio, then makes theatrical actions to imply he'd shot the radio. Laughing, he dramatically pulls the barrel up to his mouth to blow away the imaginary barrel fumes. *Bloody Christ, you busted-up little prick*, I grimace silently at Samir's buddy, or maybe at Samir… probably both. I couldn't much care at this stage, because right about now, I don't know whether to spit, shit or go blind.

I quietly move back into the building proper, then run to my office as fast as my rattled mind and legs can carry me, locking the door as I close it behind me for what it's worth. I frantically grab my day backpack off the desk with my travel items, files and the two hard drives in it. Then I pick up my jacket as well as the satellite phone. I'm about ready to bolt out of the office fire door when I realise I still might have Serge on the landline phone. I hurry to the desk, pick up the handpiece and call out to Serge in alarm to see if he's still on the line.

"I'm here, Ned. What's happening?" Serge asks anxiously, clearly sensing my unease.

"No time. Urgent. PQE… NOW," I almost yell, then slam the phone down dramatically, completely missing the receiver cradle.

✦ ✦ ✦

I hurriedly leave via the fire escape door at the back of my office. Well, it isn't really a fire escape, or a real door for that matter. We'd months earlier joked around about not having a fire escape for the entire building, so back then, I'd just smashed a hole into my back wall. Then we called up a local tradesman to fill the hole with a fire door. This turned out to be a narrow, thin, wooden non-fire door, which sort of works from time to time. Today, it thankfully works. I hurry out into the downpour, howling wind and overcast sky. Slamming the door shut, I lock it, then pick up a small, rusty, bent child's push bike frame laying in the sand against the building. I ram it into the ground, then jam it against the door knob. I'm hopeful it might delay any would-be pursuers for a little while at least, if any are likely to be actually looking for me. Who the hell are those other two bloody guys, for crying out loud?

Walking as fast as my panic-stricken legs and brain could carry me over the main road in the pouring rain, I continue towards the beach foreshore area, then, I'm thinking, hopefully to the Oasean Hotel in Cansado. I break into a run. As I do so, though, a peculiar sensation occurs. My brain begins to quieten, heart rate settles somewhat, body becomes less tense and I slow to a fast walk, then to just a casual stroll, albeit still a nervous one. Self-discipline has begun to take control again, which I'm most grateful for, aiding me to commence formulating a sort of forward plan.

Walking along the side of the poor excuse for a main road in a sheet of rain, I see an opening in a small break of low acacia trees near the foreshore. Ducking into it and sliding down through it, I partially hide amongst the sand dunes. The mound boasts a pungent mélange of rotting organic matter and foul-smelling garbage that's been dumped or washed up from the nearby Port Autonome area. The rain slowly eases to a mild shower as I gingerly steal a brief glance over the rubbish pile back to the office. I can't see any activity around the place. Lights are still burning inside. The fire exit door is still closed with the metal bike frame in place.

Opening my backpack, I retrieve my old worn blue *thobe qamees*, the local traditional dress for men, kind of like a fancy kaftan robe. I store my jacket along with my satellite and mobile phones into the backpack, strap it over my chest, pull the thobe on to cover me and the pack. I wrap my faded dark blue tagelmust scarf around my head and lower face. With my sunglasses on, it will hopefully make me look more like a local, hiding my real identity. The only twist in my outfit is my Red Wing work boots. The locals customarily wear open-toe sandals, so I'll keep my thobe pulled down as low as I can to try to hide my boots.

I suddenly recoil in shock upon hearing the harsh electric crack of a single gunshot fired somewhere nearby. I steal another furtive glimpse back towards the office, through a narrow shaft of light amidst the leaves of the tree and scattered rubbish. It comes as no surprise really to see the fire escape door now busted wide open, splintered into pieces. In spite of the broken exit, I can't see any sign of Samir or his two cronies, though. It's anybody's guess who fired the shot, or why. Or where it might have ended up. My plan now, though… is to get the hell out of here. Out of this whole area as quickly as possible, without being noticed. Although as rattled as I'm feeling about the very recent occurrences and now with the shot just being fired, I force myself to slowly, cautiously, mooch along the shoreline, in the fashion of the locals, as best my nervous system can accommodate. Walking amongst the more challenging aromas and ripe fragrances of dead fish, offal, fish guts or just general garbage splashing back and forth in the oily waves. For me, there are few aromas more pleasant than the wonderful classic tangy salt smell of the ocean. I just let it wash over me, reassuring me somewhat. The signature briny scent of slightly sulphurous or maybe iodine-type aromas from the bacteria in the seaweed, plankton or sea grasses along the shoreline is a stand-alone soothing odour.

Restraining myself as best I can, I wander in an unhurried fashion, amongst the masses of small colourful fishing boats beside the many fishermen fixing nets or repairing boats in the light rain. I view with interest the profoundly weathered faces and weary eyes of these men. Heavily wrinkled, creased, sunburnt to buggery, well beyond their number of years. Looking less like lives actually lived than barely survived, battered by the harsh work environment. They aren't seeming to pay any specific attention to me or my movements, which is what I'm really trying to determine. I wave a friendly gesture to some of them, who simply ignore me as they work away. My ignorant mistake. Locals aren't used to waving greetings to each other like westerners do. *Stay on top of things, Kelly,* I warn myself yet again.

The rain seems to be gradually coming to an end now, the normal, intense humidity quickly recommencing, creeping back into the day as the sun slinks out of the pale overcast sky. It's now possible to more clearly see the countless rusted and deserted hulks of ships or old fishing boats floundering or grounded out in the bay graveyard. Hundreds of them… probably many hundreds. Ambling my way slightly faster now around the debris amongst the beach sand and seaweed, I try to maintain a sort of veiled watch over the world behind and around me. To reassure myself, I suppose. I'd not been seen by Samir or his cronies as well as not being followed by them or anybody else. I don't think I am, although confirmation is key at the moment. A wide variety of sea birds catch my attention, screeching and flapping frantically around the boats and nets, looking for fish scraps, indifferently harassing the fishermen as they quietly chat, smoking away while working, anchored boats wallowing in the periodically slow heaving sea.

My basic plan now, I guess, apart from continually checking behind me for Samir or his accomplices, is to find a taxi or maybe just a ride of any type to hopefully get to the airport for my 2.30 flight. To hell with going to the Oasean Hotel now, as it still leaves me here in Nouadhibou. Exposed to whatever the hell is – or might have been – going on back at the office.

I get disturbed by an extremely bedraggled cat lunging out from under an upturned fishing boat, scarpering away on three spindly legs through the nearest sand dune and into the nearby sea grass. I'm unsure as to who's more distressed by this happenstance, me or the mongrel cat. I hope it's OK, though, because

I'm bloody not. I just about shat a brick to go with the heart attack on the spot when it ran out. As a result of this innocuous encounter, I'm becoming more agitated about my lack of success getting to the airport on time or just getting there at all. The temperature is now becoming increasingly hotter and much more humid, adding to my frustration.

Somehow, I finally manage to hail down what is left of an old, beat-up and rusty Mercedes taxi… well, I'm being charitable. It's more of a sort of facsimile taxi which one way or other smells more pungent than the aromas along the shoreline. We drive off towards the airport. Our bloody progress though, is also a kind interpretation. It's painfully slow. The driver has to continually stop and lift his bonnet to put water in his radiator, which is leaking like a witch's tit. At one point, when he's refilling the radiator, Samir's two Arab cronies from the back of the workshop pull up at a nearby roadside shanty stall about a hundred yards away in my Westra 4WD.

They're almost opposite us, and with no Samir. I'm not at all clear about what this tells me except I'm sure as hell not happy to see these two. They harass the stall owner about something, lot of hand waving, yelling. They then move back out to the 4WD, looking up and down the road, contemplating where I'd got to, possibly. I stay hidden, down below the taxi back seat window frame, which is not hard, as there are no springs left in my seat to support me at the usual height, anyway. I pray like mad for my driver to hurry up with his latest radiator refill. The sound of the 4WD starting up then roaring off in a burst of spinning wheels and grinding gears allows me to breathe again, almost normally. The taxi driver finally gets back in the car, getting me to the airport in one piece in the end. I pay him and thank him profusely. Then I thank the spirits, Allah and any other Gods who might be listening in today, just for good measure, for getting me here, hopefully before my plane departs or the two wayward Arabs find me.

Check-in is quick, painless for a change, just in time before flight close-off. I make my way to the departure lounge or, as it turns out, the line-up to board my aircraft. Eternally grateful for my success to date, I try to stay as unruffled as possible under the circumstances in the departure line-up. Occasionally stealing a very nervous glance out the corner of my sunglasses into the general public area beyond the departure lounge. Plenty of men in uniform or local dress are hurriedly moving from place to place. Enough for a fertile or suspicious mind such as mine to easily interpret as Samir's henchmen looking for me. Except, in reality, I can't see anybody actually standing or staring at me or any others in my departure line. I exit the building to walk over the tarmac to my plane. I know I shouldn't be concerned, as they wouldn't be looking for someone dressed in old, faded traditional clothing. I'm just being paranoid, I guess, or more so than normal.

I heave a colossal sigh of relief as I collapse down into my seat, waiting impatiently for all of the pre-flight theatrics to be completed, almost crying with relief when the plane finally leaves the runway for the hour or so flight to Nouakchott. Relaxing deep into my narrow uncomfortable seat, an incredible wave of exhaustion or anxiety washes over me, encouraging me to fall almost instantly into a restless, exhaustive power nap. I find myself wondering how in the hell am I so blessed and fortunate enough to constantly end up in these never-ending challenging situations.

I sleep fitfully, waking, sleeping, waking again. I revisit why I'm working in West Africa in the first place. The nation of Western Sahara itself is a disputed territory on the NW coast in the Maghreb region of North and West Africa. My interpretation, as limited as it has been explained to me, in effect, it's Africa's last colony. Around 20% of the territory is controlled by the self-proclaimed Sahrawi Arab Democratic Republic or SADR ostensibly, while the remaining is occupied and administered by neighbouring Morocco. All kind of confusing for anyone not involved. Nevertheless, it seems to sort of work one way or another, I'm told. Morocco seized control of most of Westra way back in 1976, I understand, following the departure of the former colonial power of Spain. It now refers to the territory it controls as its 'southern provinces'.

We, as in Castelle, are currently consulting with an Australian electrical engineering contractor titled Marinetti Electronics from Melbourne, the home of Serge. We're commissioned to oversee and monitor the contract for the installation of the SWR system. As for the system, well... it's fundamentally a non-line-of-sight radar, extremely high-quality electronic surveillance tool. Its sole technical purpose in the universe is to methodically survey the maritime and aerial coastline using electronic wave pulse processes. The industrial rationale of the SWR is to detect and identify illegal fishing vessels trespassing into sovereign waters, located beyond the visible horizon. This is unlike conventional radars, which are limited to only line-of-sight detection. SWR provides a unique capability for over-the-horizon detection of surface and sometimes air assets as well as measurement of sea surface conditions. Its extended range coverage makes it ideal for the management of the Westra and Mauritanian EEZ fisheries, which are being illegally plundered. Horrendously so, by multiple nations.

In particular, for the protection of those local fishing assets, it's a reliable early warning system against potentially illegal vessel entries or for monitoring ship and fishing boat traffic through the joint EEZ's. It's all about trying to detect and where possible intercept other national sovereignty interests wanting to steal the vast local fisheries. It appears they not only want to steal the local resources; on the contrary, they are actually overfishing them almost to extinction. Overfishing as a general characterisation we're told, is the removal of a species of native fish from a sovereign fish habitat at a rate greater than what the species could ever possibly replenish naturally. Resulting in the species becoming increasingly underpopulated, depleted or sometimes even non-existent in the area.

I've been led to believe that the excessive fishing results in what they call resource depletion, reduced biological growth rates and low biomass levels, all too technical for me, though no doubt devastating to the local communities. Sustained overfishing can lead to critical depensation. This apparently means that the fish population is no longer able to sustain itself, leading to the upset of an entire marine ecosystem, along with the long-term loss of a stable food source for the local communities and the loss of income for the various government agencies that administer fisheries.

At times, the manner in which this theft is conducted is so intensive, that it includes scraping of the ocean floor in bottom-dragging nets, which also devastates coral, sponges, kelp or other slower-growing species that struggle to recover quickly and which provides a habitat for commercial fishery species. I read about all this with interest – about how this destruction can alter the functioning of an entire ecosystem, permanently altering species composition and biodiversity.

Apparently, 'bycatch', the collateral capture of unintended species in the course of fishing which represents about a quarter of all marine catch, is typically returned to the ocean, only to more often die from injuries or exposure. However, it now appears this 'bycatch' is no longer being returned to the sea. It's being macerated or pulped into fishmeal, with all manner of preservatives and probiotics added to the pulp, then it's exported around the world at exorbitant cost to feed fish like salmon, tuna and snapper in coastal fish farms.

After having completed the initial trials; Ben and I were going to Laayoune for briefings, then to fly to Casablanca, because I wanted to visit the bar where Humphrey Bogart is supposed to have said the famous line, "Here's looking at you, kid," to Ingrid Bergman, in the movie Casablanca. Yeah, I know, a bit kinky. There it is, though, all the same.

After this, I plan to go straight home to have a well-earned rest with my gorgeous wife Carla, my daughter Katerina and dog Goliath. It's going to be a bit of a challenge, I think, to now make that planned trip back home, in the short-term, anyway. I'm far from happy about it.

Chapter 2

I ARRIVE IN NOUAKCHOTT drained, feeling more exhausted than I did before I left Nouadhibou, probably due to my agitated sleep/wake/sleep attempt on the plane. Whatever, I'm here now, hopefully one step closer to being safer and away from whatever on earth was transpiring back at our office. Also, hopefully away from Samir and his cronies. With no baggage other than carry-on, I deplane without delay towards the exit doors; however, the arrivals lounge is in absolute bedlam. It's frenzied. Crowds of people standing around everywhere, many police officers as well as armed soldiers. The line-up to exit the area is long and widespread, with no apparent headway being made as the police are checking everything and everyone.

I gently, politely, pull a police officer aside, one with the most spectacular single thick eyebrow above his dark brown eyes I've ever seen. We grip each other's hands once, along with transferring a handful of US dollars to him. As best I can, I explain my situation while trying to find out what the problem is in the airport, or more importantly, will it be possible to work our way around it? Though polite, he gives little away, just smiles at me with brilliant white teeth, then slowly walks off, pocketing the money I gave him. Shrugging off my disappointment, I mingle a bit more with the cosmopolitan crowd, who are all impatiently waiting. As usual, though, the conspiracy theories and rumour mill exceed all expectations. There'd been an attempted coup, a terrorist threat or attack, the assassination of the President… and so on it went.

Then, right out of the blue, my police officer waves me out of the line. I'm not sure whether to be fearful or pleased as I warily walk towards him. In broken, quiet English he suggests I follow him – which I do – right out of the tinted side glass door of the departure area into the outside concourse zone. He smiles at me, I smile back, grip his hands again in thanks, along with transferring another handful of US dollars. He points to an old green Mercedes taxi standing some way back from the main frantic taxi rank, then turns and slowly walks away. I stall a bit before hailing the old green Mercedes taxi he'd pointed to, as I thought I heard gunfire in the distance. *Maybe not,* I reflect as I get into the taxi. We go straight to the Hotel Tfeila, located about 30 minutes from the airport, on the Avenue Charles de Gaulle. It's right in the heart of the city and sur-rounded by a veritable host of international embassies and minis-tries. Improbably, though, the usually chaotic city is almost deserted by the usual feverish traffic. The only vehicles moving on the street are the very occasional private car, taxis and many police or army vehicles, with armed soldiers everywhere.

The lack of cars driving around is worrying and extremely unusual for Nouakchott, as it is an oddity in relation to cars. Usually, there are more Mercedes cars on the roads here than probably in the whole of Germany where it hails from. Right now, though, the streets are almost empty of cars; well, not so much empty as just very little moving traffic. I can see plenty of cars parked in all manner of precarious positions, just none rushing around in a horn-blaring traffic jam as usual. Part of the Nouakchott quirkiness is that many of the Mercedes cars appear to be beaten to within an inch of their lives. However, they still perform as required by some means, held together with gaffer tape, string, wire or tec screws. It's quite the spectacle to witness, this many dilapidated cars all in one place, many of them stolen from Europe. This sounds like a big assertion, I know, but it's what the locals have told me on more than one occasion. I suspect a coup of some sort is underway, so I try to quiz the driver about what's going on. All I get are a few mumbled Arabic words, along with a shrug of his shoulders. Whatever it is, he wants none of it, especially after we hear a loud exchange of machine gunfire nearby – which definitely has my attention; the driver's too, as he noticeably accelerates.

Without once having to stop to fill up the radiator with water, we arrive safely at the Hotel Tfeïla in one piece, somehow avoiding being shot, arrested or harassed. Getting out of the old green taxi, I'm reminded how hospitality is pretty much natural to Mauritanians. Evident as I walk into the hotel entrance and I'm once again greeted warmly by Alioune, the Hotel General Director, who seems somewhat anguished. On previous visits, he's ensured everything is taken into careful consideration for my stay, usually personally, always making me feel welcome – safe, more importantly – until I'm not, I guess. I can see they've recently invested in some sort of a security upgrade, with the installation of security cameras around the lobby. People are gathered in small groups everywhere, some in larger tourist groups, with baggage strewn in piles all over the place, masses of it.

"*Is-selaamu aleykum,* my friend," I say to Alioune, wishing peace upon him. We grasp each other's hands and hold them for a short time, as he doesn't shake hands up and down like western-ers. Then we both touch our hands over our hearts as a gesture of goodwill and peace. "What on earth is going on here, I mean in Nouakchott, not just your hotel here?" I ask, as I wave my arm around at the bedlam in the reception area.

"*Is Alaykum el Salam,* Mr James," Alioune replies, also wishing me peace. "It appears we're experiencing a coup." He stops instantly, as we can both hear a short burst of loud gunfire not too far away. He begins again in his broken English. "As I say, we are not fully aware of all circumstances, although airport now closed, with all flights can-celled. This is why we still have all departing guests anxiously still here. City almost in lockdown at the moment. However, no curfew imposed, that we know. I keep you informed when I know more," he says, waving one of the porters over to escort me to my room. It feels like he's in a hurry to get me out of the way.

Once in my room, I'm cognisant of the requirement to focus on my own overall situation, not just the coup-related obstacles, as I clearly have no influence on those outcomes. Nonetheless, I've not been in this sort of situation before, running from whatever was going on in Nouadhibou and now in a coup lockdown. It's going to be a tough call to try and work out exactly what might be involved to effectively move forward, especially given my limited understanding of whatever is actually going on with Ben, the minister or Samir and his cronies. My first task right now, though, is to try and find a temporary hiding place for the hard drives, somewhere, anywhere really that might present a reasonable hiding place in the limited space available in my small room, just in case anybody comes looking into my meagre possessions and finds them. I gently undo the screws of the ceiling air vent for the air conditioning system with a tea spoon from the condiments drawer. It's a reasonable space where at least I can hide one of the hard drives in. I reach up into the space to where the conduit bends off sort of at right angles and place one of the drives just around the bend. Then I carefully replace the ceiling vent and screws without damaging the paint on any of them.

Rounds of gunfire and muffled shouting echoes up from the street outside, sending yet another jolt of alarm through me. This is not something anyone here is accustomed to, nor something we're likely to become used to anytime soon. Warily, I go over to the window and partially pull the curtains aside to see what's happening. Nothing really to see as I begin to pull the heavy curtains back across the window again, I notice a fold in the street side of the curtain, which has a small tear near the bottom of the inner cloth. I try my luck inserting the second drive into that opening, and it fits perfectly, dropping down slightly inside the curtain fold, fully hidden. Happy with my find, I'm reasonably confident it's unlikely to be exposed, not easily anyway.

My next task is to call Serge, get his take on the situation, see if we have some idea on where we think we are with everything or what we might be needed to be done in the next stage of finding Ben, whatever that might be. It will hopefully then assist us to develop a clearer, more flexible strategy, one we can change on the run if necessary. I try to call Serge from my mobile. There is no service, which is very unusual. With all the international embassies and ministries around this neck of the woods, the reception is ordinarily exceptional. Maybe another by-product of the coup? I then try him from the room landline, which thankfully works.

"Where the goddamned hell… have you been Kelly? I've been going nuts here trying to track you down," Serge screams full on class A anger down the phone at me, no pretence of calmness. I abruptly move the phone away from my ear. "What happened to the plan to go to the fucking Oasean Hotel in Cansado? You know, the strategy supporting the PQE, for the love of Christ? They told me you hadn't made it to the hotel. I've been absolutely frantic trying to work out how to find you. I contacted RJ at Castelle, and she had no idea where you bloody were either. Now she's trying to chase you down as well," he yells. The image in my head is of copious balls of tiny spittle flying out of his mouth and nose, covering his phone and anything else in the near vicinity.

It would have gone on and on forever, so I just hung up the phone, then took it off the cradle so nobody can ring me either. I wait 15 tense minutes, then call him back, to try again to explain everything, mostly composed, as best I can in the agitated state of mind we're both in. I comprehend his angst, totally. I really do. Except there simply wasn't any time back then where I might have been able to call him while trying to… well, escape really. After some time, Serge sort of quietens down, sort of being generous. There are other difficulties charging up his nervous system, as it turns out, facilitating the elevation of his anxiety levels.

Serge continues. "My liaison in the Westra Environment Ministry in Laayoune has no idea what the hell I was talking about when I mentioned the old double-barrel minister and Ben being missing, possibly kidnapped," he says, not so tranquilly.

"How the hell can that be possible, Serge? It's their own damned minister!" I think I say this more out of astonishment that it can actually happen than anything else. "You know what I'm thinking, it's those guys who have the tail on their own minister. Do you reckon they're just outright lying to you like usual, or maybe they're really not sure themselves? What do you think?" I ask seriously, not really believing what I'm hearing… coming out of my own mouth. "I bet they've got their arse in a sling now trying to find him, which will piss them off mightily. Hearing their minister is missing from an outsider, bugger me, they'll be ropable, Serge."

During a miniscule break in conversation, another short burst of machine gunfire can be heard right outside in the street, not too far away at all. Serge heard it as well.

"What the hell's that? Are they gunshots I just heard?" he almost yells again. This just added another element of stress to his day, no doubt, as well as mine.

"Yeah, it is. Not at me though… yet." I try to explain the attempted, or maybe successful, coup underway here, which stuns Serge into a temporary silence.

"That probably explains why I can't get in contact with any of the Fisheries Department guys when I've been calling. Screw the lot of them. It all seems to be one big messed-up world everywhere these days, doesn't it?" Serge says angrily at me, as if it's my fault. "How long ago did this all happen?"

"I have no idea. Nothing seemed to be happening in Nouadhibou when I left. It was well underway by the time I got here, though, so my guess is it wasn't too long ago. I'm not going to be able or allowed to go anywhere for the time being. All flights in or out are cancelled. We're pretty much in total lockdown. Mobile and internet services are also cut off at the moment. I can still use the satellite phone, except they'll have communications tracking in place, in which case, I'd rather only use it in an emergency. So then Serge, if you want me to do anything while I'm stuck in here, let me know, as limited as it might be."

Serge took another deep breath. "That's not the worst of things, though. Those Westra guys from Dakhla backtracked all the way to the office in Nouadhibou to try and locate Ben and the minister, or their vehicles. No go with any of that. However, they found your best mate Samir shot dead in your office, lying in a pool of congealed blood with a single shot to the head. The place was all busted up, apparently. Rented 4WD is missing, and the office has been ransacked. Evidently, all electrical equipment, CCTV, computers… everything, all gone, stolen. Now you know why I've been in such a panic. I thought you might have been taken as well," Serge utters, a little more calmly.

OK, so I now appreciate the shot I heard when I'd been hiding over by the beach was more than likely aimed at Samir. Why? I felt a pang of guilt. My thinking back then… he'd probably been part of whatever the hell was going on with the other two cronies in the workshop. Serge has brought me back to the moment with this tragic news.

"I'm really sorry, mate, I didn't mean to put you through any of this. I just bolted asap. There simply wasn't any time to call you, not while I was on the run, Serge, and hiding out. The single shot, though, I heard it when I was hiding down near the beach." I explain all the details about the other two Arabs, Samir not answering the radio phone, the single shot, my escape to the airport instead of the Oasean Hotel. He seems to take it much better than I thought he might.

"Give me a second, my other phone is ringing." I can hear voices mumbling something indecipherable in the background, and then he's back. "That's RJ. She sent one of the locals she knows around to the office in Nouadhibou. He disappeared in a hurry, apparently. Local cops and military everywhere." He took a breath. I can't find one to take right at this minute.

"Jesus, Serge, do you think this all has something to do with those unofficial trials? What the hell have the guys found out there beyond the EEZ that's creating this much havoc?" It's exasperating, not knowing anything about those runs or who ordered them. What were they looking for? Or, more importantly, what the hell was it they discovered? All of it was coming with its own particular morsel of ugly intrigue and anguish as well.

✦ ✦ ✦

"A question, Serge, have you been in contact with Ben's wife? You know, to tell her he's missing?" Already guessing the answer, although I think it's essential for me to ask anyway, to light a fire under it, so to speak.

"No, not yet, if ever," Serge declares, almost mumbling. "I guess you know they're having marriage difficulties? I'd rather not add to her stress levels at the moment with supposition or without giving her some sort of direction we might plan to take to find Ben."

"Who bloody cares, mate? They're always having marriage difficulties. Every damn time Ben goes away on a job, Rikki's out there shagging her arse off with every Tom, Dick and probably Harry." Wow, a bit rare for me to spell out my thoughts like this, isn't it? "However, it doesn't absolve us from not giving her a heads-up, mate… does it?"

Or do you know something I don't, Serge? Like maybe it's Tom, Dick, Harry and Serge, I wonder to myself cynically.

Ben's thrice-married wife Rikki is a first-class, gold-plated, jumped-up, never come down, well-known master philanderer. She hates being left on her own for any length of time – like, beyond a minute or so. In this case, she finds company anywhere she can when Ben is away, which is a lot. It's also possibly why he goes away… a lot. How do I know? Well, her periodic offers for me to partake in 'friends with benefits' with her has given me a bit of a clue. The vitriolic response when I've declined her offers has given me a much clearer indication about that. Extremely nasty bit of work, this one, when she can't get what it wants. The entire happenstance made me feel quite miserable and kind of depressed when it happened, to be honest.

"Bigger fish to fry right now, Ned, like getting a plan in place for what we need to do next. We've got to find some IT specialist over there to get the data off your hard drives. Then to get the info to me to hopefully see what we're dealing with."

"Yeah, yeah, I know. You're right, Serge. Things might soon get a bit messy with those Westra guys now running around headless and without their parental supervision. So, what do you propose we do, touch up our nearest Embassy?" I'm expecting hesitation. However, rule one in my book old mate, is to have a plan. Never waste a good crisis is something our Crisis Plan prompts us to do, usually, though, only when we have more detailed information that can be validated, like if we can confirm Ben has really been kidnapped or is in any sort of genuine danger.

"Yeah, well, the first two things on page one of my list, Ned, are the data retrieval off those drives of yours, then to escalate our concerns further up the Westra government food chain to see what we can find out about our two absent ones," Serge replies, then he just hangs up.

Yeah, well, the first bloody thing on my list is to get some sort of plan in place. In the upshot, we have to do something else other than sit around scratching our arse while waiting for somebody else to come along and scratch it for us. I need to do something, so I call RJ.

"Good to hear you're still in one piece, young man. What's more importantly, you're still in the land of the living to enjoy it. Give me an update, can you please?" RJ sounds jovial enough, considering the situation with Ben. I fill her in on all the details about what I thought has been going on, as best as I understood it myself, anyway.

"Sounds all bitter and twisted over there, doesn't it? So, no idea at all with what they found the other night during the unsanctioned trials out there… beyond the EEZ?" she queries.

"Not a thought. Do you have anybody here in Mauritania who can do any of the tricky work on the data retrieval from the hard drives I have here?" If anybody can expedite something like this, it'd be RJ is my guess.

"Hmmm, yes and no," RJ murmurs, clearly thinking of who might owe her a favour or two that might be able to do this for her.

"Hit me with the 'yes' bit first then?" I suggest.

"Well, I've got a super contact in the UN there who owes me a few delicate favours." *Bingo*, I thought, laughing to myself, the 'favour' overlord.

"She can and will do it quietly for me," RJ says, more to herself, I think.

"OK, hit me with the 'no' bit then," I ask.

"Well, the 'no' part is the bigger problem. We are not the owners of the drives or the data on them. They belong to Marinetti Electronics or maybe even the two Governments. It'd be an egregious and flagrant betrayal of trust for us to do it without Serge's approval. If you can get his blessing, though, I'll kick the other thing into gear and get it sorted." I hear her taking a breath, giving some energy to the thoughts rattling around inside her.

"We'll require some form of documented approval sign-off from Serge. In order to protect us in case this turns into a deeper political dispute, got me?" RJ says, almost tongue in cheek, I thought. I've been told she's pretty famous for 'egregiously' stepping on other people's toes without a care in the world about it to get exactly what she wants or requires. Something is very different about her concern with this particular issue, though, to suggest this path.

"Got ya. Leave it with me. I'll see what I can do. Gotta go, someone at the door," I say, as I hear a loud double thump on my door. At almost the same time, I hear another short burst of shooting, which seems to be quite some distance away this time.

I look through the newly installed, door security peephole to see Alioune, the Hotel General Director, standing alongside a military or more likely a police officer out in the corridor. I greet them both traditionally as I answer the door. Alioune returned my greeting then turned to introduce me to Colonel Ould Cheikh Aziz – I think; he mumbled – who I note doesn't appear to wish me peace nor a greeting of any kind. He marches into my room uninvited, smoking a stinking cigarette, the thick grey-blue smoke trail and stench hanging in the air like a very matured fart, clinging to him as he walks around the room self-importantly.

"Is there a problem?" I query politely, looking at the Colonel, then at Alioune.

"Not if you cooperate," Colonel Ould Cheikh Aziz says briskly in broken English. Least, it's what it sounds like he says.

"More than happy to, if you can guide me on what you'd like me to cooperate with," I suggest, smiling in my typical gracious and charming way; polite in my tone. However, it appears to have been misinterpreted by the good Colonel.

His manner changes somewhat as he ambles silently around my small room with his entourage of thick putrid smoke pursuing him, glancing at my meagre collection of belongings on the bed, then examining my backpack, rifling through my things. If I didn't know better, I'd have sworn he's searching for something, maybe something specific, like the hard drives, which are now hopefully hidden well enough out of harm's way. He then goes into his spiel again in broken English about the coup and how the country is now under total control of the military. No Westerners are in any danger, although we're all confined to the hotel grounds for the time being. At least until the night-time curfews are lifted and flights can possibly resume.

"You have only small bag. Why?" he asks me, suspiciously.

I have no logical answer to give to his question, as I'd no intention of being in Nouakchott this morning at all, with any bags, or with a coup underway or not, so the only answer I can think of is to fake it, for now anyway.

"I only planned to be here for a day to meet up with a senior manager from my company in Australia. I wasn't expecting I'd need many things for such a short trip. I wasn't aware of the coup when I left Nouadhibou, so my intention was to return possibly today or early tomorrow, then on to Laayoune for meetings with our management and the Western Saharan government," I reply, with fingers, legs, testicles and toes all crossed. I was living in hope my nonsense explanation has some miniscule level of credibility about it. At least enough for the Colonel to not see straight through it at once and ask where my manager is staying.

"You must remain here in this room until I advise when you can leave. I will check your story with my colleagues in Nouadhibou. Good day," he says stiffly as he walks out of my room. A wispy trail of fetid grey smoke chases him. I look at Alioune, and we both shrug our shoulders.

"I'll return soon and explain everything to you. Right now, I must escort the Colonel to meet other guests," he utters nervously, appearing very uncomfortable with his current situation.

I likewise feel very uncomfortable with my current situation as well, along with the stinking fog of cigarette smoke still hanging around my room. Not happy, Colonel. Time to ring Serge.

Serge's unpleasant mood has not seen any improvement, for whatever reason, so I ignore his verbal onslaught about the Westra authorities, Ben, me and the world in general. Bugger him and his worldly problems. I've got enough of my own to deal with. I delve straight into what he's organised with the data retrieval from off the drives. Nothing, it turns out, as his contacts in West Africa – or more specifically Mauritania – seem unreliable. Uncontactable is how I interpret his statement. As we talk, I hear someone speaking loudly out in the corridor. Once again, I ask Serge to hold on the line while I investigate. Looking into the security peephole again, I can see two armed soldiers standing guard outside my door, talking in Arabic in yet another fog of tobacco smoke. It's not helping my anxiety at all. I quickly pick up the phone again and explain to Serge what has happened earlier and what seems to be happening now with the guards. I also explain briefly about the potential data retrieval support from RJ.

"No way, Ned, it's not as simple as just hooking the hard drives up to any basic computer and then downloading the info. The computer needs to have particular software on it with the correct associated applications and authentication credentials that support the specific database system. This is not easily found in off-the-shelf PCs. Hence you guys weren't able to simply interpret the data each day on the computers you have in Nouadibou. You realise my problem here, Ned?" Serge asks, almost indignantly, his frustration surfacing like a massive self-inflicted wound.

"Yeah, I get what you're saying, Serge. Nevertheless, in my limited involvement with computers, these highly skilled technical guys, you know, the guys who play in this space every day, can typically figure out some sort of workaround to override any technical hitches. In emergencies, so to speak. Are you saying it's not possible with this type of material, Serge?" This technology is all well above my interest or pay grade. Nonetheless, there must be some way around it, is my thinking.

"I don't know, maybe. The high-level scientific processes involved are managed by our technical team. I'll have to talk to those guys to see what they think. Let me get back to you shortly. Do not do anything until then, though. I can't afford a third-party having access to any data on those drives if they hold compromising information or potentially illegal data." He sounds desolate.

I get it, especially if it's likely to be a legal issue for us later. "Yeah, no worries. One thing I'm not grasping, though, Serge. Isn't everything backed up off-site? I mean, my interpretation is no matter what the data is, everything from all of our computers in Nouadibou is automatically backed up remotely somewhere, every day, right? Maybe in Melbourne, or here in Nouakchott? Can't you access the info from there?"

"Yeah, it is, except it's not all part of the overall system we control here in Melbourne. I'll check with the guys in Italy to see if there is a redundant process somewhere else, although I don't believe so. I'll get back to you shortly. Problem being, though, if the data didn't arrive from you guys, there's nothing for us to access on that backup," Serge says, then hangs up. I'll leave him to think on it for a bit. I'd be bowled over if there isn't some sort or back-door process these whizz kids know that might help us out. I bloody hope so, nonetheless.

I'm impatient for some sort of positive circuit breaker, so I call my wife Carla at home and lay it all out to her. She's such a marvellous sounding board with everything else that happens in our life, so time to share. It's worth the call. I feel much more revitalised after tossing around my situation and any likely options. Getting her valuable feedback is a boost for me. Bloody hell, I just love my wife to bits. After my talk with her, I feel a little more optimistic about what might possibly lay ahead and how to potentially deal with it. Time to test the temperature of the guards outside. As I open the door, I can only see one guard now. He instantly points his rifle at me, nods his head and the barrel of the weapon once to suggest I should go back inside my room… like right now, if not sooner. I comply.

I call Serge again, and to my astonishment, his disposition has now reached an exhilarating level of irrationality, fuming about some new obstacle that has just entered his life. I'm not yet focused enough on our earlier problems to want to venture into this latest bit of absurdity at the moment, so I try to pacify him. However, he's beyond it at the moment.

"Bugger it, Serge, you deal with your problems at your end, and let me deal with mine at this end. It's paramount that we get the data retrieved off those drives. I'm going to take RJ up on her offer, I'll stay with the process the entire way to ensure no one else gets to see what's in the data download. OK?" I offer.

"NO! No fucking way, Kelly. The more pressing issue we have right now is the Army Commander in Nouadhibou, he has just been in contact with me, which is my latest drama to deal with at this end. He's investigating the killing of Samir. It's only going to be a matter of time before they come knocking on your door about it. When that happens, it will complicate the hell out of your life… and mine. Disappointingly, there's nothing you or I can do about it right at the moment. It's not possible to get you out of there with all the flights cancelled, not to mention they have that damn coup chugging merrily along as well. What a giant master-class cock-up!" Serge variously yells and almost whispers this latest round of grief to me as my gut sinks to the floor.

"Fact is, Serge, none of us have been in a situation like this before, so it's going to be tough to work out exactly what might be required for us to achieve a successful outcome in relation to these drives and the data. We've got to come up with some sort of a plan to move forward all the same. Any goddamn plan." I hope he'd compose himself enough for some rational thought to creep in. Some General once pronounced, *"In battle, plans are useless. The planning, though, now that's indispensable."*

"It's critical, Serge. Let's give some thought to what might work here with those bloody drives, then develop a clear plan subject to how the situation evolves. We can change our line of attack later, if required, in a measured way as we go." I sense he isn't listening, or hearing. Same outcome.

"Whatever. A forward plan is only as good as the info supporting its development. We don't have anything of that which is credible." As Serge says this, another prolonged burst of machine gunfire can be heard just outside, in a very nearby area, nonetheless.

It seems the once tranquil streets of Nouakchott have become a sort of urban battleground, covered in a pall of grey smoke. Looking out through a gap in the curtains once again, I can now see barricades being installed at armed checkpoints at the end of the bitumen road out front. This whole situation is challenging my resolve, especially if there's the likelihood of being interviewed, or more likely interrogated, by either my close and dear friend Colonel Aziz, or the Nouadhibou Army Commander. Or perhaps more sensationally compromising, both.

Chapter 3

I'M AGAIN DISTRACTED BY another couple of loud knocks on my room door. Looking into the security eyesight, I see Alioune standing outside. Alone. Opening the door, I quickly usher him in.

"Things seem to change, Mr Kelly. Violence, it appears to ease. I think rebels may be kill-ed or arrest. Or perhaps fled? I not know," Alioune says in his version of English. "We see many soldiers leave hotel. Maybe not safe outside in streets yet, perhaps safer from before, still not safe for you though." He takes a breath and then continues. "We are ask-ed by other expats in hotel, if possible, to move to alternative hotel room, off premise. For best security. You know, in case soldier come back, want to search belongings. Or worse, to arrest them for whatever. Will you maybe interest in this also?"

My heart just about missed a beat and tripped over itself. I'd bloody jump at a chance to avoid any likely pleasantries or ultimate interrogation by the Colonel or the Nouadhibou Army Commander.

"Where are you suggesting this might be? I'm assuming it's a safe place?" I query. Probably a bit too eagerly, I suspect, although I do try to contain my willingness to participate. "Are there communications at this location, so I can stay in contact with my company?"

"Location very safe. Journey there not so far. May be not so safe as still many soldier patrol street. We try to have everything ready to go tomorrow morning. House is in compound of United Nations, part of the African Mission. It very good communication. There is, of course, a cost to this," Alioune states matter-of-factly, shrugging his shoulders, raising his arms slightly, palms upwards in a perfectly executed French shrug. His way of expressing uncertainty or indifference to the amount of money it is likely to cost, I guess.

"So, how do we get this into motion? What do you want from me or for me to do?" I query. I have no doubt the costs will be substantial. Anyway, let's worry about that aspect later.

Early the next morning, I recover the two hard drives from their hiding places, pack my meagre belongings and go down to the reception area. I meet the other two expats who apparently are the instigators of our looming escapade. They introduce themselves simply as Rob and Lee, no last names. Both look well, fit, one a healthily preserved 60-plus-year-old, bald American named Rob; businessman, he says. The second is Lee, a much younger ex-military-style man, maybe in his mid-40s. Whatever his age, he's wearing it dreadfully. More like it's sagging off him. He has a spectacular moustache and a thought-provoking haircut that to me, quite frankly… well, it just looks unfinished, like half a basin cut from the 50s. An unusual look all-round, I feel. Seems as if he rushed off before the barber had a chance to complete the task. *Whatever works for you,* I suppose.

Both are from the same organisation, something 'Omega'. Involved in the supply of oil drilling and production equipment, apparently. Observing them interact with each other and the hotel staff, neither put me at any level of unease. I'm not in a position to be choosy at the moment, anyway, so it is what it is. They both appear, to me at least, to be quietly spoken, enthusiastic, charismatic and unassuming individuals not at all what I'd have expected American oil businessmen to be like, who I imagine to be loud and pretentious. They are not. Both are dressed in well-scuffed dark denim, quasi-military-style fashion clothing, loose-fitting cargo pants and shirts with multiple utility pockets everywhere. No company logo in sight. The military fashion look is complete with both wearing similar, practical sand-coloured lace-up leather boots.

Our security briefing from the Hotel Tfeila security advisor Dhabe is enlightening, to say the least. Typically, during periods of political or civil unrest, it's almost always advisable to avoid being on the streets ever, if at all possible. However, in the dire situation where you may find yourself out there, as a general rule, it's critical to avoid any roving groups of locals and to stay away from overcrowded areas. It's also prudent to stay well clear of any potentially volatile situations such as barricaded road blocks, armed checkpoints or local protests. As important and wise as these standard recommendations seem to be, nonetheless, on this occasion, it appears we're going to rashly ignore all of the usual advisories. We'll dress and act like we belong in the local community, allowing us to avoid drawing any unnecessary attention to ourselves. There's also a fear that any private vehicle transport will most likely attract unwanted attention and probably inspection by police, army or both. So, to avoid that from occurring, we'll all gradually walk in a small group to the UN compound. We're told it's not far away. Let's see. Back home in Australia, when someone says something is 'not far away', it's likely to mean anything from 1 km to 500 km.

Dhabe has prearranged for us to quietly mingle in amongst a group of friendly locals and hotel staff who, interestingly, seem totally oblivious to the armed soldiers patrolling the streets or the carnage on them. They're still venturing out and undertaking their normal daily routines – pastimes unchanged from one generation to another – wandering around the alleys and backstreets as if nothing at all is going on with the coup. I guess there's no requirement for them to stay indoors anyway. No curfews or restrictions are in place that we're aware of during daylight hours.

I'm just so bloody nervous, breaking into a perpetual sweat thinking about this walk on the wild side. I'm visualising any number of barriers that might possibly arise or things that could go wrong during our 'not far away' walk. This is going to be way more than just an interesting venture. The key for us, Dhabe advises, will be to remain composed throughout. Do not engage in any discussions, confrontations or provocative behaviour if we're approached by anybody, especially any soldiers or police. Dhabe and a couple of the hotel staff accompanying us will deal with any of these interventions as we proceed to the compound. Mid-morning, 11 a.m. to be precise, we walk nonchalantly through the back of the hotel and out of their maintenance workshop, dressed traditionally, only carrying backpacks under our Saharan djellabas. This delivers us to a wide sand service road at the very rear of the hotel. It's littered with a few abandoned cars and carts, assorted plants and weeds, copious amounts of plastic and paper bag trash blowing everywhere in the light, dusty wind. The view, as we begin to cautiously meander down the road, is mostly of dust, desert and sparse woody vegetation. Jagged sandstone rocks dot the edge of the road and out into the low sand dunes. An occasional goat herd moves around the dunes in the near distance. Closer to us looks to be a small, makeshift camel and goat day market in progress, with perhaps 50 tethered animals, although very few customers this early.

We're initially in a small group, chatting quietly amongst ourselves in either English, French or Arabic, in the same manner as the locals we've joined. There is no obvious hurry, I observe. Air is already stifling hot and dry, aided by a faint scent of earthy dust in the gentle breeze blowing past us. A small whirly wind is beginning to build up steam down towards the end of the road we're on, drifting dust and all manner of paper and plastic debris erratically into the air and across into the desert dune area. The sun is already getting intense at this early hour, beginning to beat down on us, reminding me just how oppressive it is likely to become later in the day. My head is already hot under my tagelmust scarf, so I try to loosen it off a bit to let some air in.

"Must not, Mr Jam—es. Keep tight. Keep clos—ed," one of the hotel staff instructs me brusquely. He pulls the scarf tighter around my face so all that's showing is my eyes, covered by my sunglasses. I feel chastised for my actions, except, *bloody hell, I'm likely to die of heat stroke in here,* I'm thinking. I'm not finding it at all easy walking out in this heat, especially all wrapped up like I am. The wind is also picking up a tad, creating a swirl of thick choking dust around us as we disturb the sand while walking over it.

Our accompanying local staff and Dhabe casually greet and chat with other groups in the traditional way as we pass them, the same as they do on any other day. The dirt service road widens into a broader, well-used, loose, heavily potholed gravel road which will ultimately lead us to the UN compound, we're told. We've already been walking for a little over an hour, and in the increasing heat, it's exhausting. We stop at a small, wheeled handcart, which gives me the impression of it having been permanently stranded on the roadside sandbank forever. It sits amongst the collective rubbish, spindly weeds with dust gusting around it. There are two dishevelled almond trees beside the cart, struggling to stay alive, persisting on remaining relevant in their own way. The cart is surrounded by many locals, all sipping Maghrebi mint tea, a green tea flavoured with mint and various other exotic herbs and spices. Fabulous thirst-quencher normally, just not when we three expats are desperate to get off the streets and safely into the UN compound.

We all duck down in shear dread as our ears are assaulted by a long, loud burst of machine gun fire very close by. It's brief, extremely nerve-wracking, although seemingly not directed at any of us, thankfully, as there is almost no protection available to anybody.

Surprisingly, Rob begins to lose his nerve a little and wants to get up and go back to the hotel, he says. One of the staff members grabs him gently as he tries to stand, pleading with him quietly to sit back down and wait for just a few more minutes. Lee joins in to help calm him down. Rob reluctantly sits down on the sandy edge of the road, shaking in alarm. I can smell the fear and uncertainty oozing out of him. It isn't something I'd have expected to see from him, a seemingly capable adventurer. After a few more quiet minutes with no further gunfire, Dhabe rouses us up, and we gingerly begin moving down the dirt road once again, with a slightly increased sense of urgency. Rob seems to have settled somewhat, now that we're moving again. I stay close to him anyway, just in case.

"You OK, Rob?" I query. I think I'm more worried he's going to arc up again and give us away than being concerned for his mental health. I know, I know, not my best thoughts of the day.

"Yeah, sort off. I've been through that goddamned shit-fight in Somalia not long ago, so my reactions to close gunfire let me down periodically. It always settles. It's just that sharp, surprising bark when it hits my ears, sends me a bit off like a mad dog. I'm OK, though," he answers awkwardly. He isn't really looking OK to me.

As we advance down the road, one side is now lined with a variety of low, modest structures of mud, stone and cinder block. Some give the impression of being homes, their facades weather-beaten by years of intense sun. Most have rusty, ornamental metal gates with various intricate designs welded on them, paint and rust peeling off everywhere. An abundance of weathered trash, paper litter and thriving weeds have permanently built up in the desert sand around the bottom edges of the buildings, along with another almond tree. I note some structures have profoundly chipped and faded paint; eroded by an eternity of sandstorms, it looks to me. Others have heavily sun-bleached artistic patterns etched into their walls. It appears like this artwork is from very long ago, given its extreme distressed look. Some small businesses are being conducted out of a number of the buildings, their very colourful and vibrant signs attached to a few outer walls, child-like visual depictions showing off the shop's wares. The high walls of the buildings provide us with a brief reprieve from the intense sun. We all seem to be quietly thanking the universe and whatever Gods are involved for it. I do, anyway. Street noises are slowly coming back to life after the earlier close burst of gunfire. I can hear echoes of children laughing and adult chatter slowly drifting out to us from open windows and doorways.

We apprehensively arrive at the junction of our dirt road and yet another, wider and more heavily pot-holed dirt road to our right, all of us chatting quietly as our collective unease heightens the further from the hotel we get, mine especially, as well as Rob's, I notice. This particular road is cluttered with an accumulation of parked or abandoned cars, trucks and motorbikes, all scattered haphazardly along the roadway edges. One motor bike is still burning slightly from an earlier fire, while two other cars have been heavily shot up. Another has – what looks to me – a pile of crumbled blankets on the ground next to an open car door. On second thought, judging from the several emaciated dogs periodically attacking it, I think the blanket pile is more likely to be a dead body. The dogs are tearing away at it ferociously, in between anxiously scurrying back and forth, while keeping a suspicious eye on us walking past. The entire road looks somewhat cataclysmic, in fact; it radiates an 'end of the world' apocalypse-like sensation in me, amplifying my collective unease.

"No look there," Dhabe murmurs to us. "There is nothing worthy to see." He urges us to continue walking, a little faster, and to ignore the grotesque scene. The dogs become emboldened in their efforts as we walk further past and leave the area. We're clearly no longer seen as a threat to them.

"You may see much more of such very bad situations. It is not respectueux to let your eyes rest on such things. Keep talking to each other. Just walk, slowly forward," Dhabe says to us softly in his broken English.

"*Respectueux* is French. It pretty much means it is not respectful… for our eyes, to see such terrible things," Rob explains to me, rolling his shoulders around as we keep walking. I'm completely onboard with this comment. I'd seen enough of such things in Vietnam.

We continue slowly walking for another 15 minutes or so when we hear, drifting in on the slight breeze from somewhere behind us, the local muezzin starting the midday call to prayer in a nearby mosque. His call is loud, coarse, also slightly melodious all the same, reaching out from the speakers attached high up on the outside walls of the minaret. He's calling all those nearby to stop their activities and to respond to the call by performing the prescribed prayer, demonstrating their commitment to the faith. I notice our local support guys start to prepare themselves for the second call to prayer for the day, out of the five in total, the first being before dawn. This is something we hadn't addressed at all prior to departure – a colossal oversight. Lee and Rob both look at me bemused, hands on hips, elbows jutting out in a questioning manner, indicating their surprise and frustration at the situation. Both quickly looking wild-eyed back and forth at each other and at me… with significant concern.

"Too bloody late to worry about it now, guys," I say, shrugging my own shoulders in dread. This is very bad planning on our behalf.

I know the local guys plan their daily activities around these prayer times, so I'm not appreciating how the hell I missed this consideration in our pre-departure briefing. I watch nervously as they casually get into their routine, their spiritual preparation of performing the ablution, the ritual purification of washing certain parts of the body with their water bottles, which is necessary for performing the formal prayers. All of our people begin to lay down their prayer mats and start their prayer process.

"Time for us to get into it ourselves, guys," I say, shrugging, as I immediately drop onto all fours in the sand. I try my best to imitate the actions and the proclamation sounds from Dhabe, who is praying right next to me. Lee and Rob do likewise, trying to imitate me, trying to imitate Dhabe. My only prayer request is for no one to be observing this comical albeit potentially deadly charade.

Once the call to prayer has been met and all of the guys roll up their mats and mutter amongst themselves, Dhabe calls for us to all move on slowly. He looks at me and smiles, I think now recognising the prayer oversight, he simply says, "Inshallah." If God wills – we're talking Dhabe's God that is, not ours.

We do indeed see many more of such unworthy sights as we slowly advance down this dusty, litter strewn road, now into hour three. An old, armoured vehicle is parked crossways over the entrance to a pot-holed bitumen road to our left, blocking access to the road with its small canon and machine guns. Quite a few armed soldiers mingle around casually. Most seem to take little notice or interest in us, thankfully. In the background of the armoured vehicle, I can see the shell of another burning car, smouldering still, so again not a recent fire episode. There appears to be a number of charred bodies sprawled on the road next to the car. Dhabe again quietly instructs us to not look or react, to keep walking slowly, casually, down towards the secondary road. It is his hope for us to avoid the watchful eyes of any soldiers who might be observing our movements, he says. For the moment, as a distraction, he goes over to the soldiers, joking with them as he shares a cigarette with one that he seems to know.

We continue to slowly stroll along the edge of the secondary road, where I can thankfully now see the UN compound from our position. The sand under my feet feels different here, it's softer and loose like a sort of beach sand, giving away every now and then to small pebbles and coarse sand grains that shift with each step. All I really want to do is to run like the devil himself is after me, as fast as I can to the compound. Nonetheless, I don't, and won't. I know it would more than likely prove fatal. I keep a very close on Rob, in case he has the urge to do the exact same thing or anything else similarly crazy.

Before I know it, we're thankfully at the compound gates. Two heavily-armed Indian UN security guards are standing watch inside, looking at us and each other blankly, nodding their heads from side to side, almost comically. Dhabe has now caught up with us and quietly talks to them about the arrangements he has made, and talks, and urges and talks some more. The guards finally stop nodding long enough to unlock and open the gates. Dhabe, Rob, Lee and myself eagerly walk through them into what we hope to be a safe and secure location. I breathe a massive sigh of relief as I look back beyond the gates while the guards close and lock them again. A number of small tumbleweeds roll idly past and down the dusty street, torn pieces of plastic, paper and cloth hooked up in their barbs. It all seems so surreal, even though we haven't been exposed to any real confrontations, incidents or physical threats during our journey this morning, the entire three-and-a-half hours felt enormously menacing the whole time.

"So where the bloody hell are you now, Kelly? I've been trying to ring you at the hotel, and they tell me you checked out. How the hell can you even do that during a coup?" Serge rages, full of piss, pills, bad manners and a very shitty attitude.

By the time I finish trying to explain what has happened and where we are now, he's settled down, marginally. I tell him I'd intended to call him last night to advise of our plans; however, Dhabe suggested we not tell anybody of our intentions, especially over the phone. This is in case the phones are being monitored by police because of the coup.

"So, here we are, then, new location, hopefully safer and, with a bit of luck, where the police or army will not be looking for me," I state. "And all being well, in a place where you might be in a more pleasant bloody frame of mind to talk about things a bit more civilly," I add cynically.

Serge ignored my caustic remark, completely. "We have bigger fish to worry about now, Kelly. I reluctantly spoke to Ben's wife last night. She told me he'd sent her some sort of encrypted file the night before last, one she didn't know how to open. I wasn't thinking much about it at the time. Anyway, I got it picked up early this morning. It turns out to be the very data file from the unauthorised runs the night before Ben and the minister left. The guys are still trying to decipher the full run as we speak, although the interim feedback suggests the radar picked up a significant accumulation of vessels just outside the EEZ. Like less than a half kilometre outside. It's as if they knew the radar was looking and there was a limit to its nominated reach. The bizarre part is that by some means, it seems they may have identified the radar signal when it locked onto them. Technically, this is supposed to be impossible. It certainly looks like it once we lock on though, there's an immediate separation of the midsized vessels away from two large motherships."

"What the hell is going on there, Serge? How do they know we're searching for them, or anybody, really, let alone tracking them at that very time? Maybe they'd been in the process of separating anyway, when we locked onto them?" I suggest, knowing it's probably a stretch, saying it anyway – what the hell?

"No. Gets worse. Some of the data already deciphered suggests another highly intensive electronic signal of some type immediately comes back at us. Without really knowing, I'd say it's as if they're attempting to destabilise our radar signal. I didn't think it was doable, although it might be some variety of electromagnetic disturbance or deflection device."

"You mean like some sort of an electromagnetic pulse attack… on our signal? Something like that? As in, a weaponized version?" I ask incredulously.

An electromagnetic pulse (or EMP) is a short burst of electromagnetic energy that can disrupt, damage or sometimes completely destroy any electronic device or system it is aimed at. It releases a rapid and often highly concentrated burst of electromagnetic radiation, generating a powerful rise in electrical currents, commonly leading to high-voltage surges. If these surges exceed the tolerances of the electronic components, it causes them to spectacularly fail or significantly malfunction at a minimum. The sensitive semiconductors like the integrated circuits utilised in the radar system are particularly vulnerable to such high voltage spikes. How do I know all this? Well, we used a very early, experimental version of an EMP weapon back in my Vietnam days. I can tell you, though, even way back then, I'd been bloody impressed with how destructive it was at totally frying Charlies' electronic systems effectively. With apparently no possibility of repairing the systems, it was so efficient.

"Yeah, that's exactly what I mean, and I'm not referring to the natural bloody type from sunbursts or lightning. Our systems have really high-quality shielding. It's then supported by advanced grounding technology and surge protection measures to enhance our resilience to naturally occurring EMP disturbances," Serge replies. "Who knows how well all these elements might handle an intense, weaponized version that's deliberate and directional, like maybe a laser or whatever this thing is. I guess if the energy is strong enough, it can temporarily or maybe even permanently disable some or all of our electronic equipment perhaps. I'll have to talk to our designers in Italy to get their feedback on the potential impacts of a deliberate attack with one of these things. It's irrelevant if whoever they are do actually have a directional EMP weapon. That's one scary as hell scenario, I can tell you. That's a very high-level and serious threat to our operations in my book."

"What has all of this got to do with Ben and the minister going missing? Admittedly, the timing seems to be incredibly coincidental, doesn't it? How all these occurrences just happen within hours of each other? Don't you think?" I challenge, unease and probably a tinge of apprehension creeping into my thoughts, particularly as we have no control or even input into any of it.

"Buggered if I know, to be honest, Ned. I've found, though, sometimes, when a series of complications occur simultaneously, there's a natural inclination for us to automatically assume they're connected. Sometimes, they just aren't. I'm desperate to find out all the same. You're going to have to sit tight where you are for a while, I suppose. Once this coup settles down and flights open up again, get yourself back here to Melbourne, and let's see what we can kick into gear as a team. In the meantime, maybe you can get in contact with our nearest embassy or consulate and explain what we think has happened to Ben and the old double-barrel minister. See what sort of reaction it generates with them, if anything at this early stage. Talk later today, Ned." Serge hung up before I had the chance to think about anything else to say or ask.

"Yeah, I'll see what I can do. Talk later," I reply robotically to an already dead phone. I thought about what Serge had assumed. You know, though Serge, sometimes, when a series of complications does occur simultaneously, they may bloody well be actually connected. Time for me to ring RJ again for a bit of encouragement and to bounce a few thoughts off her. First, I want to call my wife Carla to let her know I'm safe and what's going on.

Later in the day, I reluctantly make contact with the Australian Embassy in Rabat, Morocco. I already know the unconfirmed issues are going to be a very hard sell; not surprisingly, it is, in particular, with the limited information I currently have, or that I can share, none of it verified as yet. I also do not want to include any mention of Castelle in the conversation at this stage. This is because it's more than likely to then turn into a giant cluster screw-up of vast political interference of the highest order, right out of Canberra.

Before calling, I repeatedly go over and rehearse my explanation of how Ben is missing and presumably in some sort of trouble. Like maybe being kidnapped, somewhere in Western Sahara. I spin myself every yarn I can think of to try and make my claim sound rational and articulate, to me at least. When I finally work up the courage to call, I speak at length to a senior consular officer named Ryan, who I must say is very patient and accommodating. He firstly wanted to talk briefly about the circumstances surrounding the coup, if I felt safe, why I'm in Nouakchott, the sort of questions I'd expected and prepared for.

Then to Ben. "He's travelling with the Western Saharan Environment Minister. Both departed Nouadhibou to go to Laayoune. Somewhere between Nouadhibou and Dakhla, they appear to have gone missing," I say.

"How do you know they're missing?" he interrupts me.

It's a very fair question and one I'm also expecting. It's just not something I really want to delve into in any great detail, although I have little choice. I briefly explain how we imagined things unravelling. The check post at Dakhla, how the two vehicles hadn't arrived as planned, the way we were contacted by the Westra representative there to advise the loss of contact, the inability to contact them via any of our communication devices. We can't confirm they're missing or maybe kidnapped, except nothing has been seen or heard from any of them in nearly 4 days. All of the expected questions are asked. "What is the full name, age and nationality of your missing Ben, his passport details, provide a detailed description of his physical appearance, height, weight, hair and eye colour, any distinguishing features, blah, blah, blah." Ryan methodically went through the whole check list of items I expected.

I give him as many of the details he asks for as I can. Then I explain how our MD in Australia contacted the Westra Government officials he has been dealing with to enquire after the minister and Ben and asked to actually talk to the environment minister. "The official simply declared he's not available, denying anything is amiss: the minister is on extended leave and that Ben is not with him," I add.

"What is the name of the minister? What date, time and location were these persons last seen?" he probes.

I give him all of the particulars we have available about the location and the minister, which is minimal anyway. Also provided are the contact details for the communication devices that are in both vehicles and with all of the guys.

"Any recent photographs of the missing people? Your Ben? This minister?" Ryan asks.

I haven't got any with me, so I suggest I'd arrange for something to be sent to him, then clarify, "No ransom has been demanded or any communication received from anybody since they went missing. Although it is confirmed that both vehicles were, and are, still missing."

I'm already regretting my decision to make the Embassy contact, although I know any information I can provide is critical to aid a potential investigation. There is just an extremely frustrating feel in my gut about how little I do actually know for sure. Or more significantly, I suppose, how much other information I know that I'm unwilling or unable to really share with Ryan at the moment. Like the earlier strange call from Ben, then the escalation into Samir being killed in my office, my escape from Nouadhibou and the unauthorised radar runs. Now, though, well, now bugger it, I have the Army Commander wanting to interview me.

"What information can you give me about the circumstances surrounding their disappearance, like any suspicious activities or warnings prior to them going missing, any threats, or unusual occurrences? Can you think of any potential motives or individuals who may have been involved?" Ryan puts to me, now delving into the very nuts and bolts of what I'm not yet prepared to share. Or more specifically, what I don't know enough about to share without muddying the waters further.

I explain briefly about what we're doing in Nouadhibou and Westra, omitting the specific details likely to lead me into difficult or hard to explain territory, like Castelle. I give Ryan all of Serge's details and bravely suggest he call Serge to gather any more recent information he might have received. Ryan suggests the query might be jointly managed by the Paris and Rabat Embassies, as this particular incident kicked-off in Mauritania, which is handled by Paris. The relevant consular officer will use the information I've provided to assist in coordinating with local authorities to try to find the missing persons, which Ryan states technically now numbers four, if we include the two security personnel in the escort car. Who knows why I haven't given those two guys any thought at all? I feel regretful about it as I sign off from Ryan and hang up. Really, counting Samir, we have five people heavily involved.

Chapter 4

BETWEEN ALIOUNE AND DHABE, they kept us regularly updated on matters linked with the status of the coup and any military administrations. Alioune did explain to me nonetheless, how Colonel Aziz was far from pleased to find I'd mysteriously departed the hotel against his orders to remain in place. It also emerges Rob and Lee were likewise ordered by the Colonel to stay in the hotel until he returned. All very dubious of the Colonel, or maybe it's just a plain healthy degree of paranoia taking over yet again.

Regardless, to the collective us, it already sounded like the coup was gradually blowing itself out over the following few days after we'd arrived at the UN compound. It even seemed to be relatively free of violence and gunfire from what we can hear on the outside. Within the week, the coup was indeed declared over. It was possible to see from the safety of the compound, Nouakchott begin to return to the crazy busy Arabian cosmopolitan city it had been prior to the upheaval, little by little.

I note that Rob and Lee are relaxed, although bordering on impatient to get out of the country, as soon as possible. Their plan was to seek refuge over one of the nearby borders, they suggest, by any means achievable. And it sounds like they have multiple options available to them. I'm shocked at how extraordinarily well-informed they are about the goings on of the coup in particular. More so about the potential, possibly illicit exit strategies available to get out of the country and the manner in which to expedite their way out.

Unpredictably, they invite me along. These two are full of such surprises, as my ongoing discussions with them uncovers while in the compound. I'm of the very strong belief both Rob and Lee are far more than just oilfield equipment suppliers. They display a remarkably high level of knowledge about various industries, indicating to me they're extraordinarily well informed.

The moment the situation begins to stabilise, Rob and Lee commence organising a host of – what I thought to be – curious activities to expedite their discreet departure. On concluding their research and consultation with their various contacts, they decide the country of Mali to the East was going to be their exit point. They share with me their thoughts about it being the closest and safest point out of Mauritania. Also, where we'd hopefully attract the least amount of attention on arrival. It also turns out to be the country where Rob and Lee miraculously have some very good connections amongst what sounds like an extremely dubious network of acquaintances, as I soon find out. All of this subterfuge, is imperfectly designed and haphazardly executed in an attempt to avoid the potential impacts of the police or military investigators who frantically want to *interview* all of us, it seems. Mind you, I'm likewise anxious to get out of Mauritania as well, in particular without becoming victim to the likely overzealous police or military investigators looking for me. In my case, it'll ultimately be about the circumstances surrounding the killing of Samir, my Westra government supplied driver. Him being a Western Saharan citizen, found dead in the office of an Australian guest worker in Nouadhibou, Mauritania. Nothing to worry about here… like bloody hell.

For Rob and Lee, well, something else entirely seemed to be going on with my two American co-conspirators and why the good Colonel wants to *'interview'* them once again. As it turns out, Rob and Lee both speak fluent French… another little surprise. I'm not sure why; it just is, not that it matters, in fact my thoughts lean to this discovery being in our best interests at some point.

Obscuring ourselves still in the traditional indigent clothing and headwear, our exit from the UN compound initially involves being furtively transported out in the back of a type of truck that, to me anyway, seems unlikely or incapable of taking us too far. We ultimately transfer to a bigger semi-trailer that still does not impress on me, the likelihood to be able to take us much further either. Who knows? The primary objective is to get to the closest border town to our east, to the small town of Néma, still in Mauritania, then cross the border into another small town, Nara in Mali. Rob and Lee both assure me, theoretically and technically, it should be a no-brainer. Yeah, well, let's keep a careful watch out for old mate 'Murphy' is my advice to them. That would be the mythical Murphy's Law, which typically states, 'Anything that can go wrong will go wrong, and at the worst possible time.' It's only a saying, not grounded on logic, scientific laws or anything else technical. The problem, though, is it too often comes to visit uninvited and when least expected.

The trip is an agonisingly slow, dusty, swelteringly hot, turbulent and chaotic 14 hour ride. All three of us cramped into a stifling compartment behind our wrinkled and ancient driver Ibrahim Brahim. The space was probably his bed at some time years ago – more profit in passengers using it than him. The only glass window in the entire truck cabin is the heavily cracked windscreen. All others are covered in various forms of billowing plastic curtains or cloth screens. Like many trucks we saw on the route, ours – an old, beaten-up, dark green Renault semi-trailer – is heavily overloaded. Mostly, this is with sacks of UN food aid grain or flour and some local cargo, plus an abundance of local travellers and their goods and chattels. It's hard to say if the locals are free-loaders or if they'd paid a bribe of some sort to have a precarious position lolling about way up on top of the cargo, seemingly not caring either way.

The journey, around 430 km or so, takes us along possibly the worst road I'd ever been on… in my life – largely sandy dirt to sometimes heavily pot-holed rock-hard gravel or clay sections. The journey is inundated with various forms of broken-down or slow-moving traffic and intermittent wildlife like gazelle and antelope grazing. I'd never seen these spectacular animals before and I'm impressed with their markings and the various shapes and sizes of horns they display. I think any other time, I'd have enjoyed just sitting there and watching them, taking it all in with my camera, just not today. We stop repeatedly to offload and reload local cargo and 'passengers'. These intermittent breaks allow us to get out and uncoil our crooked, kinked up bodies and to gather a breath or two of welcome fresh, albeit dusty air. The atmosphere of staleness, body odour and bad breath in our cramped compartment space is, well,… it's challenging.

At each stop, we're habitually briefed by our heavily-armed Tuareg 'guide' Ousmane. He wears a distinctive indigo turban made of some material known as mud cloth, called a *bogolan*. Apparently, it's made from handwoven fabric from his clan and dyed with natural pigments Rob advises. I obviously have to know all this. This particular one is decorated with faded intricate patterns, depicting his family story, evidently. His task is to safely chaperone us through the border into Nara and then on to Bamako. In addition, his role extends to paying off all of the relevant officials and their hangers on various handfuls of cash. He has a lot of it, all provided by Lee; no shock there again. To me, Ousmane looks more like your quintessential hard-as-nails African mercenary. Not that I'd know what one looks like – but if I had to guess…

As we approach Néma, my mobile phone whistles loudly, startling all of us out of our stupor. It's good to know we're back in mobile phone network range, no longer crippled by the outcomes of the coup. The whistle tone indicates it's Serge. *What the hell?* I decided to take the call.

"Where are you now, Kelly? Fill me in," he squawks, voice distorting. The fact he calls me Kelly and not Ned suggests he's in a lousy mood… There's something unexpected… not.

I quickly explain our circumstances and advance plan. "We intend going to Bamako. Our ballpark time frame is to be there in the next couple of days all being well. If the various Gods on duty are onside, I hope to be going home within 3-4 days. Any news on Ben or the minister?" I try to ask quietly. My screw up, though, mentioning the minister. I'm cognisant of both Rob and Lee looking at me and probably hearing every word. Should have kept 'that' word out of it.

"Unfortunately, yes. The escort car… well, it's been found abandoned and semi-buried under drift sand in behind some dunes at an old resort called El Argoub, or something like that. It's on the coast. Samir's Westra guys who had been monitoring the minister's progress in Dakhla along with RJ's local mate found it yesterday. The minister, Ben or their car have not been found, nor any of the escorts themselves. I've just spoken to RJ, and she advises the escort car is not damaged, as in it isn't shot up or damaged by a collision or car accident. No blood in or on the car, so who knows where the escorts are. My money is on them being in on whatever happened to the minister and Ben," he states while I listen with unease. This is not making any real advancement. Every bend in this potential damn kidnap scenario just leads to another piss poor outcome of ever-increasing magnitude.

"OK, thanks. Look, now is not a good time to talk. Your voice is dropping in and out. I'll call you later, when we get to Nara," I lie. I can hear him pretty well. I'm just uncomfortable discussing it any further in front of the guys.

"Dang, your buddy still missing, eh, slick?" Lee asks indifferently. Who knows where the nickname 'slick' comes from or what it means. It's a new one for me. One of many. We'd talked a bit about Ben being missing back at the compound before we left. Not in any great depth. Just enough to make conversation. "He with a

Government Minister as well now? Both missing. Can't be good for the blood pressure? Anything to do with the coup ya think?"

"Yeah, he is with a minister, but one from Western Sahara – not Mauritania – the Minister for Environment. They'd been on their way to Laayoune for a briefing. As I mentioned back at the compound, they went missing along with their escort on the way. That call was about our guys finding the escort car, minus our escorts or anybody else," I state.

"Sounds like your escort guys might be the ones who took 'em. Know anything about those guys, who they work for normally?" Lee asks.

"Yeah, my thoughts as well. They're the minister's own security guys, so who knows what's happening there." I'm not sure why I feel the necessity to share this with them, or any of it, really. I think I just want to air it in my own head to sort of get things into a clearer focus myself, so I tell them about what we're actually doing with the radar.

"Hmmmmm… Your biggest problem out there, bud, is not the fish pilfering, although that's no doubt mammoth. By far, though, all of the other crap, like the people trafficking and organ harvesting, illegal wildlife trade and drug running blows the fish pilfering out of the sky – or out of the water. Then there is the big one. Gun running, along the entire coastline there, all the way around to Tunisia and Libya," Rob says, disturbing the hell out of my train of thought. As I'd thought before, these guys are remarkably well informed and not at all what I'd have expected American oil businessmen to be like. I'm cementing my earlier thoughts that these two are into much more than just oilfield equipment suppliers… Not that this is an issue, I don't think.

"You want to elaborate a bit more on that, Rob?" I ask, looking at both of them in disbelief, I suppose. Rob is about to continue when the driver yells out abruptly, pointing to a roadblock just in front of us on the bend, at the outskirts of Néma. *Cannot possibly be good,* is my immediate thought. *Because we're still in bloody Mauritania.*

Our Tuareg 'guide' Ousmane reacts first. He'd been asleep in the passenger seat next to the driver. Alerted, he instantly sits upright and speaks to the driver in rapid Arabic. The driver produces the most superb French shrug, with both continuing to converse for a second or two more. Ousmane turns and speaks to us quickly, in French – not helpful for me. He doesn't seem to be too bothered all the same. Ousmane turns back to see about a dozen police casually walking out onto the road. He unhooks his shoulder holster and handgun, placing them on the floor of the cabin. The truck slows down and then comes to a jerky stop in the centre of the road, in a swirl of our own thick dust catching up and encircling us. Ousmane steps down from the cabin and casually walks over to the police desk, smiling a greeting while lighting up a cigarette.

"Police roadblock, Ousmane reckons they're probably looking for coup plotters or escaping coup members," Rob mutters.

As I look back out the windscreen at the police and Ousmane talking animatedly, I smell something I haven't for a very long time, gun oil. Followed right away by the unmistakable click of a gun slide being pulled back in order to load a cartridge into the chamber from the gun's magazine. I look down at Lee's hands to see the gun – an ugly black pistol. A Glock, I think. Looking over at Rob, I see he's likewise loading another one. My heart just about stops. I speculate where these guys have got their guns from, first of all, then more importantly, why the bloody hell have they armed themselves?

"What the hell, Lee? Rob?" I say, exasperated. I can now more noticeably detect the strong smell of the gun oil in the confined space. I'm irritated to buggery, especially because I know I can't do anything about it. More importantly, there is no win for anybody if this turns into a gunfight between these two... or us three, and the multitude of police outside.

"You want one? We have one for you. Think about it, pal. We're just outside Néma, and if need be, we do what we have to so we can get over the border into Mali. Once over there, we're home and hosed. You OK with that, pal?" Rob asks. Menacingly, I feel, adding 'pal' as another nickname for me to the list.

"No, I'm not bloody OK with that, pal! I'd very much prefer letting Ousmane do his thing instead of turning this into a gunfight between us and the whole bloody police force out there," I snap, waving my arm angrily out towards the group of police and Ousmane.

Ousmane, who in this very instance seems to be shaking a bulky hand with the senior officer, payoff proceeding. "Let's see how he gets on first, eh?"

I already know if Ousmane isn't successful in bribing the officers, things are likely to get very deadly, quickly. I put my hand out for the other gun they're proffering to me. I check it out and load it. Ready for… whatever anarchy is about to wash over us if it all turns to crap.

I get the impression Ousmane has probably donated the magic number of bills to the officer, seeing how they are now laughing and shaking each other's shoulders and forearms. At the sight of this laughter, Ibrahim Brahim, our truck driver starts up the truck once again, readying to depart. Ousmane finishes his cigarette with the officer, laughs some more, briefly shakes arms again and casually walks back to the truck, steadily stepping up into the cabin. Always a very tense moment, this, when you turn your back on a prospective adversary as you walk away. If anything is ever going to come undone, this is the most likely time. Today is thankfully not the day.

Ousmane cautiously obtains our exit visas from Mauritania and our entry visas into Mali, with no questions asked, from what we were able to see, anyway, just discreet handfuls of local cash. It's obvious to me that he's clearly done this before, possibly many times, as he's very efficient at his role. We roll over the border into Mali and the town of Nara with no further awkward situations, at least none obvious to me, all bribes appropriately bestowed and the recipients delighted with their good fortune. Exit and entry visas all seem to be correctly and officially signed or stamped and handed back with no fuss. Watch out for Murphy, I remind myself.

It's gradually getting darker now as we drive into the main township of Nara, and our transfer vehicle to take us from Nara to Bamako has not yet arrived. After a while, it's decided to get Ousmane to arrange for some accommodation for the night while Rob and Lee chase up their ride, which has apparently broken down. What did I say about Murphy?

Nara is a relatively small, remote settlement with limited infrastructure, even fewer public amenities and absolutely no tourist trade. We'd already figured accommodation options for Western travellers are likely to be few and very basic, if any, reflective of the rural nature of the region. Guest houses are scarcer, and those in existence likely offer simple rooms with minimal facilities. However, the capacity of Ousmane and of ordinary Malian citizens emerge as our salvation. Ousmane has convinced some locals to provide us shelter for the night. I guess another successful pay-off has been appropriately bestowed and gratefully accepted.

Our shelter is not luxurious by any means, very welcome all the same. It's a mudbrick, thatch and wooden hut of dubious construction proficiency, centred in a high-walled family compound of various living quarters, food storage huts, communal spaces and animal shelters. It seems to house several generations of one family or clan, with the compound owned by a senior clan elder. So in accordance with cultural traditions, the chieftain makes us welcome and feeds us enthusiastically, then leaves us to ourselves for the rest of the cold night. Once we've settled down into our hut, I want to revisit my earlier query to the guys.

"So Rob, you OK to expand a bit more on what we discussed before the roadblock, about the fish pilfering?" I ask, while I look at both him and Lee, then Ousmane.

"Yeah, well, about that. We have a little bit to do with some oil industry colleagues who work extensively in the region. Their biggest concern is the gun running in the sector and the organisations fronting those enterprises. These guys seem to be from a mostly disparate lot of militant Islamist groups wanting to build their own little Islamic fiefdoms in West and North Africa. They have a significant piracy impact on our oil exploration and production activities, particularly in Algeria and Libya of recent times. So yeah, don't get me wrong, although I think the fish pilfering is a major issue, it's less of a big issue for us… well, at the moment, anyway. The build-up of militant groups and their various misdeeds is more an issue for our industry," Rob replies, looking at me in the glow of our oil lamp.

"I'm wondering then why the Mauritanian and Western Saharan Governments might be more interested in chasing the overfishing concerns than the gunrunning or other equally undesirable concerns to both countries."

"Is all same," Ousmane utters. I look over the oil lamp at his eerie face in wonder.

"What do you mean, Ousmane? What is all the same?" I query genuinely at his comment. This is the first time I'd even heard him speak English.

Rob steps in before Ousmane can comment further. "What he means is that all of those activities going on outside of the EEZ are pretty much conducted by the same bunch of parasites. It's just different types of income streams to them, that's all. Controlled by a few different organisations. It's how they fund their Islamist ideologies – via terrorism. Each one of those schemes provides a share of their income to the organisers, who help control all the activities out there."

"The controllers have no regard about the moral aspect of these ventures, slick. You know what I mean, like the organ harvesting or child trafficking, they just want their cut so they can buy more weapons and boats or bombs and things of that nature. The more of the shonky schemes they can get their hooks into out there, the more money they make. Easy peasy," Lee adds.

"How the hell do you guys know all this? There's no bloody way this all comes from working as oilfield suppliers. It's hard to bloody believe," I say, mostly humour in my voice.

"Believe what you want, bud. Don't matter to us. We're simply well-versed oilfield equipment suppliers who keep their well-tuned ears to the ground is all, slick." Lee smiles at me in the subtle glimmer of the lamp. Rob joins in with a little laugh and then Ousmane. I can see the funny side of all this. Regardless, I'd be more comfortable knowing what they really do for a living. Like, are they CIA or something similar?

"OK, let me give you an example that a good maritime friend of mine, a ship's master, revealed to me recently. The fish pilfering is still very big business, no matter what. It appears to have turned another commercial corner these days as well. For instance, apart from the best of the best fish being kept, frozen and sold, the rest of the bycatch is macerated up into fish meal, massive great ship's holds full of it. It then has some synthetic antioxidant additives introduced to it, something called EQ. I can't remember what it is at the moment. Anyway, it also apparently has the occasional steroid and preservative added before it's sold. This is by the ship-load full, mind you, and fed as fish feed to multitudes of aquaculture farms all over the world. Your own country included, I think, down in some place called Tasman, something like that? All for extremely high profits. In the end, though, bud, it effects the live fish it's being fed to. It seems this EQ product somehow lowers the quality level of Omega 3 in the fish, which is the whole purpose of why most people eat fish in the first place, yeah? So you see, the rorts are endless for these guys," Rob alleges, smiling again.

We, as in Castelle, were already cognisant of this swindle. We'd been made aware of it long before we mobilised onto the project. Nonetheless, I think I'm probably more stunned that these guys are across so much of it, especially the supply to our most southern state, Tasmania. However, I have other more puzzling concerns.

"What about this organ harvesting you mention? I'm guessing this is the removal of fresh healthy organs from the dead, or the living, possibly even without their consent? How is this possibly done out there, outside of the EEZ. Won't the organs perish unless they're transplanted quickly?" I really haven't any idea how this macabre scenario might actually come together. I'm keen to know if the guys are across it along with everything else they seem to have a handle on.

"Yeah, well, it's another crazy ugly story. It's also one we know little about other than it mostly involves plenty of exploitation, coercion and – more often than not – copious amounts of violence. My loose understanding of it all is Albino body parts are specifically valued, as they're supposed to bring all sorts of riches, success, power or sexual conquest. Macabre, isn't it? It's also rumoured some of those body parts are used in superstitious witchcraft rituals, or something along those lines," Rob says, raising his eyebrows. "I can't remem-

ber, but I think I might have actually started that rumour myself."
Rob and Lee both laugh at this.

"We've heard from some of our industry mariners that one of the motherships somewhere out there has a modern hospital onboard. It's probably closer to Algeria, Morocco or Tunisia is my guess. From there, they use helicopters to fly the ice-packed organs to the recipients onshore. Or maybe fly the recipient out to the ship for the swap. Who knows? Any thoughts, Lee?" Rob queries.

"Nah, I'm pretty much the same. I know it exists, just not much about the machinations. I do know the illicit side of harvesting makes huge profits, though, from recipients in frantic need of those organs for their specific transplants. I read an article recently about it. Seems a very lucrative business for those OK with putting their ethics, moralities and principles aside," Lee adds.

"Anyway, guys, that's me. It's been a big day, I'm dog-tired. Happy to talk some more tomorrow if y'all want. Right now, though, I'm done," Rob says, as he lies down onto the traditional sleeping mats provided for us, made from grass and straw, spread out on the dirt floor. They're thin but nevertheless comfortable enough to sleep after spending 14 hours in that bloody truck.

We're woken in the very early hours of the next morning to the excited chatter of massed birds feeding off the nectar of a tree right outside our hut. They're tiny, multicoloured, beautiful and very vocal, a sort of metallic green on the head and back, while the chest is a vibrant red, bordered with bright yellow. What a great way to kick off a new day after the past vile week we've just been through.

"Sunbirds," Ousmane says in English. "Feed upside down." They are indeed feeding upside down. There's so many of them vying for attention that I'd missed that unique feat.

As we're standing at the door of our hut watching the mass of birds, our ride finally arrives, complete with a European driver, maybe Russian. Whoever, he seems, smells and gives me the definite sense of being massively hungover, or possibly not yet at that stage, still drunk. Maybe he's suffering is some sort of aftereffect malaise from repairing a broken-down vehicle… while getting drunk. Whatever, I'm still not in a position to be choosy, I guess. The ride itself is an old, although seemingly well-maintained Peugeot station wagon. Ousmane tells us it's "most best for Mali," mainly for its toughness in the harsh local conditions, I assume. Then apparently, there is the other factor. Mali has so many of them around the countryside that spare parts are easy to obtain, a bit like all the Mercedes in Mauritania. I don't care, I just want to get moving, as do Lee and Rob.

I'm beginning to feel a bit more inspired, little by little – excited almost – the closer I get to hopefully going home. With only the journey from Nara to Bamako in front of us, the rest hopefully will be just flights, unless of course Murphy gets involved, which is not entirely out of the equation. Our Bamako escapade is about 300 km of what we're told can often be especially challenging road surfaces on Route Nationale 1. 'Especially challenging' is a distinctive bit of terminology offering a variety of thought-provoking images in my mind's eye. None of them reassuring, suggesting perhaps the journey might quite possibly offer mostly very poorly maintained paved sections of road. Undeniably, it does have exceptionally poor maintenance of the paved sections. More spectacularly, we're then faced with literally awe-inspiring sections of completely unpaved and unmaintained road. As a result, we anticipate our journey to take us about 6-8 hours.

We are so wrong.

Some latter parts of the route do in fact have… reasonable tarmac surfaces, I suppose. While the remote rural sections… bloody hell, they're so much worse than the road from Nouakchott to Nara. Some sectors are particularly brutal, huge dust-filled potholes, deep rutted tyre tracks. More ominous though are the multi-layers of seemingly bottomless corrugations in the road. These are a series of bumps and ruts, causing the vehicle to bounce and shudder violently all over the place even at very slow speed. The constant shaking and vibration are enough to make us periodically lose traction, regardless of how slow we drive. The shock is so severe, at one stage. It shatters the rear window of our station wagon, loudly, like a gunshot, alarming the hell out of us all. At that very moment, it wasn't clear to us if we were under attack, with the sound truly suggesting it is a gunshot. We piled out of the car defensively, armed and ready to attack, only to find no threat towards us other than the bloody dusty road and a busted window. We have nothing to cover the broken window space other than a couple of shirts, so we continue driving slowly through the dusty conditions, with all windows now wound down to try and avoid any further breakages during this perilous and unpleasant stage of the journey. With the choking dust now billowing in, it demands we drive even slower and with extreme caution for our own health and safety. We continue, just much slower, while encountering hordes of nomads on foot and a wide variety of vehicular traffic.

We also come across more wildlife, stony sand dunes, gibber plains and masses of broken-down cars, tractors, trucks and trailers everywhere. Multitudes of them. No doubt the breakdowns are primarily due to the savage punishment rendered by the inferior road conditions and more likely from even more dubious driving skills. Navigating through this quagmire takes us significantly longer than anticipated, well over 10 hours in total. One matter delaying us, though, is not the road or driving conditions as an end result. It's the build-up of traffic outside of Banamba, about 145 km from Bamako. It clears periodically, but slowly. Then frustratingly builds up once again. Lee and I decide to take a stroll along the line of stalled vehicles with Ousmane to see what the hold-up is being caused by. To our incredulity, it's a peculiar 'tax collection' roadblock instigated by some of the local enterprising and rebellious Tuareg tribesmen. This 'tax' roadblock holds up traffic intermittently, interestingly by dragging a simplistic chain of connected tumbleweed over the road to hold up traffic. It's probably one of the most bizarre occurrences I'd ever seen. You could quite easily circumvent this by simply driving right over or around and past this woody chain without a problem; it's the dozen or so heavily-armed Tuareg tribesmen on the other side that discourage this. On arrival at the riotous setting, Ousmane quickly pulls us aside and explains to Lee what is going on, in fast French.

Lee explains to me, half laughing. "Ousmane says these are his people. They're Tuareg, from up North and from over the border in Niger. No danger here, not for us at least. They're doing this to send a message and to be confrontational, to irritate the hell out of the government in Bamako, to let them know they can just do such things whenever they want. Especially now, as economic and political conditions have worsened for the Tuareg, triggering their grievances to escalate. They'll collect a bunch of Francs from those drivers who can afford it and then disappear long before any military or police arrive, come back another day and do it all over again somewhere else," I'm stunned at the boldness of the tribesmen to simply hold traffic to cash ransom in order to try and survive tough economic times.

Ousmane eagerly arranges for us to divert our car around the mired traffic jam and the dreaded weed chain, doubtless for yet another generous handful of money gratefully received by the tribesmen. We begin to make our way again towards Bamako, Ousmane laughing hysterically at the madness of the moment.

"So, what on earth was that all about, guys? It sure appeared to me like some sort of bizarre and dangerous scheme by the tribesmen, isn't it?" I ask, laughing along with Ousmane and the guys. Rob talks to Ousmane again in French, querying from his own interest as to what the hell it was all about. Ousmane replies, animatedly to Rob.

"OK, it seems a rebellion by various Tuareg groups commenced back in 1990, and it's still going strong today, in one form or another. It's spread from Mali over into Niger, with the aim of achieving autonomy or at least forming some sort of their own nation-state. It pretty much sounds as if the Tuareg have been marginalised by the government over the years, promising any number of solutions, all broken. So now the Tuareg are firing up again, into another nationwide rebellion. I think that's what he means," Rob says.

"What with holding traffic to ransom for a cash tax on the roadside? Not much of a rebellion, is it?" I ask, a bit dumbfounded.

"Nah, I think that's just to piss the government off. Probably also to distract them a bit while other groups get more seriously engaged in building the rebellion. Ya gotta admit, that's a hell of a way to piss the government off, though. If you pull that roadside tax thing in multiple locations over a week or two, or many months, damned hilarious, don't you think?" Rob chuckles, instigating a group laugh-in all over again.

I'm not so sure of the hilarity angle. Then again, I'm less sure of the local Tuareg politics behind this previous or impending rebellion. I'm all in for a good old-fashioned fight for rights though, so good luck to the Tuareg nation, I say. We finally arrive into the congested and polluted traffic of Bamako mid-evening, booking ourselves into the Hôtel Nord-Sud, which is relatively close to the airport. It's a seemingly popular choice for European travellers, as it offers hot running water and a bath, which is all I want after these past days on the road.

Later that night and well refreshed, I reassure Carla all is well in the world… well, sort of, anyway. I also update RJ on everything that's happened since our last contact. Next, I venture down to the only space that passes for a bar at the hotel and order a beer. I engage with Rob further about the unusual activities off the coast of Mauritania and Westra. He seems less inclined to talk about it now, at least in any great detail such as I'd like him to, anyway. I put forward how their unique oil sector focus could make certain aligned information available to them and their industry colleagues. Enough probably to develop a depth of awareness of the critical hitches hypothetically impacting their operations and other offshore industries, like ours, and I say so.

"Yeah, you're sort of right, except we're only focused on our own specific patch of complications and how to minimise the impact to our industry operations. That in itself is a big enough pain-in-the-arse for us to deal with. Lord knows we struggle more than we'd like as it is without diving into anybody else's business. Unless, of course, it presents a direct threat to ours," Rob states dryly. "We continually wrestle at times to try and manage the level of risks thrown at us in general. You probably know what I mean, things like the attacks on exploration drilling rigs, the floating production facilities, the transfer pipelines getting the product back to onshore facilities, the list goes on. Our biggest concerns currently are the suicide attacks on support boats and slow-moving bulk shipping tankers. There has been an enhanced strategy towards these of late for some reason," Rob reveals, sounding somewhat dejected.

Lee adds, "Trying to protect those assets is proving harder for us every day as an industry. A close colleague of ours recently lost one of their heavy-duty support boats to Islamist pirates off the coast of Algeria. This vessel boasted some significant deter and repel equipment onboard, so we're perplexed as to how the pirates actually gained access. Unfortunately, these are items we will no doubt see turned back on us and our industry if they ever figure out how to deploy them." Lee looks at Rob and shrugs, then at me ruefully.

"Well… if for instance you're possibly referring to an EMP, an Electromagnetic Pulse device, used as a weapon, then they have already figured it out. Sort of, anyway. Something of this nature was fired against us the other day, the last night we ran our radar system in Nouadhibou. I believe with no significant negative outcome. This time," I say this while looking at the bewildering expressions on both Rob and Lee. "By the look on your faces, I'm guessing I've nailed it?"

They both nod forlornly in agreement.

So I go on to explain – what little I knew, anyway – about the recent EMP effects we thought we'd been impacted by. They both listen to my explanation without interruption, looking blankly at each other and nodding periodically.

"Well, right there is a whole other world of hurt we weren't expecting or wanting… or needing. Certainly not so soon, at least. Hell, we're still trying to figure out how they took possession of the vessel. That all seems a bit redundant now, doesn't it?" Rob replies solemnly, raising his arms in frustration, looking somewhat overwhelmed.

"Something else you should probably be aware of," Lee adds, lifting his eyebrows as he looks at me, then at Rob. "There's another piece of equipment onboard the vessel they now have. It's called a long-range acoustic device, or LRAD." Both look at me more despondently, if that's possible, to see what my reaction is. There's none – yet. What the hell's an LRAD?

"Before you ask, an LRAD is an ultrasonic directional weapon using intense and targeted sound to incapacitate a human threat. It's an extremely high-powered sound wave blast, like a sonic boom. Capable of damaging or destroying eardrums and causing severe pain, disorientation and nausea. So then, between the device that destroys electronics and the other one destroying eardrums, they have formidable weaponry available to them." Lee frowns.

"Bloody hell, guys." I'm actually stunned. The only tangible expression I can muster is fear, I think, and probably anything else in between. "Why'd one of your industry vessels require this sort of equipment onboard? That's almost military grade weaponry, isn't it? What else have they got a hold of while they were at it?"

"Nothing else of note we're aware of other than the usual small arms standard for those vessels. As for why they're onboard, both those devises were being transported out to an offshore oil storage facility for installation, for their protection. Because we lost comms with the vessel, we're not sure if those bits of gear had been functioning during the transit. If they'd actually been operating, you can probably appreciate why we're a bit troubled as to how they might have captured the vessel while it was on the move," Lee replies.

"Insider onboard, maybe, part of the crew? Someone who's privy to how to get his Islamic hoer buddies onboard, undetected?" I suggest, as I look out the bar window at the twinkling city lights. "I honestly wouldn't know what to think any more about any of what I'd heard over the past few days. Although I do acknowledge now, the fish pilfering seems the least of the harmful threats outside the EEZ. Which makes me wonder if the radar searches for the fish pilfering fleets were just some sort of subterfuge? Perhaps to enable an enhanced interpretation of where all the other activities are being conducted out there?"

"Yeah, our thoughts also. Now you can probably gather why we think the illegal fish pilfering threat is further down the food chain for us too. With these sorts of weapons in the hands of the terrorists, things are only going to get more difficult for us to defend our industry operations out there," Rob says quietly.

We continue discussing a number of different angles for another half hour or so. Then after exchanging our various contacts, I bid them farewell. I'm flying out very early the following morning and want some rest. I also desperately want to talk to Sergio and RJ about tonight's discussions and more importantly to chat again with my wife.

Chapter 5

ALL IN ALL, IT took me almost three harrowing weeks to weave my way around one perilous morsel of misadventure after another to finally get from Mauritania to Melbourne. Why? Good bloody question. Starting by subtly fleeing Nouakchott to Bamako, the capital of Mali, then from Mali to Tunisia, Dubai and lastly to Melbourne. I finally arrive back in Australia after those harrowing weeks enroute, unsure if I feel relief or just plain exhaustion. Maybe a bit of both. Pretty much the same, anyway. The trip from Mali to Tunisia then to Dubai was all as expected, then it all fell into a hole. Our home leg from Dubai to Melbourne ended up being diverted to Singapore, as a result of an onboard medical emergency, then a monumental layover in Singapore while everything got reconfigured to get us all to Melbourne.

Now in downtown Melbourne, and battling the brisk, biting cold gusts sweeping along Elizabeth Street this not so fine morning. Myself and all other pedestrians find ourselves with no other choice other than to rush through the annual invasion of nature's allergy season. This cyclical period sees a surge in the unremitting airborne pollen and other allergens from countless London Plane trees. It sets the stage for an uncomfortable day ahead, marked by itching, sneezing and intensified discomfort. I literally run into the building entrance where Marinetti Electronics operate from to try and escape the environmental barrage on the street, only to be confronted by cigarette-smoking desperadoes lingering in their self-induced grey fog barely inside the entrance. Really, in this bloody weather, with all this crap already in the air and in their lungs, getting a last puff in before going to work… some people are just seriously asking to be publicly abused, aren't they? I take the stairs two at a time up to the office. Apart from coughing, wheezing and sneezing my lungs out as a result of inhaling the pollen, I have an overwhelming sense of doom and gloom for some reason. A bit like a heavy bout of Monday-itist… on a Thursday. The scars of recent misfortunes, since taking Ben's call weeks earlier, are now beginning to welt up on my psyche, making me feel uncomfortable in my own skin. I greet Helen, the very well put together elderly office manager as I walk past her desk into Sergio's private office. A soft waft of her perfumed scent drifts along with me. I wonder what Serge might have discovered after my call to him from Bamako a few days ago. I'm not anticipating it to be good news.

"Morning, Serge. How're you doing there today, mate?" I query, closing the door, then proceed to wheeze, sneeze and damn near blow my head off as I walk over to his desk, dropping my backpack with the hard drives onto the only clear space available. I'm a little shaken at the sight of him, to be honest. He looks an absolute bloody wreck. "You look a bit haggard there, old boy. You OK?"

In fact, he presents as positively ill – white like a ghost, fidgeting, mumbling to himself quietly, moving piles of papers back and forth.

"No, I'm not the best this morning," he says irritably, flicking imaginary hair out of his eyes. "I've just got off the phone from that Consular guy in Rabat, what's his name – Ryan, I think." Serge almost sobs, wringing his hands as he mentions this. "He's heard, unofficially, from some of his acquaintances in low places; it appears the minister has been found – very dead."

Serge just sits there then, staring. Saying nothing, looking straight at the office door, squeezing his hands. This doesn't look, or sound like a very good outcome, especially for Ben is what I'm imagining.

He begins again, sluggishly. "No real big shock there, I suppose… him ending up dead, that is, except it… it's the manner of it, Ned, which concerns them… and, and, and me, to be honest." Serge stutters, then shakes, or shivers. Hard to work out what the hell's going on with him. I'm becoming increasingly concerned all the same, for both Serge and what I'm about to hear.

"Yeah, his throat was cut, tongue cut out, ears cut off and eyes removed," he says, shaking violently as he bursts into a soft sob. "Nobody else found. I guess Ben and the two security support guys are still missing… or whatever they are. What in the name of Jesus Christ is going on with all this, Ned?" Serge stutters again, sobbing mournfully, wiping tears from his face against the back of his hand. "I'm an electrical engineer for Christ's sake, not a bloody policeman or soldier… or, or spy. I don't know how to deal with all this mess that's happening." Serge cries as he jumps up from his seat and begins pacing around the office, sobbing quietly.

"Serge, sit down, mate, please. Let's just talk this through for a bit." He doesn't seem to hear me, as he keeps pacing. I suppose I'm not so shocked about the minister being dead. Alarmed a little at the brutality, just not entirely disturbed. I'd almost been expecting something like this to materialise at some point in time, I suppose. Him turning up dead, I mean, just not something quite so brutal. Certainly nothing like this. I'm more shocked at what I'm seeing with Serge at the moment, though. Phew. He seems to be on the verge of an epic breakdown of some sort. I'm not sure who to call or what to do. I know I can't leave him on his own at the moment, though. I look out of the glass office petition to try and attract Helen's attention. However, she has her headset on and is looking down, clacking away furiously on her computer.

"Well, mate, this bit of mischief is the object of very ancient history, of legend. It's what they call ritualised symbolism. Basically, it has cultural meanings going way back, associated to early savagery. A very specific message is being sent amongst that bit of butchery," I state, watching an expression of shock slowly creep across Serge's face. "It's principally sending a message to all others to see nothing, hear nothing and say nothing. Or… maybe in the minister's case, perhaps he should not have seen something, heard something or said something, or maybe not done something?"

Serge fidgets with his phone. His behaviour is becoming more erratic, so unlike the Serge I've got to know.

I continue, "I speculate, old mate, the minister has been tied up in all these shenanigans off the coast, one way or another. When we tagged those boats outside the EEZ, it's put a very dramatic cat amongst the Islamist pigeons, and it's come back to bite him in particular, leading to his murder. Classic cause and effect aftermath, Serge."

I don't know if he hears me or if he's still churning the latest news around inside his mind. Whatever it is, he still looks positively ill and not improving.

"Come and sit down for a bit here with me, Serge, mate, please. Let's kick this around some, eh?" I suggest again gently, patting the seat next to me. Bloody hell, he looks like he should be in some sort of medical establishment under intensive care or in a full-blown care home right at this very moment. He's coming unravelled before my eyes at a very fast rate of knots.

"No, screw it, Ned, I'm OK – sssort of," Serge stutters.

He's definitely not OK from what I can see. I don't think whatever it is he's suffering from is seasonal depression either. This is something way more serious.

"Head Office told me last night they're going to pull the plug on the contract over there. In its entirety, effective immediately. I'm still trying to get over the shock of it, I've been working my way through the likely breach of contract matters this morning… when this bloody call from Rabat came in," Serge says gloomily, pointing a shaky finger towards the phone on his desk.

I take a second or two to digest this peculiar bit of information myself. It seems a very odd position for Marinetti to take. "What has made them get all anxious on this so suddenly? Nervous enough to want to bail on the contract?" I ask Serge. This is definitely not something I'd been expecting to hear at all.

"I don't know. I just don't bloody know why, Ned… Why would they want to do such a thing? I don't know anything anymore." He sobs again. "This whole thing is so screwed up, and I don't know what to do next," Serge cries.

I'm becoming far more concerned with his behaviour, looking out at Helen again, still busy clacking away.

"What have they said about it, Serge?" I ask, trying to remain composed, looking out at Helen again to see if I can get her attention.

"Nothing specific. I guess… well, you know, with Ben and the minister going missing is probably key. Then those bizarre unofficial runs, Samir's murder, the office being ransacked and you being hunted by the police and army ticked one too many boxes for them, maybe. For me too, to be honest. They're going to have absolute heart failure when they hear the minister's dead… and how he died more specifically. That, my friend, is going to be very difficult for them to digest," Serge states almost triumphantly, cackling eccentrically.

I'm desperately trying to stay calm and composed, or at least to seem like I am. The crazy laugh, though, it's tripped a wire for me. I'm not sure I'm a stable presence at the moment, for him – or for me. I'm listening carefully to what he's saying, only I'm not hearing anything rational. Best thing I can do for now, I guess, is just to let him talk and express whatever it is he's trying to get out, if it works for him. I don't know if I can leave him alone, though, while I get Helen to come in to help, I don't know what he'll do next or how he might react to me involving her. This guy is in a serious crisis. I believe he's experiencing some sort of mental breakdown, and I have to do something soon. He really requires some sort of professional help… so will I pretty damn soon, I think.

Bugger it, I'm going to take a punt on including Helen. "Serge, I'm going to get Helen to come in here with us so we can all talk it out together. You OK with that, old mate?" I doubt he heard a word I said, as he keeps weaving around his desk, mumbling to himself then letting out this eccentric laugh every few seconds. I open the door to ask Helen to join us… urgently.

The next half hour or so is demanding and extremely worrying. Helen hasn't ever come across Serge acting in this manner before and has no suggestions to offer on any immediate remedy other than to be there for him. She calls in a couple of other senior staff members, who have likewise never seen Serge like this, or anyone, carrying on like this. We're collectively in the dark. All we can initially do is encourage Serge to sit down and relax, to try and talk to us, Helen holds his hands while he mumbles away to himself. He's becoming more agitated and disconnected as time goes by. Helen knows a local doctor in the same building and calls her to see if she can assist. While waiting for her to arrive, Serge falls onto the floor into a foetal position and begins to sob uncontrollably. Time to ring for the ambulance.

Between Helen, myself, the other senior staff, the local building doctor and the ambulance paramedics who sedated him, we finally get Serge off to the hospital. It's something none of us want for him at the moment, as the Ambo's inform us that Ambulance ramping around Melbourne is something new to most of us, although apparently it's totally out of control these days. Unfortunately, we have little choice in the matter other than to send him off on what is expected to be a very long wait outside whichever facility they're directed to. At least he's sedated for the moment.

Helen is especially shaken by what's happened, so we talk for a long while after Serge has been taken away to try and put her and myself at ease a bit. It's difficult to decipher what's gone on with him, or maybe the business, to ultimately put him into this state of mind enough to require him to have medical intervention. We talk about what we can, could or should possibly attempt to do next, both for Serge, Ben… and the overall contract. We're both still pretty shocked, so neither of us has any real idea of what to do at the moment. Again, neither of us has a clear picture of what Serge might have been working on or handling himself, or if the senior management in Italy knew anything about his state of mind or are doing about it.

All I really want to do at this very moment is go home to my family in Adelaide. Unfortunately, it looks like that is not going to happen. As much as I don't want to, it unfortunately feels like I'm going to have to immerse myself into the issues here to attempt to resolve some of the overall problems in order to try and find Ben… hopefully alive. Time to call RJ again.

RJ makes a sort of sympathetic sound concerning Serge's condition and hospitalisation. I can't help but feel she's possibly still just a little rankled about him not permitting her contact in Mauritania to help interpret the data off the hard drives when we had the chance. More interestingly, though, she's not at all shocked about the minister turning up dead and less astonished about the manner in which he'd been killed.

"We'd heard faint whispers around the traps a little earlier about the potential demise of said minister. I figured it to be largely true, although it hasn't been possible to confirm it with anyone reliable. We couldn't substantiate anything about the status of Ben either. I tried to get in contact with you at the time to let you know, it might have been during one of your flights I think. As you can imagine, it's not the sort of information I'd like to leave on your messages," RJ disclosed.

I agree. "So, what sort of whispers did you hear, and from where, can you reveal?" I query, not really expecting anything – not anything honest at least.

"From my old colleague Diop in Mauritania. When he told me about it, he'd been a hundred percent certain the information was legitimate. Just wouldn't disclose his source. Not at this stage, anyway. He believes he has a remote lead on where Ben is being held or is possibly going to be held," she announces. I'm wondering about this Diop character – who he is, what favours does he owe RJ… or what is he getting out of all this.

"Well, that's got to be a good thing for us, yeah?" I query enthusiastically. It sounds to me like a very positive outcome for all of us, especially for Ben.

"Depends on who has him, I guess," RJ replies quietly, giving us both a bit of time to think about who it might be, or more specifically why they have him.

"Another factor to consider, I suppose, is where they might have him, and what they want in return for him to be released," I suggest. "Why knock off the minister, though? That just doesn't make any sense at all to me… You agree?"

"Yes, I agree. However, I don't believe this is your ordinary, everyday garden-variety kidnapping scenario, James. I very much doubt there'll be a demand for a financial ransom, as it simply doesn't feel like that sort of situation. If I were to speculate, a bit earlier in the piece, the kidnappings seemed to me… I don't know, a bit more like some sort of political pressure being applied to the minister or his department, and Ben was just collateral damage. As you say, though, killing him, that's way too much out there for it to be political, I think. You have any thoughts on it you want to share, James?" RJ asks.

"Not really. I'm still trying to get my thoughts around the attempted EMP attack on the radar. Then all of the other crap happening out there Rob and Lee mentioned."

"Hmmm, yes, about all their points, can you word me up on those matters a bit more? Serge gave me some vague dribs and drabs of what you told him. However, I think his thoughts were more active on other subjects – or on no subjects at all. I detected a few gaps in what he'd been trying to tell me. Hopefully, you'll be able to do a more effective job of it? I've got time to listen now if you're interested?" RJ invites.

I look out of Serge's office window at the windy, pollen-infested day outside. Hordes of colourful people coughing and gasping their backbones out while trying to walk their fragile lives up and down the wind tunnel of Flinders Street. I can see a number of small tour boats on the Yarra River. A couple of rowers are sculling their way fiercely downstream in their tiny, impossibly narrow racing shell, or are they called skiffs or boats? I think I'm trying to appreciate the simplest of life's pleasures, so far removed from the bizarre happenings out beyond the EEZ. After another moment's hesitation, off I go to retell the extraordinary tale of happenings in a distant land as relayed to me by Rob and Lee. In the reiterating, I find much of what the guys have told me to be, I don't know… still almost unbelievable.

"Wait. You say much of this activity is coordinated by a group of aspiring Islamic terrorists for funding? Is that what these guys are trying to suggest?" she asks sceptically.

I see right away where her thinking is taking her. I remember having similar disbelieving thoughts and queries myself about the level of Rob and Lee's knowledge on what happens outside the EEZ, so I explain further about my suspicions on them being well connected to the seedier side of life, more than just oil field suppliers. I describe the encounter with the guns at the border crossing and any number of other minor giveaways I'd detected – or suspected, at least – about them during our discussions and time together. Then I elaborate on the seizure of the EMP device and the sonic boom weapon they told me about, the ones misappropriated from the hijacked oilfield work boat.

"Bloody hell, James, are you for real? Get me in contact with these guys will, you?" RJ demands impatiently. "I'll see what they might be able to find out for me on other matters. Maybe we can align the information from Diop and them. It might possibly pinpoint where they're holding Ben and the security guys."

"Yeah, I can organise it. About the security guys, I really know nothing about them. Rob, Lee and myself believe they're in some way involved. Either voluntarily or under coercion. Maybe they're being forced to participate in whatever is going on… who knows? My guess though, RJ, whatever is going on outside the EEZ has bugger-all to do with over-fishing. This is way more sinister than just that."

"I agree, especially now that we have potential Islamic terrorists involved in the overall picture. It changes things dramatically!" RJ exclaims, almost gleefully. "Get those intros to the guys organised, can you, without delay? I'm going to chase up Diop some more. Time to get him working another angle on this, OK?"

"Got it, I'll get back to you shortly." I am amazed once again as to what the hell I've got myself into this time.

Over the next hour or so, Helen secures open access to Serge's mobile phone and laptop computer for me. I'm keen to see if I can find anything or do something to maintain some sort of momentum with the data assessments and maybe keep the contract alive.

I wish I hadn't.

If I'd thought the world to be a wonderfully wacky place before getting access, once I began reviewing Serge's information, in particular on his phone, the world emerges as a far gloomier and more ominous place than I'd originally thought possible.

My earlier very brief and mischievous notion Serge might have possibly participated in a bit of extra-marital curricular activity with Ben's thrice-married wife Rikki regrettably proved correct. There's all manner of strange messages on Serge's phone that I wasn't aware existed or were possible to have. Some sort of e-messages from Rikki – dozens of them, maybe more – about their 'relationship'. It wasn't going well, though, by a long shot. It appears Serge has been trying to get out of whatever arrangement they've had going for quite some time. I think maybe the initial excitement of the affair was probably beginning to diminish, as he mentions a number of times that the constant secrecy has taken a toll with him. Rikki on the other hand left me with no delusion she wanted to escalate it, to get bolder in whatever it was she craved. It's been going on for a long period of time. I note the timing of the initial correspondence is well before Ben was kidnapped. This distresses me far more than I understand why.

I don't know the technical process with how these messages can be sent to Serge's phone, whatever the means are, there is a plethora of them. I stop reading any further though. I can't anymore, actually. I feel embarrassed or ashamed or... I don't know, something; like violating their privacy, maybe. Possibly guilt for reading the private and salacious content in just the small amount I'd seen so far. I'm mortified, in fact. I don't want to know about it at all. Unfortunately, it's something I can't unsee now or get out of my thoughts. I know Rikki has been massively unfaithful to Ben over the years. Nonetheless, it takes two for a protracted affair like this particular one to happen and to continue unabated. I thought more highly of Serge than to fall into Rikki's infidelity honeytrap. There we have it, though, I guess. I'm establishing a bit more of an awareness about what might have brought on his breakdown this morning.

Unfortunately, other information I soon view on Serge's computer quickly takes my attention into another undesirable realm entirely. He'd been liaising with the kidnappers!

There's a dreadful black and white photo of Ben on the computer, just an appalling image. He's somewhere in a semi-darkened room or some sort of small cell or space. No furniture, no other identifiable bits and pieces are visible. He simply looks shocking. Abandoned. My heart sinks as I view his picture. Scraggly, dank hair dishevelled over his filthy gaunt face. Hands bound in front of him, not that this would've been necessary, as he looks to be so fragile as to not require any restraints. He's emaciated, with torn, filthy clothes literally hanging off his thin scrawny frame. I'm so distraught at what I see, and to be honest, I'm not at all sure what to do next. Why does Serge have this photo, and why not tell me about it? How long has he had it, I wonder? More importantly, where the bloody hell has it come from?

Then it hit me. Serge had mentioned the head office in Italy notifying him yesterday that they're pulling the plug on the radar contract over there in its entirety, effective immediately. He referenced something he'd been occupied with, about working his way through the likely contractual legal difficulties this could likely throw up. This was probably right before the call came in from Rabat about the demise of the minister.

"Shit!" I scream as I slam my fist down on the top of the desk, much louder than I intended. I believe now that Italy probably sent Serge the photo. They're the ones in contact with the kidnappers. Why the hell could they possibly be doing this and not notifying us? My gut says this is why they want to pull the plug on the contract, because someone has Ben as leverage.

"Is everything OK, James?" Helen queries cautiously as she knocks and walks into the office a little nervously, concern over her face at my outburst.

I flinch in alarm. "What? Oh, so sorry, Helen. I'd just been thinking about Ben and his situation and kinda thought and acted out a bit too loud. Apologies if I scared you. All is fine," I lie.

All is in fact far from fine. My head is spinning up one way, and my guts another, free falling to the floor. I think I'm in a massive state of shock. In fact, I know I am. I've got to talk to RJ about this ASAP, as Ben is in reality an employee of Castelle contracted to Marinetti. So in this case, why the hell hasn't Marinetti been in contact with RJ?

"OK then, if there is anything I can do to help, let me know," Helen says cheerfully as she turns to walk out the room.

"One thing, Helen, Serge mentioned he'd spoken to Italy last night. Who does he generally liaise with over there? Do you know?" I ask as blandly as possible. I don't want to alert Helen to any of my growing misgivings.

"He always talks to Fazio. He's the owner and MD of the company. Do you want me to get him on the line for you?" Helen offers.

"No, thanks. Well above my pay grade I'm afraid. I'll leave all of the contact between him and RJ. Thanks anyway. I'll keep working on his phone and computer to see if there's anything I can help with in regard to the strategy going forward," I say, pointing my hand at Serge's laptop.

Helen smiles at me, then quietly closes the door, slowly turns around to face me, her back to the door. "It's quite possible you may find some things in either his phone or computer that might leave you a little puzzled James. I'm not suggesting you will, although you might. If you do, please call me if you'd like to discuss it? I'm a very good listener. OK?" Helen looks at me with a sorrowful gaze, suggesting, guardedly, she knows about Serge and Rikki.

"Hmmm, I think I may have already found what you're probably referring to. If you're implying these things might involve Rikki, that is?" I look at the slight change in Helen's face, almost of relief.

"Yes, it's what I'm referring to," Helen says softly as she sits on the edge of the desk, clasping her hands in front of her skirt. She looks incredibly forlorn. "Serge has shared some of his dilemma with me. Not in any great detail, mind you, just that something is, or has been, going on. He regretted it, although it had been happening for quite a while. Serge is a good man, James. Yes, he's weak in regard to the mysteries of the forbidden flesh. Other than that, in almost all other aspects, I believe him to be a decent person. Rikki, on the other hand, well… let's just say she's simply a very sad and shallow person, quite possibly even treacherous. In particular relation to Ben's situation, I'm deeply disappointed in both Serge and her."

"I'm likewise disillusioned in them both. What about Serge's wife, Liliana isn't it? Is she aware of what's been going on?" I query, probably already knowing the answer deep down.

"Yes, unfortunately. Per favour of the deceitful Rikki once again, apparently. I haven't probed, although I believe they are now separated. Liliana has taken the children and gone back to Spain, where she comes from, a couple of weeks ago, ostensibly for a holiday. It's very uncivilized, sad and messy, James, isn't it? This morning's episode is possibly the culmination of all the self-inflicted burden he's been carrying around with him." Helen cries softly, a couple of tears gently roll down her cheek. She wipes them away with a tissue and sniffs as she looks at me with a heart-wrenching expression.

I really feel sorry for her, being inadvertently caught up in the ripple effect of all this appalling unfaithfulness. "I'm just so stunned. It unfortunately looks to have still continued after Ben's kidnapping."

I'm enormously offended by the entire episode. The betrayal is of an incredible magnitude and has actually shaken my trust in Serge.

"Do you think Fazio is aware of this particular situation, Helen?" I ask, as I'm wondering if I should confide in her about what else I found on Serge's computer.

"I don't think so. Who really knows, though? I only in truth became aware myself recently, because Rikki came in here ranting and raving one day not so long ago. Carrying on something dreadful. Serge brought her in here to quieten her down. They talked… and talked. She eventually left, angry, at least peacefully all the same. We all thought it might have been a reaction of some sort to Ben's kidnapping, initially, anyway. I soon became aware it's about something much more entirely. Serge called me in after Rikki left to tell me about what he and her had been up to, about what'd been going on. I'm enormously troubled by what he told me, as I have a high regard for Ben, less so for Serge after hearing about the infidelity. Not so much for Rikki – not at all, really."

Helen turns to leave the office. I want to comfort her. However, I don't want it to be misinterpreted.

"Do you think Ben knew about what'd been going on?" I had to ask the question. The entire thing just blew me away; it's treachery of a monumental form. I'm pissed at them both and struggling to cope with the intensity of the knowledge.

"I'm sure he must have at least suspected, don't you think? He loves Rikki, I believe. Nevertheless, I honestly don't think he cared if he suspected or had known for sure."

"Had he been ill, Helen? Ben, that is? He seemed unwell from time to time when we worked those long hours together in Nouadhibou," I query.

"Not so I'm aware of. He never spent much time here in the office, so it's not been obvious to me he might have been in poor health." Helen shrugs her shoulders miserably then walks out the door, closing it quietly behind her.

I chose at this point not to share the image I'd found in Serge's computer, mainly because I don't want to add any further burden to her existing level of anguish. In addition, I'm still trying to deal with the shock and enormity of it myself. I know I have to share it… eventually, with someone. Nevertheless, not with Helen. Not just yet, anyway. I want to talk to RJ about it. However, when I try to call her, she isn't answering the bloody phone at the present time.

I keep searching Serge's computer, only my thoughts are in such disarray over discovering Ben's photo earlier, I don't think I'm taking much notice of anything I'm observing in reality, not until I discover the technical analysis assessment and feedback report from the unauthorised trials. I can see the electronic images of the radar searching a largely vacant and blank ocean. Suddenly, it zeroes in on a large collective mass of white, fragmented light images. This is the radar signal being bounced back towards the radar antenna from a solid object, or objects. From what I can remember, the radar measures the strength and round-trip time of the microwave signal emitted by the radar antenna, as it's reflected off a distant surface or object. In this context, it's what seems to me like the accumulation of many vessels massed just outside the EEZ. It gives the impression that there are possibly dozens of them. I can't interpret enough definition in the electronic signature to be able to establish how many vessels or what sort of activities were underway once the radar picked them up.

Nonetheless, within a few seconds, all hell seems to frantically break the collective loose. The white mass instantly begins separating in all directions, as it turns out there are in fact probably more than 50 various sized vessels involved. I'm pretty much convinced now that my earlier thoughts of them already beginning to separate when we tagged them were incorrect. Just as suddenly, the hazy radar signal becomes radically distorted after the image fractures significantly to the point of complete disruption. This is likely the assumed EMP burst that Serge referred to in our earlier conversation. So it's real. This is quite possibly the EMP weapon stolen from the oil industry support vessel.

One of Serge's earlier concerns of it being technically inconceivable that somehow those boats outside of the EEZ were aware the radar had tagged them, hence their immediate separation… how could this be possible? I begin to speculate about the now dead minister. Did he know those boats were operating just outside of our contractually designated target zone all of the time? Is this why he's been murdered, and so brutally? He knew about it, or even condoned it, and for whatever reason, it seems he possibly violated whatever mutual arrangement or covenant he'd put in place with the terrorists, or whoever it is out there, not to light them up on the radar? I also wonder now if he'd been tortured before being murdered. Was he alive still when they committed all that carnage on him?

With nothing else to see from the radar image anymore, as it's pretty much lost, I refer to the technical assessment report, which confirms the disruption is most likely the result of an EMP strike. The feedback report proposes: *'The disruption of radar signal is most likely from the release of a targeted, high strength burst of electromagnetic energy. It disrupted and overloaded the sensitive electronics in the radar package which has led to a temporary loss of signal. This has made the task of tracking any detailed technical data in the target areas impossible for the operators or for any analytical data interpretation'.*

The technician preparing the report also suggests: *'At this stage, there doesn't appear to be any permanent damage to the radar infrastructure'.* He further advises in extreme cases, a powerful EMP such as the one that struck us might possibly, in all likelihood, permanently damage the radar enough to render it inoperable. Given the strength of the EMP attack, it is likely to reduce the radar's effective range, making it difficult to detect our target objects at the nominated distance. This could ultimately lead us to require either finding an alternative method of tracking our target area or to abandon the operation entirely.

Is this what has prompted Italy to abandon the contract, I wonder. Reading further into the report about signal interference, it states: *'The EMP introduces a significant "noise" interference into the radar system's signal. This makes it almost impossible to distinguish between genuine nominated target zones or false signal echoes, creating confusion for the radar operators to interpret'.* The report continues to detail what countermeasures or backup systems might be available to minimise a potential future EMP impact and how we might best respond to the threat, in particular when we already know it exists. It's a most bizarre state of affairs, reading this information in the report. To then try and correlate it all in my thoughts, with so many other recent peculiar happenings that've occurred, I rationally tick them off, such as the unauthorised runs, Ben and the minister going missing at the same time, Samir's murder and our office being ransacked. Then, there I am, being hunted by the Mauritanian police and army during a coup, all while trying to escape from Mauritania through Mali with two very suspect oil field workers, to being back home in this most current mess. Bloody hell, it all reads like some pathetic over-sexed passe novel for immoral delinquents. Now, we have the brutal murder of the minister to add to the plot, the pitiful infidelity business with Serge and Rikki, then Serge having a massive breakdown of whatever origin. More importantly, though, finding the photo of the kidnapped Ben has twisted me off more than I care to admit. One too many boxes ticked off for Serge. A few too many extra for me as well, to be honest. I sit in Serge's chair, contemplating what to do next, when my phone seems to scream at me, injecting yet another layer of nervous tension into my day. I assume RJ is getting back to me. I probably sound drunk or drugged, because I'm simply unsure which part of this curiously eclectic set of circumstances to lead off with, stuttering and mumbling over various story elements.

"James," RJ screams down the phone. "Whatever the hell's going on right now in your head is not helpful to either of us. Tell me exactly what's happened, straight after we hung up from our earlier telecon today. OK? Just begin there, got it?" Her voice quietens down; it's almost soothing now, kind of like only a small out of control chainsaw.

Off I go again, trying to explain every morsel of what I'd learned since our earlier telecon, all the grimy bits including the findings in the technical report about the EMP attack. RJ seems to be listening intently, with a few hmm's and ahh's along the way. She doesn't interrupt me until I pretty much finish, although I've probably left great big chunks out.

"Fucking hell, James." RJ utters, which is highly unusual, as I don't think I've ever heard her swear like it before.

"I know, I know, it's a bit of a circus, isn't it?" I say this, knowing full well that there are most likely a host of other bewilderments drifting around out there in the universe just waiting to drop into our laps. "Anyway, I've now sent you the photo. As you'll see, he seriously looks like shit. My guess is he's probably deteriorating by the hour. At least he's still alive, for now, which is a slight bonus I guess. The photo has a date stamp on it of 3 days ago. Look, amongst all of this, my primary concern is still for Ben. However, until we can get a bit of clarity on where he might be held, we're just spinning our wheels. There's nothing we can really do for him, is there? What about your friend Diop? Have we heard anything back from him about where they might be holding Ben?" My suspicious thoughts about Diop are still hovering around in the background.

"Diop is going to get back to me later this afternoon on a couple of other matters he's checking for me. He suggested that Ben is possibly being held on one of those old rusting hulks out in the ship graveyard at Nouadhibou. I don't know if it's his gut telling him this or maybe it's his confidential contact in his ear, whoever the hell that might be. At any rate, he's trying to get some sort of confirmation on the issue by this afternoon." RJ takes a breath and, without missing a beat, continues. "I'm also waiting on some feedback from your old travelling cronies Lee and Rob. Wow, as you mentioned, are those two ever extremely well informed. They left me with the impression that there's probably some really handy connections at their fingertips in the netherworld we might have to make use of at some point down the track."

"Bloody hell RJ. Is that what your guy thinks? That Ben might be out in the graveyard at Nouadhibou? It's as if he hasn't really left the goddamned place. Whoever it is, probably picked them both up not far from when they left the office that day." I'm stunned. If in fact it's true, he's been captive out there somewhere in a no-doubt dreadful environment for over a month now.

"So tell me, RJ, with all of these bits and pieces of information we seem to be accumulating, what's going to be our likely strategy if we get confirmation that Ben is actually being held out there somewhere? Are we then going to take this to the Mauritanian authorities, like the police, navy or army to deal with, or… what?"

"Honestly? I really have no idea… yet. Let's see what Diop comes back with this afternoon and after my chat with Fazio. I'll then kick it around with my people higher up the food chain here in Canberra. OK then, back to business. I'm going to get in contact with him right now, bang a few heads together, see why he hasn't bothered to touch base with us about the photo. More importantly, though, where has it come from, and when? If in fact it was them who actually did relay it to Serge. I'll call you back shortly," RJ says as she hangs up.

I'd like to be a fly on Fazio's wall during this conversation. I doubt it will be a pleasant 'chat'. It's a very odd situation, all the same. The fact he hasn't contacted us about the photo and to explain how he obtained it, if in fact it originated from him. I'm really hoping Fazio is not involved in all this, or worse… Serge.

It doesn't take long for RJ to get back to me, a little over an hour, and she's not pleased with the world. Pretty fired up, actually, over whatever she'd found out.

"OK, listen up, James, a lot of factors have unravelled since we spoke earlier; not much of it advantageous, especially for Ben," RJ declares in an angry tone. "Fazio tells me some unknown person contacted him, a man with poor English skills. Happened the afternoon before last, completely out of the blue, from a phone with no number identified. In any case, the caller demanded Marinetti remove themselves from the radar contract in Westra without delay."

RJ took a breath for a couple of seconds.

"He asked – Fazio, that is – asked the person who he was and why he's making such a demand. What impact was the radar having on the caller? As Fazio isn't in a position to simply switch it off and contravene the contract on a whim. It sounds like the caller got all bitter and twisted at his questioning, screaming all manner of obscenities down the phone at him. Adding threats of violence as well. Suggesting dire outcomes if they don't. Then he hung up. Not long after, Fazio tells me a courier arrived at his office to deliver the envelope with the photo in it. Words were scrawled on the back in poor English handwriting "Cancel Contract or he Die". At the time, he had no idea who the image was of, apparently. He doesn't know what Ben looks like, anyway. What's more, at that point, he hadn't known about the minister being killed either… not until I told him, nor about Serge's breakdown. He's contemplating his own nervous collapse at the moment as we speak."

"What a bloody mess, RJ. This has snowballed into a whole new world of grief, hasn't it?" I exclaimed, almost in disbelief. "I don't know, do you think this might still be connected to those unauthorised runs one way or another?"

"Yes, I do. He wasn't aware of those other runs being conducted either, or who might have sanctioned them. He apologised profusely about not being in contact with us as well. Like he stated, he'd no idea who the photo was of. He was just so horrified to see it. Strange, though, don't you think? It seems Fazio hadn't connected the dots with Ben being kidnapped and possibly being the subject of the picture. Anyway, after receiving the threatening call, he spoke to Serge about it. They apparently discussed the threats; except they were not initially going to shut down the operation. They'd still apparently been kicking around what to do when the courier arrived at his office. He faxed Serge a copy and tried to call him to talk about it to see if Serge recognised who was in the photo. He tried. Only couldn't get him on the phone this morning, though."

RJ sounds flustered. I don't blame her. I'm way past that stage.

"Probably because he was in discussions at the time with Ryan from the Australian Embassy in Rabat about the minister. Then right after, he decides to have his monumental melt down."

I'd noticed his mobile phone was switched off when Helen gave it to me this morning. Not sure if Helen or Serge had done it, not that it matters.

"Not surprisingly, like I said, Fazio has absolutely no idea about the minister being dead. The news shook him up quite a bit, unfortunately. I decided not to share how he died at the moment. He's endured a couple of challenging days lately. I don't want to push him closer to the edge," RJ mutters. Remarkably sympathetic of her with this sentiment, I felt. Not like her at all.

"Anyway, back to business. I've also heard from Diop. Although he's still awaiting firm confirmation the kidnappers are holding Ben out on one of those old rusting ships or somewhere else nearby. He can confirm, however, we're not dealing with your average low-life money-for-hire kidnappers. As Diop tells it, these guys may be "spectacularly unintelligent". However, seemingly, they are considered the real deal. Looks like they're part of some Islamic extremist group of one militant species or other out there. You mentioned this earlier too, didn't you?"

I'm unsure if RJ sounds excited or nervous about this state of affairs. Hard to judge.

"Well, I guess no big shock wave there, I suppose. Not really. Yes, Rob and Lee highlighted the fact that these guys can be pretty active out past the EEZ. Probably small in numbers, they seemed to think. Only fanatical in whatever their wacky ideology might be this week. I just don't get the kidnapping angle with them, though, if they're not after money. Most of these radical mobs kidnap for ransom, don't they, to help fund their revolution or whatever they call it?" I asked RJ. I'm not at all sure where this is likely to be taking us. However, I have a stronger suspicion now that Diop is far closer to whatever's going on out there than he's letting us know. His information is too precise.

"I'll get back to you shortly. That's Diop on the other line again, I'm guessing," RJ says, just before she hung up. I can hear another phone ringing in the background, where ever she is.

Well, things seem to be hotting up. My query still remains – what are we going to do if we confirm Ben is being held in the ship graveyard? I very much doubt this is something Marinetti or Castelle have in their bag of tricks. Rescuing kidnapped people from Islamic terrorists? I shudder at the idea. Do we ask the Australian Embassy in Rabat to assist in whatever way they can? I know they probably won't want to get involved in the rescue itself.

They may possibly help coordinate things with the Mauritanian authorities, as Ben is being held captive within Mauritanian jurisdiction? What are they likely to do, negotiate with the kidnappers? Or maybe go in there all guns blazing and attack the terrorists, because they are terrorists, not really kidnappers? Much more likely outcome, I think. Not the best for Ben, as he may be killed in the crossfire or be executed by the terrorists when an attack commences. I don't have to wait long for an answer, as the phone screams at me again in a way that I feel is trying to relay an extreme sense of urgency to me: Pick me up NOW. Creepy. My guess, it'd be RJ again.

"Things are on the move, James," RJ says quickly. "We've now received confirmation that Ben and a number of others are in fact being held on an old rusty hulk out in the graveyard. Diop has provided the exact coordinates. He can't confirm how many there are at the moment, unfortunately. It appears they move them around quite regularly in the process of selling them off or trading them or whatever it is they do with the hostages. One thing Diop mentions is that nearly all of the hostages are westerners. They're more valuable as a trading or trafficking commodity. All sounds very ominous, doesn't it?"

"Yeah, it does. Well, at least there's confirmation now. I'm not really across the thing with the guys being traded, though. What does it mean?" I had a bit of an idea, except I like to have these sorts of tenuous theories tested by others a bit closer to the pointy end of business.

"Yes, I was curious about it as well. From what Diop briefly explained, it seems this involves some semi-aligned or rival extremist groups within the wider Muslim factions, each with their own twisted interpretation and focal differences of the Islamic ideology, evidently. They see westerners as valuable bargaining chips only, that's all. Or shock fodder by beheading some of their captives on camera as a terror tactic, to showcase their actions in propaganda materials."

RJ took a breath and was silent for a few seconds, doubtless shocked herself by the dramatic, abstract image of her own statement.

"You know what I mean in regard to them only seeing westerners as valuable bargaining chips, don't you, James?" RJ asks.

"Yeah, I think I do. It's just a bit difficult trying to digest all this into context while I'm sitting here all comfortable in Serge's office in cultured old Melbourne, living in a safe space and surrounded by life's amusements," I reply. "Yeah, I get it's the immediate source of instant revenue by trafficking them to quickly obtain funds for their causes. Trading the westerners for guns and ammunition or other trinkets they might want, including intelligence between each other?"

"Yes, I get it's apparently far more preferable to negotiating with authorities or family for an acceptable ransom. This is much quicker and also has a psychological element, as they get rid of their hostage burden faster and easier, and it's also going to another kindred group with similar ideologies," RJ mumbles, her attention elsewhere. "Anyhow, look, I've asked Diop to try and follow up further with his contact about which group or groups we might be dealing with. You never know, this might help us to identify someone who may be able to apply some sympathy pressure into the whole thing, possibly getting Ben released to us a bit easier."

"Question then, RJ, what now? Do you have any plan, now it's confirmed Ben is being held in one of those old wrecks? I'm sure this isn't something Marinetti has ever been involved in previously, right? Neither have we, I suspect? Rescuing kidnapped persons from armed Islamic terrorists is a whole different ball game from what I'm led to believe Castelle is about," I insinuate.

"Castelle does have some capability in this area. It's by the use of a third party that we've utilised before to get Aussie business people out of Senegal in '89, Kuwait in '91 early in the gulf war and again in Rwanda during that bit of unattractive genocide recently. We've used a company named Ortega, based out of London. Run by a group of ex-SAS and special forces guys. I've been in contact with them to do a preliminary availability check and planning strategy request," RJ says.

I wince at the suggestion of hiring mercenaries to help with getting Ben released. "So, do we use Ortega for the negotiations on our behalf? Is this the plan?" I probe, already suspicious of this as a tactic, no matter what their involvement.

"No, not the negotiations. Although they're very capable of doing this. We'd be looking at an entirely different approach from them, if we can get their assistance. I know you're probably thinking mercenaries. Nonetheless, they prefer to call themselves Private Maritime Security Consultants or PMSCs. Interestingly enough, your cohorts Rob and Lee also use the same company. They contract them for international shipping lines and the oil industry to protect their oil rigs, oil facilities and ships operating in or traveling through a particularly hazardous region," RJ says, throwing more fuel onto my suspicions about this tactic.

"Why not ask the Australian Government in Rabat to assist us? I'm guessing they're unlikely to get involved in negotiations or any rescue itself. However, they may possibly help coordinate things with the Mauritanians. Ben is being held captive within Mauritania, isn't he?" I question.

"What do you think the Mauritanians authorities might do if we get them involved? I very much doubt they'd negotiate with the kidnappers, because that's not what they are. They're terrorists to them, not kidnappers. I suspect if we involve the authorities, we'd lose all influence over every aspect of it. Very likely, we'd be completely left out of the loop − unreservedly is my prediction. What do you think?" RJ snarls over the phone, not sounding like she is really seeking my thoughts on her suggestion.

"Yeah. I know… I know. I've been trying to consider the various angles. There doesn't really seem to be any approach likely to benefit Ben. He may still end up getting killed regardless. Either accidentally by friendly fire or deliberately by the kidnappers," I protest.

"Not if we employ a more precise approach, James. Very specific planning, using well-trained and experienced personnel, utilising modern strategies and resources, extremely quick plan of execution. That's what I'm suggesting here. I don't believe handing over the problem to an authority who is ill-trained, ill-equipped and with a singular focus on taking out the terrorists will be of benefit to any of the hostages. Saving Ben in that scenario, if it were to happen, would be a bonus, only not necessarily the key element in their plan, I suspect. You do get it, James, don't you?" I can tell RJ's getting irritable with me. Fair enough, so she should; I'm likewise the same about this bloody plan.

"Yeah, I do, although hiring a bunch of mercenaries to rescue Ben may end up with the exact same result – Ben dead. Don't you think?" I question, probably less enthusiastically than before.

"As I've already explained, they're Private Maritime Security Consultants James, PMSCs, not mercenaries. Although I'd probably still put my hand up for them whether they were bona fide mercenaries or not. We have to fully control the narrative here, James, the entire sequence of outcomes. That is the only way we might be in with a chance to get Ben back alive." I can tell it's time for me to stop now. RJ is getting beyond agitated, and that's not going to help either of us going forward.

"Listen up, James, put the PMSCs in a box for the minute. There is a much bigger fish here to deal with. It's a complex environment as to why Islamic extremists kidnap westerners and sell them to other extremist groups, and I don't want to get into it here. As you're aware, though, we have the religious motivation amongst all this as well. I know, I know, it's important to avoid reinforcing a stereotype, to avert portraying all Muslims or Islam as extremist. The fact remains, as Diop has made clear to me, and he is a Muslim, many of them can have an incredibly twisted interpretation of their own religious beliefs and needs. This often motivates various influential individuals or groups to commit such acts. You still with me, James?" RJ queries indignantly.

"Yeah, yeah, I get all that. It's not why I'm concerned about using the private guys. My alarm is that whatever we do, using these guys in Mauritanian waters and armed to the teeth is just dangerous. It's not sanctioned by their government or military, or ours. So, my thoughts are more towards if it all turns sour and their government does ultimately get involved, where does that leave everybody?" I feel I have a valid point.

"We'll deal with that specific issue if the time comes, James, or I'll deal with it. I've already got a couple of strategies in play.

So, let's just focus on crossing the t's and dotting the i's with the planning phase, can we?" RJ then hung up on me, not for the first time. I'm sort of getting used to it now. My prediction is the 'strategies in play' will involve our well-connected friend Diop. I haven't finished wondering about him and his involvement yet. I'll likewise put that in a box just for the moment.

Chapter 6

I NOW FIND MYSELF in Tarifa, an unbelievably picturesque and unique Spanish town located at the southernmost end of the Iberian Peninsula, in the province of Cádiz, so **RJ** tells me. I don't much care to be honest. I'd been planning to be home with my family, not here. The beautiful Tarifa is also apparently the closest point in Europe to Africa, with the distance between Tarifa and Morocco just 14 km at its narrowest point seemingly. Like I give a toss right now. Additionally, it sounds like it's quite famous as a popular destination for wind and kitesurfing. Maybe I'll dip my toe into that adventure another day – NOT.

On this trip, however, I'm meeting up with **RJ** and a host of other co-contributors… or is that co-conspirators? Who knows. In regard to this, I'm introduced to all the others at such a pace, I regrettably can't keep up with their bloody names, old age and disinterest catching up with me way too soon. Our objective with this meeting is to go over Ben's rescue plan. My words, not theirs. The plan… yes, well, to me, it sounds like it's going to be a bit out there. From what I can interpret so far from RJ's current brief, shifty explanation, it's probably more accurate to describe it as being very way, way out there.

It now definitely includes the use of the private army from Ortega of London. The image I still have is of mercenaries, of course. Screw 'em if they don't like to be called this in today's world. I've since spoken to Rob and Lee about their thoughts on Ortega when they contract them for their oil industry interests operating in the Med or the Atlantic. They both enthusiastically extoll the virtues and skill set of Ortega and their personnel. More so an appreciation of their results, Lee emphasises. In other words, good operators. Oh well, entertaining times to come.

Interestingly, the PMSCs station themselves on temporarily anchored albeit very mobile 'arsenal ships' in international waters. When called on for urgent assistance, which appears to be quite regular, they're either helicoptered or mobilised by high-speed motorboats to a client rig, facility, freighter or tanker to protect the cargo, crew and the operations. Once onboard, they assume the role of 'active security defence'. Hardening whatever the facility or ship is with extremely high-pressure hot salt water jet spray guns, razor wire – sometimes electrified, sonic booms, EMPs and high-calibre firepower. After the threat passes or has been 'neutralised', the team returns to its arsenal ship and awaits the next call out.

I get the impression that as these types of threats increase, so does the extent of the arsenal the PMSCs have access to, increasing their fierceness and success rate simultaneously. Subject to requirements, I'm advised this can at times include privately-owned and armed helicopters and fixed-wing aircraft, in addition to small high-speed anti-piracy interdiction or retired combat naval vessels that can actually hunt and kill the pirate vessels before they get a chance to attack. It's a very different world these guys live and play in, and one I'm totally unprepared for or familiar with.

Anyway, back to the plan. Here's how it's expected to work, as far as I can comprehend it at any rate, with what RJ explains. "On this occasion, the security team will depart from the arsenal ship via motorised rigid-hulled inflatable boats (or RHIBs). You probably know the type, James, all very military gung-ho sort of craft, heavily armed, high-speed, high-buoyancy, extreme-weather craft with the primary mission of effective insertion/extraction," RJ says, like a lecturer. She goes on about how they're built for mission survivability and success, whatever all that really represents. It enables remarkable high-speed tactical turns and excels in the roughest of sea conditions, apparently. As if I really want to know all these details, RJ. Jesus!

"However, before you go and get yourself all jammed up, James, it's important for you to know a few things, so please note. There will be no legal or jurisdictional considerations addressed in this operation in order to avoid any territorial repercussions, OK?" RJ says in no uncertain terms. "Although it's likely we will contravene any number of international laws in the process, a conscious decision has been made not to coordinate through, or to make contact with local Mauritanian authorities to attempt to have our actions legally sanctioned. This includes maritime enforcement or any other government agencies. That is simply not going to happen. Trusting governments to properly and professionally do their thing is what led us into this position in the first place." RJ looks at me, expecting, I guess, for me to be horrified at this stance and to speak my thoughts.

I'm a bit disturbed by the decision in a way, although no more so than many other inexplicable things that've happened over the past few weeks. I say nothing, just raise my eyebrows and shrug.

"As the operation is being controlled by London, using their resources, there will also be no requirement for us to be in any sort of contact with the Australian Embassy in Morocco or Paris. James, you OK with this? Whatever comes after we get Ben back, we'll deal with it then, regardless of any legal or ethical implications that might arise, got it?" RJ actually smiles at me, as if she believes I'm fully onboard with all this lunacy.

RJ and I fly out next morning from Tarifa to one of the arsenal ships, the MV Arguer, by a Sikorsky S76c helicopter, covered in a type of naval grey camouflage. A very slick aircraft, modern, fast, comfortable, reasonably quiet and surprisingly, well-armed with a nice little under-hang of rocket pods and who only bloody knows what else is tucked away. We are accompanied by six other serious looking, unobtrusive guys, who I'm told are rotating out with some of the guys onboard the ship who are going on leave. It takes nearly 2 hours to get to the Arguer. We disturb a large flock of seabirds resting on the edge of the ship's helipad as we approach and settle gently down onto its cargo net. The view is of a vast calm expanse of open, empty, tranquil turquoise sea, stretching out to the horizon in every direction. We land just in time to catch a pod of dolphins diving and careening playfully around under the helipad. Lucky timing… hopefully good luck for us as well.

From a brief glimpse, the ship is compact, single main deck with an elevated superstructure. It's festooned with multiple shaped antennae and another distinctive feature – a big white ball on top called a Radome. The dome covers the various radars and satellite equipment, protecting it from the weather… and prying eyes. How do I know this useless bit of information? Well, what I'm looking at reminds me of a much less refined version of this on the Riverine assault boats or PBSs way back in my Vietnam days.

This ship looks to me like a retired naval vessel of some sort… or maybe not yet fully retired, just temporarily relaxing. It's flying a main flag and a couple of pennants, none of which I am – or probably should be – familiar with. My guess is they're undoubtedly linked to some friendly country or another as a distraction and protection. Crews wearing camouflage uniforms wait to assist us to disembark and to take our bags. Below the helideck, I see blue metal cargo containers spread around in neat lines. A small crane is sitting idle with other cargo-handling equipment attached. As we walk down the grated stairs of the helipad, the crew unloads the cargo from the Sikorsky and begins refuelling it for the return flight.

We're guided below deck into the mess and galley area. Again, it's a neat, functional space designed to provide meals and a place for the crew to relax. The seating and tables are permanently fixed to the floor to curtail the risk of any movement during rough seas. The ship's kitchen or galley is also a pocket-sized space with all the necessary features a fine fighting ship is likely to want. The decor and overall ambiance of the area is simple, a trace of military and maritime style decoration here and there. The traditional brass bell hanging from the ceiling, photos and shoulder patches for personalisation, plus a couple of old blunderbusses and swords attached to the walls. There are also several extra-large TV screens fastened to the walls, along with multiple clocks and noticeboards. My guess is these are for operational purposes, not leisure.

The one thing standing out for me is just how well maintained this ship is. Everything is stored neat and tidy, clean. Unusually for a ship that spends its life at sea, I see no great big seams of stained surface rust on the vessel like I've seen with many ships.

We're introduced to the assault team; I prefer to call them the 'rescue team'. I guess it's OK for us to differ on this minor terminology point. We meet the Team Leader 2IC Captain Padraic Collins, or call him Taffy, he says softly in his musical Irish lilt, and here I am thinking it would've been Paddy. The names of the rest of the team of eight various nationalities flew past in an Irish blur until Taffy points his head at one big hellishly ugly guy and then nods to me.

"He be your wingman. Name's Gustav. Ye can call 'im Gus," Taffy says to me with a grin.

This is the first earth-shaking instance I recognise I'm to be included as part of the assault… or the rescue team. I feel a sudden, intense emotional reaction to this unexpected news, enough to just about give me constipation. This is not my thing, anymore at least – hasn't been for a very long time – and I'm of the very strong belief it's not something I want back in my life. I admit I'm disturbed at the casualness of his statement. I don't know why, but I am for some reason. I should have expected it, I suppose. Bloody RJ. I'm not so thrilled at having Gus as my wingman either. He's got more tattoos than teeth and looks permanently half asleep. I'm trusting he'd turn into all sorts of crazy killing machine when any action starts up. Time will tell, I guess. Just so long as I'm not with him. I pull RJ aside for a quiet, vibrant chat.

"What in the bloody hell is this about?" I ask quietly, politely, granted in a slightly animated tone and with my back turned to the others. I'm jolted and pissed off all in one. I just don't want to show it to the other guys onboard.

"Settle, James," RJ hisses. "You're not part of the assault. I want you along to be support for Ben and to also identify him in amongst any other of the multiple hostages, which is the indication we have been given by Diop."

RJ quietens, then continues to speak, just in a less menacing icy tone.

"It's also highly likely that Ben and the others will have underlying medical concerns due to no physical exercise while in captivity. You know what I mean. Wounds, infections or chronic illnesses, possibly other ailments such as temporary blindness. Our intelligence suggests neither Ben nor any of the others are ever taken out on deck for physical activity or to get any fresh air or sunlight. So due to his prolonged exposure to darkness and lack of visual stimuli, we believe this might lead to temporary visual impairment and reduced depth perception. He will therefore no doubt require your help. Got it?" RJ looks at me for any questions. None to offer. Nothing of value to add at this point.

"On top of it all, they'll be disorientated, and their emotional state of mind will no doubt be in the sewer. So, man up, James. You'll be on one of the rescue craft, not backing up the assault team. You're there to take care of Ben and maybe some of the others if required. This will allow the rest of the team to just focus on what they have to do to keep everyone safe. I know you can do this, OK?" RJ almost demands of me in her eloquent manner.

"Whatever. However, my main concern here is I don't know if I can do it. It's been a bloody long time, OK? Regardless, it's still far more preferable for me to have been consulted on the matter before any decision like this is made. Or before Gus is unceremoniously dumped on me! Got it?" I snarl back, turning to join the others as they all walk inside.

Our initial briefing is short, to the point, although very clear on the team tasking. The MV Arguer, with its ship identification system turned off, will slowly steam to within a half dozen miles or so from the extreme outer rim of the graveyard and then anchor, alluding to engine electrical problems if anyone challenges why the vessel is temporarily anchored there. The team will then conduct a quiet RHIB approach to the abandoned target vessel, where a dynamic entry assault will be initiated.

Now, dynamic entry evidently is the highly refined art of a swift, more often violently explosive and precise tactical breach. It's a high-risk, high-reward strategic activity, or so I'm told, typically applied to rapidly gain shock access to confined spaces, secured areas, structures, buildings or facilities. Namely, our abandoned shipwreck in this instance. It seemingly requires skill, strategy, split-second timing and decision-making to instantly and successfully penetrate a target. The goal in this case is to apprehend or preferably kill the kidnappers cum terrorists, rescue Ben and secure the high-threat area, if only temporarily, until we can all safely depart... all of us.

"Alright, lads, gather around now and listen up. For ye information, communications with te kidnappers has now ceased for God only knows what reason. Not tat God could have been much use to us, anyway. Look wa happened to him, eh?" Taffy laughs along with his men at his own sing-song joke.

"Negotiations seem ta have been waddling along fine like, rapport building all tickety boo, ten it just stopped. It's enough to make ye want ta puke, isn't it, eh?" Taffy laughs in his Irish intonation. "Anyhoo, I'm reasonably informed tat if possible, attempts wee continue to try and negotiate ta safe release of ta captives. All good with tat?"

This is all alarming news, to me anyway, as I'd no idea any contact or negotiations were being conducted with the terrorists, or the kidnappers... or whatever the hell they are. I look at RJ standing next to me, eyebrows and shoulders raised. She whispers softly to me. "These guys are quite routinely contracted by family members to make contact with kidnappers to try and negotiate the release of certain hostages. This communication he's referring to is not about Ben. It's about someone else, a German national, now assumed to be either dead or sold on, unfortunately."

"Now… 'tis our emotions, ye see, 'tis what I want ta talk an remind ye about, as usual. Mainly about how tis can affect ye proficiency in a fekking gunfight, particularly during a high-stress dynamic entry like tis wee one. Tat can vary significantly, yeah?" Taffy looks at us all again with a serious expression, one by one. "It all depends on what's in ye toughts. Sometimes, tis ye training and ye worldly experiences too, yeah. So ye know the drill? Mainly tho, no matter what ye let get into your damn head, ye have ta make sure ye mind runs te body, yeah? Not te other fekking way round, got it? All ye guys have been here before, plenty o' times, yeah? Not on tis piece o' shite job, I know, and not all of ye have worked together previously either, ah?"

I'm not sure, but it seems Taffy lost his breath halfway through talking. He still keeps going, breathlessly, regardless of his bit of a gasping hiccup.

"So ten, ye see we need to familiarise ourselves with each other in ta short time we have. See our mate the great big fekking dinosaur over ter?" Taffy points his head towards me. "Well, he ain't been in one of tes encounters for a century or so now," Taffy says, pointing his head to me again and laughing softly along with the rest of the team.

"So ten, no enjoying ta craic. Let's get ta looking after him, can ye? Precious goods 'tis one. We got ta get him home in as big a piece as possible, along with young Ben. Both fekking alive and all, mind ye, as well as all ye lot." They all chuckle again lightly. I'm hoping they're laughing with me, not at me. I think the reference to 'craic' meant to not be enjoying themselves too much during the assault, like in not making a party of it.

"So, to help us with that, Kelly and old mate Gus here are going to be on the outside looking in, to stop any of them fekkers escaping or coming at us from the outside." He points his finger at Gus and nods, then looks around to ensure everybody understood.

"So, we all know the deal in a dynamic jobby like this, we're likely to suffer a fekking great surge of different stuff, all sorts of sensations 'n adrenaline in ta body 'n ye head. Let's prepare ta body for action wit tis rush ten, yeah? Let ye heart rate increase. Don't try ta manage it. No deep breathin' or such shite. Just let it do its ting. Let it be ta boss, yeah. Let it sharpen ye focus 'n heighten ye senses. Make ta best use of ye fight-or-flight effect." Taffy looks around at the team to ensure everyone is paying attention.

"We have to maintain an intense focus on ta key threats and ye immediate surroundings as well as ta mission's primary objectives, yeah? That being to neutralise ta fekking ragheads while minimising harm ta our hostage 'n ourselves, got it?" Taffy barks, looking at everybody as they mumble their acknowledgements.

"Once we get onboard, concentrate on following ye plan, got it? Communicate with each other clearly and identify ye targets. Now rest up for a wee bit while the team leaders get this little escapade all jissied up." Taffy laughs, as he waves me and two other guys over towards a portable table and chairs.

"Oh, by ta way me cherubs, remember to respect our confidentiality here, yeah? You know ta drill. No sharing any fekking information or discussing ta situation openly with ye boyfriends or girlfriends when ye talking ta 'em on your fekking bat phones. Got it? I don't want tis op fekked up by any of ye with big gobs. Got it?" Taffy shouted this last bit as he pointed to each team member, me included, with a fierce look in his eyes. Everyone sullenly nods their agreement as they wander off to their quarters.

In the background, I can hear the helicopter winding up and taking off back to Tarifa. Onboard are the few guys going on leave, maybe to even test out the wind or wave surfing there. The sound of that helicopter departing leaves me with a feeling of deep isolation and loneliness for some bizarre reason.

I was never involved in a dynamic entry gunfight during my Vietnam days, so everything about this is going to be new. And challenging, a very risky venture. In the canteen of the Arguer, we meet the overall Team Leader, Oscar Harrison, or "Harry," he says to call him. Another Aussie. He commands all of the operations flowing out from the Arguer, his particular arsenal ship. They have three such ships, Harry tells me, one in the South China Sea, another in the Arabian Sea and the Arguer, which is commonly based around Morocco and Algeria in the Med. I'm pleased to meet another Aussie who's going to be part of this little rescue operation cum nightmare for me.

"Remember, it's important to note this type of operation is highly complex and dangerous. Everything about it is unique, so for us to carry out an assault on a grounded ship, it's crucial to follow a coordinated and carefully planned approach. To assist in this, we've got a couple of our local lads doing some unobtrusive fishing from their little wooden pirogues all around the wrecks for the past few days. They're observing the goings on in the area in general, just more specifically with this particular wreck." Harry takes a break to sip his tea.

"They've gathered some valuable intel about the exact location where this wreck is amongst that massive great pile of rusty ships. However, there are a lot of unknowns with this op. For instance, we don't have any actual internal ship plans to base our strategy on. Nonetheless, we've assessed the layout of the old ship from similar types. We also identified a few potential hazards and the likely defensive positions the *jihadis* could take. We can't yet confirm how many hostages are expected to be onboard or where they might be held, nor do we know for sure how many of the extremists are onboard at this point, as it keeps changing. We figure about three."

Harry stops momentarily as we listen to the clanking of the Arguer's anchors being raised in preparation to get underway, the ominous jangling of the chains sounds not unlike some bloody scary movie scene we're all about to enter into.

"Our information is they're mostly young guys, though, not your apex predator types. Possibly low down in the food chain and untested. However, we're regarding them all as full-blown, real deal islamists." Harry states, looking around at all of us to see if there are any questions.

"Tactical have planned their potential entry and exit points, one forward and aft. So our routes and tactics are taking these elements into account to minimize casualties and maximize success." Harry took a sip of his tea again while waiting for any questions.

"A question, Harry. What about me? I've not been involved with this sort of thing for well over 10 years. I don't know if I've got the juice left in me to be part of it. More importantly, I don't know anything about the weapons or equipment you guys use these days. You planning on giving me a bit of guidance on them?" I ask anxiously.

"Yes, I'll be doing it with you myself, James, along with the RHIBs and the night vision equipment. We still have plenty of time. We don't intend to kick off until early morning the day after tomorrow. You'll be up to speed by then, I promise," Harry assures me.

I can now feel the motion of the Arguer as it gradually begins steaming off on its long journey towards Nouadhibou.

"Once we all sign off on the plan and it's in place along with all the necessary preparations made, the assault can be initiated. Tactical have all the essential firearms and associated tactical gear. They're well-trained and skilled in dealing with these high-risk situations. We'll be moving swiftly, taking any tactical advantage we can, employing all necessary force only as a last resort to ensure the safety of the hostages," Harry reiterates. I half suspect most of this high-level briefing is for the benefit of RJ and myself. I imagine these guys do this sort of thing pretty much all the time and don't need to be reminded.

The next day and a bit disappear in a blur of intense activity onboard as the Arguer makes its way to an anchoring point off the coast of Nouadhibou. It's especially hectic for me, as Harry put me through my paces with all the weapons these guys typically use – 9mm Heckler & Koch MP5 submachine gun, the AK-47, the Mossberg 500 series shotgun – sawn off, and the SIG Sauer P226 handgun. A very nice piece of work, the last one.

I am, however, pleased to note a welcome transition from older, Vietnam-era firearms that I'd used in another life to the more modern systems these guys have access to. To be quite candid, it appears to be the latest and most advanced firearms and equipment available. I'm impressed… Yeah, I know, I'm easily impressed. After learning the safe handling, clearing jams and any other ins and outs of each of these weapons, Harry felt my skill-building update was complete enough for me to be involved 'as backup on the water.' Ah, great, a whole different set of words to explain my role in this to what both RJ and Taffy employed earlier. I just love such surprises.

Harry then instructs me on the use of the night vision googles, or NVGs, then I'm kitted out with all the relevant gear I'm likely to require. This surprisingly includes a couple of items I'm not expecting – a stun gun and a pepper spray. It's a very different world from my last venture into this neck of the precarious woods – or waters. Granted I'm not part of the assault team, I still hope like bloody hell I'm up for the support task, nonetheless. My nerves are a bit pessimistic about it all, as they're flying around inside my body like a shithouse rat on payday right at the moment.

During the transit, I'm also given another level of education with basic RHIB training by Taffy. I won't be the RHIB operator, I'm advised. However, I'm still required to be acquainted with it enough to take over if Gus gets injured or otherwise incapacitated. This instruction comprises all the relevant skills of operating during high-speed evasive tactics and quick extraction manoeuvres, as well as maintaining control in various sea conditions. We then recover the RHIB at sea back to the Arguer, which we will do for real and under pressure after the rescue. My immediate thoughts when discussing all this with Taffy, about the RHIBs approach to the rusting hulk, is the likelihood of the *jihadis* hearing us coming. "Couldn't they? With our outboard motors?"

"Ne worries, lad, ta RHIBs use quieter motors for ta stealth ops. We've modified 'em and ta exhaust wit silencers ta reduce our noise even more. Plus, we use low-speed approaches 'n low RPM to minimize noise, ten we switch ta oars for ta final approach if need be, ye know, ta maintain silence?" All of this information, as optimistic as it sounds, still doesn't put me at ease. I really don't want to be doing this; only I'm committed now, or I've been committed, so let's get on with it.

I'm stressed to buggery already with the intensity of being involved in the rescue in the first place, more so now with trying to focus on the volume of military type guidance I've been given over the past day or so. At the back of my thinking, I'm still trying to absorb all of Serge's shenanigans, which is not working well for me, crashing around inside my head.

The Arguer arrives and anchors at the 'jump off' point, as Harry calls it, late on the second night. This is the staging location for the assault team to do their final preparations and gear checks before 'jumping off' to actually conduct the assault operation. I nervously enter the mess for our final briefing as Harry clarifies any last-minute details or revisions.

"We're gonna approach the wreck slowly with two ribs from the southern shore side, one from the northern ocean side and a fourth as a standby from the east, around 4 a.m. I don't really want to involve four RHIBs. Nevertheless, we have just been updated on a sandstorm weather pattern we've been monitoring for the past couple of days. It's now approaching a little faster from the east. It's unlikely, although there is some potential it might interfere with our plans. It's still a very long way off, only these things can be very unpredictable. I'd really like to stall the op until after the storm passes. However, we're so exposed out here now, anchored up where we are. I don't want to attract any more attention than can be helped." Harry looks at us all to see if there are any questions so far. None are forthcoming.

"The other issue is that we just don't know how many hostages we might have to evacuate, so the more resources we have available on the water for us to utilise, the better. We'll be taking whatever advantage we can of the darkness and any moon shadow cover to avoid detection by moving in and around the other wrecks

out there. Hopefully before any of this sandstorm descends on us."
Again, Harry looks around for any questions. Nothing from me,
except what the hell am I doing here, and really, how bad can a
sandstorm possibly be… over the ocean?

Harry continues his briefing. "There'll be plenty of ambient
noise in our favour on or around our wreck. You know, things
like the creaking and groaning of the old rust bucket itself, plus
all other the wrecks in the near vicinity will throw in their various
sounds as well. Wind and sea conditions will likewise aid in mask-
ing our approach. However, let's keep in mind complete silence is
not ever going to be achieved no matter how hard we try. There's
always a risk some prick on the wreck might be up on deck having a smoke or taking a piss and hear us if they're paying any
sort of attention. So, let's stay on the ball, guys. Get your gear
double-checked and let's get ourselves ready to go." Harry seems
remarkably composed. They all do, I guess, compared to me.

Just before 4 a.m., we set off in the RHIBs in total darkness,
with the moon well hidden behind a menacing cloud cover. The
scent of saltwater and sea air is strong and strangely soothing… for
me, anyway. I crave it as I'm about to venture into the refined art
of being fearful for my life once again, forced back into this confrontational type of environment after all this time. I can already
feel the weather beginning to get up a bit; shallow choppy waves
are building, which might slow us down slightly, although not by
much is my guess. Gus turns out to be a very capable RHIB operator and soon gets us skimming relatively smoothly through and
over the chop. We're originally the fourth boat coming in from the
east. However, the plan changed somewhat at the last minute, due
to the impending sandstorm. Additionally, once the team commences the assault, the Arguer will now weight anchor and steam
slowly towards the target wreck in order to pick us up much closer
than earlier planned.

My adrenaline rush is as high as a bloody kite during our
approach to the wreck. We're not going to be paddling to keep our
noise down; not necessary, as the wind has picked up further and
is making a hell of a racket amongst all the wreckage. Wind and

waves are smashing many of them – the ones that are still sort of floating – up against each other in a terrifying, awesome display of destruction, already broken wrecks now shattering and grinding away their splintered, rotten wood and heavily corroded metal. Gusts are howling in between the bent and buckled masts, whipping rusted wire rigging around violently on some of them. I've got hyper-alertness coming out of my ying-yang at the moment, desperately trying to convince myself I'm ready for any potential threat, urged on by natural fear and a massive lung full of apprehension – I guess somewhat for the unknown, although more so for the known, the bloody terrorists.

In particular, I'm anxious about the possibility of engaging the hostiles on the wreck after all this time out of the game. Am I still able to handle this sort of thing? It's nerve-wracking, especially in these high-stress weather conditions; at least for me it is. The rest of the guys seem to be steadily taking it all in their stride, as I'd expect. We're no longer maintaining radio silence during the approach. What's the point? We can hardly hear each other talk, anyway, so highly unlikely the *jihadis* will hear us in this wind. All the same, we're still communicating far quieter than normal – in whispers and with the occasional hand signal where required. Once the guys are all on to the wreck, I know from my own past familiarity that crystal clear communication is going to be ever more important.

Right before we come alongside for the actual assault to commence, one of the operators in an adjacent **RHIB** activates a telecommunication jamming device. It's designed to disrupt any nearby communications temporarily. Once set in motion, it sends out a type of signal which interferes with the *jihadis* external communication equipment. It deliberately searches for and transmits interference signals on the same radio frequencies as their mobile and satellite phones. It's intended to disrupt the electronic communications between their mobile phones and the relevant base stations. It effectively disables all mobile phones within the range of the jammer, blocking them from receiving signals or from transmitting any. The resulting disarray at their end once they become aware, or if they become aware this has occurred, will hopefully bring the rest of the team some valuable moments to proceed onto and into the ship, increasing the chances of a successful rescue.

Before the assault commences, the plan is for each team to conduct a final briefing to confirm the operational objectives and communication protocols. God only knows if this happened given the current deteriorating weather conditions. It doesn't happen on our RHIB. The entry teams have now confirmed they're at or near their positions, ready to initiate. Non-lethal distraction devices like flashbangs are ready to be used to disorient and distract the *jihadis* if they become aware of us before we're ready. Unlikely to happen in this weather. Doubtful they'd want to be out in this stuff is my thoughts. Upon Harry's signal, all teams will simultaneously penetrate their designated entry points. Maintaining situational awareness in this increasingly hostile weather is going to be a monumental task, as a gun battle between us and the terrorists is likely to be ferocious. I do not kid myself. This is not going to be just a high-risk state of affairs, it's going to be an utterly ballistic nightmare.

Harry initiates the kick-off signal over the radio. Hearing it in my headset sounds ridiculously loud given the harshness of all the other conflicting weather noises of the night. "Arguer, we are GO, GO, GO – over!"

I watch anxiously as the teams swiftly board the wreck in total darkness. They enter into the stairwells forward and aft, leading to the bowels of the old rusting hulk, preparing to encounter any immediate resistance. They're not disappointed, as initial shots are fired by the *jihadis* within seconds of the assault commencing. Harry earlier estimated we're likely to encounter three or four of them onboard. On the contrary, from the very first contact, I get the impression there's quite a few more. My heart is beating like mad, pounding away violently with a mix of anxiety and just old-fashioned fear as we hear the guys engage. This is not my bag these days, that's for sure. Knowing this, I still trust I'm up for it if the need arises, as I don't want to let anybody down, especially myself. I can periodically hear echoes of the wreck's buckled and rotten wooden deck planks creaking beneath the guy's boots, enhancing an already eerie atmosphere. A bright moon moves out gradually from the back of the heavy clouds and now casts long gloomy shadows, intensifying the sense of desolation for me.

Gunfights provide an all-consuming sensory overload, this much I already know and remember – way worse in the dark. They're always loud and boisterous. The environment becomes extremely disoriented with the assorted muzzle flashes going off all over the place in the dark. The flash is intense, very briefly illuminating the near vicinity around the muzzle for a fraction of a second. Hearing the actual gunshots and ricochets themselves, the yelling and the intensities of various explosions along with the smell of gunpowder and the physical effects, the sudden flash of light and sound has a psychological impact on anyone in the vicinity – these sensory inputs are overwhelming, inducing fear and anxiety. I remember from my own previous dangerous undertakings how fear and anxiety are common emotions in any gunfight. Right now, nothing has changed for me in this context. I'm once again scared witless.

After several minutes of almost continual gunfire, much of it partially silenced by our guy's weapons, I hear, "Victor, prepare to assist; I repeat, Victor, prepare to assist – over."

Victor is my call sign. My level of anxiety has very successfully achieved a whole new, inconceivably exhilarating level of intensity upon hearing that instruction for me to deal with Ben. I don't want to answer – more so, I'm not ready to assist. Not just yet. I'm still trying to get myself emotionally sorted out here.

"Ack, Victor good to go. I confirm, Victor good to go. Standing by – over," Gus acknowledges the call for me, as I'm still somewhere off in an uncertain cerebral wilderness with the pixies. I turn to abuse Gus for answering, and in doing so, I instantly see a bloodied jihadi stagger up onto the deck above him with his AK-47 dragging alongside. I don't have time to think or react. Muscle memory kicks in, and I simply lift my sawn-off shotgun towards the guy and blast him off the deck at point-blank range. It looks to me like I blew him completely up and over the rusty wire railing on the other side of the old wreck, while his AK-47 skids harmlessly along the deck and lands in the sea next to our RHIB. My brain cleared just like the snap of my fingers. I'm back in the game now, well and truly – at least I am until the shock of what I'd just done triggers in my brain.

"Victor, GO, GO, GO – over." I hear Harry's voice yell urgently over my headset, and it's still not what I want to bloody hear right at the moment. Gus looks at me and nods his head up towards the deck as he holds our rope ladder in place for me to climb up. Bugger it, here we go again, I guess. Reluctantly, with each step, I assess my specific situation, thinking about what limited moves I might have available to me if some jihadi hoer pops his head up while I'm still in the process of climbing onboard.

I recall how time often feels distorted during the initial moments when I've entered the amphitheatre of a gunfight. Sometimes, for me, anyway, everything seems to just happen in slow motion, which is fine. Then, at other times, it feels like it flies by in an instant, a result of the adrenaline rush and ultra-heightened focus relevant to the threat, which is not so fine. I also remember the physical stress of a gunfight can be exhausting. It initiates a certain level of psychological fatigue, challenging to maintain attention and make split-second decisions… the right decisions, at least.

Oddly enough, though, during previous gunfights, I have been acutely aware of my surroundings, or at least more than I am when not in a gunfight. Constantly scanning for any hazards, assessing concealment and monitoring teammates' positions so they don't accidentally shoot me – or get shot by me. This sense of heightened awareness – or fear, I like to think of it – is absolutely crucial for my survival. It's also a powerful motivator to stay alive in my case. Some guys go through contact with tunnel vision. Their focus narrows on immediate threats only, ending up with reduced peripheral vision, making it ever more important for each of us to communicate with team members.

Once inside the stairwell, I can feel right away how cold and damp it is in here. It's uninviting. Hostile. Mouldy stale air stinks the place up and makes me want to throw up. I wrap my scarf more tightly around my face to protect my nose and mouth from the stench and any pollutants in the air. The harsh sound of a firefight breaks out again somewhere down below me. Muzzle flashes suggest it's more towards the back of the wreck, and it's a heated, prolonged exchange of fire. I cautiously step over the body of another dead jihadi – no child this one, now not likely to ever have any either. Rolling him over slightly, I view him in the hazy green vision of my NVGs. He comes across like a very seasoned player, a seriously dead one, not an untried child such as we were anticipating.

Entering further into the claustrophobic bowels of the old wreck, I encounter a labyrinth of dimly lit corridors and rats, masses of the stinking rodents. Old, rusty and rotting rope lies around in the passageway, spread out everywhere, doubtless the cherished home of the rats. I carefully pick my way around a tangle of debris, littered with rusting equipment and other obscure objects that have either broken off, shifted or fallen down over time.

At one point, I'm instantly affected intensely by a nauseating stench, causing me to tear away my shemagh to dry retch as it washes over me like a wave of filth. I don't know what the hell it is. Nonetheless, it's a disgusting, overloaded odour. Almost certainly includes putrefying flesh, maybe rotting food, acrid faeces. It's a confusing and ugly mixture. Mingle it all up with an overpowering stench of fuel, oil or maybe grease from the ship's old machinery, and we have the stench of Armageddon. I can hear other fluids of some sort, perhaps seawater, sloshing around inside of the wreck's hull below me.

Various forms of marine life have colonised themselves into the wreck. It's possible to vaguely make out some unfamiliar objects. Maybe corals? There're also curious-looking sponges and other organisms I can't identify, all variously attached to the rusting surfaces. A few crabs or other types of marine-like crawly creatures scurry around in the sediment sloshing about in the deeper part of the wreck. Fear is having a pretty good time surging around my veins at the moment. Gotta remember the mantra – the mind is the boss of the body. I try to press on regardless, driven by the desire to save Ben, I think… and myself. It's like I can almost hear the ghostly whispers of the hostages pleading for their release, spurring me onward… yeah, right, leave me alone, you guys. All the same, I can assure anyone who cares to listen, I do not want to be here, in this place, at this very moment.

A blurred green figure emerges from one of the cabin doorways to my left, a faint glow behind him. My shotgun is already swinging towards it. I realise quickly it's one of ours, not as quickly as he realises I'm one of ours as well. He nods his head down towards the back of the ship. At the same time, he comes out with a small computer and a bag of something else not easily identifiable. Our tasking also involves the collection of any intelligence related to the wreck and whatever the hell else is going on here with the terrorists. The intention being to somehow surreptitiously pass this intelligence on to the relevant authorities, possibly via Diop, to launch whatever investigation they might wish to at a later date. Any intelligence collected during the operation might be crucial in this process, although we're all highly sceptical anything would transpire – nah, we know it won't.

Shooting stops for the moment, typically indicating the less accurate are now ruing their decision to engage and are probably dead or dying. Little by little, I move my way over and past three more dead jihadis, two young and one old this time. I glance at the face of the old one. Even in death, with rats crawling over him, he looks cruel, maniacal… fanatical. Still dead all the same. As the dynamic entry progresses, I can see where the teams have systematically cleared any likely dangers in the cabins and other spaces in all areas as they'd work their magic, signing off with a chalk X on the walls. I move forward. It now appears they've ultimately secured the entire wreck, which for my brain at the moment is a comforting thing, although they're still searching for any likely booby traps, concealed compartments, hidden jihadi hoers or other potential dangers. The goal at the moment is to just maintain control and to prevent any of the jihadis from regrouping. This might be difficult for them anyway, as it looks like most if not all of them are now dead.

Amidst the earlier gun battle, the teams worked intensely to find Ben along with any other hostages. The rescue of captives, I'm told, is a delicate process, requiring careful target discrimination during clearance. I'd heard earlier over the radio that they'd found Ben, alive. When I ultimately get directed to him, hidden away in a dank, secluded, gloomy and corroded compartment, I can tell from his teary red eyes that he's bearing the full weight of his endless suffering.

He's coughing loudly, initially a dry, rasping cough, gravitating into a kind of moist, wet, hacking sound. A glimmer of hope ignites within him as I approach with my soft red beam flashlight calling his name. Red beams are easy on his eyes, unlike the harsher white light. It won't impact my eyes either, preserving my night vision, and the same with any other team members in the area. I'm sort of overwhelmed by a surge of empathy – or something. Maybe it's simply determination against the *jihadis* who'd unquestionably not want us to rescue these guys. Whatever it is, I swiftly work to free him from his rope restraints, trying to speak words of encouragement to him as I work away, aiming to rekindle his focus and my concentration.

After releasing him, I give Ben a colossal hug to let him know he's safe. He's shaking like mad and is reluctant to let me go. I can relate to this; I'd been the same after being rescued in Vietnam. I give him some small sips of sugar water. It'll help restart his rehydration process. Before I can do anything else, though, he heaves up a massive, hoarse cough, producing a mouthful of blood-saturated mucus, abruptly lapsing into difficulty with his breathing. It's rapid and shallow. My immediate thought is that he probably has pneumonia, and bad. I'm quick like that some days.

I have a spare quilt jacket to put on him along with another shemagh scarf to cover his face and to try to warm him up a bit. My next step is to urge him to gently move to the forward area passageway, slowly, in order to finally disembark onto our RHIB. I speak to him as calmly as possible throughout, which by the way is quite the feat for me, as I'm anxious as buggery myself and keen to get the hell out of here… like post-haste. I then notice to, my dismay, he has nothing on his feet. I hadn't thought to bring any extra footwear for him… bugger, bloody idiot.

The rest of the team is concentrating on the other captives who likewise require considerable comfort and help to move. I struggle a bit with Ben, because he's so weak, wobbling from side to side, I'm unable to support him properly. Actually, I'm struggling a bloody lot with him. I try to hold him as steady as I can, except I'm not doing much of a job of it, given how weak he is. I ask one of the other team members – Alex, I think it is – if he can give me a hand. Not going to happen.

"Can't, dude. We got eight guys in total in here to try and get out. Not something we expected – not at all. Maybe two or three, definitely not eight, that's for bloody sure."

I then hear him tell Harry over the comms about how many they've found. "Will require all boats and hands in for this – over," Alex clarifies.

"Ack, will coordinate – over," Harry acknowledges calmly.

Suddenly, there's another, brasher announcement, this one clearly sounding like Taffy. "All comms, all comms, listen up. Fekkin dust storm has picked up ta pace 'n changed direction. Tis gonna be on ta us afore ye know it wit high crappy sandy winds. Get movin' all. We gotta spin tis up and do it now! Over."

Our original plan, if possible, was to provide medical attention to anybody who might have serious or life-threatening injuries. I guess now with the early arrival of this bloody dust storm, it's taken that very limited opportunity away. Another nice little challenge then for us all with this impending storm. Again, how bad can it possibly be, I still wonder? A windy sandstorm over the ocean? Continuing to push and pull Ben is a big ask for me. I do as best I can, as I can see he's now completely exhausted and struggling to put one step in front of the other anymore, especially barefoot. Deteriorated basic motor skills and muscle weakness limit his ability to move at all now. I'm amazed he got this far. I'm quickly becoming likewise drained. Only thing left to do now is to pick him up in a fireman's carry over my shoulder and barge my way around the debris and up the steps to the top deck.

It always seems to take forever, doesn't it? We do finally get up there all the same, exhausted, although I feel a profound sense of relief – or maybe elation – at actually achieving it. The emotional release is intense, and from my previous endeavours in this space, I'll probably feel a bit despondent once the adrenaline drains away. It almost becomes a physical thing. Bugger it, I'll deal with it when it happens. I lower Ben to the rotting wooden deck and take a deep breath in to get my own composure and equilibrium back… and abruptly choke on the foul, sandy air. How bad can the sandstorm over the ocean possibly be, I asked earlier. Bloody hell, enough to bugger up your night is the answer I can now tell myself. I tighten my shemagh scarf and then do the same with Ben's, pulling out and putting on a spare pair of goggles for him.

My deeply cathartic emotion of safely rescuing Ben is rapidly turning into a nightmare of significantly reduced visibility amongst the foul sandy air storming around us. It's difficult to see more than a foot or so in front of us in the sand-blown darkness. Then add the turmoil of not being able to breathe fresh air. What a bloody predicament. I'm guessing it's going to be especially treacherous trying to find our way back to the Arguer. I live in hope that Gus with no teeth is super proficient with all the GPS navigation on the **RHIB** to get us to where we have to be to meet with the other guys and get us back to the ship.

I slowly drag Ben over the deck to the edge of the wreck, and to my astonishment, Gus's big, ugly, toothless and tattooed face is almost level with the edge of the deck… momentarily, anyway. The next ferocious wave crashes him against the wreck, then takes him down again, to be about six feet below us, probably more. So then, this is going to be an intensely interesting experiment… not. Gus and I try to discuss over our radios as to how we might manage this violent swing in storm surge, given the limited time we have available to us – except it's almost impossible to hear each other with the wind continually whipping our voices away. Our communication efforts are reduced further in the next few seconds when three terrified kids exit the stairwell and join us… all young teenagers. One doesn't seem to hesitate; in a wild panic, he either slid or fell over the side of the deck into the shocked arms of Gus, as the **RHIB** once again comes up nearly level with the deck. Screw it, I jump at the peak of the RHIB's rise and drag Ben with me into the boat.

We're quickly followed by the other two kids literally diving over the rim of the wreck as the wave we're riding recedes. One of the kids – looks like the smallest – lands on top of my back, then completely losing his balance, simply rolls over the edge of the RHIB into the ferocious sea. I dive for his arms that are thrashing about in the air, only to see him go straight under as he hits the raging water. It's almost like the sea erupted with increased fury, churning like a furious cauldron of lathered white froth. Giant waves emerged over the top of us before crashing down on where the poor kid went in with a deafening roar. In the midst of all this tempest, our RHIB seemed tiny as it bobbed around helplessly at the mercy of the turbulent seas. The kid doesn't even partially surface again. Both Gus and I frantically scour the waves next to us with our arms and oars for his frail body, with no success. My guess is the poor little bugger was so exhausted, there was no fight left in him to try and get back to the surface. I doubt he knew how to swim, anyway. With all that'd been going on around us this night, I'm absolutely gutted at the tragic loss of this youngster who I hadn't got the chance to even meet… or to save.

I'm devastated. Worse, I'm stuffed if I know what the hell to do next after that crushing episode. Gus, on the other hand, made the decision for me, or us. For whatever reason, he propelled the RHIB forward at a great rate of knots, throwing us all off balance, down into the hull as it lurched. This is literally seconds before another RHIB races in to take our place against the wreck. Now I get the urgency of our swift departure. I can barely see the other team members on the wreck getting ready to board their RHIB. They're accompanied by two more guys they have freed. These look like adults. Laying on top of the two kids and Ben down in the hull, I'm holding onto the lifeline ropes on either side for dear life. We erratically ride the foam crests of the bleak sea over the next 30 minutes or more. I struggle to communicate with Gus. I can't hear anything over my comms unit. In trying to readjust it,

I realise it's gone, possibly yanked off me by the young kid falling over the side, the thought of which just saddens me all over again.

We're smashed all over the place, driven by the intense and endless jarring and heaving sea, flinging us about in the dark turbulent water and the sand-strewn atmosphere. I'm damned if I know how Gus is maintaining control in these extreme conditions and strong winds. Bloody impressed at his efforts, nonetheless. Our RHIBs inflatable collar provides me with some minor confidence we'll remain buoyant and stable no matter what. All the same, pounding around in my thoughts in these radical waves and sandy air, gives me the uneasy feeling that at any second now, one or all of us might possibly be either thrown out of the RHIB, be swamped or the RHIB is capsized. Fearful of this occurring, I get the two kids into life vests, which is easy enough given their size. Then I cover them up with the RHIBs tarpaulin and provide them each a thick field bandage to cover their nose and mouth from the sandstorm. Getting Ben into one is more of a challenge, as he's so exhausted. We finally get there all the same.

Eerily enough, I can just make out the beginnings of the first light of a new dawn break into the horizon. It's unsettling as the token scrap of light I can see is entirely shrouded in a soft, orange tinge from the sandstorm, creating a menacing haze. I partially turn to try and see how Gus is getting on. He notices me through his wild-looking motorbike goggles and gives me a thumbs up. He has his shemagh scarf wrapped around his mouth and nose to prevent the sand particles from chafing him or getting into his throat. I check on Ben to make sure his scarf is secure and he's breathing OK, he is. Beyond that he's not doing well at all. Nevertheless, there's not a lot I can do about it at the moment. I feel for the poor young kids. One is throwing up, still crying his heart out and shaking uncontrollably. The other one seems, well, jeez, I don't know, he's almost excited with this adventure.

Another RHIB races alongside and scares the hell out of me. Clearly, I'm not maintaining my situational awareness like I ought to. Looking back into the sandy mist behind us, I can just make out the other two not far back. The operator of the RHIB next to us gives a signal of an open and closing hand three times as they race ahead, suggesting around 15 minutes until we rendezvous with the Arguer. I hope he's right. I'd been concerned communication with the Arguer or the other RHIBs was probably difficult or maybe totally compromised in this weather, the signal from the other RHIB is reassuring comms are still working.

All of a sudden, on the horizon in front of us, there's a massive flash of light and a dull hollow thud echoed in the atmosphere, seemingly from an explosion of some sort. My most immediate and unsolicited impression is it must be the Arguer. Maybe the *jihadis* have found and attacked it? I turn again to look at Gus to see what his reaction is. He just put a hand out in front of himself and waved it down in a reassuring motion. He clearly knew more about the explosion than I do. Another of the RHIBs caught up to us and flew past at high speed, which in these conditions is no mean feat. The last RHIB settles down alongside us with the operator giving us the thumbs up, indicating to me all is well in the world of RHIBs in rough seas during a sandstorm.

From out of the eerie orange gloom in front of us, there she is, the Arguer, steaming into partial view through the storm-whipped horizon, all lights blazing, towards us, under full power, I imagine. As it gets closer, I can see it's got the first RHIB swinging wildly on its lifting davit as it's being winched up out of the turbulent sea and onboard the ship. Seeing the Arguer is quite simply a spectacular and most welcome sight. If I wasn't hanging on for dear life, I might've stood up and cheered like some lunatic. What the hell was that earlier massive flash of light and dull atmospheric thud, I wonder. Right now, who cares, I suppose. Mission criticality is to recover all the RHIBs and all personnel safely onboard. It takes nearly an hour to get the rest of the RHIBs stowed onboard. Although there's a real sense of urgency in the methodology to get it done, the weather isn't being sympathetic or cooperative to our efforts. Once the remaining three RHIBs arrive at the ship, the strategy is for each to tie off alongside temporarily as the Arguer quickly turns about. We're then towed alongside, as the Arguer steams full ahead towards a designated anchor point way out in international waters. One by one, each RHIB carefully manoeuvres up into position to attach to the davit, then each is safely winched onboard and secured. We're the last one to be picked up.

Both the kids are crying uncontrollably and throwing their hearts up by the time we're finally on deck. I give them a small hood they have to initially wear to minimise the potential for them witnessing any of the people onboard or any detail of the vessel itself. We are likewise also wearing our masks to avoid any accidental observation of our faces. I gently guide them both and Ben down into the mess area so they can warm up and towel themselves off. They're pretty much beyond it, though, especially Ben. They're all absolutely exhausted, not only from the terror of the sea escape venture; no doubt their primary suffering belongs to the distressing kidnap effect itself. A further upsetting aspect to their newfound freedom is the obligatory wearing of the security hood to ensure none of them can see the faces of their rescuers or any of the ship's details while they're onboard. This is for our protection and their safety and security once they arrive home.

It's pretty apparent to me that extensive psychological support is going to be the bigger requirement once we can get them out of here and on the way home, wherever it might be. This isn't something we can deal with right now, not onboard… if it's ever likely to be addressed for some of them. Readjusting to the outside world again is going to be a tough call for them all, I believe, anyway. Probably for me too.

The Arguer continues steaming towards our anchorage. Uncannily enough, not long after all the RHIBs are finally secured onboard, we begin to sail out of reach of the heaviest part of the sandstorm environment. The seas likewise become slightly less unruly.

After a brief respite of a shower and a feed, we all meet again in the mess. The purpose being for an after-action assessment to analyse the operation's success and identify any areas of concern while the events are still fresh in our minds. The only thing really fresh in my thoughts is the loss of life of the poor kid. I'm going to have to work on that. A key aspect of our briefing is from the ship's Captain Adam Timson, a plain-speaking English naval man of some lengthy career duration seemingly.

"Congratulations all. Job exceptionally well done. Everybody is now back safe and sound, especially our rescued guests." I don't want to raise the fact we lost one rescued child. It's not something I want to think about, as it'd just make me deep dive down into despair once again at the loss of him. Then there is the possibility that they all might still feel somewhat unsafe because they have to temporarily wear their hoods for everybody's protection.

"So then, you're probably all wondering about the little flash bang glow of twinkling lights and energetic atmospheric thump you may have witnessed out there this morning? Well, as it happens, while transiting to meet up with you guys, tending to our own business as we were, we picked up a medium-sized, high-speed craft on our radar. It was moving a bit erratically but largely towards us, unfortunately. When it got close enough, the crew hit it with our newly-installed non-lethal deterrence, our high-powered anti-piracy strobe searchlights. We saw quite a few armed Islamists onboard, probably a dozen or so, some wearing masks, all with firearms, some with RPGs."

He paused momentarily, with a wry smile on his face.

"Now, the power of our new weaponised searchlight beams is pretty respectable, having a tendency to cause any uninvited guests with an uncomfortable outcome – intentionally. They create an environment where our visitors are left a little helpless and unable to see… at all. We believed ourselves to be under a potential pirate attack at this point. Anyhow, for whatever reason, once we lit them up, they chose not to take evasive action, electing instead to blindly open fire on us, sending bullets ricocheting off the ship everywhere. So our crew returned fire – heavy fire, actually. We also utilised our own water cannons and RPGs. Consequently folks, the glow of light and energetic thump you may have observed is the result of our RPGs hitting the target. I regret to report, there were no survivors. None that we saw, anyway. So then, any questions?"

RJ put her hand up. "Do you suppose they just stumbled on us, Captain? Or do you think they might have been on their way to rescue their colleagues being attacked on that wreck and spotted us while in transit?"

"Hard to say. My guess is they were already on a similar course to ours when they saw us. They may have been going to assist, except with comms being jammed on the wreck, I doubt anybody onboard would've been able to raise any alarm. I think they were routinely out doing their regular pirate excursions to see whose day they could screw up. OK, if there's nothing else, Brian here – one of our medics – also wants to talk to you about a few things."

Some guy called Eric, I think his name is, put his hand up. "That bloody sandstorm, Captain. How the hell did we not know it'd be on to us so soon or be so bad? It was brutal. It hit us like it actually hated us."

"Good question. Brian will explain more about the sandstorm and any medical precautions we may have to take as a result of fleeing through it. Brian, I'll leave it with you now," Captain Timson says as he hands over to Brian and then walks out of the mess, giving us a soft salute as he goes.

Brian, our most senior medic onboard, I've been told, gives us an overview of what the sandstorm was about. "That bit of environmental mayhem hitting us this morning is actually an annual occurrence that sweeps across the Sahara Desert from East to West Africa. It typically originates in the Red Sea area of the Sahara-Sahel region of North Africa and moves towards the Atlantic coast. Right where we happened to be operating. It's commonly known as the 'Harmattan', which I believe means from 'coast to shore'. It's a dry and dusty trade wind, and as we all noted, it carries a significant amount of fine airborne sand, dust and pollen type particles and any other detritus it can pick up on its way. It's been known to blow continuously for anything up to a month or so and is in fact a notable meteorological phenomenon in this region. This event apparently aids in the pollination of date palms and other trees requiring stimulation." Brian pauses, probably to see if anybody wanted to ask any questions, had any interest… or is listening. We all seemed to be listening at least, just no questions – yet.

"Now to our own personal interface with this exciting and sandy occurrence, it's known to move and change direction very fast, as we're now well aware. It just so happens, this year, it arrived earlier and moved way faster than normal. We'd been monitoring it for days. Even while doing this, it regularly changed course swiftly enough to catch us out, particularly when we're already committed to a mission timeframe. Operating in it can be a potentially dangerous encounter, especially for anybody who might already have any minor existing respiratory concerns. Inhaling this dust and fine sandy pollen infused particles can play havoc with your lungs." Brian again pauses and reviews the room for any feedback. All quiet, or at least there are no questions, lots of coughing, gasping and spluttering nonetheless, including from me.

"However, operating in a sandstorm like this, even for the short time as we did, may have long-term health implications for some of you, subject to any of your existing individual health problems. Inhaling the particles is likely to irritate your airways, possibly resulting in conditions like bronchitis, asthma or chronic obstructive pulmonary disease or COPD. Additionally, the sand or dusty pollen can lead to skin irritation or more severe conditions like dermatitis. So, anybody having breathing difficulties, or you observe any of your colleagues with these types of symptoms, let's have a look at it ASAP, got it? Have I got your attention, everybody? What I'm saying is not to just brush any of these likely symptoms off in the long term. Get them looked at early, OK, before any overall decline in your physical health?"

"So what are you suggesting here, Doc? Should we be getting regular health check-ups to monitor the long-term effects of being exposed to all this shitty sand and particles? What is the worst case here? We get cancer, asthma, maybe die from breathing all this junk in and screwing up our lungs, that your point?" I can't remember the name of this guy who asked the question, I can see he's a bit agitated about the situation all the same. I don't blame him. He and a number of us are already wheezing and coughing up brown phlegm every few minutes.

"Yes, regular check-ups, just to monitor any potential adverse effects on your respiratory system. In an ideal world, we wouldn't have triggered the op when we did. As Harry mentioned, though, before we left, we'd have preferred to stall until after the storm had passed us by. Regrettably, we were already too exposed out where we anchored up, and we simply hadn't wanted to attract any more attention than necessary. The dust and fine particles can irritate the lining of your nose, throat and bronchial tubes. It can also reduce your lung function, especially in individuals with pre-existing respiratory conditions, like I mentioned. It will in due course make it harder to breathe and is likely to degrade lung efficiency. It can also lead to lung scarring, impairing your lung function. I have to stress the point here, though; this is generally in extreme cases of prolonged exposure to high levels of this dust. We weren't exposed for a long period of time. Nonetheless, we feel it's necessary to address it with you so you're at least aware of the down side of exposure, to be on the safe side."

"Yeah, right, well, I'll tell that to my lungs every time I cough up another gob full of this muck. Maybe a ration of whiskey might help to cleanse it up and kill it off?" A few made half-hearted attempts to laugh at this comment from another of the Brits in the teams, whose name I don't remember either. Most of us are too busy coughing and wheezing already to add to the dialogue, although the whiskey option isn't such a bad idea, or going home to my wife, now this is a far worthier one.

"OK, come see me after in the aid station if you have any concerns. In regard to another matter, I want to discuss our rescuees and what they're likely to be going through. None of it's going to be good as you can probably already imagine. So, in a nutshell, although their freedom has now been secured, nothing is going to be easy or straightforward for these guys. They must still remain secluded from the majority of us, and we must continually wear our masks when around them or when any of them are present." He pauses again for any questions… any interest, or are we listening still? We are.

"They're currently undergoing a basic medical check onboard, evaluating their physical and psychological well-being, seeing if anything has to or can be addressed straightaway. Not that it'll affect us in any way or that we might have any influence over things. It's still beneficial for you all to note how their anguish may rub off on us a bit while they're still with us. The long-term emotional toll of their captivity will quite possibly lead to trust anxieties, depression and isolation. They're likely to have difficulty with social reintegration and in rebuilding relationships with their families and friends or trusting us while they're still onboard. The complications for them may include anxiety, panic and other stress-related symptoms, nightmares, maybe flashbacks. So all, please keep this in mind if you have any interactions with these guys, especially any negative ones. They're dealing with a lot of untidy emotions and will be for a long time. They'll also resent wearing their hoods, so wherever possible, let them remove theirs, and you guys wear your masks, OK?"

After the briefing concludes, I sit down with RJ over a coffee to see what her plan of attack is for Ben going forward, if there is one yet.

'My primary focus, I suppose, is to provide him with any emotional support I can. I'll need your help in achieving that. He's already been asking me if he can call Rikki to let her know he's safe. I told him I've spoken to her about his safe rescue. Goodness me though, James, her response wasn't what I'd expected, I can tell you. It's like I'd just told her about a luncheon invite or something mundane like that. *"Oh, OK, thanks for that. I'm glad to hear he's fine,"* RJ mimicked nastily. "Then the shallow little bitch just hung up on me. He's way too fragile at the moment to be talking to her and getting that appalling sort of response, you agree?"

"Bloody hell, the little bitch. She'd bring him completely undone with her arrogance. I know she's a cow, RJ. But even for her, though, that's a whole new level of ugly. How do you want to deal with this, then? I mean deal with the whole saga, you know.

The long-time affair with Serge, who's now in a facility to help him work through his spiritual breakdown. Not to mention that Serge and his wife have also separated as a result of all these shenanigans. On top of this, we then have the dead minister and all of the skulduggery linked with it. Where the hell do we begin with any of this, RJ?" I begin to question if I actually want to be part of all this going forward.

"I know, it's a problem, no doubting it. First things first, though, let's get him into some sort of facility so they can work on building his strength and health back up. I'll feed him a near truthful white lie for now as to why he can't talk to Rikki. Then, the next step I guess is going to be pretty tricky. We have to debrief him about what happened from the time he and the minister drove off from the office in Nouadhibou. This must happen, James, without sending him into a deep depressive state." She's saying this to me why? I'm not the right person to quiz him about those circumstances, that's for sure.

"Are we taking him home to recuperate? We'll have to conjure up a pretty good tale to keep him away from Rikki is why I ask." And keep the shallow little bitch away from us as well.

"No, I don't think that's wise. We'll take him back to Australia, ultimately. For now, though, we'll have to look after him somewhere else. Somewhere secure. I've been talking to our evacuation provider, International Recovery Services, about where the best secure facility might be for us to take him for both physical and psychological care. They're suggesting some sort of private trauma centre in either Spain or France. They'll get back to me once they confirm availability." RJ looks at me, I think to see if I approve of this strategy… or if I'd been paying attention. I have no idea whether it's a good idea or not, nor do I care much about one solution or another. I just want Ben looked after, so I just nod and shrug my shoulders.

"I guess these places offer specialised care for people with physical injuries, malnutrition and emotional suffering like the extreme stress Ben is suffering. They have in-house professionals to provide ongoing therapy, counselling and any other forms of psychological and health support he might require," RJ whispers, trying to sound confident. *I'm confident I want to go home.*

"OK, so on another matter, are we going to do anything about the jihadis' and all of their mischief-making out past the EEZ and what they're up to in the graveyard? Especially now they've stolen that bloody EMP? Do we do anything about the connection between this massive screw-up and the minister being murdered? Anything? What about any of the intelligence we took from the wreck? Who does that belong to now, and who is going to interrogate the data?" *The list of concerns I have seems endless. My brain has this necessity, though, to compartmentalise some of it in order for me to move forward – as fast as possible.*

"The intelligence is being examined as we speak by one of the whiz kids onboard here. It belongs to all the stakeholders, although primarily to us as we're funding this operation. Once we decipher all the data, I'll pass on as much as I can to Diop so he can then furtively pass it on to his contacts in dark places within the Mauritanian government. Hopefully, this might generate some interest amongst any of their ministers who aren't on the take. Ortega will also take a copy to their contacts within the UK government. We'll consider at a later date if we should quietly give the Westra authorities the same information. As for the rest, James, we chip away at it, step at a time."

We talk some more about Ben's current condition. He hasn't been treated well by his captors; none of them had been. It appears he and the others were given little access to any quality food or water. The conditions of his confinement I witnessed had been appalling; probably the same for all of them. His physical health has deteriorated considerably from when he left Nouadhibou and was first taken. He's clearly malnourished, emaciated and extremely weak. Then there's the amount of weight he's lost. He looks so gaunt. To be honest, he looks almost ghost-like after being kept in the dark environment for so long.

We already knew that, because of their prolonged inactivity and confinement, Ben and the others' muscles would have most likely atrophied, leading to reduced mobility and strength. We'd anticipated this earlier in the planning phase, aware they might have difficulty walking unaided or just moving around in general. While a plan was in place to try and manage this, it's been difficult to achieve, as there are so many more of them than predicted; add to that we have the extreme effects of the sandstorm impacting us and them, to complete the mayhem.

RJ voices her belief that the prolonged captivity and isolation will ultimately have a severe psychological effect on Ben. I can see this is going to be an issue for all of them in reality, already exhibiting signs of anxiety and, according to the medical team, symptoms of extreme traumatic stress. I know a bit about this myself from my own previous harrowing encounters in Vietnam. The guys seem to be emotionally disconnected from their world, or our world, not just the fact they've been rescued and are now safe; it seems from their entire captive involvement almost like a sort of denial. They're highly distressed, completely withdrawn and already having difficulty communicating with us and, more concerning, with each other. They have all now been given the opportunity to bathe the stench and ingrained grime out of their bodies and to dress in fresh clothing in an effort to lift their emotional self-esteem.

"So, who is going to be responsible for looking after the rest of these guys? Us, as in Castelle?" I ask, already probably knowing the answer is no. "Because I'm not good at doing any of that. Plus, I want to go home to see my family, not hang around with all this for weeks on end. It's been a long time since I've been home RJ."

"I get it, James, and I agree. I don't know for certain who will take the lead on this, to be frank. In the planning phase, we put our hand up to look after Ben and any other people held captive. At that early stage, we anticipated at least one or maybe two additional captives, certainly not this. Anyway, regardless of the numbers, I guess it's going to have to be Castelle, because we've arranged and funded the rescue. So, yet again, we'll talk further to International Recovery Services, as they have all the people and the skills to manage this from an ongoing perspective. You and I are not equipped for this level of support for Ben or for any of the others either. I'll get back to you on this soon."

"Another point of consideration, I suppose. How do we keep any of this out of the press?" I ask. Not an area I'm too familiar with. Getting it into the press, I'm fine. Keeping it out – not so fine.

"Yes, well, in regard to this, we tell no one… no one at all, James. This is important. Everything about this is off-limits. It's going to be essential for us, all of us, to handle this extremely sensitive topic with great care and deliberation, especially for the well-being of the rescued and their families. In particular where it involves the young one who drowned. The ethical implications of this as a media money-spinning story once it gets out into the mainstream will be nothing like what actually occurred, that's for bloody sure. They'll all be on their three-wheeler trikes dashing around, yelling about any number of fucked up or concocted stories, competing with each other just to sell more coverage. So we tell no one," RJ says, almost angrily.

Not for the first time I've noticed an increase in her swearing, which is something spectacularly new all-round. Another week or so, and she'll be swearing like a trooper. Either she's spent way too much time in my profanity-strewn company, or something else entirely is going on, as she has previously been dead against the use of vulgarity. However, I reckon I'm a pretty improved species in that space now myself… I like to think so, anyway.

Chapter 7

FINALLY HOME, WITH MY family, for over a month now. Slowly decompressing. Recovering really… well, trying hard to anyway, after the disconcerting events in West Africa. Endlessly humoured nonetheless, by the universe allowing me to get caught up in this never-ending cycle of life-threatening crises. The last few months over there have taken their toll on me, though, both psychologically and physically this time. I'm pretty certain I'm sort of on the way to recovery, though I keep going over in my contemplation the enormity of what has been achieved… and lost.

The kid, though. I keep getting myself bogged down about him immensely, in the nightmarish scenario of him falling off me into the sea. Crazy, I know. Nonetheless, I keep beating myself up over it – unnecessarily, I'm fully aware – because I didn't prevent him from falling overboard or rescue him once he was in the sea. It feels almost like I've acquired some sort of moral injury because of it. The psychological impact of this particular singular harrowing encounter sits well above all of the other high-stakes situations and apprehensions I've tried to deal with over the past few months. It's as if I've bloody well betrayed the poor kid, because we – or

I – didn't save him… again, right after he'd just been rescued from being a hostage, bloody hell. I do realise it's not unusual for this type of emotional impact to occur. It's like some sort of a lapse in my own deeply held ethical beliefs and values has negatively transpired against me – what the hell am I thinking, here?

The rest of the operation sits pretty fine with me. It's just the after-effect of the poor kid dying that's messing me up, for now. We're all well aware of the other potentially more serious repercussions of conducting the operation without notifying authorities in Mauritania, so no need to lose sleep on that aspect. Violating sovereignty and international laws are very sombre concerns that'd crossed our thinking and our discussions often enough from the outset. The large number of captives onboard is what genuinely complicated our plans, prompting an urgent rethink of our intended approach. Then, along came the bloody sandstorm over the goddamned ocean.

I continually rehash the successful elements of the operation, as encouragement. The fact that post-rescue, those liberated were submitted to immediate medical assessments and an initial discreet debriefing. Crucially, these were conducted in isolated cabins, with our personnel wearing their masks for both their protection and of the rescuees ultimately. Our aim being to try and prevent any unintentional recognition or disclosures by our guys, likely to compromise our identification, or what the rescuees might inadvertently divulge about us on their return home. What they don't know or can't confirm is unlikely to get them into trouble… or us.

Due to the intensely covert nature of the rescue, liaising with any authorities for the next phase to be successfully achieved wasn't an option. So, to expedite matters without any potential blowback on any of us, and to furtively attempt to shift the focus elsewhere, we'd enlisted the assistance from a derivative of the International Red Cross Society. Their role, in a confidential funding arrangement, is to look after any ongoing medical and emotional health support, counselling and to ensure the well-being of the now-freed captives, managing all this while arranging their repatriation and a safe return to their home countries and families.

Regardless of the potentially endless legal and diplomatic ramifications our actions in Mauritanian waters may attract, we prioritised the safety and well-being of those rescued above all else… and of course ourselves. Our use of force, though no doubt subject to various layers of international law, was justified in our eyes by the very real threat faced by the hostages, in particular Ben. In the targeted mission against terrorists, international humanitarian law and the laws of war do not come into play as far as we're concerned. While irreversible harm has befallen the terrorist kidnappers, any legal consequences are highly unlikely. Our personnel, officially unaffiliated with any specific country, face minimal risk of diplomatic protests or extradition demands – catch us if you can, basically.

Media scrutiny, however, is going to pose, and probably will continue to pose, a challenge if not managed correctly. The 'mysterious rescue out of the blue' narrative may have some negative influence on the rescuees' well-being once they return home. There, it all ends, though. Controlling any information released to the media is crucial. It is being carefully stage-managed. None of our debriefing statements from those rescued will ever make it to the media or any other agencies. Regardless all this information was carefully scripted anyway, controlled and managed at the highest level to safeguard our personnel's identities and information about the vessel and its operations.

The potential legal complexities arising from our actions are considerable and may involve international counterterrorism laws and infringements of UN Security Council resolutions. Our disregard for certain legal frameworks, combined with the extraterritorial jurisdiction of a home country, as unlikely as it is that it might ever be determined, might further complicate the situation. In summary, the aftermath of the rescue operation is intricate. Considerations range from maritime legal consequences leading to in-depth, long-term media impacts and ruptures in diplomatic relations. All of this is critical in the context of safeguarding the well-being of the hostages and maintaining the confidentiality of our operation. Another potential issue likely to arise for Castelle is the fact that it's a quasi-Australian government entity. One which is unlikely to survive a high-level government investigation or a Senate estimates enquiry, should the government become aware of our involvement.

And then there is Ben, who has been hastily and safely ensconced into a private care centre in Madrid, Spain. From the frequent feedback provided by his medical team and RJ so far, it appears his recovery is progressing slowly, nonetheless favourably, in most aspects of their specific recovery program for him. As anticipated, Ben has gotten more and more impatient about wanting Rikki to be with him during his convalescence. He's apparently getting quite demanding in fact – who wouldn't have expected that was going to happen? RJ and I both spoke openly and frankly with his Care Team Leader, Professor Antonio Baltony – several times, actually – about the hypothetical complications of this occurring. My biggest concern, I bluntly advised the Professor, is given her colourful history, there's no doubt in my thoughts, Rikki will falter. Within days, if not within hours, I say to the Professor, she will be screwing one of his young, good-looking medical staff, right behind Ben's back during his recuperation. He was initially appalled at my candid assessment, though he'd already been made aware of her indulgences – or her peccadillos, as he calls them. I do think it gave him pause all the same to consider whether to allow her to come to the facility. I bloody hoped it to be the case at least.

Professor Antonio told us he had spoken directly with Rikki several times, and at length, apparently, about the possibility of her coming over to join Ben. I can only imagine the shock he'd been subjected to with her responses to that conversation. He didn't want to share with us what they discussed or how he chose to word his questions to Rikki. Regardless, and unsurprisingly, a blanket ban was soon put on any possible attendance by her at the facility. The Professor further ordered no communications to be undertaken with her or to be accepted from her. The health and recovery of Ben is paramount and overrode any other wants or desires by any other parties, including Ben's.

As Ben slowly recuperated and began to progressively build up his mental and physical strength again, Professor Antonio finally allowed RJ to visit him, initially just as a social call, to assess his reaction to entering back into the real world. Ultimately, however, RJ was permitted to begin debriefing him about his experiences from the time he and the minister left our office in Nouadhibou. This is a critical phase in understanding the various links in the entire episode. RJ wanted me to come along, but I declined. My own slow convalescence was more important to me and my family at the moment.

Chapter 8

SLEEP, OR ANY OF its likely derivatives, has often been difficult to come by since I returned home, especially tonight for whatever reason. I'm as restless as hell, something's bugging me, something not quite right, I'm not sure what – it's hard to place at the moment. It's problematic though to achieve any sort of rest when the legs and the brain are fidgety, and it has plenty of things to deal with at the moment. I'm continually turning over and over the outcomes of the past couple of months – well, the past two years with Castelle, really… and the loss of the kid.

I don't know why tonight is so bad for me though; it normally isn't this intense. I simply can't switch off these most recent events, as much as I'd like to, especially my thoughts about the poor dead kid. Anyway, my tossing and turning antics are now aggravating my gorgeous, heavily pregnant wife Carla. She normally loves me madly, although I sense not so much tonight while I'm disturbing her sleep. I'm not sure if I feel something is out of the ordinary or if I'm just having a rough night with my thoughts. Whatever it is, the high winds outside hammering away at our old tin roof probably play a part to my disquiet. It seems my dog Goliath is likewise having a challenging time as well, undoubtedly my agitation is influencing his. He quietly prowls between our bedroom and our daughter's. Maybe he's the reason why I'm restless. I don't know… who knows? Maybe I'm the reason he's unsettled? Laying on the floor next to my side of the bed, he utters a long, low lingering growl at the wind and thunder outside. Swinging my feet out of the bed and resting them next to his head on the floor, I pat him softly. Quietly shushing him, I put my jeans on, listening to the hellishly howling wind and rattling tin roof.

I'm not alarmed at anything with his growl. I just assume he's annoyed or sympathetic to my edginess, or he's as irritated at the wind as I am, until I notice the very faintest of a moving silhouette reflected on the passageway wall from the soft night light. My instant thought is that it is Katerina – discounting it immediately, unless she'd recently grown taller and taken to carrying what seems to be a handgun. My heart rate rapidly accelerates, completely out of any logical range… ballistic even. Goliath and I both, in chorus, bolt for the door, having absolutely no idea why or what I intend to do once I get there. I'm just so outraged that someone is intruding into our home uninvited… with a gun. Given past experiences, I can only assume that whoever it is has but one reason for being here – to do me and my family harm. The solitary thing to think about is their safety.

Leaping forward, I scream like a bloody banshee as I stride out, whatever the hell they sound like. Add Goliath's highly intense barking, and we clearly take our intruder by utter surprise. This in turn takes me by complete surprise as well to realise he isn't alone. Our heads unfortunately collide heavily at the bedroom door, knocking us both to the floor violently in the process. I partially scramble up in a heavy daze, trying to grab for his gun hand, realising then the gun has a suppressor attached. I smash it a couple of times against the door jam, hard. Regrettably, he doesn't release the weapon. To add to my misery he's strong, the big prick. Surprisingly, though, agile or not, he's not recovering anywhere near as fast from our brutal head impact as I am; hardly at all, in fact. By some means, I manoeuvre my hand around his gun enough to get a bit of a finger into the trigger guard to try and stop him from actually shooting me, while my other hand is busy trying to gouge one of his eyes out. I sense, though, he's really struggling to recover from our collision, which has got to be a good thing, I thought. Well, a very good thing for me, right? For him, not so good. I'm figuring he's possibly heavily concussed.

In the process of all this occurring, I vaguely recognise Carla screaming in the background. Lights come on in our bedroom and along the passageway. Goliath, though, is no longer with me. Strange how the mind registers some minor things such as this during times of extreme distress, isn't it? Like no dog, although me crushing my thumb into one of the intruder's eye sockets as hard as I possibly can doesn't seem to distract me. He grunts noisily, painfully, then screams, signalling to me I'd achieved some degree of success. There's an art to eye gouging, I'll have you know. It's called enucleation, or evisceration, or exo-something or other. Can't remember the specifics. It's not as if it matters. We were instructed extensively on its use during our close quarter combat training back in Vietnam. Some things you never forget. This is one of them. It's deadly, intensely painful, and moreover, if you manage to actually extract the eye out with your thumb, it's irreversible.

I know, I know, it's a very untidy, gross thought and a worse image to have banging around inside your head all by itself and unsupervised at this hour of the day. It's a handy self-defence tool nonetheless, so my sympathies at this stage are with the success of my thumb, not the outcome of the intruder losing an eye. Given my apparent success so far, I apply further pressure into his eye socket. His scream increases as he tries to violently bump me off him. He then tries to savagely pull his gun hand away from my hand, except the silenced weapon discharges, and the intruder screams. I scream as well, except it isn't my intruder who screams—well, not the one I'm trying to deal with. It's the other one, the one further down the passageway, now leaning against Katerina's bedroom door frame, with Goliath attached to his leg. In the blink of an eye, I see him collapse in a shrieking, writhing bloodied heap onto the passageway floor. Howling loudly, screaming. Trying to hold his lower stomach in with both hands covered in blood and gore while Goliath tears at his leg.

I can now also see my intruder a bit more clearly with the lights on, removing my thumb hurriedly from his eye socket in order to be able to smash the point of my elbow into his throat as hard as I can. This time, I'm far better rewarded with a distressing sound of crushing cartilage or bone… or whatever the hell it is in there. Who cares I say; a reward is a reward in my book. He chokes and gurgles violently as I smash my elbow down again and again until he goes limp. I only then recognise Carla screaming at me to stop, pleading with me, telling me the police are on their way. So I stop. I feel the threat from him has passed. Heaving for breath, laying on top of the intruder – the big prick, I snatch his black balaclava off. However, I don't recognise the face, or its origins. Not Russian or Japanese. More Arab, if anything. Great, that's all I need. Now Muhammad wants to kill me.

I know I should have been more worried; I just don't actually fear for my own life during all this. Bizarre, isn't it? I do for Carla and for Katerina's lives, however. Let's face it, when there's a lunatic or two loose in the house with guns, it's probably time to fear for my own life as well. I simply don't. Not right now, anyway. I know it's a terrifying ordeal. Nevertheless, my brain was not yet registering it as such. I'm unfortunately, regrettably, very much back into my brutal Vietnam fighting mode, just like that! Interesting how the hell this just happens – or maybe it's not?

Above the screaming noise of intruder two, I hear a big car skid to a halt outside – it's some sort of vehicle with a big throbbing motor at least. Spreading gravel all around with its braking wheels. Unsure at this point if I'm relieved or distressed at hearing the sound. Is it the police already? Surely not? One car door opens then closes quickly. There's no subsequent sound of anybody moving about, though. I pick up my intruder's gun, pointing it down the passageway just in case. I believe now a threat continues to exist, and yet, it's not possible to see anybody or hear anything other than the racket intruder two is making while dying from his gut shot. Nothing happens for a few seconds. Then, the car door reopens, slams shut, with the car then speeding off in a shower of loose stones and grit, spinning wheels and over-revving big engine. It slams into something solid outside, maybe my tractor or the corner of the shed. Whatever it is, it's a very solid crunch. It backs up furiously, then races off in another eruption of spinning wheels, high revving engine and flying stones. I've no idea what the hell it was all about, although my money is on it not being very favourable for us anyway.

My intruder seems to be in a deep unconscious state, really struggling for breath. Going grey in the face, not dead – not yet, anyway – and I don't want the big prick dead, not just yet. He's definitely not with us at the moment all the same. His chest is rising then falling ever so slightly, with difficulty. More importantly, it's the gravelly sound wheezing out from his mouth, throat or nose, which suggests to me he's unlikely to be amongst the living for much longer. He's in huge distress is my assessment. His subconscious just hasn't probably accepted it yet… it will, though. I only realise at this point that I have also been shot by my intruder. Not badly, though, I don't think. Seems to be straight through my side. Looks more like a deep graze than the full impact. It's bleeding away merrily, but heavily all the same. Now I understand why I'd screamed earlier as well. Judging from the flame burn marks on my skin and clothes, the gun was very close to me when he fired it, probably touching me, causing the shot to go straight in and out of me.

Slowly, ever so slowly, I get to my feet – awkwardly, feeling incredibly disorientated, multiple points of pain around my body now registering in my brain. I haven't overexerted myself in this way in a very long time. I sort of limp and slide my way down the passage, my hand gliding along Carla's freshly painted passageway wall for stability, dragging my bloodstains along with it while pointing the gun at intruder two. Approaching him cautiously, I can see there's blood everywhere. The coppery, sickening stench is penetrating deep into my psyche and my memory bank, reminding me of the dry, sweet metallic pungency from incidents in my past. In no time, it will dry off and take on a vile odour that will oppress the senses and seize my breath away. Until then, I have other things I have to do.

I think about what has just happened. Lungs heaving, staring at the second intruder, who's staring back at me in agony, behind his mask. Desperately trying to get my breath back slowly, I lean uneasily against the wall on one bloodied hand. When I feel strong enough, I reach over to him and rip his balaclava off as well. Again, I don't recognise the face, although it appears to be another Muhammad by his looks. I do however, recognise the pink frothy bubbles coming from his nose and mouth. This guy's likewise in serious strife, except he and his subconscious do know it. I can tell from his terrified eyes and the amount of blood exiting between his fingers as he tries to hold his gut together. There does not appear to be an exit wound. My best guess on this then… the shot is a hollow point bullet. Designed to expand on impact, to produce a larger wound, thus inflicting more internal mutilation to a target, which I assume was meant to be me… along with my family, possibly. I'm astounded it didn't expand as it went through me on the way to Muhammad the second. Dumb luck today, I guess.

My sympathetic nervous system has released so much adrenaline during the encounter, my emotional response, my 'fight-or-flight' reaction, is totally out of control. I pick his gun up as well, also silenced, put it into the back of my jeans, then lean down and slowly press the end of the suppressor on my gun into his wound… hard. Yeah yeah yeah, I know, I know, very unkind. Screw the dog, though. I want to know a few things, and hopefully before he dies.

"Who sent you?" I scream at him, louder than his screams of pain. Mind you, his screams intensify with the new and highly exhilarating insertion of the gun suppressor into his gunshot wound. His eyes bulge out, as a long stream of pink bubbly saliva dribbles down from his mouth. The froth also coming from his mouth increases, stronger now, much brighter with thicker blood in it than before. I know this guy is done for – he definitely knows it as well.

"Who sent you?" I scream at him again, pushing the suppressor in deeper… my mistake.

His eyes do a bit of a fluttery thing, along with a massive sigh escaping his bloodied lips, as the face goes white, his eyes roll back into his head at the same time, as he succumbs to the pain… or whatever. I'm not happy at my eagerness. Unsure if he's dead or just fainted from the pain, either way, I'm not going to be getting anything more out of him just at the moment. Or maybe ever, as I now hear the faint sound of sirens in the distance. Police are once again attending my property in relation to an incident relating to someone dying. *This cannot look good on my local community integration scorecard*, I mock myself. I don't know why I think it's sort of humorous. I know I'm about to enter into whole new world of grief, or maybe just another phase of the same old existing one.

Between my panic, plus my nervous system clanging away at an alarming rate, I slowly limp over to, by now, a hysterical Carla. Holding a distraught Katerina close to her on the floor, just inside of her bedroom, both are crying uncontrollably and shaking intensely. I reach out to try and comfort them both, except Carla pushes me away, violently, with a strength and venomous look more appropriate on the faces of the thugs than my gorgeous wife. I'm shocked at her reaction. I don't know why she's responded like this. I'm stunned. It'd appear that, once again, I'm the source of bringing mayhem and violence into our family home. I get it, I do. Nevertheless, I'm obligated to protect myself and my family when this sort of thing happens. I just can't seem to stop it from happening… therein lies the issue, I guess.

At the very same time, I look around for Goliath. This wonderful family connection is missing. No barking or running around to comfort Katerina like he habitually does. I stand shakily and stagger my way back out of Katerina's room to the second intruder, where I'd seen Goliath last. I find him, partially hidden under the passageway armchair, next to the comatose body of the second intruder. Goliath is dead. Broken neck it seems, probably caused by the intruder kicking him or maybe falling on him when he got shot. I'm doubly devastated. I kick the intruder as hard as I possibly can in the head, which I have no doubt hurts me far more than the intruder, as I'm in bare feet.

✦ ✦ ✦

I bend down to pick Goliath's body up just as I'm interrupted midway by police surging into the passageway. Guns raised, screaming at me to get on my knees and to put my hands behind my head. I meekly do as directed; no point trying to protest my innocence at this stage. I can't blame them, I suppose. I probably look like hell – dishevelled, blood all over the place, covering much of my torso. Imagine this image along with my intruder's blood-spattered gun poking out the top of my jeans while the second intruder's gun stuck into my back beltline. No questions are asked of me initially. Just shoved flat to the floor, handcuffed, lifted up roughly, minus my intruders' two weapons.

I'm frogmarched over to a chair in the kitchen at the end of the passageway and pushed into it, all the while protesting about my gunshot wound. It's obvious these guys are as shocked and as nervous as I am with the scene they've just encountered, as I look back on it. More police arrive to add to the already chaotic scene.

This has just been the most terrifying ordeal for me… for all of us. I'm trying to run my mind over things, all while I'm sitting on my kitchen chair bleeding miserably away. Striving still to recap everything I can about these two-armed thugs wearing black balaclavas forcing their way into our place of safety, our Kasbah, at 4.30 in the morning for crying out loud. However, as I reflect on it, this does not look or feel like a robbery in any way. Although they had created a climate of extreme fear amongst us, it felt much more like a political or violence-motivated attack. As I consider the confrontation, I'm struck by how desperate the armed invaders hadn't been. They just weren't panicked or reckless, not to me anyway. This was a very calculated intrusion, very professional, very something else, just not a robbery.

One of the police officers' snarls at me to sit down again and shut up when I try to stand up to explain about my wound,… and to also remind him I'm one of the victims here, not the perpetrator. I return his attitude right back at him. It seems to have little effect, a reaction he's probably mostly immune to, unlike his crotch-scratching antics, which seem to be a permanent fixture in his life.

"Uncuff him, now please." This is spoken quietly from a police sergeant with a name tag of Rutledge walking up beside me as he comes into the kitchen from outside. I recognise him straightaway – he's one of the officers who'd attended here many years earlier, when someone else died in this very same kitchen. He'd been respectful back then, and again now it seems. He's followed by two ambulance paramedics, at least one of whom I think is female, maybe both. Hard to tell these days, not that it matters. Neither of them appears to be those who attended way back when to take the dead away.

"No offence, Mr Kelly. Normal reaction, I guess, when the guys are confronted with a scene like this," he says quietly as he stares at the carnage in my passageway while the snarly officer glumly unlocks my handcuffs. Sergeant Rutledge turns to one of the paramedics to ask her to look at my wound. I'm grateful, although more concerned for Carla and Katerina. I'm about to refuse the treatment and insist my paramedic and her blue hair go see how Carla and Katerina are first, just as the second paramedic comes out of Katerina's room with them both, wrapped in a grey blanket. Carla is shepherded past us, without any glance or acknowledgement of me at all, to a waiting ambulance outside. Its red and blue flashing lights reflect off the kitchen windows as my paramedic works away on my wound.

My blue-haired medic advises me, "This is not a graze, young man. You have actually been shot, through and through. Nonetheless, it's a deep wound. We'll need to take you to the hospital so they can check it out for any organ or deep tissue damage. You are likely to require surgery. Regardless, you're going to require multiple stitches for this wound. In addition, you've lost a lot of blood. What the hell are all these other wound marks here? You're covered in them."

I don't bother answering. How do you explain any of my past misdeeds in a few brief words? She begins patching me up as best she can for now. I'm experiencing a slight case of gunshot déjà vu, although I'm sure I'll adjust.

Another two paramedics make their way into the kitchen, weighed down with their bags of trade, working their way into the passageway to administer to the two home invaders. I get up off my chair again to be escorted out to a waiting ambulance, just as two more cars arrive a few seconds apart, all complete with flashing lights to add to the dramatic sound of dirt and dust spraying everywhere as they brake. Doors slam shut. The detectives I guess, as I look at the kitchen clock. 5.20 a.m. They sign in with one of the police officers at the door and make their way inside the house. One of them talks to Sergeant Rutledge, while another two walk into the passageway, snapping on what looks like kitchen gloves, asking the paramedics about the status of the 'these two guys'.

What, these 'guys', are they being considered the victims? "HEY! The victims here are me and my family, OK!" I shout at them angrily. Unnecessary, I know. Really, though? Is this the most ideal approach these guys can apply at first glance? While I'm still present.

"Sit!" A detective standing in the kitchen barks at me, pointing to a chair, pushing his oversized horn-rimmed glasses up his nose. I take my time to look from the angry stares of the detectives in the passageway to him. Thinking momentarily, I recognise him from the earlier incident years before – the interrogation from the detectives back then. This guy is grossly overweight though, so I don't think it's him. Or if it is, he's been resting up in a very healthy paddock of recent times.

"Tell me the story," is all he says, which in a nutshell isn't a problem. It's just the manner he chose to use, almost as if what he really means is *tell me your bullshit version of the story.*" This grates on my already hypersensitive and adrenaline-pumped nerves. I stay standing, glaring at him, as he again pushes his glasses up his nose.

"I said sit!" he almost yells at me this time, pointing angrily to the chair again, pushing his glasses up yet again. Jeez, get that fixed dude, will ya. It must drive you nuts, because it is me. Worse than the earlier crotch-scratching officer.

"No," I respond quietly, politely, or as much as the moment allows. No yelling, no harshness in it, no anger in my voice. The look on his face is worth the reprisal I'm likely to have come my way. Bugger him. I'm very reluctant to talk about any of this whole hostile encounter with this guy, for all the obvious reasons.

"Sorry about that, I hadn't meant to put you offside in there," I turn to look at one of the other detectives from in the passageway as he walks up and stands next to me, pointing his thumb over his shoulder to mean 'in there' being the passageway. "We sometimes become a bit desensitised to these things. Not as self-aware of our surroundings as might be helpful."

His smile seems genuine, maybe somewhat regretful. I'm OK to see where this ends up, although I doubt anywhere good for me.

"I've got this, Alex. Can you go and work things over with the guys, thanks," he says with authority, nodding towards the other detectives in the passageway. Alex is not a happy little chappy about this change of circumstances. I think he's actually very pissed about it and is struggling to keep it under control. I sense he'd been relishing the task of pulling my fingernails or whatever else it is they have in mind for these types of situations. I say nothing, although appreciative of the positive intervention. I just look at the guy to see where this is still likely to lead, if anywhere.

"I'm Detective Sargent Raymond Tallis. Call me Ray," he says, not putting his hand out to shake or anything, just standing there, staring at me as he retrieves some plastic bags from his jacket pocket.

I nod, responding by not offering my hand either. 'I'm James Kelly. I live here.'

Raymond Tallis slid the small plastic bags over my hands one at a time, holding them in place with a couple of heavy-duty rubber bands, very tight ones. "Apologies for this. Forensics will want to check your hands out. I'm cognisant of your emotional agitation at the moment, Mr Kelly. Violent crime is extremely disturbing for all people concerned. Particularly where it involves an invasion into the one place in our world, where it is psychologically imperative to feel safe – our own home," he says, looking slowly around the kitchen and nodding his head.

"Yeah, I know you probably get all that. It's just I've got my own version of emotional suffering coming out of my ying-yang at high speed at the moment. So the last thing I want is for you guys to be talking or looking at me as the potential offender here," I say this kindly, quietly, although my entire being is busting to scream it out in frustration. "We endured this assault with our two-year-old daughter present in the home. When these pair of pricks invade our private space, violently threaten and attack me, it's going to leave my family with a fear I'm certain will remain with them for a very long time… if not forever."

My protestations are interrupted by blue hair. "We have to take Mr Kelly now for potential surgery and treatment of his gunshot wound. Now if you please, Detective?" she states simply, much to Raymond Tallis's dismay, I can see. I think if he held the power right there and then, I'd be staying exactly where I am, bleeding away. I'm once again grateful for the intervention, although less thankful for the pain visiting me during the transfer from the kitchen chair to the stretcher then into the ambulance.

"I'll be seeing you in there later this morning," Tallis says quietly, giving me a two-finger salute to see me off.

I'm guessing the immediate treatment of my gunshot wound probably takes precedence over any interview or interrogation Ray has in mind. I'm wishing this to be the case at least, as the pain relief drug blue hair has administered starts to take effect.

Chapter 9

I AROUSE SLOWLY IN a hospital bed, feeling an all too familiar delirium, lethargy and grogginess of post-operative recovery and not thrilled about it. I vaguely recall waking up some time earlier in the actual recovery room, pain-free but a little confused, a lot nauseous, instantly drifting back to a drug-induced sleep then.

The same old typical, somewhat chaotic machines, wires and thin clear plastic tubes are all hooked up to me once again. Curious lights blinking and flashing, alarms periodically buzzing, other machines beeping as they monitor my vital signs. I'm coupled to a machine administering some welcome painkillers at the press of a button. A wonderful new innovation. This I'm particularly pleased about. I blearily recognise I'm in a private room, which although as much as I appreciate this comfort, I find it equal parts threatening and disquieting for some reason… buggered if I know why. The other item I recognise about this scene is my loving wife Carla and daughter Katerina aren't here, leaving me with an empty sense of foreboding. Remembering now the fierce look of rejection Carla flung at me back in the house earlier in the day, or was it yesterday?

A nurse in a soft green loose uniform is walking around slowly, humming quietly to herself next to my bed, busying herself checking charts and all the lines attached to me and the rowdy machines. She's tall, attractive looking, slim, with fiercely pale blue eyes, almost white. I ask her if my wife Carla might optimistically be outside in the waiting area.

"She may be, lovey. No one is allowed in to see you at the moment other than our staff monitoring you. The police at the door are restricting all access," she replies cheerfully.

Now all by themselves, just those few words, all at once, cleared any bleariness. "Am I under police guard? Is this what you're suggesting, like as in under arrest?" I query the nurse, tentatively, my voice mildly hoarse – from the surgery, I guess.

"I don't know, lovey. I just know there's been a policeman outside your door since you came back from surgery. They're not letting anyone in at the moment. They haven't actually told us what's going on," she comments, less cheerfully this time.

I shiver intensely and not because I'm cold. I think it's because I'm extremely anxious at what I'd just heard. The earlier incident is now flowing back to my front of mind in a monumental shower of shit. Instead of beginning my recovery and possible discharge process as I'd have expected, an empty, volatile gut feeling suggests everything is about to turn into a pile of orchestrated chaos of the highest order.

"Can you perhaps let the officer know I'm awake?" I ask the nurse, reluctantly.

"Are you sure you want to do it right now, lovey? You've just woken up. You also seem very shocked, perhaps a bit distressed to hear you have a policeman at your door. Do you not want to give yourself some time to gather yourself and your thoughts?" she suggests kindly, with a soft smile bordering on conspiracy.

I think about her suggestion. She's right, of course, and I agree, already feeling I'm beginning to fade again, welcoming the reprieve of darkness and peace.

When I wake again, I'm not sure of the time, although it still looks light outside my room window, so probably still the same day. Feeling a little more alert now at least. Well, enough to notice the policeman is now standing guard inside my room and not outside my door, for whatever reason. He just stands there, staring at me, saying nothing in reply to my 'G'day mate.'

He simply turns and without delay walks out of the room. Returning a few minutes later with Detective Tallis along with someone else in medical scrubs who I guess is my doctor.

"How're you feeling, Mr Kelly? A little more improved now, I hope? I'm Dr Kenrick. I'm the surgeon who saw to your wound. The operation went well. It was a close impact penetrating injury; a bit of powder burn and detritus on entry. Exit wound is quite large and somewhat irregular. It pierced various tissues, including muscle, a couple of blood vessels, nerves, causing significant damage along its path. There is, however, no major internal damage that we weren't able to fix during surgery." He says this with a sort of a sad smile, as if he's disappointed there wasn't something more seriously wrong with me, something he'd have been keen on endeavouring to fix. "You're very lucky being so close to the gun. I believe it was an expanding bullet, a dumdum, I think they call it? Fortunately, it kept going straight through you to then hit and expand inside another person, I understand?" I think he's making a statement, not asking a question.

"You may still suffer some minor side effects, in particular some extreme pain as you begin to move around. We've removed multiple bone fragments from where the bullet impacted a rib. There may still be some minute slivers presenting as time goes on. We have you on medications to reduce any infection and the pain along with any nausea." He almost murmurs as he reviews the notes at the end of my bed, then looks at all the machine read-outs that are monitoring me. "We should have you out of here in a day or so, subject to the wound not becoming infected. You feel up to chatting with the police for a bit?" he asks, more seriously now, looking into my eyes with a tiny torch.

"Yeah, I guess so. Might as well get it out of the way," I say, looking at Tallis leaning quietly against the back wall of my room with his arms crossed, looking serious himself. "Can you tell me where my clothes are, Doc? I have some special phone numbers in my wallet. I'd like to make some calls to those people."

"All of those items are in the care of the police for the time being, including your shirt, which was pretty much ruined I'm afraid," The doctor says as he looks at me then at Tallis. "OK then, I'll leave you guys to it. Please don't overdo it, Mr Tallis, if you don't mind. Our colleague here is still quite weak," Dr Kenrick mutters as he slowly walks out of the room, reading more notes.

Tallis doesn't move, just stands there quietly against the wall, still with his arms crossed. "I don't think this is going to get out of the way as quickly as you might be hoping, James. You OK if I call you James?"

My gut sank momentarily after he says this. *"This is not going to get out of the way as quickly as I might be hoping"* has a rather extreme, almost obstructive tone to it. "You can call me whatever you like, Ray. However, before you call me anything, can you explain where my wife and daughter are? I'd like to see them first if I can."

Tallis sort of smiles at me, or maybe it's closer to a scowl. "That's not going to happen in the short term, James. They're being kept informed of your progress. However, while we sort out the shenanigans of this morning's events, you are not permitted any visitors."

I'm about to arc up and participate in the discussion before Tallis cuts me short, holding his hand up in front of me in an officious manner… like a traffic cop.

"You can get your bra and knickers in a knot all you want, James. However, nothing, and I'm here to tell you, I mean nothing, is going to move forward until we get a decent interpretation of what actually happened today and why. You have been subjected to a highly unusual and volatile situation, which we don't typically see around here, around this part of the country I mean. So we have to dig a bit deeper into what might have been behind it," he says, too quietly. I'm not liking this situation.

"Well, if this is the case, aren't you supposed to read me my rights or give me some third-degree warning against saying anything stupid or incriminating, something like that? Plus, what authorises you to seize my personal items? Don't you have to present me with a court order for this type of thing?" I object.

"Let me try to explain things, James, to de-stress this particular situation just a bit for you. First of all, I will not be giving you any criminal caution, which is what it's called, as there is the impending issue of self-defence very much active in this scenario. I'm going to instead talk to you about what happened to get your take on how you think you saw things unfold. This is to try and determine what, or who, you think might have been at the bottom of it. I'll record this for later analysis with my team. Are you OK with this?" Ray asks confidently, continuing before I have a chance to answer.

"Secondly, we've seized all of your clothing for analysis, as we're entitled to do in situations such as this. Furthermore, we have taken blood samples upon your admittance to the hospital, for toxicity analysis against booze or drugs or both. We have these unique powers in South Australia, James, under the Summary Offences Act, to be used in certain circumstances without requiring a court order. Are we now clear enough on those particular points for you, James, or do you want me to go all formal on it? Happy to oblige, in order for you to be able to challenge what we have done here?" He delivers this statement more brusquely.

"Hmmm, yeah well, whatever. I guess it has to be fine. In this case, then, maybe you can try to explain what you just said a minute or so ago. What does *'this is not going to get out of the way as quickly as I might be hoping'* actually mean?" I'm not feeling the love, nor the level of control Tallis seem to have with the situation. My temperament is all shot to bits at the moment.

"Right, then, let's clarify some more detail. Hombre number two is dead. You'd remember him, I'm sure?" Ray hesitates momentarily, probably wanting to see what my reaction is. "In addition, your personal favourite invader is dying of extensive blunt throat trauma. They tell me he has multiple fractures of the cartilage structure of the larynx or trachea or whatever it's technically called. Apparently, these fractures can cause air to escape into the neck and chest, leading to significant respiratory compromise. He's unlikely to ever regain consciousness," he says this as he reads from his small notebook, pushing himself off the wall to slowly walk over towards my bed.

I watch him observing me with his policeman's eye, trying to comprehend what my reaction is no doubt. I'm giving him nothing.

"Anyway, back to the bullet in hombre number two. It lodged near his spine. Except on the way there, it expanded as intended, ripping through his intestine, pancreas, spleen, stomach, diaphragm, along with his lung," he quotes, as he looks up from his notes. "I believe I've pretty much got it right. Tissue in every one of those organs was substantially damaged, and blood also leaked into his chest. He was always going to die from his wound, James. No matter what." He again hesitates, staring straight at me, waiting for any feedback I might wish to contribute – or not.

"Here's the thing, though, James. You see, the doc I spoke to who performed the emergency damage assessment tells me he also suffered a massive tissue disruption around the entry point of the bullet. Like something large had been brutally inserted into the wound itself, for whatever reason. This is after the bullet has gone through to do the other spectacular damage, you got it?" He just stares at me again. I mean, like the real deal, the 'no blinking' type stare. He must have practised the hell out of this act in front of a mirror at some time, as he's got it down pretty well.

"There is no suggestion his death isn't a result of the gunshot wound from intruder one shooting him, as you have suggested. However, judging from the blood found on the end and inside one of those gun suppressors, there is now a query as to how it might have got there? Or, more importantly, if it may have been a factor or exacerbated his situation? Do you know how this might have transpired, James?" He waits for my reaction. Still none.

I'm giving nothing away. Anything I've got, I'm keeping to myself. "Is there a reasonable question in amongst all this flimflam somewhere, Ray? Or anything else to add with any real purpose?" I ask glibly, already knowing where this is probably leading.

"Well, yes, there is James. The question is yours to answer. Do you have any idea how it might have occurred? How the blood got there? I'm asking you if you know how his blood might have got onto and inside that particular suppressor?" Tallis asks, still doing the staring, no blinking thing.

"No," I reply solemnly. "I have no idea how it might have happened. What's more, I have no interest in providing any further comment on this interrogation without a lawyer present. I think I can see where you're trying to take this, Ray, which is not looking at all favourable to me," I say as unruffled as possible.

"Look, I get your sentiments at the moment, James. Nonetheless, we have one dead body, with another one hanging in the wings. In all likelihood, he will die very shortly. So the issue, I guess, will later be from the viewpoint of a police prosecutor. It may well come down to whether there is justification for your level of self-defence actions resulting in those two fatalities. They will have to determine if there's any evidence the perpetrators were intending violence towards you and your family. Their intent may have been to only to rob you or to maybe scare or threaten you for some reason?" he says to me, in all sincerity.

I just lay there, in absolute disbelief. Staring at Ray and his stupid statement, in incredulity. "Are you out of your dog-fucking-mind, Ray? Do you really not grasp what you just suggested? The guns are theirs. They're loaded, with suppressors attached, and not loaded with soporific bullets, Ray, were they? One of those pricks shot me and his partner with a real bullet in that violent home invasion, not a burglary or a robbery – or a scary night out." I nod my head in astonishment and slowly lay back on the pillows on my bed. I'm not feeling great anyway, and listening to this diatribe isn't making me feel any more agreeable. In fact, a timely weariness is slowly creeping over me.

"So… let me try and get this right… if I can. According to your bizarre interpretation, the fact there were two of those guys, with silenced weapons, wearing balaclavas and all the other

Mickey Mouse black paraphernalia, is challengeable? At least to you guys? As it appears, it doesn't mean, in the eyes of your precious justice system, they intended to do me and my family any harm, just probably rob us or scare us for some obscure purpose? Are you seriously delusional or just plain mad, Ray?" I challenge, gently starting to slip away again.

"I want to see my family, and I want a lawyer, Ray. And I want this to happen NOW! You got it, Ray?" I reply, as I feel the fog in my head becoming more incoherent, welcoming the sleep of the post-operative drugs that I'm frantically clicking into my system to overwhelm me yet again.

Chapter 10

"HEY, HOW'RE YOU FEELING there, young James?" a surprisingly soft, female voice says to me, or I at least think it's what I heard how it sounds. I try to answer, except there's nothing available to me. Not a bloody thing coming out. Head is numb, vacant, overwhelmed, with a peaceful, drugged-up hollowness of post-operative pain relief. I do notice, however, Detective Tallis or the other ever-watchful police officer is not in attendance. Well, not inside the room, anyway.

The voice spoke again. I recognise it now. It belongs to Alison Jordon Renfrey, or RJ, as she likes to be called for some reason. RJ is my direct line executive from Castelle, who I work for now, or had worked for. This might now be subject to where all this mayhem ends up. She's not who I bloody want to be speaking to just at this very moment. I want to see… I desperately have to see and talk to my wife and daughter. Only, it looks as if it's not to be at the moment, for whatever reason. I open my eyes and look at RJ. Standing there in all her six-foot-two splendour, dressed as usual to the max, as stunning as ever. Lofty in her overdressed and expensive pastel outfit, and as always, accompanied with her customary bold fire-engine red lipstick and fingernails. She's changed quite a bit since I first saw her, a couple of years or so ago. Aged a lot, really… she still looks pretty presentable all the same. It's beyond me how she does it. There it is, though, right before my eyes. I watch her take a pair of spectacularly-coloured framed glasses off and slide them into her top jacket pocket.

"Feeling on top of the bloody world, RJ, as you'd probably have already guessed. Respectfully though, old girl, you're not who I want to see or talk to right at this very moment. No offense, I'm sure you know what I mean? Where is Carla? I want to talk with her and comfort them both after all this frightening misery they've been through," I moan.

"Not going to happen anytime soon, James. Carla and Katerina are both in police witness protection at this very moment. They have to be. They must stay there until we can decipher whatever the actual threat really is and where it's coming from… and how to neutralise it," she says this to me quietly, like I'm a child.

"Piss off, RJ, will ya. I just want to talk to my wife, and I'd like to do it now, if you don't mind?" I ask irritably. "It's all I ask of you, for now, anyway, please?"

RJ states again, "As I said James, this is not going to happen. I mean it. Your Carla and Katerina have both been put into a heavily-guarded witness protection program. Need I remind you, this is specifically due to a very delinquent situation unravelling around you early this morning, James? Quite possibly escalating at this very exact moment. We don't know. They have to be protected, and they'll stay there until we can work out what happened and why. The police have been instructed to give serious consideration to all of your ongoing protection situations, because clearly, there is some sort of a threat to you and your family. Their safety is the police's paramount consideration." RJ took a gulp of air, trying to recharge.

"I've just been talking with Detective Tallis outside here," RJ says, directing a finely boned finger delicately towards the door. So they are still here on guard, which bothers me. "He tells me they're no clearer to identifying the suspect vehicle you heard, or the people in it, the one that crashed into your tractor while frantically departing from the scene. They've been door-knocking your neighbours about it with no success. No big deal there, I suppose, given they're a long way from your place. They're still conducting their evidence trawl through your property, though, which I assume they commenced soon after you left."

Bloody hell, I'm still trying to absorb all of the earlier comings and goings. Now I've got to try and take in this new intimidating information… Witness bloody protection, for crying out loud?

"So James, any thoughts on who this might be, or why? Do you think this has anything to do with the recent West African or Indonesian jobs you've been on, maybe? Or possibly your earlier venture with your Japanese colleagues from Vietnam?" RJ queries.

"I honestly have no idea, RJ. I haven't yet given myself the time to fully digest everything that's happened. I've been too distracted by my family not being here to pay much attention to the rest of the situation. Well, not entirely, I'm concerned about my legal position in all this as I continually replay the scene over and over in my head. The incident is like some sort of broken record taking me through it, time and again. I'll admit, the Arab thing staggers me a bit, though. Maybe there is some connection with our results in West Africa, or maybe the Indo job. I just don't know, RJ," I reply honestly, although my gut is now picking up on the possible ramifications of RJ's suggestion… Bloody *jihadis.*

"Well, as for your legal status, I've arranged for one of our contract lawyers to represent you for the time being, James. He's one we've tapped into on quite a few occasions, name of Chris Connor. He's an ex-copper, swapped sides years ago. However, he knows the ropes from their side pretty well. He's very good at what he does and with the results he delivers, although he can be a bit esoteric at times and a lot cryptic. So please, James, just try to take it easy on him when he hits you with some of his more unusual thoughts, OK?" She smiles at me with those great big eyes and bright red lips as she opens the room door, the same door someone is now knocking on.

She introduces me to this Chris Connor, who has just walked into my room, right behind his great protruding stomach, the one sticking out between his very stressed shirt buttons, bare hairy skin escaping just above his belt line. My lawyer, huh? Well, my lawyer for now. We'll see how things evolve before I commit to him for the long hike. If I do, he'll have to clean up his overall dress act, including his frenzied dirty hair thing, pushed off to one side – all awry. Include in this image the cheap and filthy shoes, the dirty pressure-stressed shirt – well, not so much dirty, just not clean – which ultimately is fine, I suppose, as it matches his old suit. Now this, well, this is dirty. It hasn't been cleaned or sponged off for a very long time is my first guess, if ever. He may have actually slept in it recently, perhaps often, judging from the multiple deep creases in the fabric. In fact, I wouldn't be surprised if he's just got out of bed while still wearing it.

"In terms of criminal proceedings, the occupant of a home, as in you, is not normally civilly liable for any personal injury or property damage inflicted on or suffered by a home invader while acting against the home invader," Chris says slowly, as if lecturing a class of dumb homeowners. The hoer hasn't even introduced himself yet, or looked me in the eye, which is concerning.

"What does this actually mean in normal English, Chris? Forget all the fluffy legalise or lecture speak. Am I in trouble or not?" I have little patience for this type of double-talk at the best of times, especially coming from someone who appears like this guy does and who won't look at me.

"It is lawful for an occupant of a dwelling to use any force or do anything else the occupant believes is necessary under partic-ular circumstances, including *'to prevent an intruder from breaking or entering the dwelling'*. So yes, it is legal for you to fight off your home intruders. Still, unless it's a 'you or them' situation, it's best to try not to kill them," Chris says. Me,… I'm already feeling the lon-gevity of him representing me does not seem to be strong in the future of our tea leaves.

"I feel it's pretty bloody preposterous, also wholly unreason-able for your irrational legal system, in all its wisdom and pompous glory, to expect a householder to use their person as an evidence exhibit with regards to a violent assault." I try hard not to yell this at him, almost achieving it. He's infuriated me, as he still hasn't looked at me yet. "I shouldn't have to get shot, stabbed, beaten up or threatened in my own goddamn home in order to convince you guys or your screwed up law. 'WE' are the innocent victims here." I do yell out this time, as I look at him then at RJ.

Chris finally looks at me, momentarily, vacantly, blank… as if I'd said absolutely nothing, or anything he'd understood. Then the moment evaporates just as swiftly, and he nervously looks away again. I don't know if it's shyness or some sort of anxiety phobia hindering him from looking me in the eye. Regardless, I find it awkward.

"My home is my castle, you guys. I know we all say it, except I actually believe it… I live it. I love the fact every person must have the right to personal privacy and security in their own home. I recognise the puzzling philosophy of how the wider public should be aware the police cannot protect them everywhere all of the time. I get it, I really do. The consequence of this philosophy, though, is we're left to try to protect ourselves, up until such time as the police can assist." I'm struggling a bit here, with the lack of rationale in the law and it's flip-flopping about who can, could or should be to blame. Meanwhile, the drugs are still thinning out the blood in my body and my brain, which is not making my perception of what's happened here or my life any clearer.

"I'm on your side here, James, and the long answer is probably yes. We'd just have to ensure there's strong evidence your life and the lives of your family or anyone else in the house were in life-threatening danger. We're going to have to demonstrate those home invaders had a serious intent to harm you… or your family, not just rob or threaten you," Chris says, incredulously, talking to me without looking at me still.

"Are you for real? I'm not the one who turned the home invader's weapon against him. He tried, and as you're aware, succeeded in shooting me and, in doing so, also shot his own partner in crime. This wasn't me doing it, dude. Even if it had been, I'd still bloody call it very reasonable self-defence. When some criminal decides to go into someone else's home with a weapon and with intent, then bugger it, they don't get to cry foul when that very same weapon is used back against them."

"I appreciate the terror of these types of ordeals can be overwhelming, James. In amongst it all, nevertheless, we still have to establish an 'evidence trail of the alleged perpetrator's violence or persistence'. In this, the perpetrators themselves have created the evidence you require," he says in his lecturer's voice.

"So how can we still call them the 'alleged perpetrators' when they're found inside my home, armed and violent?' I ask. "There is nothing 'alleged' about it, is there?" I demand, pointing to my wound, looking at the silent RJ.

Without answering my question, Chris fires off another adjunct series of information. "We've been advised a bit earlier by police they have just left your property. CSI has been there for hours, since just after you left, in fact. Doing the usual, you know, taking a million photos, swabs of just about everything, all manner of samples and seizing whatever material likely to be relevant or they feel will be required to further their investigation. They've now apparently completed all of their initial scene examinations and spoken to your wife." He takes a breath, before firing off again.

"As you're aware, she's the only witness. They need to establish how both intruders received their injuries. One guy is still in hospital, very critical and yet to be interviewed, which in all honesty is unlikely to happen, I believe. And the other is dead, which you're already aware of, yes?" He does actually look at me this time, fleetingly, to see what my reaction is about this news.

There's no reaction to see. I'm sort of pleased… just not going to show it for any hidden cameras which might be lurking in the room. Paranoia alive and well right there, yeah I know.

"I want you guys to leave now. I need a break to take my mind away from all this crap. Especially from you, Chris. I have to try and rebalance myself a bit, so give me a break for a while can you?" I almost whisper. I'm tired – past tired, in fact. I'm exhausted from all the crap of the past 12 hours or so, and I've still got the visual of this poor kid drowning interfering with my head periodically.

"Yeah, sure, we have an update meeting planned with the police shortly anyway, James, so we'll leave you in peace for a while. We'll try to sort out what they intend to do as we enter into the next phase. Take it easy. We're all on the same team here, and we'll help get you through it," RJ states, as she smiles at me with her bright white shark teeth, ushering Chris out of the door. I'm glad to be alone. The peacefulness is what I want – for now, anyway. To see my family is what I really crave, and I'm becoming far more anxious about it not occurring. Not being able to talk to them on the phone is stressing me out enormously.

Several hours later, RJ and Chris come quietly back into my room again. They wake me up to tell me intruder A's life support has been turned off due to his deteriorating condition. I slump slightly when told, more for their effort than for my own emotions. I don't, however, allow myself to appear happy, pleased, upset or stressed about the news. Good riddance is my most immediate thought. Both intruders are now dead. I'd have preferred for them to have both stayed alive, at least long enough for us to find out who sent them. Bugger 'em, it is what it is, I guess.

"RJ, I'm sorry to hear this, I really am. I'd been hoping he might've been able to tell us who sent them, or more importantly, why? Let's put it aside for just a moment, though. Can we? I desperately want to speak to my wife and daughter. I'm aware they're in witness protection. I know this. Surely though, there must be some mechanism for me to be able to talk to her by phone, yeah? They must likewise be frantic not being able to talk to me?" My anxiety is leaching out of my pores. I'm becoming very distressed about not being able to see them, to comfort them… it's pissing me right off actually.

"I get your anguish, James, I sincerely do. Carla is being kept updated with your situation by the police all the same, I assume by Tallis. However, the police won't even let me talk to her on the phone on your behalf. I guess they're trying to shield her and Katerina from the impact of what has happened and what is likely to materialise going forward. I know it all seems somewhat wet and emotional. Just let things settle down a bit, can you? Just for a day or so until you get out of here. Then I'll push for you to either join them or at least talk to them on the phone. OK?"

I'm not at all pleased with her suggestion, only with little other options available to me at the moment, I guess I have to just wait. It all sounds a bit too peculiar, though. No contact at all allowed after such a life-threatening event? Who the hell decides that?

"So how do you think this will pan out now then, Chris… now Muhammad and his camel-shagging offsider are both dead? There's no possibility for this to become a case of "I said versus they said" is it?" I query. "From my limited knowledge, under our contemptible criminal law system, self-defence is a totally legitimate justification when defending myself against someone wanting to cause bodily harm or more importantly, the potential for loss of my life. I acted in self-defence, so this cannot possibly end up in a murder trial, can it?" I ask, hopefully.

Chris answers slowly, again without looking at me. "First of all, I'd like you to refrain from using racist or bigoted commentary about the deceased. Now, I believe you almost certainly won't be prosecuted for murder. It's an open and shut case of self-defence. However, if excessive force is considered to have been used and the intruder or intruders are killed in the process, as it is in your case, in those circumstances, the charges are customarily reduced from "murder" to 'manslaughter'." He adds obliquely.

"What! Jesus bloody Christ, Chris, I don't want to be prosecuted at all. For manslaughter, farting in public or anything else for Christ's sake. We were being attacked in our own home, while we slept, unarmed. There can be no other outcome here that works for me other than self-defence, Chris. If you can't achieve this, then tell me now so I can fire your arse and go find myself someone who can. You got me?" I'm yelling again now in frustration. "We didn't have the means or the time to remove ourselves from a situation of potential harm, even if it is expected we should do so. They were already armed, already inside our house when I woke up for crying out loud." I'm flabbergasted at his senseless suggestion.

"The prosecution will have to prove beyond reasonable doubt you hadn't. Otherwise, it'd result in a 'not guilty' verdict. As always, precedent or interpretation are the key aspects in legal matters. There's only your wife as the witness to give any evidence to a hearing, from her perspective, points the prosecutor declared are normally dealt with at trial."

"I don't want to consider going to trial. I want to be released as a free man, not convicted or condemned or acquitted. I want the whole bloody thing set aside as a successful result of self-defence. End of story. If you can't arrange this let me know… now," I goad, thinking this guy just doesn't get this… or maybe I don't get it?

"The thing is, James, for my money, the home invasion was just a bit too pedestrian when I think about it. If they'd wanted you, or all of you, dead, why bother sneaking into a place in the wee hours of the morning, one that has a dog inside? Why not just rock up in broad daylight, out in your remote location, walk right up and knock you, or all of you, off? You see what I mean? There is something out of sorts about this entire scenario." Chris looks at me for a change, oddly, like he doesn't get it. Welcome to the club, because I don't get it either.

"I have to talk to you about something else, James − a few things in fact. Firstly, it's my understanding you have been in the past a highly trained and skilled special forces soldier in Vietnam, am I correct in this?

"Yeah, many years ago, I've been a soldier in Vietnam. Highly trained is questionable. Special forces is a no. What else do you want to discuss?" I can already see where this is going.

"OK, so the soldier fact is true. Now, the police have also alleged you spoke to them at the scene and uttered something to the effect of '*The second prick was in my daughter's room… what would you do if you caught some arsehole in your young daughter's room. Do you have kids? It's fortunate the other prick shot him, or I'd have tried to do it'.* Is this correct? Is this what you remember saying, James?"

"I've got no idea what I might have said during that particularly stressful time. I was agitated to hell right at that point in time, OK? What else have you got to discuss before I kick you pair of clowns out of my room, again?" I'm already done with him, again. If this is what RJ thinks is helping me, then screw them both.

"Thirdly, what has already been raised with you by the police, apparently, the doctor who carried out the emergency surgery on intruder number two has suggested he also suffered a massive tissue disruption around the entry point of the bullet. Like something large was inserted into the wound itself post the bullet entering, something like the suppressor from intruder one's gun. Considering the blood found outside on the end and inside of the gun suppressor, there is now a query as to how it might have got there or if it maybe intensified his chances of dying? They're suggesting you deliberately inserted the suppressor into the guy's wound, torturing him until he died. Is this what happened, James, to the best of your recollection?"

"I honestly don't know. I don't remember doing it. What the hell, though. I was angry as hell about what'd been going on, hyped up to the eyeballs. I may have, although I'm certainly not admitting to it, that's for bloody sure." There's a vague stirring in the fog of my mind about this. I'm damned if I'm going to say anything else until the fog clears.

"Look, number two received emergency surgery en route to the hospital, which I guess could've further complicated his bullet wound and recovery prospects. From my perspective, though, it's highly unlikely any doctor or pathologist will give determinative evidence that this unquestionably furthered his chances of dying. No matter if they do, it's still the gunshot to the internal organs which killed him, not you poking around in his bullet wound. At the very worst, it might be considered an assault," Chris says, staring at my life support instruments blankly as they bounce and squeal a bit after his comments.

"In all seriousness, though, this particular issue aside, how far can someone go to protect themselves or their family inside their own home? I want to know how far we can legally go to protect our loved ones. Whether I have been a soldier way back in the past, or whether I babbled something under extreme duress, it's what this is about, isn't it? It's not about me being a former soldier?" I'm already looking at any other forward options minus his assistance, unless he pulls something pretty spectacular out of his arse in the not-too-distant future, like really soon.

He seems to give some thought to my question, then apparently disregarded it. "My final query is for my own personal interest. You call your property 'Kasbah'. So, from my brief research, in Arabic, it essentially denotes a fortress, citadel or the fortified quarter of a palace or property, or a settlement of some sort, although it appears to be a historically flexible term. Can you enlighten us on why you chose the name? Given the relevance of your intruders both seemingly being of Arab extraction, I'm sure you can see the credible connection?"

"There is no connection. At least none to the best of my knowledge, anyway. I called it that when I first bought the property, years ago. As a type of talisman, a lucky charm title sort of thing. To superficially protect me from the demons hovering over me from my Vietnam nightmares. It's also intended to symbolically shield me from all manner of tempest. Things like cold and heat, bushfires and wild storms, crazy winds or crazier people. I'd been in a very debilitating bit of space at the time, recovering, with some difficulty. I wanted to try and safeguard myself rationally, from any other external influences I didn't want in my life, you know what I mean? Especially those things likely to disrupt the harmony and well-being I was desperate to have back in my life," I answer honestly, remembering back to the time momentarily, vividly all the same.

Chris stares at the wall as he thinks about my response. "OK, thanks for that. I can wholeheartedly appreciate it, given what you'd been through over there. You can see the significance, though, can't you? Of the fact your intruders both seemingly being

Arab, and the name of your property having an Arabic nickname or moniker? I'm sure the police will ask you, or me, about your choice of name. It being denoted as a fortified residence which at times housed military garrisons, when we then look at the outcomes of the home invasion, implicating an ex-soldier?"

"No, I see no reason why they might connect any of those separate topics simply by what I named my property years ago when I purchased it. There is just no connection. I don't have any weapons in the house. I didn't use any weapons. The shot came from the intruder's own gun, the one in his hand. The one he fired, not me. I also got shot too, remember?" I'm again getting a little frustrated at this line of thought.

"It will always be up to the police or more likely the Director of Public Prosecutions, the DPP, to make this decision. They'll decide if the level of self-defence applied against the home invaders was necessary, warranted or lawful. As we have already discussed, generally, people are entitled to the safety their home provides, they're allowed to use reasonable force to protect themselves or their property. No doubt a 'reasonable person' would've likely felt very threatened and feared for their family if they disturbed an intruder in their home like you had. Especially two who are armed as yours were. However, we now have the additional element to contend with where you are a formerly trained soldier, with the police now possibly thinking along the lines you may have taken your attacker's gun and shot intruder two."

He looks kind of stupid serious at me, waiting for some sort of reaction, I guess, acknowledging I'd heard what he'd just suggested. Bugger him, I'm already sick of hearing this line. "So, what is their theory now, or maybe your theory? That I bloody shot myself as well, with the intruder's gun? Is this it? Is this what you fruit cakes are trying to cook up?"

"Look, James, I know this might sound a bit too fluffy around the edges for you. Regardless, and despite the laws being in place to protect homeowners in danger, we know people can still face the possibility of being charged or maybe going to jail for using excessive force against an intruder." He looks at me briefly, trying the sympathetic expression again. I have an inexplicable sort of sensation Chris might actually not be fully on my side with this matter, or on anyone's side… maybe he doesn't know how to pick a side? I remembered RJ suggesting he can be a bit off with the pixies. I can definitely agree with this.

"Defending your home, family and you fall in a legal grey area throughout the entire country. As a general rule, though, home-owners are allowed to respond with a degree of force if they fear for their safety or those of their loved ones. Which clearly you did." He looked at me probingly, hoping for confirmation his theory is correct. I gave him nothing again… for now. There seemed no point. My accelerating blood pressure is telling me to shut the hell up.

"The key issue here is whether your perception of danger led you to believe the use of extreme defensive force was reasonably necessary, if your belief was based on reasonable grounds," he concludes.

"Are you seriously mad, you and Ray, both with the same stupid question?" I'm fuming again now. "It should be whatever reasonable force is required by me as I perceive it, in the situation… at the goddamn time. My response should not be determined reasonable or otherwise in those circumstances as to how you guys or your madcap legal system perceives them. Because you weren't there, nor under any threat or in danger!" I yell at them both. "Now get the hell out and leave me alone."

They both turn to each other slowly, shrug and move quietly towards the door, like puppets on a string, under instruction.

"A quick word with you, RJ, before you go." I want to clear some air.

RJ stops walking through the door, whispers something quickly to Chris, turns and moves back into the room, closing the door gently. Before it closes, I just catch a glimpse of a police officer standing up out of his chair, outside my door. So I'm still being monitored. I'm not sure yet how this makes me feel.

"Fire away," RJ says softly.

"Firstly, what's the go with your mate here? He mumbles a lot and doesn't look at me when he talks to me. Is he some sort of a wacko, or maybe a bit autistic? What?"

"No, he's certainly not that. For your information, he's got an IQ of over 150, which to you and me means he's highly gifted, intellectually. He does suffer marginally from a type of social anxiety, which limits his social ease and confidence in some situations, except when he's in court. This can make it difficult for him to make eye contact one-on-one, because he feels uncomfortable or self-conscious in social interactions, leading to the avoidance of eye contact. All this aside, he's a brilliant lawyer, probably the best I have ever worked with. What is your primary concern with him?" RJ asks smoothly. She doesn't normally ever get defensive, although I detect a slight change in her expression as she speaks. She's probably not liking me very much at the moment.

"No big deal, really. I just feel uncomfortable in myself when dealing with people who don't or won't look at me when they talk to me. I'll have to take your word on the brilliant lawyer thing, because he hasn't impressed me yet, I can tell you." I don't want to push this any further for now.

"He's trying to very delicately weave his way – well, our way, actually – through the maze of your potential culpability with both the police and the DPP. You're probably not aware, however, the DPP has two main priorities when considering whether to lay a murder or some other similar charge on you in this particular situation. Firstly, whether the prosecution is in the public's best interest. Secondly, and probably more importantly, whether there is the likelihood of a successful conviction if he does charge you over this matter. For my money, it'd be a no on both counts if I was required to vote as part of any jury. This is what Chris is pushing for, on your behalf." RJ raises her eyebrows as she concludes, querying if there's anything else to discuss.

"OK, thanks. I'm not aware of how this all works. I've been more focused on getting out of here and to see my family. Which is the matter I wanted to talk to you about. Once I'm free to go, am I going to be reunited with Carla? In their witness protection, what do they call it, WitPro?" I ask, hopefully.

"Well, here we bump into a bit of a conundrum. It appears Carla does not want to be reunited with you – at the moment at least. Or so it seems. She's advised the police it's not to happen. For the foreseeable future, anyway. They're both so upset by the distress of yesterday, she has to balance out her equilibrium on this incident, I guess. Doesn't want to talk to you, or me, or anybody else for that matter, it seems." RJ looks at me compassionately.

"Were things all well and good at home prior to this matter disrupting your lives, James?" RJ queries caringly.

"Hell yes. We're about to have another baby. As far as I'm concerned, all is well and going in the right direction. Why do you ask, RJ?" I tense up a bit over this question. This is not a situation I'd thought about or considered I might have to, previously. We're all good, as a family… aren't we? I all of a sudden question myself now.

"No particular reason for concern. I just detected a brief sense of evasiveness from Detective Tallis earlier when we met and I asked him if he can get you connected by phone to Carla. He momentarily stalled, then mumbled something about having to get approval. I assume he meant from Carla. When I spoke with him on the phone before I came in just now, that's when he suggested she doesn't want to be reunited for the time being."

"So, what happens with me when I get released from here tomorrow? Where do I go? Do I perhaps have a choice in the matter? What if I don't want to go into their program?" The cold, hard hand of dread is slowly clawing its way up my throat. Nothing about the past 24 hours feels right, and I doubt it's going to feel any more improved going forward in the short term.

"I don't actually know, to be honest." I always feel uneasy when RJ talks about being honest. "I guess you should have the right to decline participating. They're typically voluntary, so I guess you're not obligated to enter into it if you choose not to. However, participation does require your cooperation and agreement. Keep in mind, though, it's worth considering there may be potential implications and risks associated with refusing the protection. Things like people wanting to harm you are still out there, so a reduction in your personal security is not helpful. We'll have to check with Ray before you make a decision on this, young man," RJ replies.

"I wish you'd stop calling me that. I'm almost as old as you are. Find another term, will ya?" I sense a crankiness intruding on me.

"Get over yourself, young man. It's a term of endearment, something we're all collectively far too short of these days," answers RJ, with her own crankiness beginning to encroach on me as well it seems. "I'll leave you now to ponder on what you might like to do going forward. I'll talk to Serge, now that he's out of that rehabilitation facility, to see if there's anything he can add to this potentially being linked to West Africa… or maybe check deeper to see if it's because of the Indonesia audit. You guys executed a great job on that West African assignment, by the way. It really disrupted their entire corrupt operations. Very effectively achieved." RJ smiles as she stands up to leave. "I'm hopeful this recent incident is not rippling down from that." Me too RJ. I'm praying to any of the various Gods who might be listening in today this isn't the case.

"While we're on the subject of West Africa, when do you intend giving me an update on your debrief with Ben?" I ask.

"You've got enough on your plate at the moment, James. Let's deal with this conundrum first OK? I'll tell you anything you want to know. All in good time. I do, however, strongly recommend you take up the offer of WitPro. For the short-term at least, until you get your head and health back together enough to function by yourself. I'll talk to Ray about getting you connected with Carla as soon as practicable. Talk later." RJ turns to leave, swinging her two-finger salute once again as she walks out, dragging the soft waft of delicate perfume with her, closing the door as she leaves.

I scrutinise my bland room, probably for the very first time. It wasn't important to have observed it in any detail before, now either really. Nonetheless, I want to distract my attention away from my encroaching thoughts of Carla not wanting to speak to me, or worse, to see me. I look at the clinically bland, pale 'comforting and safe' décor and the 'cool' awkward furniture. This is undoubtedly more relevant to my visitors than to me as the patient. Next, I reflect on the soothing, nondescript artwork and a couple of leathery-looking plastic plants attempting to create a soothing atmosphere. I take in the slate grey tint of the hot twilight sky outside and a high-rise crane working on some nearby construction site. There's a faint set of contrails blending into the horizon from a recent jet passing over, reminding me of the B-52 contrails I used to see in Vietnam.

I can't begin to imagine how both Carla and Katerina must be feeling, so shocked over the home invasion itself. I desperately want to comfort them. I'm beating myself up over what might have created this situation. What the hell is driving this, I'm wondering. Is it only because of the home invasion incident itself? I honestly don't know how else I might have dealt with it. I had no control over any of the narrative from the second I got out of bed.

Or is it something else, some other deeper, murkier issue? I love my family deeply and will do anything to keep them safe and happy. In doing so, I speculate how I might've somehow isolated myself from the very family I love so dearly? I've been away so much lately, involved in the Indonesian and then West African jobs and all of the bloody mischief and misery associated with both of those. My life seems to be one long obstacle course at times, with me as the primary hurdle. This has to be fixed somehow.

An odd notion drifts into my thoughts. Carla has an old girlfriend who has recently come back into her life – or our lives, really, in recent times. This girlfriend has not long ago lost her husband to some cancer or another. I initially felt she'd been turning to Carla for some comfort to ease her grief at her loss. It hadn't taken me long to realise there was little to no anguish or any sorrow at the loss of her husband. She's already dating other guys interstate within a couple weeks of burying her husband. I rebuked her about it on a couple of occasions, although there was little interest from her in my comments. I'm hoping her recent intrusion into our lives has nothing to do with this change in our circumstances.

My reverie is disturbed by a knock on the door yet again. Annoyed, I yell out for whoever it is to enter, and Chris pokes his head in the door. Of course he does. "So James, good news. Any potential manslaughter charges have been dropped over the demise of your home invaders. I've been briefed by the Office of Public Prosecutions, the OPP, who have decided to withdraw any prospective manslaughter charges against you."

"Yeah, as I'd have bloody well expected, Chris. I can't work out how or why there might have been any other option considered," I say quietly, still seething it was contemplated anyway.

"The OPP advised us it would not have been possible for the Crown to disprove your claims. You know, your reactions being anything other than an act of self-defence. There will be no necessity for a jury trial to make the call on the charges to determine guilt or otherwise," he says clinically. It seems to me he's parroting his words right from an OPP statement.

"I've declared all along, my ability to safely retreat from the immediate threat with my wife and child was just not available to me – us, not while being attacked by those two pricks."

"Yes, well, they've thankfully accepted your position. I'll leave a copy of their media release here for you to read at your leisure. On another matter, the offer by the police to put you into protection must be addressed, James," Chris states this as he places a formal looking sheet of paper onto my bedside table.

As I've already said, "the WitPro thingy is not for me. Unless it's with Carla and Katerina, I'm just not interested. I'll take my chances at home."

"Look, it is true, participation in WitPro is generally up to you to decide. You cannot be forced to enter the program against your will. However, it's important to note the decision to enter into it is often a complex one, and I encourage you to consider the latent risks and benefits. Ray will work closely with you to develop an appropriate security plan. For now, the plan will not require any changes to your identity, just relocation to a different area and other physical security measures."

"Not gonna happen, Chris," I emphasise.

"Think about it at least. Consider the dangers of not entering into it. Especially as there's already been a very credible attempt on your life. Now, in particular, the risk is likely to be enhanced, as you're probably perceived by whoever these people are to have killed both of their professional killers. This is likely to encourage them to try a little harder to get at you for whatever it is this is all about. Hey, it's ultimately up to you to make a decision based on your own assessment of the situation. For my money, though, I'd be kicking the door down to get into it. You just have to be cognizant it will not be with Carla and Katerina. That's just not going to happen at the moment, OK?"

"Then it's just not gonna happen, Chris. I won't consider it," I reemphasise. "Time for you to go. I'm worn out and want some rest. Thanks for the media release. I'll check it out later. For now, though, you can just leave me in peace."

"As you wish, regardless, please consider the offer, at least until we find out who is pulling the strings on this and why. OK? I'll return in the morning to walk you out of here. Have a good night," Chris says, as he slowly gets up out of my 'cool' visitor's chair and leaves the room, without once looking at me. I pick up the OPP's media release. It just looks and sounds like more weasel words to me, simply making me angry all over again.

Media Release – Office of Public Prosecutions

"The decision to discontinue a prosecution is never taken lightly. The frightful set of circumstances surrounding the attack on Mr Kelly and his family were taken into consideration at the time, and the charges were dropped. After careful reflection of the evidence, and after unsuccessfully seeking any views from either of the victim's families, who we can't identify as yet, a decision made by the Crown proclaims it would not have been able to disprove self-defence to the criminal standard of proof – beyond reasonable doubt. Accordingly, there are insufficient prospects of conviction." The Director of the Office of Public Prosecutions, Andrew Callahan said this morning.

Mr Kelly's lawyer, Mr Connor said, "My client has acted in an appropriate way in response to the irrational behaviour of the violent men who are now deceased. This lends significant support to the self-defence argument."

I don't know how I manage it with the level of anger inside me at the moment. Nonetheless, I drift off again into a bit of a narcotic-induced slumber.

Chapter 11

MY DRUG INDUCED THOUGHTS venture into a kind of safe obscure daydream space, where I recall originally meeting RJ, at home on our farm. I'd been working in my garden when I heard a car pull up in the front yard. Thinking it's maybe Carla coming back early from visiting neighbours, I went out to greet her. I'm taken aback to see it's a tall, very attractive woman unfurling herself from a tiny car.

"Good morning," a gravelly voice says, smiling at me, with a face all lit up by the smile and her bright red lipstick. Slowly walking around the front of her small car, she looks warily at it. "Damned rentals, all they had left. You book a truck, end up with this toy, not to worry," she announces while now taking in the sites of my rudimentary landscaping efforts around the homestead. "Nice. Your own work?" Her arm pointing to the work. I'm not sure if it's because she's impressed with my efforts, or not; neither mattered to me right at this moment.

"Can I help you?" I ask politely, albeit without my usual honied charm I keep tucked away somewhere for special occasions.

"Yes, you might be able to," is the reply, also polite, as she put out a well-manicured hand, offering it to me as a handshake. "Are you James Kelly?" The bright red lips ask.

"Who would be asking about that?"

"Alison Jordon Renfrey is my name. RJ for short. I work for a company called Castelle. There are some very specific opportunities within our organisation I'd like to discuss with you if you have the time? Ones I'd like you to consider. I don't require an answer right now. At least let them roll around inside your head for a while and bang away amongst the cobwebs for a time," Alison Jordon Renfrey, alias RJ the Englishwoman says, sounding not unlike a new age travelling snake oil salesman, direct from the war zone in Vietnam days.

I took her big delicate hand with the brightly red painted nails and jangling bracelets, we shook, not firmly, just courteously. Not unnecessarily muscularly as I'm expecting from her, although I'm sure she'd be quite capable of it.

"So why don't you tell me what Alison Jordon Renfrey, alias RJ, is famous for, or why I might be interested in such opportunities with a company called Castelle?" I ask, trying to work out how she gets "RJ" out of Alison Jordon Renfrey.

"Yes, yes, I think I can do that. Well then, as a bit of a backgrounder, I'm a close friend of an old colleague of yours from quite some time ago. Greg Masters." RJ pauses for a few seconds to let that name deliberately sink into and rattle around my psyche. I give no reaction, although there is indeed one already rock 'n' rolling its arse off in my consciousness, coming direct to me free of charge from all the way back in my Vietnam days.

"As we both know, he died of cancer many moons ago. Much before his time." RJ took a deep breath at this point, possibly remembering her friend Masters. "In spite of my accent, I am actually "a true blood Aussie"; one who has lived and worked out of the UK, Asia and Europe for too many years. Primarily in numerous roles with the Australian Department of Foreign Affairs. My role, such as it is, has mainly involved supporting Australian companies eager to do business internationally in general, although predominately in the southern hemisphere," RJ says, dabbing at the perspiration on her neck with a colourful kerchief.

"I met Greg during some diplomatic razzamatazz or other in the early 70s. I was still a junior back then. By some strange means, we'd been thrown together and struck up an unlikely friendship, which we maintained until his untimely passing. He gave me your contact details just before he died, along with quite a glowing testimonial of your skills," she discloses. "I hasten to add he and I were never, ever in the same line of work by any stretch of the imagination," she added, declaring this gem of information while smiling radiantly.

I admit my nervous system has been doing a bit of a classical two-step up and down my spine at the mention of Masters. I purposely kept looking out at the horizon so as to not show RJ my concern or anything else I might have on my face to show. I chew on this new bit of information – or intrusion before answering.

"So then, there's an interesting connection, bit of a shocker, although I don't know why it should be, knowing Masters I suppose. Why now? He's allegedly been dead for quite a few years. On top of anything else, I'm comfortable here, not to mention safe. I'm enjoying the chance to spend as much time as possible with my wife and daughter. What makes you think I'd want to change this or consider giving it up?"

"I'm not suggesting you should consider giving it up. What I'm proposing, though, is perhaps viewing opportunities to have both. Get involved in some of our more interesting ventures plus still maintain the lifestyle you have here," she says this while waving one of her well-manicured hands around to indicate 'here' being the lifestyle element of her discussion. "There will of course be some travel, and always a possibility for a touch of danger, nothing like the distractions you've been involved with previously, no war zones," she says, smiling.

I wonder, just how much she really knows about my history? I don't bother asking, suspecting she's probably well informed by Masters. "So, why me, and again, why now? I've been living here and out of any sort of 'game' for nearly 10 years?" I emphasise the 'game' with my hyphened fingers. "There must be a truck-load of younger, more eager and fitter roosters out there you can approach? Ones who don't have the 'lifestyle', as you call it, which I have here? Besides, they're probably far more eager to get involved in some of your undertakings. Happy to help you find them if you want?" I suggest quietly. I'm slightly flattered at the offer I guess. I'm just not following the rationale of 'why me or especially why now'.

"I thank you for your offer, James. However, the primary reason I'm approaching you directly is because of the way you are you see. The manner in which you handle occurrences or how you conduct yourself in different… sometimes challenging situations. How you manage those demanding situations," RJ says genuinely. "You seem to possess an inner comfort zone, which allows you to deal rationally or calmly with uncertainty. My guess is it's in your genetic warrior DNA." She says this while doing a similar raised eyebrow as Masters used to do. I groan at the sight of that one single act.

"Hmmmm, on this subject alone, I have a theory. Let me share it with you, if I may? It goes a bit like this. If something sounds a lot like crap, smells like it and feels just like it, then there is a fairly good chance it's something I'd rather not step into. Your last comments seem to fit this characterisation uniquely. Do you want to try again?" I suggest, while offering her a rocking chair on my veranda to sit on. Right away, I'm unsure if the ancient old chair will survive her size, which I put at around six-foot-three.

"Well, it may sound, smell or feel like all those things to you, James, however, I can assure you, my intentions are anything but. I'm very selective with who I have working arrangements with. Castelle, on the other hand, is much more selective about which clients we work for. We don't like to take on someone else's unnecessary baggage, so to speak," she adds quietly.

"OK, all this is fine, if true. So then, why don't you fill me in a bit more specifically on 'why now'?" My thoughts briefly drift me way back to when I asked another interesting person in a past life those very same questions, so many years ago in my kitchen, right before he had a heart attack and died on me. I pray the same does not occur again today.

"Yes, OK, I can do that. Well then, at the most basic level, when you're over there in amongst it all with all your warrior mates, at various times of threat, you probably wished to be anywhere else in the world except there, yes? However, when you are somewhere else in another softer or more peaceful wilderness, you prefer to be back out there in amongst the hunt hmm, getting your adrenalin fix? My guess is this emotion back then was perpetual, yes? Nowadays – well, right now, James, I predict no matter how great this life here is," she says, again waving her athletic arm around indicating the farm and the rustic artwork on the outside veranda walls. "You're doubtless once again drowning, or you're more than probably desiring to be back out there amongst it, just not at the dirty end. Maybe a more selective end that gets the old adrenalin charged up again? How am I doing so far?"

"Go on," I say noncommittally, agreeing with her to some degree, in silence.

"Castelle Corporation was founded way back in the late 50s by a group of political strategists, originally established back then to assist Australian companies, who were keen to expand into international markets and developments. What we do today, where possible, is to help them get set up in those markets and with the relevant international partnerships. Once they're up and operating, which can take considerable time and effort, we then support them where required to ensure they avoid any matters likely to creep into the picture that can destabilise the success of those efforts. Like corporate corruption, fraud or other conceivable and possibly unethical activities likely to have the possibility of impacting their business endeavours, compliance requirements and the Australian Government's efforts… or reputation. This necessitates us to get involved in a whole range of different activities, things like work scope profiling, relationship assessments and contractor management reviews. We participate in a whole host of undertakings to assist the relevant business in minimising negative impacts on the organisation's opportunities for success, reputation and achieving their desired bottom line. Still with me so far?" RJ gazes at me intently.

"Go on," I say again, more noncommittally this time. It's already getting a bit dreary for me. However, she's come all this way, I'll give her some more time.

"We support these businesses operating globally in times of rising geopolitical risks. As you probably know, the nature of global conflict evolves, continuously. We're seeing more and more non-traditional players emerge to threaten global safety and international business stability. Our activities are conducted internationally and often, not always, often enough though, in uncertain, sometimes hostile environments. Still with me?"

I nod yes, although it's not getting any less tedious all the same.

"Dealing with disreputable conduct requires a disciplined level of simplicity. Especially when it's impacting one of the Australian companies, we've helped to partner up with another nation's companies to get into a venture in the first place. Or worse, if it's one of those companies we support who are misbehaving badly. Our remit is broad. It includes commercial corruption and cross-border crime, where it has an interface with our Australian companies' international undertakings. We basically try to hold the powerful and corrupt to account, relevant to our partner development plans. This involves significant forensic accounting to investigate fraud, corruption and other unethical acts of bastardry, which our on-ground guys – like maybe yourself – do the background research, conduct the risk assessments and investigations, kind of like a "clean eyes review". That then leads to us also being involved in preparing financial briefs of evidence for the Government to try to remedy any non-compliances."

I nod again. It's now becoming a little less dreary.

"Although our main office is in Canberra, we only conduct engagements overseas primarily. We try to future-proof our government's business support strategies, by reimagining how those partnered-up approaches might successfully work across boundaries," RJ says, looking up as Carla and Katerina drive in immediately in front of a cloud of thick dust trailing behind, back from her gallivanting around the neighbourhood.

The next hour or so is taken up with introductions, explanations about who RJ is and why she's at our farm, having coffee, tea, snacks and storytelling. The latter mainly by RJ with her many global exploits and Katerina with her many farm adventures with all manner of her imaginary friends.

"These audits and investigations your organisation does Alison, how do you actually get involved with them, and why?" Carla doesn't like to use nicknames. She prefers to use a person's proper given name regardless of how they like to introduce themselves.

"Well, we initially get engaged if there is any hint of non-conformance or potential fraud indicators with the partnership deliverables that have been agreed upon. Unfortunately, these frequently centre around one form of corruption or another. We've also exposed all manner of theft and smuggling by multinational companies as well as by organised crime syndicates who slither their way into the ventures. We've conducted dozens of investigations into corruption or misuse of assigned funding, abuse of power and human rights or contractor exploitation. All in relation to our major international operations.

"We're highly regarded for our work exposing financial corruption in our endeavours. Of late, however, we've also used our cross-border collaborations to assess any emerging or trending influences. You know, to address any number of other important global complications the Australian businesses might become unintentionally exposed to or inadvertently involved in. This is where you might wish to participate, James? These areas include the extreme human rights abuses I just mentioned, cash-for-contracts scandals, contractor fraud, bribery, poor contract security strategies and political corruption. The list goes on and on, James, Carla, forever and a day."

I see Carla's eyes light up slightly at the mention of the varieties of thought-provoking challenges, the type she knows is likely to be of interest to me. I remember well, all the encouraging lines being part of what RJ told us at the time, before she hired me. What drivel. In the long run, as I got totally immersed into these assignments, and time went on, l realised, they're in actual fact, simply a different although an enhanced version of the people I'd been involved with in Vietnam so many years ago.

Chapter 12

My revery is disturbed by yet another knock on the door. Surprisingly, being lost deep in my thoughts helped me peacefully sleep the night away. RJ stuck her head in to ask if it's OK to enter and disrupt my life once again.

"Yeah, come on it, RJ. What positive news do you bring with you today?" I ask, with a plastic smile that I've begun to refine.

"Well then, you're sounding a bit more chipper this morning. James, you must have got some pain-free sleep last night?" RJ queries with her massive red lipstick smile.

"I have, funnily enough, RJ. I've been running a bit on fumes lately, stressing about my family. I'd also just been contemplating a few minutes ago, about how you turned up at my place one day not too many years ago to introduce yourself and Castelle into my life. I'm still undecided, old girl, as to whether or not I'm grateful for that occurrence or I should kill you for it," I say deviously, still with a smile of sorts on my face. "So then, any news about reuniting me with my family?"

"None that you want to hear about at the moment, James. I'm still trying to work my way around this maze with Ray Tallis, about you joining them that is. Has the doctor been around to clear you for discharge yet?" I noticed RJ has completely ignored my comment on how we met. Entirely bypassed it.

"So if we haven't got that sorted out, then the next step is for me to return home, RJ, 'cos I'm not going into WitPro without joining them. Something is going on here, RJ, something that you know about and you're not sharing with me, old girl. Give," I demand.

"The something I know about is not in relation to your family or WitPro. It's linked to the two home invaders, James. They're Syrians. Well, actually, they're refugees from Syria. Their families escaped some years ago and ended up being relocated to Albania, well over 10 years ago, it seems. I got their post-mortem photographs from Tallis and sent them on to Ortega in London, who have done some highly classified background checks for me. These two are most undesirable characters, as it turns out," RJ says, looking at me mournfully.

Bloody hell. It takes me a while for that bit of information to actually sink in, to register.

"Albania. It's in the Balkans, isn't it? So we're getting a clearer, more appreciative picture now, aren't we, bit by bit? The Balgary Construction Consortium, BCC. The contractor in the Malukun Islands job in Indonesia, a mixture of Chinese, Korean and Balkan companies." The last mission I focused on before going to West Africa. It was another screwed-up assignment we dramatically pulled apart, immensely upsetting the corrupt apple cart. "Bloody hell, RJ, what's the final washup from that nightmare? What has your ultimate forensic audit discovered?" I appeal. I'm happy just to have got away from that in one piece, it's way worse than a nightmare. I can't think of a single memento I might possibly have wanted from that horrendous time, not one. Nothing I'd want to bring back into my life now to remind me of it.

"Damn, James, it's still ongoing. I can tell you though, the primary contractors, BCC, have been suspended, and a caretaker construction contractor from Singapore has been bought in to complete the build phase. BCC is absolutely ropable it seems, not that there's anything they can do about it, as their entire operations are now so contaminated by their bad faith behaviours, culpability and impropriety. Datuk Malawi, the principal of the local partner company in PT Indolian, arranged for both the military and the local police to come in and arrest all of the BCC senior management. Unfortunately, this included our colleague Raymond Cook and a couple of other senior expats on our side. Seriously, though, the investigation that you kicked off so brilliantly still hasn't concluded." RJ rummaged in her slender, although elegant leather briefcase. "I've got a copy of the preliminary report here somewhere," she says as a sheaf of papers surfaces in her hand. "I'll leave the opening statement here for you to read. The rest is technical jargon. Unlikely to be entertaining reading."

"Yeah, well, it looks like it should now include other aspects, doesn't it? A natural conclusion might easily be drawn here, suggesting the home invaders may have been sent by BCC? With the intent to possibly instigate reckoning against me, I guess, for setting this thing off in the first place?" I pose to RJ, shrugging my shoulders.

"Yes, well, there does seem to be some sort of a link here. For your information, while the auditors continued their inquiry, they began receiving all manner of anonymous threats. This escalated into a number of face-to-face warnings urging them to cease the investigation. Some of the auditors unfortunately reported being followed by mysterious people, raising serious concerns about their personal safety. In response, though, BCC, probably recognising the severity of their situation, attempted to downplay the allegations and discredit the auditors. They asserted the auditors misunderstood the complexity of financial transactions, deeming the corruption accusations as baseless and the allegations of threats to the auditors' safety as ludicrous. Interesting times, James?"

"Yes, there does indeed seem to be a link from there with what is going on here with me. So what is the next step, then?" I query.

"Hmmm, yes, let's not get too carried away just yet, James. I've passed on our information to Tallis, who I believe will now share it with the Feds and whoever they decide to bring into the loop. I must admit, though, it certainly looks like BCC might have got their knickers in quite a tight knot here for them to want to contemplate this type of action," RJ says soberly, looking at me with concern.

I strongly believe she had earlier considered all this home invasion issue stemmed from my earlier post-Vietnam difficulties, while I suspected it originated from the West African fiasco. Both of us are alarmed to find it might be coming from an entirely different angle.

"It sort of makes sense to me now. Chris mentioned earlier, something about how he felt the entire episode seems very pedestrian to him. Why didn't they just come in at any old time, anonymously, and just kill me up front or from long range, or all of us? These guys wanted me to know who it was from or what it's about. I think they probably figured it's simply bad manners to allow me to up and die without knowing why or who is responsible for it. That's what this is all about, RJ. These guys aren't just closing off a link to all the corrupt findings. This is about ego. These idiots seriously want me to know what it's all about. Bloody hell, they're going to be mightily pissed now, aren't they? Now they've lost both hitters the other night, with no message being delivered?" I ask.

I can see she's about to say something when her phone rings. RJ looks at it, sighs, apologises and takes the call, speaks for a few seconds, then excuses herself from the room.

Ten minutes later, she comes back into the room slowly, forlornly from taking her call. A grey solemn look, one of despair, on her face. Cogs in there churning. . . at very high speed. I see it all in her anguished eyes and facial expression.

"Bad news?" I probe, needlessly.

"Worse, way worse. Very grave news, I'm afraid, off the scale bad. We've just lost one of our guys in a murderous ambush attack in Karachi, Pakistan. Along with three other oil client personnel and their local driver," RJ says mournfully. "Seems they'd left the client's office after completing another fraud and corruption audit and were in transit to the airport to go home. I'm not fully aware yet of any of the findings. It seems they may have similarly identified some massive fraud with one of their major ventures. They were attacked apparently while going over some public bridge called the PIDC near the Sheraton Hotel. You know it?" she asks, raising her eyebrows.

I shake my head no, nor do I want to, by the sound of it.

"Bloody Karachi. It's a grubby port city of about 14 million people. Can you get your mind around just how many people this actually is? It's insane, all living over the top of each other in the same city. It's been wracked by ethnic and religious violence for years. I think it's the closest thing to an indisputable basket case I've ever seen. Irreversible is my speculation, for the exact same reasons of what has just happened today. It's pretty much lawless," RJ declares. It's clear she's mourning the loss of her colleague… heavily.

"You personally know the guys, or at least our guy?" I ask quietly.

"Yeah. Been with us a long time. Way too long, it appears now. He'd been planning on retiring next year. Got a couple of kids, plus a couple of grandies as well. It's going to be tough for all of them and us to try to navigate around this. Our consular guys in Pakistan are arranging for the return of his mortal remains. At least it's something we can do for him and his family, I suppose."

RJ is looking decidedly uncomfortable with what has just occurred. This is probably the first time she's ever lost anybody really close with her missions.

"You want to talk about it, RJ? What's his name, our colleague?" I ask sensitively.

RJ hesitates. "Christopher Mansell, hell of a nice guy, not ex-military or anything gung-ho like you guys. He came to us as a civilian from police forensic accounting many years ago. He's exceptionally good at what he does… or what he used to do," she states despondently, recognising the change in status with what she'd just said.

"Is it time we dug a little deeper into why we're experiencing these sorts of high-level threats more frequently and how we might be able to more effectively manage them, RJ, to protect our people?

You know, like me in Indonesia, Ben in West Africa, Christopher in Pakistan, and didn't you have some security hitches in Rwanda? There's a definite pattern accumulating here, don't you think?" It's also one I'm wondering if I need to have in my future.

"Yes, you're right James, it's something we've been kicking around for quite a while to be honest. Unfortunately, our theories of providing additional security for when you go on these types of jobs is unlikely to have prevented any of the problems you just mentioned from still arising." RJ's about to continue when she's disturbed by my doctor walking in the door with his entourage of staff doing their morning rounds.

RJ excuses herself softly, gives me a bit of a one-finger salute this time and leaves the room quickly. The staff commence their poking and prodding, viewing my wound, reading charts, hitting me with questions upon questions and rebandaging my wound. It's then decided one more day of convalescence is required. I protest profusely, only to now find out the final arbiter after my doctor signing off on my discharge, is of course Ray Tallis.

I lay back onto my pillow, thoughts about the poor kid drowning immediately coming to front of mind again for some reason. I force them aside and pick up the sheets of paper RJ left for me to read the 'Draft Executive Summary of the PT Indolian Energy Corporation Audit Report', it read.

DRAFT EXECUTIVE SUMMARY AUDIT REPORT – TIANG FORENSIC SERVICES

FOR PT INDOLIAN ENERGY CORPORATION'S BOARD OF DIRECTORS

Independent auditors, Tiang Forensic Services (Tiang), of Singapore, were commissioned to scrutinise accounts of PT Indolian Energy Corporation's joint venture (JV) project between Indonesian and Australian partners, in the remote Ankara oil field, on the Island of Seram, Maluku. The scope was for a deep, clean eyes review of financial records, contracts and critical path completion compliance. The primary concern of the audit was to avert both PT Indolian JV partners and relevant Departments of the Australian Government from becoming embroiled in a wider corporate corruption scandal.

Auditors uncovered an extraordinary level of corruption within the JV. As a result, PT Indolian has officially suspended operations of Balgary Construction Corporation (BCC), the multinational entity contracted to build the production facility, following the triggering of dispute resolution mechanisms. Tiang have discovered compelling evidence of widespread corruption at multiple levels, exposing a pattern of excessively inflated invoices for goods and services. Its suspected funds were siphoned off via these inflated charges, causing a substantial burden on the operation's financial resources. Further investigation has exposed complex kickback schemes and money laundering involving high-ranking local officials. Funds have now been traced to accounts held by individuals closely connected to the host government.

In the face of heightened threats against exposing the level of corruption, the auditors have provided damning evidence to host Government officials, police and investigative journalists. The release of this evidence additionally exposes enormous human rights abuses within the construction phase as well. The resulting media coverage has garnered international attention, prompting calls for investigations by regulatory bodies and human rights organisations. This situation underscores the dangers faced by auditors when exposing high-level corruption in sensitive industries like oil and gas. Unfortunately, there is an overhanging menace of professional retaliation likely to be agitated against the auditors, resulting in threats of physical harm to auditor personnel.

In the case of the PT Indolian Ankara field, situated in a remote, emerging domestic market, oil and gas assets are technically controlled by the state-owned PetroStar Energy Authority via their Production Sharing Contracts (PSCs). Bid-rigging and improper payment schemes often pass through these ventures as a direct result of poor due diligence programs and flourishing unethical practices. Economic challenges in the region contribute to ineffective accounting controls which have allowed multiple suspicious transactions to go unchecked, fostering corruption via bribery and kickbacks. PT Indolian's deficient financial governance along with their inadequate enforcement of standard protocols have influenced these fraudulent practices.

Environmental: Social impact concerns have also led to fraudulent environmental practices impacting local communities. A submission by local Sawai tribal elders have claimed gross negligence by BCC and PT Indolian, asserting the collective mismanagement of the site waste water and septic system which has and continues to have a significant public health impact on tribal families living down river from the construction site. (Note: A further report is being prepared by the World Health Organisation on these impacts and associated compensation claims.)

The scandal is expected to cause a sharp decline in market value, with the venture not yet producing. PT Indolian faces challenges in accessing capital markets to continue to fund it through to completion. The fallout from this scandal has broader economic implications, as investors may lose confidence in the company and in the development.

END OF SUMMARY

There's nothing really stunningly new in the summary for me, although when I read the initial findings in conjunction with what I already know, it's devastating for Indolian and for BCC. This prompts me to reflect on our recent home invasion incident and where all of this might end up, given both of the shooters are now dead. They're not thoughts I want wandering around inside my inner self at the moment. I force my thinking to deviate to the sad circumstances around Christopher Mansell's recent demise… and how we might overcome some of the high-level risks we continually face. Christopher's disastrous encounter reminds me for all of the wrong reasons of my initial tasking with Castelle, which seems to have come back to severely bite me in recent days with the home invasion.

Chapter 13

MALUKU ISLANDS, MY VERY first outing with Castelle, alone. My task is to conduct a basic commercial threat assessment and compliance audit of a new oil and gas facility being constructed by a joint Indonesian and Australian company, PT Indolian Energy Corporation. The venture has been introduced and supported by our shadowy Australian government business development group, Castelle. It's located up in the highlands of the West Papuan Maluku Islands, the famous Spice Islands. The site itself is near a small town called Bula on the north-eastern coast of the Indonesian island of Seram. Bula township is in the vicinity of the now-depleted Bula oil fields, established in 1919, so I'm led to believe during my research. PT Indolian's field is called Kanara, it's nearby and by all accounts its going to be massive.

Flying from Saparua Island to Bula, my adventure commences early, very early. Like the minute we fly over the coastline to enter into Seram airspace. As usual, before I go out on any new assignment, in any of my careers, I sleep terribly the night before. I'm desperately trying to recover some of the forsaken kip when the grumpy Dutch pilot of our Cessna Caravan charter plane interrupts the peace and tranquillity of our flight and my attempt at sleep.

"Your attention, please. We have been ordered by the Indonesian National Army to divert to a new and unknown destination, in the jungle, just ahead. I have no idea why," he says in his broken English, sounding very agitated about this occurring. "I do not understand why they order us to land. We must not disobey their instruction, however. Please be calm," he says, although he seems to be the only one amongst us not composed at the moment.

As the fully loaded plane with our 14 passengers, mostly local nationals, gradually descends towards the approaching forest canopy, we collectively begin to become extremely agitated. For all intents and purposes, we appear to be attempting to land directly into the steamy thick lush green canopy. Our communal anxiety develops into raised voices of concern to much more direct yelling of abuse and reproachment towards the pilot from these very same, previously calm people.

He addresses us again, more forcefully this time. "Please, please to be quiet down, please. I not know where we are meant to go yet. I see landing strip to front of us in bush. We be OK," he lied – well, I felt he'd lied anyway.

My co-travellers settle down somewhat as we nervously observe a narrow scar, a minute slither of a dirty brown scratch become exposed in the impenetrable emerald-green jungle canopy in front of us to ultimately reveal a short dirt runway. The plane hits the ground hard, like bloody hard, I believe with a greater speed and force than in a normal landing. I initially thought the pilot maybe panicked a bit and lost either total or partial control over the aircraft. I relax a little once we slow and bump to a halt, then wobble around and bounce our way towards a clear area surrounded by an army tent city and perhaps a hundred Indonesian National Army or TNI soldiers, possibly more.

As we're taxiing to the parking area, our pilot advises, "I'm instructed to taxi to small clear pad off side of runway in front of us. Please be patient. I try to sort out whatever is issue. We are safe." He again lies. More intensely this time. He has no more idea about what's going on than we do.

In front of us in the clearing are another half a dozen armed soldiers in green camouflage uniforms, lounging around on two large metal trunks. An older single-engine aircraft of indeterminate heritage sits on the same cleared area next to them.

Our pilot addresses us again. "We ordered to disembark. Please do as request. Remain polite to soldiers when here. No trouble. I tell you everything soon," he says over his shoulder in his broken English, as he drops the airstairs to exit the plane.

We all nervously trundle out after him and anxiously stand in a communal huddle on the muddy clearing right next to our plane. We're all quickly moist from the tropical humidity and clammy air carpeting us. Meanwhile, the TNI soldiers with the trunks stand up, then walk straight past us and the pilot to begin loading, with some degree of difficulty, the two large metal trunks into the main cabin of the plane. Meanwhile, our pilot speaks to their commanding officer.

It turns out, as the pilot informs us, "It is cases full of cash, wages for soldiers being issued to each field camp around island. Small charter aircraft over there fail to start when they attempt to leave, so they commandeer… or requisition or hijack our aircraft to still do journey." We all just stare at the pilot in disbelief. How are we all going to fit into the plane is the most obvious question we're all faced with.

This became very clear, very quickly. Four of our local passengers and their luggage are unceremoniously removed from the plane, under significant protest from them and the pilot, to no avail. They're out, and the six soldiers with their boxes of cash are in, end of story. We depart from our unscheduled diversion soon after. The soldiers are sitting in the now vacated seats as well as two on top of their trunks of cash placed in the centre aisle of the plane. We climb up into the muggy grey sky again in search of Bula, our next landing point, or maybe an alternative TNI induced adventure. Who'd know? Finally, we circle the Bula airport. However, as we approach, the plane encounters a colossal, almost impenetrable smoke haze, sometimes grey-white, other times wafting from black to brown. The plane air-conditioning sucks in large gulps of the smoke, which I don't think is supposed to happen. It isn't clear at first where the smoke is rising from, as there are multiple streams of the acrid emissions climbing up from various locations. Equally unclear is what might have caused it – land clearing burn-offs perhaps, or errant out of control bushfires. Whatever the origin, there are too many locations for it to be a single source for all this amount of smoke.

It then became evident to me however, abruptly, where this blanket of smoke plume eddying skyward is originating from. Though the spiralling toxic smoke haze almost obscures much of the ground from view, it's obvious to me as we descend lower and get closer to landing. I can see it distinctly; it's coming from multiple burning houses and buildings in the township of Bula. I'm presuming it's an out-of-control bushfire that has hit the small town, slowly working its way through the thatch and wooden houses, shacks, huts and long-houses… churches as well. The peculiar aspect for me, though, is there doesn't appear to be any effort being utilised to bring the smouldering fires under control, which I find particularly odd.

I become far more aware of other ground anomalies as we get a closer and lower view of our surroundings, at the same time the air around us changes violently. While the plane slowly descends through the turbulence, the whirring of the propellor blades stir the humid smoky air, carrying with it the acrid stench of smoke and decay of dead bodies into the cabin with us. On our approach to land, the air around us becomes even more unsettled; this is just prior to another rugged landing, which I'm confident is definitely due to pilot error and nervousness this time. I'm likewise sure the multiple dead bodies I can now observe laying around the streets in various distorted forms are not the result of any bushfire.

Only my washing lady will later fully appreciate how alarmed and anxious I am becoming, at a great rate of knots right at this very moment. The aircraft taxies to an abrupt halt in front of a modest airport terminal, already burnt out, although still smouldering away. I do not want to leave this aircraft! I am not going to leave this aircraft, I tell myself, as I watch the pilot carefully try to clamber his overweight frame over the soldiers sitting on the trunks mid-aisle. The soldiers in turn seem wholly undisturbed by the smells or the macabre scene outside our aircraft or in the surrounding village carnage.

"Is OK, unrest is last night. All gone. All in peace now. Is OK to leave. Is safe," the pilot says, lying through his bent teeth once again, seemingly oblivious to how outrageous his comments are as he lowers the airstairs. The oppressive smell and heat cloak us immediately; it's thick and suffocating, heavy with the scent of burnt wood, smouldering debris, and the unmistakable, sickly-sweet odour of death.

"Not bloody likely, old chum. What I'm looking at out there is not what I consider to be safe. I'm not going anywhere. Let's get the hell out of here. Back up into the air, bloke," I reply to our pilot, who I have now lost complete and total faith in.

As I point my hand towards the obvious carnage outside and then up into the sky, I briefly observe, with some amplified degree of angst, a large 4WD Toyota utility truck hurtle amongst the wafting smoke. It thunders past the smouldering road entrance from the airport boundary road, onto the airstrip and skids to an abrupt halt next to the aircraft. With a heightened degree of relief, I notice it displays the logo of PT Indolian, the company I'm here to assist in the threat assessment audit. Except, I now already know what the bloody potential threats are though, without having to grace the site with my presence. They are all right outside of the bloody plane window, very easy to observe.

"You go now. You driver here. We cannot wait no longer," the pilot urges in his appalling English, a shroud of fear and sweat washing over him… and me. He then changes tack to begin talking to one of the TNI soldiers, one who is displaying all the signs of likewise wanting to discuss my departure – the commanding officer is my guess.

From the truck I hear, "C'mon James Kelly, get in the bloody truck, will ya man. We gotta get the fuck outta here," the Kiwi company driver bellows at me out of the small gap in the driver's window, urgently appealing to me, almost angrily. "It's all quietened down here for the moment. Nevertheless. I don't want to be hanging around here like a swinging dick any longer than necessary. So let's be getting mobile." It's a loud coarse command, not a request.

I can now see the TNI commander and his soldiers becoming more agitated as well. I feel a direct command from either him or the pilot is imminent. I dejectedly try to rise from my seat, only to realise my seatbelt is still clasped; even my seatbelt doesn't think it wise for me to depart. I reluctantly unlatch, collect my bags from under the seat and unenthusiastically leave the aircraft. I tentatively stumble down the airstairs and almost run from the plane to the truck, briefly glimpsing the desolate surroundings. In these microseconds, the full horror of the attack becomes apparent to me. Bodies, some partially covered by hastily thrown blankets or makeshift shrouds, lie where they fell. The victims, a mix of men, women, and children, show signs of violent deaths, primarily gunshot wounds and brutal hacking lacerations. The sight is both heart-wrenching and nauseating, a stark reminder of the cruelty inflicted upon them.

I dive into the passenger seat of the large 4WD truck and before I'm even fully seated properly, it speeds away in a flurry of spinning wheels, revving engine, flying dirt and disturbed thick swirling smoke. Off to the side, I can hear the plane beginning to rev up its engine in preparation to depart, probably rapidly… from this supposedly 'safe place now', as the pilot describes it.

"I'm Rojer Hoag. Leave your window up, 'cos the stink will fuck you up. Lock the bloody door. Don't stare at anyone. We'll be outta here before ya know it," Rojer says gruffly. I thought he might have looked across at me at least to see who I am. He doesn't.

I gaze across at him nonetheless, at a heavily tattooed, perspiring Rojer Hoag. Three things profoundly stand out at first glance. He wears a sickly yellow complexion, accompanied by similarly coloured eyes, all uncomfortably so. Possibly disguising a pharmaceutical miasma of some sort. On top of this, I notice he's old. He must be in his very late sixties, or maybe early seventies, all wrinkled up to buggery. The third aspect I notice is Rojer probably hasn't missed out on too many meals during his long life, if any. His ample stomach caresses the bottom of the steering wheel as he attempts to manoeuvre his way around the now taxiing aircraft. He speaks to me matter-of-factly, whilst I'm pondering if he's about to die on me, or maybe already has, given his age and alarming skin tone.

Apprehensive about his pallid appearance, I look across at him again. Rojer has one sickly hand gripped tightly on the steering wheel, with a Rolex Oyster watch attached. I reckon it's probably the real deal, not some knockoff. The other hand is on the gear shift, both hands being manipulated furiously as a monsoonal downpour releases huge grape size rain drops onto us, like small silver water bullets thumping onto our truck and the area around us. I notice Rojer has also over-dressed for the occasion in an old torn dirty blue short-sleeve shirt with faded company logo, complemented with dirty work shorts and muddy boots. He's unshaven, which simply enhances his glowing looks. He also has a cow lick in the front of what's left of his hair.

So, on top of all these choice findings, when I scrutinise the inside of his truck, it gives me the immediate expression that at some point in time, it has collided heavily with an epic life of disorder. There is debris and grime everywhere – on all of the truck surfaces, seats and in the foot wells. The entirety of the interior surfaces of the cabin are filthy, including all the windows, inside and out. I'd just perceived it's likely Rojer hasn't missed a meal in his life; conversely, his poor truck looks like it's forgone every opportunity in its existence to have ever undergone a cleansing of any description.

His comment about the stink is regrettably correct however, while moving nervously from the aircraft to the truck, I'd already picked up the much stronger putrid foul stench of burnt and decomposing flesh. A smell like rotting meat with sour, decaying fruit undertones. I have managed to drag some of the stench into the truck with me. I'm regrettably well familiar with the gases and compounds produced in a decomposing body from my Vietnam days. They emit distinct odours, as nearly every microorganism in a body is involved in some aspect or other of the cycle in human decomposition. Yeah, gross, I know. That's what I'm faced with right now and not happy about it in any way, shape or form. I also drag along another stench when I got in the big truck, the stink of my own fear which I haven't tasted for a very long time either. The silence inside the truck is broken by the buzz of multiple flies, which I also no doubt dragged in with me.

"What the bloody hell has just happened here, Rojer? And I don't want the sanitised version, mate," I demand of Rojer Hoag, the well-dressed sallow skinned man, as he roars our 4WD Toyota straight out of the smouldering airport gates then past what's left of the burnt-out gatehouse. I feel beyond anxious – way beyond – more nauseous than anything. It's a feeling of extreme unease, of worry and mostly fear beyond my control. Likely to be an ongoing emotional state of mind for a while is my prediction. The activation of my fight-or-flight system has well and truly kicked in, although it isn't helping me right in the midst of this seemingly highly dangerous, anxious and now rain-soaked situation.

"Clashes between those radical Muslim pricks from over in Ambon and the local Muslim and Christian groups here, mate. All sorts of radical crap from both sides been going on for a few years now, bad as each other," Rojer Hoag states nonchalantly as he frantically swerves and skids to a sudden sideways halt right before nearly colliding with a group of old men carrying a dead child, possibly a little girl, who are walking across the rain-soaked road in front of us. The ground beneath their feet is a mix of mud, ash and blood, trampled and muddied by the chaos that has swept through this place over the past day or so.

"Don't look directly at them, and for Christ's sake, don't take any photos bro. It'll aggravate this to hell and back. Something we desperately have to avoid right here, I can tell ya," Rojer almost whispers, as he slowly moves the truck off again in the downpour. His unhealthy skin reflects in a slice of sunlight, which makes him look absolutely dreadful, although he doesn't appear to be in any pain, none outwardly obvious to me at least.

"Won't make any difference is my gut feel, mate. Poor kid will still be dead, regardless." There is no way I want to take photos in any case. I do however, look directly into the harrowingly saddened eyes of one of the wizened old men carrying the child, maybe the father or grandfather. I can't begin to imagine the loss he's experiencing. There doesn't seem to be any hatred or anger there, just deep sorrow. The look on his wrinkled wet face is agonizing to take in. Doubtless the result of long-term suffering or of continual lifetime losses. The old man instantly reminds me of so many similar faces I'd observed back during the Vietnam war. It's distressing to be reminded of it… always.

Looking around the township as we drive through, I can see it's literally in ruins. Buildings, some painted in bright colours, are now charred husks; walls are blackened and crumbling. Windows are shattered, doors hanging from their hinges, and the villagers' personal belongings are strewn everywhere, all over the place, maybe trying to relay the accounts of the lives abruptly interrupted by this murderous chaos. The once-lively marketplace, now a scene of carnage, with stalls overturned and goods scattered, mingling with the remnants of human lives and the pools of concealed blood.

"What's the likelihood of us being attacked as Christians ourselves. Rojer?" Seems a feasible question to me, although I'd have expected something to have already happened if this was to be the case.

Rojer glances his sickly eyes across at me for the first time, briefly. "No likelihood at all, bro. We round eyes are not the issue in this sectarian shit-fight as long as we stay out of it. The last few days saw both the moderate Muslims and Christians attacked by those radicals from Ambon. That was then followed by a series of arsons and bombings from who the hell knows. Killed over 40 people last night alone, mostly the non-radical Christians, as well as some of the moderate Muslims. We've received warnings about several more shootings this morning, a couple of bomb attacks and small-scale communal clashes. It's relatively stable at the moment though." Rojer drove like a man who doesn't entirely believe his own spiel about the degree of safety he suggests is in our stars. He's also restless, continually twiddling with his hands and legs as well as playing with a native string bead bracelet on his wrist. It looks as old as him.

"Some sort of pathetic peace agreement was brokered earlier in the year between the moderate Muslims and Christians and has held together pretty well by the local communities. Although it was screwed up a day or so ago when the fucking Laskar jihad mob launched attacks on Christians in Ambon and then came up here to Bula to do the same. Word has it the last of the Christians – thousands of the poor bastards, in fact – are in the process of being booted out of the Malukus. They're pretty much displaced persons now, in refugee camps all around the various Godless islands. I guess waiting on repatriation to somewhere bloody else supposedly safe, if there is such a place," Rojer states, as the sky opens up again in a massive monsoonal downpour.

"Fuck… This is going to right royally screw up our river crossing further up in the highlands. It's our only main road into the construction camp. Unfortunately, it's below a massive river catchment area that'll flood its arse off with this amount of rain. We'll just have to wait and see how it ends up, I guess," Rojer curses, pale skin shimmering with perspiration.

I note he uses the word 'fuck' and a multitude of other derivative curse words like a comma in just about every sentence. It's like an involuntary outburst of excessive, obscene language or socially inappropriate and derogatory remarks is how he functions. Maybe he's borderline Tourette's? He sadly reminds me of myself many moons ago in my younger days. It's going to be an interesting trip, I think.

Time for a few questions about the abstract health of my driver and his discoloured skin. "So Rojer, tell me, what's the deal with your skin discoloration, if you don't mind me asking? Some sort of jaundice?" I pry, orbiting my hand in a circular motion towards his head.

"Yeah, I do mind. Anyway, whatever, you're right, it's a bit of jaundice and some sort of screwed up hepatitis infection trickling along with it. Picked it up here a year or so ago. I've had all the treatments and still can't shake the fucking thing. Starting to break down my red blood cells now," he answers as he slows down during a massive downpour that makes it almost impossible to see anything in front of us. "Fuck!" Rojer screams at the rain.

Already hypersensitive to the atrocities back in Bula and the impact of the storm, my fear and anxiety levels haven't yet got a chance to decrease. My life now seems to hang on the insufferable whim of a vagrant weather pattern and a potential disease-ridden human cadaver as my travelling companion. Hell of a trip.

"Anyway, what the hell is this audit thing you're doing? What's it all about, hey?" Rojer's tone left no doubt he's displeased with whatever he thought my audit is about, implying perhaps he's more than just the old, grumpy and unhealthy-looking company 'driver'.

"Too much equipment and parts not turning up. Maybe 'lost'. Sometimes, they're the wrong part or are misplaced once it's here, or maybe before it even gets here, Rojer. Costs have escalated through the roof, and transparency has declined. Our mutual client, PT Indolian, wants me to chase the paper trail along with the bits 'n' pieces down to see where it leads. Or maybe where it doesn't lead to or why. Head office seems to think the Bulgarian contractors might be siphoning things off. Either way, it's a threat to the success of the venture meeting its governmental performance criteria requirements, so we need to see what we see." I'm waiting for some sort of negative reaction from young Rojer about my tasking, just not quite what I get.

"Sounds too much like head fucking office interference again to me. They should leave well enough alone, unless those pricks want to come out here and run this shit show on-site themselves. Best you ensure your audit bloody well stays away from my little patch of harmony, Kelly," he says bitterly, as he winds his window down to spit out a wad of black… something. Maybe it's chewing tobacco, or perhaps it's his arsehole, right before I get a chance to kick it in for him.

"I'll be going where the paper trail takes me Rojer, which will include your very own little patch, if in fact it takes me there. Life is full of disappointments, so if you've got anything you want to say about it, now is as good a time. Or if you have anything to share about something else which might assist me, I'd be pleased to hear about it as well," I suggest to him unemotionally, noticing the agitation almost radiating out of him as he drives a little more carelessly now, possibly gravitating towards reckless even. Now is not the time to have a confrontation with anybody up here. I can imagine everyone is already distressed to hell and back with what is going on in Bula, so I don't want to cause any unnecessary distractions inadvertently.

"I hadn't meant for it to sound quite the way it probably came out," Rojer replies sombrely. "What I meant is you bean counters seem to have a completely distorted armchair perception on how these activities actually get executed on the ground… by us." He looks over at me with a shifty-looking half-smile, probably to check if I'm paying attention. I am.

"Back there in their belltowers of privileged separation, they draw up their budgets from the absolute lowest bidders before they screw them down some more. Then they get all their ducks in a row according to the precious commercial, social and their politically correct fuckedupness requirements. Once it's sorted, they kick a few heads to get contracts approved and signed in a hurry, then off they go. Handing it all over to the operations team on the ground here to meet their bullshit deadlines, piss poor budget projections and screwed up policies and protocols," he adds bitterly, staring straight ahead as he weaves and slides angrily around the muddy, greasy road.

"I'll have to correct you just a bit there, Rojer old mate." I half-smile back at him. "First of all, I'm not a bean counter. I'm what they call a threat evaluator. I analyse and assess potential risks to the success of a venture, specifically yours on this occasion. The most critical element of this role is to try to block any trouble bubbling to the surface. I'm sure you know what I mean, the kind that might derail the entire contract? Secondly, I don't work for your company, nor do I take my instructions from you. I, in fact, work for a company tasked by a particularly grim department of the Australian Government. This department sort of vacillates around in amongst the Department of Foreign Affairs and Trade, actually. So, I'm directed by their policies, not yours—" I don't get to finish. I get really pissed when this happens.

Rojer slams on the brakes, bringing the big 4WD to a slow moving sideways skidding halt, resting on the edge of the slippery dirt road. I'm lucky I guess in one respect, as I'm wearing my seatbelt. This has counteracted me from going head first into and possibly beyond the windscreen with his extreme braking. I'm not thrilled about this turn of occasion at all. I know from experience, there is probably significant benefit in me explaining this to Rojer in a manner that he will more than likely fathom.

"What the bloody hell did you just say? You're a spy, is that what you just said? For the Government? What in the fuck have they got to do with this place? Hey?" Rojer impales me with these comments, loudly, like some part of his illness contamination, as he waves his hands around the steering wheel. A dribble of black slime trickles down his chin, which he quickly wipes away with the back of his sallow hand, confirming my earlier chewing tobacco theory at least.

"Let's get a few things squared away here Rojer, OK, right now and right up front, shall we? First up, you don't get to bellow at me or carry on like an unregistered dog towards me under any set of circumstances. Am I making myself crystal clear on this point? Otherwise, you and I are more than likely going to come apart like a flying fuck." I've straightened myself up in the seat now, and I look him square in his unhealthy-looking eyes with what I intend to be a reassuring look in mine. He just stares back at me, angrily, sallow fists opening and closing around the steering wheel. I know it's important for me to establish my authority here, without going too far over the top. Well, not too far over the top for me, which I can tend to do. I'm considering enlightening him about a few more aspects of life he might benefit from, except he strikes me as some sort of a psycho stepson of a prick who probably carries a gun or a knife or some other damn species of harm inflicting device.

"Secondly, I'm not a spy for anybody, not for your company, the company I work for or for some shady department of the Australian Government. I'm simply here to conduct, in consultation with you, a threat assessment on the likelihood of this venture achieving its performance criteria and succeeding to the end of this construction phase within budget. If it wasn't about to fall off its wobbly rocking horse wheels, I wouldn't have to goddamn be here at all in the first place." I say this now with my own hands raised in a conciliatory manner, as this is definitely not the place where either of us should be at this point in time.

It's at this very moment, I notice a black Glock pistol in a fancy leather stitched holster, gaffer taped to the driver's side door panel, just above the metal door latch moulding. In easy reach for Rojer to access with his right hand at any time he wants. I don't know why I hadn't noticed it before when I first got in the truck. It has my full attention now, though, I can tell you, although Rojer's right hand is nowhere near it… for the moment. So, my earlier thought he's possibly a psycho stepson of a prick who probably carries a gun or something similar is actually real.

"Crap," Rojer bellows at me.

"Just hang onto your well-worn anxiety hat there for a bit, Rojer. The Australian Government has invested heavily in inter-country and governmental negotiations and liaison to make the most of international trade and investment opportunities for companies like yours. It gets comprehensively involved in researching, introductions, consultation and trade negotiations on behalf of these companies. It initiates various concessions to get your company engaged as the partner organisation in the long-term viability and successful longevity and profitability of the entire life of this operation here, not just this phase of it," I declare dispassionately, eyeing an almost expressionless facade moving across

Rojer's face like a sickly mask. Something else happening inside there he's not ready to share – not at the moment, anyway, I feel.

"Screw it, Kelly. Our senior management and the primary contractor here are the major problem, not the partners. The construction activities themselves or the people here trying to execute it are at the mercy of this lot. Our senior management are the corporate maggotry getting us into these binds. Their moral hazard approach is simply too far removed from reality to be aware of or care about the disagreeable occurrences which regularly infest our lives out here." Rojer spits this at me as the colour of his face darkened to an impossible tinge of almost orange.

I'm fearful he's about to have a heart attack or give me one… or something. I put my hands up in a gesture of peace.

"It's just not so goddamned simple to get this job done to their particular manic schedules or demand patterns, their impractical budgets or a reasonable standard. I don't believe maggot central has any insight of what is important to our people out here on the ground. They only care about what they can make from it profit-wise, especially the profit from the secretive little back-pocket bonusses. Maybe they just want to avoid having to think about the level of extreme unpleasantness we're too often exposed to out here," Rojer offers, a little less angrily.

With our truck now stopped right in the midpoint of the steamy jungle road and Rojer's driver's side window down, the wavy vapour of outside humidity catches up to us in a rush, charging into the cabin. A heavy mugginess cloaks us, and the inside of the truck steams up within seconds. Clamminess becomes intense within milliseconds, our AC roaring its lungs out hopelessly, trying to keep up.

"You think it might be a good time to keep things moving along here, Rojer, eh? We can discuss all this at your camp later. Sitting here in the centre of a muddy road in the pissing rain is only likely to provoke something else to come and drop into our laps, uninvited, yeah?" I'm keen to keep any further obstructions interfering with our trip, especially those which can be addressed at the construction camp later.

"Yeah, whatever," he growls, angrily ramming the gearshift into place, completely bypassing the use of the clutch, which of course is always an exhilarating clash of technology, gears and brutish energy to be subjected to. He somehow entices the truck to roar off down the increasingly greasy track, both hands firmly grasping the steering wheel, thankfully nowhere near the gun taped to his door.

We aren't long into our resumed journey, maybe half an hour or a little more, when we arrive at the river crossing Rojer is dreading. For very good reason, I now understand. There's a significant backup of people, bikes, cars, trucks and minibuses on both sides of the river, probably a hundred or so people by my guestimate. All wanting to get safely over the raging torrent. Rojer parks our truck haphazardly, perpendicular to the rest of the vehicular line-up. There's heavy base music being played out loud by a group of young locals from one of those big boom box music blaster things you see on the US TV. Can't remember what they're called; nonetheless, it's as ugly as hell, huge and bloody loud, and the sound is massively distorted. We reluctantly walk down amongst the musical crowd to the river's swollen edge. Well, I'm the only one being reluctant, given what we'd just seen back in Bula and now with the number of locals congregating at the river's edge, mostly, if not all Muslim.

Rojer, though, well, he doesn't seem to have a care in the world. He sort of jigs and jives a bit whilst he laughs with the music guys as we pass. When we step to the edge of the bloated river, I feel about a foot taller, with all of the orange gumbo clay mud clinging to the bottom of my boots. All of us here are the same, slipping, sliding and struggling to stay upright, except those walking around in bare feet. As I'm trying to de-clay the bottom of my boots, one of the local children runs up and gives Rojer and myself a long chunk of thick, sharpened clumping bamboo to use as a mud cleaner and walking stick. I'm amazed at how much easier such a simple tool makes life moving around the mud and slush.

The swollen river, though, bloody hell, it's one scary, even amazingly fierce image. A ferocious cauldron of blood-brown flood wall of foam, mud, rocks, tree debris and logs smashing high into each other in a kaleidoscope of turbulent, violent and loud mayhem. It's frightful; nevertheless, it's also spectacular. I likewise knew from flash floods back home and in Vietnam how they're characterised by an intense, high-velocity surge of floodwaters triggered by significant torrential rain falling within a short amount of time on a nearby elevated terrain. This river, well, it ticked every one of those boxes. I watch with horror as a giant lush healthy tree, what looks like a flourishing green native Ficus to me, groans and cracks as it cascades slowly down into the turbulent river. The floodwaters have undermined its root system, a sad ending to such a majestic, beautiful tree as it's slowly carried away downstream.

Rojer seems to soften around the edges somewhat when faced with the unique flood site before him and the loss of the giant Ficus. "I'm hoping this will only be a temporary hindrance for us, especially while all that savagery is going on over this side of the river." He raises his hand and points his thumb behind him, presumably meaning the carnage back in Bula. "Apart from hampering our access, these flash floods are very destructive fuckers. Not only because of the force of the water itself, it's also the massive amount of debris swept up in and under the flow. It hurtles down at a great rate of knots, mostly hidden under the surface. We're gonna have to wait until it subsides a hell of a lot before any of us attempt to navigate across." He seems to flicker between nonchalant and anxious, almost between each breath. This is one complicated bloke, I'm thinking.

"So, the crossing, is there some sort of rock base here we drive on to get across, or do we navigate through the sand, pebbles and rocks?" I query. It looks like a very precarious crossing, regardless of what lay on the bottom.

"Nah, it used to have a concrete causeway. We put it in at the beginning of the project. Who knows if it's still here. It hasn't been tested like this until now, so it's anybody's guess as to whether it survives or not," Rojer replies, shrugging his shoulders. "Time will tell, I guess," he says as he shrugs his shoulders again and walks off to talk to some locals dressed in their hi-vis clothing.

It's a slow slog back to our truck in the mud. I attempt to clean the gunk off the bottom of my boots again as best I can before stepping inside. Still suffering the aftershock of the Bula atrocities, I've got to shake some of it, or all of it, off. Time to think outside the square a bit, so I call RJ on the mobile phone to discuss the status. There's no signal, though. I then fire up the satellite phone, and she answers. It sounds surreal to my own ears, as I cover what I'd been through and seen at Bula and Rojer's unusual infantile behaviour and disposition.

"Interesting times indeed, young man. We've heard almost nothing about the destruction you mention in Bula. We've only heard some brief oversight suggesting all of the conflict activities have centred around Ambon only. Anyway, for now, stick to the plan all the same, I think. Follow the paperwork. I'll see what I can find out about our friend Rojer. He seems to have a much higher level of comprehension into what's going on than just as a company driver, that's for sure. Stay in touch. Keep the satellite phone fully charged all the time, James. I suspect we're going to be making heavy use of it," RJ says as she signs off.

I position my seat back a little to try and relax for a while until we can get a chance to attempt a crossing, when I notice Rojer coming into view. He's walking past the locals standing around in their small groups, greeting them in their own language as he goes. Nothing unusual about it, except he's swigging from a silver pocket flask as he walks. Judging from the expression on his face after each swig, whatever the liquid is in there, its attention seeking. Another thing to be aware of, I guess. Looking across to the driver's side door as he opens it to get in, I notice his gun is missing from the holster. Presumably, he'd taken it with him to the river's edge. I don't know what to make of it, except it probably bothers me more when you combine the gun with the silver pocket flask. Add his juvenile behaviour back down the track earlier and his aggressive attitude towards his senior management. None of these items provide a healthy combination are my immediate thoughts.

"Hey Rojer, tell me, what is it you do here with Indolian? What's your actual role in it all?" I query, curious to know more about him as well as keeping his mind off the flask and the gun – hmm, the bloody gun. Let's find out about that first. "You're well-armed there, by the looks, so my guess is it's not just as a company driver?" I point to the empty holster in the door and the handle of the Glock poking out from under his shirt.

"Nothing special about what I do, Kelly. I get to look after the low-hanging fruit of the logistics and procurement aspects, of our side of things, special materials handling, for Indolian only, not for the contractor BCC. I make sure our gear gets to where it has to get to, once it's here with us, that is. You know, basic things like that, hence my earlier comment about you staying out of my little patch of harmony," Rojer says this whilst clenching the steering wheel and his teeth as he looks straight out of the windscreen.

"Yeah well, haven't we already addressed this, back there?" I counter, pointing my own thumb over my shoulder behind me this time, indicating back where we'd just come from. "I've already figured out you get to sit and play at the adult table unsupervised. However, it's what game you and the others might play is what I'm likely to be more interested in when we sit down to kick things around. You know what I mean?" I say calmly, not really wanting to delve into these matters right here on the edge of a raging river and in front of a bunch of locals who probably either don't know or don't care which side they're on in regard to the atrocities back in Bula.

"I'm not out to get anybody, Rojer. My job here is simply to figure out where things are going, why they're not going where it's meant to be going and then how to get all concerned back on their bikes functioning as required. What I don't want, though, is someone trying to convince me I can pick up this particular piece of shit from the clean end, 'cos that's simply not going to wash. It's too late. I've been sent here because it's really stinking it up now, and it's created a bit of a speed bump, which we have to flatten out. It necessitates us to get the productivity balance right again." I watch him as his hands clench and unclench around the steering wheel anxiously, something else definitely happening in there that he doesn't want to share, not just yet are my thoughts. Maybe I've hit him with one too many cliches. Time to change that attitude of his – soon.

"Yeah, whatever!" Rojer utters softly, still glaring straight ahead.

"This is not a witch-hunt, Rojer, not for you or for anybody else working here. If there are extreme impediments being considered here by the dark Government department or Indolian, they would've already sent in an attack team of some pretty high-level third-party forensic fraud auditors with their own security to crank the handle. They'd want to check every physical item as well as each piece of paper or e-document floating around the place to see who's up who and who's benefiting. This is not what I'm doing, Rojer. I'm trying to circumvent a scenario like that from materialising by exploring any ways we can limit whatever the hell is going on with the missing gear. Like I told you, so we can try to flatten out the speed bump, even if just a bit maybe," I state.

"I gotta say, though, I'm not feeling the love from over your side there Rojer. You gonna help me out a bit here?" I goad, eager for some sort of breakthrough with him… or not.

"Yeah, well, stiff shit about the love, Kelly. I just don't have the energy to pretend to like you today," he responds, although not unkindly.

"Don't want you to like me, Rojer. Just to work with me on this audit. Do ya think you can do that?" I say this whilst watching his hands once again clenching and unclenching the steering wheel at an increased tempo.

"Have you wondered why I'm out here, doing all this?" Rojer asks quietly, gesticulating his non-gun arm around, waving it at the convoy of stranded vehicles and people. "I don't think there is any benefit in letting yourself be misinformed by other's opinions of what goes on out here with these project activities. People are deceived too easily by looking at spreadsheets, flowcharts, contrived reports or self-serving statements."

"No, Rojer, I have no idea why you're out here, mate, nor do I care. It's none of my business. I don't judge. We all do things for different reasons. I have no concerns about why people make those choices, for whatever the outcomes are best for them. It's also nothing to do with my tasking here which has a specific assessment focus, if you know what I mean? Trying to sort out all the mess between opposing positions, options or objectives of the various stakeholders. Why do you ask, anyway?" He seems very self-effacing all of a sudden. I sense whatever it is he has on his mind is potentially coming to the surface. Maybe it's a bit of progress after all?

"What do you think you want to know then, eh?" Rojer growls, looking sideways at me.

Nice little bit of deflection happening here, I think.

"Well, first up, how about filling me in a bit more about the mischiefs you referred to back at Bula? You know, the history at the back of what we saw there?" I ask respectfully, although just mentioning the disturbing events makes me feel all ill at ease once again. Still, I'm curious to know more about it all, more importantly to understand how it might impact us or the success of the venture. In addition, it will hopefully keep his mind off the flask… and the gun.

After a few moments of silence, he says, "Well, the real locals, you know who I mean, the ones that've been rooting around here forever, both the Muslim and Christians, they've lived together here peacefully for over a hundred and fifty years, with next to no shenanigans. A number of years ago, however, we faced an upsurge in violence following the arrival of those bloody Laskar arseholes from Java and South Sulawesi, a coupla thousand of them. Then we also had a bunch of the TNI soldiers come over here as well to screw things up. Feedback from the villagers suggested the TNI were reportedly supporting and fighting alongside the militants. This led to calls by the Christians for a UN peace-keeping force. Other reports suggested the TNI simply turned a blind eye to the slaughter, contributing by not putting a stop to it." Rojer took a breath and lit another cigarette. I can't begin to imagine what the insides of his lungs look like.

"Most of the fighting took place around Ambon. Story has it at least 700 or so people died during that flare-up, fewer than the number killed in an earlier attack though, which was supposedly around 900. Partisans on each side have claimed the government security forces were directly supporting their adversaries, not actually taking the famous middle ground as they'd indicated."

"Well, from my own personal take on life, Rojer, that famous bit of ground is traditionally not a place you want to find yourself occupying for too long, I can assure you. I've seen it and been in it before. It's not a reassuring place," I suggest, recalling how many times I've seen or heard about the many failures associated with that specific bit of ground by the fence sitters afraid to make a decision.

"Yeah, well, there are too many different gangs of these unintelligent pricks involved in all this now. I doubt any of 'em would know how to find the middle ground or their arses with both hands and a road map. None of this is going to wind down now, that's for sure. It's got nowhere to go, really, other than to get uglier every day of the week. Over the past couple of years, there's been scores of people – from both sides, mind you – killed, beaten, raped… you name it." Rojer took a deep breath, reflecting on what he'd just imparted.

"The burning of many Christian and Muslim houses, buildings, mosques, churches and every other wonderous place of worship has driven most of this round of fighting. Massive loads of food stocks have been bloody well stolen in over two dozen small towns, villages and settlements. Both sides have pilfered thousands of cows, goats, chickens and sheep, as well as clothes, cooking utensils and other personal materials," Rojer sighs again. He's visibly frustrated at the inevitable escalation.

"Sounds like quite the predicament, Rojer. Is there no peace strategy being put in place on either side to try to remedy any of this?" I ask.

"Yeah, like I said earlier, reconciliation has been attempted plenty of times, real serious efforts too. It's been hampered by the more radical Laskar wankers, or holy warrior Muslims, they call themselves. They vehemently oppose moderate Muslims trying to foster peace with the Christians. The radicals are very anti-reconciliation and anti-Christian. It creeps into our business periodically, just not enough yet that we have to push back hard. Our partners are all local Indonesian Datuks and Sultans, so they tend to keep a lid on things to some degree. For how long, though… who the hell knows."

"You say none of this has yet really impacted these operations. What makes you think it might do so in the future?" I ask.

"Because nothing is ever certain about any of this, no-one is immune, OK? This is how stupid this whole mess is. The radical bloody Islamists attacked a police station here on Seram Island just recently, killing eight predominantly Muslim people, including officers. It was meant to punish the Muslim officers who they perceived to have been protecting a Christian village. Can you see how utterly unpredictable and hopeless this situation is turning into? If they didn't care less about knocking off a police station full of their own people, they're sure as fuck not gonna care about coming after our place, or any others in the region," Rojer says, slamming his open palms down on top of the steering wheel.

"It's impossible to attempt to save the souls of these radical militant pricks, you know, because the bodies in which their souls live are so poisoned and treacherous, they're beyond redemption, at least by any of the Gods we know about. It's like the old story isn't it? Man plans, God laughs and the Godless die," Rojer says with a slight wink of humour.

"You know what, Rojer, it sounds like these guys have been screwing with each other for so damn long now, it's hard for me to imagine someone isn't getting something material out of it. You know what I mean?" I express my anxiety over the improbability of it all. "Like money, power, territory, something like that."

"Yeah, I know what you mean."

As I sat staring out the windscreen, I notice a couple of local guys in hi-vis clothing leaning against a nearby truck glaring at us. I'd noticed them earlier, only I hadn't given too much attention to them then as we'd just arrived, I'd put it down to curiosity. Not now, though.

"You notice those pair of hoers leaning against the back of the truck over there, Rojer?" I ask, pointing a partially obscured finger in their general direction. "The pair in the dirty hi-vis gear, especially the little one on the left with the parang machete hanging off his hip?"

"Yeah, I noticed them earlier. I don't think they're a problem. The bigger unattractive prick on the right is named Rahmat or Rahman, I think. Something like that. He used to work for us at the camp, arsehole got booted for stealing about 6 months ago. I think he's a follower, not a leader."

"They both look like they have unresolved anger issues to me, or maybe it's just psychotic nervousness. In the unlikelihood something does fall off the rails here with these two, Rojer, do you have another one of those floating around?" I ask, pointing to his gun, now securely back in his fancy leather door holster.

"Nope. Never seen the need for it. I can't see much point in them getting their knickers in a knot about anything, though. I doubt either of 'em play in the toy box with those Islamist pricks or if they're supporters of the Islamist ideology. Who bloody knows, though? I'll keep my eye on the pair of pricks, anyway, just in case," Rojer says as he gives me an ugly smirk and wink.

"Let's think worse case here then, Rojer. Assume they do decide to arc up for whatever bizarre reason, what'd your plan be? Do you have one?" I query, still all hyped up about the gruesome events back in Bula.

Rojer looks at me with his smirk again and taps his gun resting in the door holster. "That, and some help from a friend in low places. See that big unpleasant looking hairy unit over there next to the bus?" he says, pointing to a tall, quite regal looking specimen standing beside a dilapidated mini-school bus. "He's the chief of the village nearest to us downstream. They've previously been affected by a few health problems with their kids down his way of recent times. I've helped him out with our medic and some essential medicines. I've already worded him up. Given our relationship, he'd fall over himself to sort out any such concerns we might have with anybody likely to raise the temperature here."

I nod, pleased at least there's some sort of plan available to us.

"You might pick up those bloody medical supply discrepancies in your audit, Kelly. It's a big part of what we do around here that's not possible to put into the cost estimates the maggots use to originally cost all this up. Same as things like the concrete causeway we put in here to ease access for everybody to traverse the river here," Rojer grumbles.

As he finishes talking, we suddenly hear a loud roar from the crowd down next to the riverbank. We both jump out and set off on a run, slipping and sliding our way through the light rain and mud, down to the river. Once we arrive, Rojer pushes his way past the crowd lining the bank. I'm not sure I'm ready for what I see. One of the locals on the other side has become so impatient, he's rashly attempting to make the crossing in his small truck loaded high with timber logs. The river is flowing less violently, but it is still flowing, still way too intensely to yet attempt a crossing, I would have thought anyway. There still seems to be all manner of debris mixed in amongst the flow, which says all it needs to indicate the dangers to the hapless driver, prior to departing from the other bank. The result is so easily predictable. He slowly inches to about a third of the way across, out into the heavier flood flow. Within seconds, though, the truck is picked up by a floating tree and tipped over, carried off downstream in a surge of filthy, foamy water, tree branches and boulders. As inevitable as it is, it's still disheartening to see the small truck roll over and over in the floodwater until it smashes into a massive boulder embedded in the midpoint of the river. There's very little of the truck left, as it's continually pounded against the rocks by its own load of logs.

"What a master-class fuck-up. Ya don't get any deader than that, I can tell ya, no matter how hard you try. What a useless waste of life," Rojer spits as he turns to angrily push his way back in amongst the crowd.

He's instantly confronted by a bunch of threatening young locals, led by the two from our earlier observations, in particular the short angry one with the machete, which is now raised above his shoulder in an aggressive stance. Before he has a chance to move forward from where he stood, a massive hairy fist smashes into the back of his neck with such force it generates such a solid cracking sound that it just about makes my eyes water. This encounter turns the angry little one's lights out straight away, eyes slowly rolling up and back into his head, literally collapsing into a small heap, on the spot, like a balloon deflating. Shocked at this action, and before any of the other youths have a chance to react, a dozen other men immerge from the crowd and drag the other youths away variously by the throat, by their hair or lifted bodily up off the ground and removed. This all took only a matter of seconds before complete harmony is restored. Well, certainly not my emotional harmony, that's for bloody sure, which is going to take a lot longer. Rojer drags me reluctantly over to meet Saleck, the huge and hairy village chief. Hands are shaken, smiles traded and a few words exchanged between Saleck and Rojer. Saleck is going through some paperwork with Rojer, which I don't appear to be included in, so I turn to wander back to our 4WD when Rojer calls out to me.

"Saleck feels this matter is more likely to have been some opportunistic attempt by Ismail at retribution for Rahman's sacking, nothing more. Ismail being the angry little machete wielding prick. It's highly unlikely to be related to the savagery in Bula earlier today or last night," Rojer says, as he lights up yet another cigarette, from the dying butt of the one he's currently smoking. "Let's hope so, anyway. On another note, Saleck reckons we'll probably be able to cross over within the next couple of hours or so. He's seen so many of these floods, he can pretty much timetable when it'll ease enough not to be a major threat to us anymore."

Chapter 14

SALECK'S CALL IS INCREDIBLY accurate, amazingly so. Within an hour and a half, even though the river is still flowing quite strongly, crossings do in fact commence, although it's slow going. One vehicle from each side at a time, gradually driving over the concrete causeway, which amazingly is still in place in spite of everything. It takes a good hour or so before our turn comes to cross. Inexplicably, we bump into Ismail and Rahman again as we leave the crossing on the other side. My immediate thoughts are, "OK here we go again." In hindsight, though, I think Ismail might have been trying to reclaim some dignity from the earlier disastrous encounter. Except, I very much doubt if he knew whether he's ever possessed any dignity to begin with, so in this case, he'd no idea where to begin. You can recover from a bad decision; rarely, though, from a badly executed encounter. His was a hugely bad mistake. Rojer wisely ignores them both and continues driving past them, up the crossing exit and finally out onto the main dirt road. In due course, this leads us to the PT Indolian construction site road. What a bloody day, and it's not over yet.

We continue our way deeper into the dense wilderness on the rough and irregular construction road in total silence. I'm contemplating Ismail and Rahman. God only knows what's going on inside Rojer's head. Sunlight barely filters past the thick canopy above us, creating a sort of a soft, mottled, everchanging pattern with us on the road, also disguising the multitude of hidden potholes beneath the pools of storm water. As we venture deeper into the jungle, other noises slowly build – mechanical thuds, metal on metal bangs and echoes, gradually growing louder. This distant drone ultimately transforms into a steady mechanical snarl. The air is tinged with the acrid stink of welding fumes, heavy machinery noise and diesel exhaust. Despite this, the atmosphere is still strangely thick with the fragrance of exotic flowers and the earthy aroma of damp soil.

Emerging from the thick vegetation, I find myself standing at the raised edge of a vast clearing, where the once glorious tropical wilderness has been turned into the semi-organised chaos of construction activities. Periodic sounds of wildlife and the calls of tropical birds high up in the trees can still be clearly heard, intermingled with the chatter of monkeys observing the human activity from the safety of the treetop canopies. Higher up, I initially heard and then saw a helicopter swinging a load under itself as it passed over the outer edges of the construction site vegetation. It gave me a slight nervous twinge hearing and seeing it, taking me back momentarily to Vietnam. It's also news to me, however, as I was not aware Indolian has a helicopter.

The construction site is an absolute shocker. No other way to describe it. It's massive and ugly, so ugly a mother would struggle to love it. It's like the biggest boys' Meccano set I'd ever seen, except man-size, so surreal. We get back in our truck and slowly drive onto the site proper, in the midst of the lush wilds. It's a bizarre, almost conflicting encounter, 'engineering creation invades amazing natural beauty of mountainous tropical paradise'… its confronting actually.

"What's the deal with the helicopter, Rojer? I wasn't aware Indolian has one. What's it used for?" I query.

"Not ours. Belongs to a South African oil company further up the bloody river. Good bunch of guys all the same. They're doing some sort of a seismic survey up there for a new oilfield. They use the chopper to cart people and equipment around the bush, it's almost impenetrable up that way. They've bulldozed a road out to their camp from here as well, so they can drop supplies off periodically for their guys who are hacking their way through by hand. It'd be a damned nightmare, that job, way worse scrub than what we have here. Mountainous and thick as buggery." Rojer shudders at the thought of it, I guess, or the various demons invading his body.

I see cranes stretching out all over the place, loads continually moving from one location to another. In the heart of this now desecrated paradise, amongst the network of narrow muddy tracks, a web of scaffolding rises skywards, surrounding partially built structures. The shell of the new mini-refinery rises up before me against the backdrop of the wilderness, in stark contrast to the surrounding greenery. Masses of workers in hardhats and hi-vis clothing move about like an army of ants, standing out against the industrial backdrop. Pipelines meander around the site, in the end they'll connect different industrial processes. Enormous storage tanks, still under construction, loom up against the backdrop of dense greenery, sunlight gleaming off them. The entire area is punctuated by clusters of temporary buildings serving as offices and facilities for the workers. A mammoth accommodation camp is situated on another patch of bare earth further down near the river. Rojer tells me it can accommodate up to around 650 workers. Judging from what I can see so far from the workers on-site, the camp is probably close to full.

Notwithstanding this industrial intrusion, the jungle doesn't yield to it so easily. It's persistent, true nature itself, indignantly asserting itself against the invasion; new vines and creepers reach out and cling to the new steel structures and stored materials. Amongst all of this commotion, I'm introduced to the PT Indolian Assistant Site Manager Asler Nunas, a Brazilian engineer who looks a bit like the walking dead. He's recovering from a heavy bout of malaria, and he seriously looks like he is almost dead, or has been… or wants to be. The primary PT Indolian Project Manager Raymond Cook is also bedridden apparently, suffering from some other malady, maybe also malaria.

By comparison, my next 5 days conducting the threat assessment audit of the operations are initially mundane, somewhat fractious at various times, nonetheless pretty routine, until it isn't. The fractious component comes about from the Bulgarian contractor site manager Borislav something or other. The entire interaction with him was awkward, and that's being kind; so unlike me. Lying, recalcitrant and obnoxious are probably words more suited to describe the frequent encounters with both him and his Nigerian security henchmen. Threatening is another word readily coming to mind. Unfortunately, as the lead contractor, he's the boss of the entire project site here, so there's no getting away from dealing with him.

"Why Nigerian security guys?" I ask Rojer.

"They're the guys the contractors brought here from their last construction job in Nigeria evidently. Also, because they're neither Muslim nor Christian, it seems, the theory there is, they can move around within either of these belligerent communities without any hassles. After the violence in Bula the other day, all this is now kinda moot, I guess. Only Muslims left in the area," Rojer scowls, clearly not a fan of the Nigerians, I'm thinking.

Not surprisingly, nearly all of the aspects I'd been briefed on back in Australia about the audit focal points and the associated, often seemingly unrelated matters are exactly as were anticipated. The contract has a number of complications. Pick a number. Any number will work, it's so bad. Some – most really – of the bigger concerns are way beyond my remit and are going to require a higher-level forensic examination. The various aspects of the facility being built, the overall management team itself and the contractors involved all seem to be struggling to meet almost any of the required deliverables. One of the biggest failures in achieving those deliverables is the primary contractor themselves, BCC, the Balgary Construction Consortium, a mixture of Chinese, Korean and Balkan companies. They appear to be operating with a complete lack of transparency in their financial and compliance dealings, and I'm only looking at the most basic level. It has made it difficult to trace funds and to detect fraudulent activities. This muddiness fosters an environment conducive to wide-spread corruption. As I systematically work my way deeper into the mire of the audit action items with Asler, Rojer comes to see me early on day 5, at the same time as the helicopter again flies over in the distance, another heavy load slung underneath.

"Saleck has asked me to ask you if you wouldn't mind coming down to his village for a meeting with him and some of his senior people," Rojer murmurs conspiringly, seemingly not wanting Asler to hear the request, who's off to the side talking to some of the work crew.

"Why would I want to do that?" I ask quietly, maintaining the intrigue, casting a cursory glance at Asler to see if he's looking at me or if he overheard what we'd just spoken about. What the hell is all this secrecy concerning?

Rojer continues cautiously. "As I mentioned the other day, they've encountered some serious health problems with their kids down there. I'd like you to discuss this with him, as we both believe there is a direct health link with this bloody place."

"How can you connect his health issues down there with what is happening up here, this being an unrelated construction site?" I question.

"As I said, a direct health related link, regrettably, inadequate wastewater treatment and improper disposal of raw sewage from the constructor's camp. Come see me when you're finished here later today, and I'll explain," Rojer whispers, as I notice Asler walking back over towards us.

"All OK, Jim?" Asler keeps calling me Jim, regardless of what I say my name is. I just go with it.

"All good here," I reply, when in fact all is not all OK here… well, not inside my head, anyway. The secrecy Rojer just exhibited concerns me.

✦ ✦ ✦

I do in fact meet up with Rojer at a time he designates later in the afternoon. He suggests we go for a walk, away from anybody likely to overhear us, I guess. I reluctantly agree. He guides me down towards the riverbank.

"So Rojer, what was all the intrigue about this morning? Why does Saleck want to meet with me? You know his village is well outside of my threat assessment remit," I query.

"Yeah, well, fuck your audit remit, Kelly. You've no doubt already sussed out some of the rackets going on around this place, because there is no end of it. Saleck's issue is different. His is a humanitarian matter. His village draws all of their drinking, cooking and washing water from the river bend downstream, next to his village. Since the construction got underway, nearly a year ago now, people from his village have been getting ill, especially the kids. They've been getting severe dysentery, diarrhoea, fever, nausea, dehydration, stomach cramps, excruciating stomach pains, you name it," Rojer says, ticking off the ailments on his fingers.

"So how does this relate to the operations here?" I probe.

"Because the goddamned contracting team have an inadequate wastewater treatment system, which ultimately leads to improper disposal of raw sewage from the constructors' camp, like straight into the bloody river. That's why, dude." Rojer flings this at me as he spits out another mouthful of chewing tobacco slime. I just can't look at him doing this. It's such a disgusting practice.

"I've seen the treatment plant. It appears to be very proficient, well maintained and operated professionally. What do you see as the issue with it, Rojer?"

"The damn thing was only originally built for a 250–300 people camp, tops. Although its initial design was for much more. We have nearly 650 people living and working here at the moment, operating 24/7, working over the ablutions system at a hundred miles an hour. The wastewater treatment plant is massively under pressure trying to cope with the overload. When it begins backing up at a particular time of day, the raw waste is then automatically redirected straight into the river. You don't have to be a brain surgeon to work out where it goes from there. Straight downstream to the bend, where Saleck's village is. This is what the goddamned issue is," Rojer states angrily, lighting up a foul-smelling cigarette as he stares at me.

"So why do you believe I should get involved. You have your own environmental monitoring people here doing their regular assessments and audits, don't you? I'm meeting up with them tomorrow. Aren't they the best people to be dealing with this?" I offer.

"You won't be meeting with the lead advisor that's for sure. He won't be coming back from leave today. He's quit. Alleges he's been regularly threatened by the BCC security team pricks to stay away from the wastewater treatment plant. His two enviro offsiders are also refusing to go there. They've made it known the plant is a disaster area. They've suggested the limited bloody resources they have in place aren't up to standard. This is all about shortcuts from the very beginning, to save money, so this very same money can then go into the back pockets of the lead contractor management team." Rojer is building up a head of steam now I can tell by the irritation in his voice.

"You know this how?" I ask.

"Because I've been here since before the fucking construction launched. I argued my nuts off back during those early days about the plant being so obviously insufficient to support future requirements. They basically told me to 'piss off' and mind my own business, as BCC is in charge. I've done a bit of monitoring myself since then and confirmed my fears. Excess volume gets automatically overboarded, unfiltered, straight into the river. I've passed this information on to Saleck after their kids all started to get ill…" Rojer stops talking. He's staring back towards the accommodation camp. I follow his stare and observe one of the Nigerian BCC security guards stomping down towards us, furious for some reason by the look of him. He's bald and has some eerie sort of wrinkles happening with the skin on his head, like a testicle is my immediate thought.

"What do you want, Boarke?" Rojer asks irritably.

"What you doing here, Hoag? You know you must have permission to come here to this secure area. Why you down here, heh?" Combined with his accompanying facial expressions, his broad African broken English speech is loud, hostile and aggressive. It's a tone I instantly take umbrage to. It just grates on me.

I move in front of Rojer to meet the approaching bald security guard called Boarke, with my hand outstretched, to introduce myself. "Hi, I'm James Kelly, the corporate auditor," I say, in my best sugar-coated voice.

"Get out of my fucking way. I talking to Hoag," the bald security guard says in his broad accent, attempting to brush my hand away and push his way past me. It isn't a good attempt; unsuccessful nonetheless. I move across further to stand right in front of him to block his way. "Get out of my way. You also not have permission to be here in this secure area," he yells at me.

"I do not require anybody's permission to go or be anywhere. I have access authority to all and any areas I choose in order to conduct my corporate audit. What is your name?" I ask, although Rojer has already enlightened me. I put both my arms slightly out in front of me, in an attempt to protect my space and stem him advancing any further.

"Do not touch me, understand. Do not fucking touch me," Boarke bellows at me.

"I haven't touched you. You walked right into my open arms. You tried to enter into my personal space in a threatening manner. So I did not touch you or push you away." I say calmly, protesting the fact he walked into my partially extended arms, not me pushing into him.

"Best you just piss off, Boarke, before you overstep your authority yet again," Rojer deliberately goads the guard, no charm in his tone.

"Screw you, Hoag. You know you not allowed be here without permission man, so get out, now. Or I deal with you both. I call in the security team to arrest you," the man called Boarke screams at us yet again.

I'm getting the sense young Mr Boarke uses abusive yelling and swearing like Rojer uses the word 'fuck', every chance they can. Time for me to put an end to this ridiculous performance so we can all move on to other things today.

"Mr Boarke, by the authority vested in me from the Board of Directors of PT Indolian, I'm instructing you to leave this area right now. Should you choose not to comply, I'll call in the local police to have you arrested and permanently removed from the site. Am I making myself clear with my instruction, Mr Boarke?" I ask firmly. Bugger this guy. I'm not in the mood for taking any more of his aggression. I'm hoping my threat works, as I have no bloody idea if I have the authority to make the threat or to carry it out, anyway.

Boarke splutters and hisses, in utter shock, I think. "You fucking want me do what?" he screams in disbelief, as he moves towards my extended arms yet again, except in a much more threatening stance this time.

"It will not be a wise move, Mr Boarke, to disregard my request. Hey, though, let's find out, shall we? C'mon, let's see what happens," I say as I drop my arms. It's a challenge to him I'm pretty open to at this stage. I'm not expecting it to have the impact it does. Boarke's face just about explodes. I thought he was on the verge of having a stroke, on the spot. He looks at me and then at Rojer with an angry glare and then back at me. He about-turns, military style, stomping back towards the camp.

"I'm pretty certain that's not gonna be the end of things, is it, Rojer? Old testicle head will be back, yeah?" I ask, already knowing the answer.

Rojer sort of sniggers at my comment. "No, he's a loudmouth that one. We've had a number of run-ins, he and I. He can't seem to help himself. He's a walking talking fuck-up every day of the week. So yeah, he'll be back," Rojer claims.

"OK then, Rojer, please explain why we're down here in this supposedly secure area, causing all this ruckus?"

"Come with me, over to the edge here, Kelly. We gotta hurry, though," Rojer insists. I assume it's because he thinks Boarke will soon be back. "See this, Kelly?" He points to what looks like an 8-inch metal pipe protruding out slightly from the edge of the bank. It's dispensing what's appears to me to be a small stream of clear fresh water into the river.

"Yes, I see a pipe discharging clear water into the river. Why do you want me to see this?"

"That clear water you see is recycled. It's processed wastewater. It's pretty clean and benign now that it's treated. It's been through the system enough times and has been purified by a multi-step technology process called reverse osmosis. This process removes any contaminants, toxins, bacteria and other debris. It leaves just the clean water which we all use here. Any excess amounts are overboarded straight into the damn river every day, once the desired purity levels have been reached. Just watch," Rojer says, looking at his watch. "Wait for a bit. You'll see what I mean."

He looks again at his watch and then back towards the accommodation camp for Boarke to materialise with his other guards. Within probably 10–15 minutes, I notice the clear fresh water slow, and then increase, turning grey. I move a little closer to the bank to take some photos. The earlier slow flow then builds and turns brown for a few minutes. It then sputters momentarily, and all of a sudden, it comes to life and surges into a powerful deluge of raw, black sewage, discharging at a high rate, straight out into the river. I take several more photos of what I'm seeing, then I have to move. I can't stand next to it any longer, as the stench is incredibly bad.

"Why now, Rojer? Why has the clean water changed to this now, at this time of day?" I ask.

"Crew change from day shift to night shift. All of those day shift guys are shitting and showering their arses off all at once. That useless wastewater plant can't handle the instant and massive increase of ablutions." Rojer stares angrily at me. "It will settle down again later in the evening back to clean water. This whole debacle you're looking at now, well, it begins all over again at the next shift change in the morning," Rojer says loudly, staring at the foul black mess discharging into the river, then looks back at me.

"I want you to get your bloody corporate maggot mind around this, Kelly. This is a twice-daily episode. Do you still not see why Saleck wants to meet with you?"

I'm gradually getting used to Rojer's aggressive manner. I note it's not actually directed at me. Or at least, I don't think so. It feels as if it's aimed at matters out of his control.

"I've said before, Rojer, you don't get to talk to me like that. I'll not say it again." I glare deep into Rojer's eyes in a threatening manner. It seems to have some sort of effect at least. Christ only knows what I'll do if he does decide to talk to me like it again. "OK, let's go see Saleck then. You organise it. I'll be available. It's important you be aware, though, Rojer, this is still way outside of any scope of work the board has sent me to look at. So, just knowing about this matter or getting Saleck's point of view on it doesn't mean to say it can or will change anything. Just be aware of this, OK?" I advise, knowing full well if I'm a board member and became aware of it, I'd be worried sick that Saleck's village will sue PT Indolian for millions due to the sustained and reckless pollution of his village by this. I'd secondly be concerned about where the hell the money went for the correct establishment of the original size wastewater plant and who's going to be required to pay it back.

Rojer organises for us to meet with Saleck and his people early in the morning of day 6. I try to arrange for Asler Nunas and the boss Raymond Cook to come along with us, which I thought would have been a no-brainer. Asler, well, he begged off due to his workload… really? Raymond Cook is still in bed ill I'm told, although I'd seen him walking around the construction site chatting to people earlier in the day. Both of the environmental assistants also begged off for obscure reasons. This seems very suspicious to me. Rojer agreed.

Early next morning, I greet Rojer at his 4WD truck in the car park. I'm ready to embark on the short journey overland to Saleck's village. However, all does not seem well with Rojer though. He's still his usual grumpy, solemn, charming self, except he also has a hell of a nice bright new black eye and another shiny bruise on the right side of his face now to add to his enchanting demeanour.

"Anything exciting happen I should know about, Rojer?" I ask, pointing to his massive black eye. I also note his gun is securely in place in the door holster.

"Nah, nothing I can't handle Kelly. Let's get going," Rojer growls, starting up the truck. The background humdrum of construction activities of the new day is already well in full swing. Shift change has been about two hours ago. Just as we begin to drive out of the car park area, Rojer's phone rings. I can see he's tempted not to take the call. Nonetheless, I urge him to take it anyway. He stops the truck, steps outside and walks around in circles, listening to whoever it is on the other end. Looking at me once, he nods and then seems to hang up without saying more than a few words. He glumly walks back to the truck.

"Change of plan. That was Saleck. It appears our Senior Environmental Advisor Andri hasn't quit. He's been found dead in his home last night, cause unknown at this stage. Saleck was on his way over here earlier this morning to discuss it with Raymond. However, the BCC contractor security pricks stopped him. They'd set up a temporary roadblock halfway between here and his village, ordering him to turn around and go back. What the bloody hell are those mongrel Nigerians doing creating a security checkpoint in the middle of the fucking wilderness, for Christ's sake?"

I think I understood. It was actually meant for us, I reckon. "Two things I'd like to ask you, Rojer. Firstly, tell me about the eye." I'm pretty sure I'm way ahead of him on what's likely to be unravelling at the moment. Given what I've already observed about corrupt kickbacks, inflated invoices and poor contractor management practices with this venture, and the primary contractor themselves, threats and intimidation are the next natural and logical currency to come into play.

"I got whacked on the side of my head last night by someone. I reckon it was that prick Boarke, although I didn't clearly see who it was. I'd been on my way over to see Cooky, you know…

Raymond? I'd heard he was crook again. As I was walking through the carpark in the dark, some arsehole up and whacked me one from behind with a hunk of wood… or something, I dunno. I was out to it for a bit, I think. Came to when one of our own security guys found me," Rojer moans as he rubs the side of his swollen head and face, clearly not pleased with what has transpired. "What's the other bloody thing you want to know, Kelly?"

"Who found the Environmental Advisor dead in his home last night?" I can see a bit of a pattern developing with all these occurrences, none of it looking good for either Rojer or myself.

"I don't know. I guess maybe it was Saleck or one of his people. Andri was advising Saleck on the level of contaminants found in the polluted waste water samples. That's where Saleck had been before we met up with him at the flooded river crossing the other day. Why do you ask?" Rojer inquires solemnly. He'd already answered my question. Clearly, the senior environment guy has been doing tests for Saleck to determine culpability, which exposes him to multiple levels of reprisal by the consortium if they found out. It undoubtedly appears they have.

"Because I'm getting the impression there's a bit of an unhealthy pattern building here. It's mainly focused around the waste plant, and it always seems to include the security guys. Someone is trying to prevent any scrutiny taking place of the plant. The thing bothering me a bit is it's not sitting on the radar of the audit I'm meant to be doing," I say. "Do you think Andri was murdered?"

"Yes," Rojer replies simply.

I dial up RJ on my satellite phone. We discuss everything that's happened over night and this morning, at least everything that's occurred since I gave her a heads-up late last night after witnessing the over boarding of the raw waste. RJ is not surprised. Irritated, just like me. In no way shocked, however.

"OK, after our chat last night, I had a bit of a gut feeling things might go a little pear-shaped. I contacted the General Manager at that Sasol seismic camp you mentioned. You're right, it's not far from you guys at all. Anyway, his name is Johannes

Du Preez. Nevertheless, if anything gets out of hand, he's quite prepared for you to evacuate to his camp. You know how to get there, I guess?"

"No. However, Rojer has mentioned it. He'll know."

"Well, my advice then is if anything does in fact get out of hand, and respectfully James, it sounds to me like it's already on a bit of a roll, then boot scoot to Bula, and I'll try to get you a charter flight. Or go to see Du Preez at the Sasol camp. In the meantime, I'll wise up the PT Indolian board members again about what's happening out there. Might be time for them to bring in the local police and Indolian's own security people. Leave that with me. Talk soon. Take care please, James," RJ says genuinely as she hangs up.

"You might have to escort me back to Bula. My guys are going to try and arrange a charter flight out of here. Something very peculiar is developing here, Rojer, don't you think?"

"Yeah, I do, except it's not simply developing; it's been working its arse off around here for quite a while, as you've no doubt picked up yourself with your audit. The culture within BCC is beyond toxic. It's bloody venomous." Rojer gives me one of his jaundiced-eyed looks, maybe a bit softer this time, I think. Perhaps we're both getting more aligned now, maybe on the same team for a change… or for the time being at least? "This whole goddamned place is utterly compromised by the way they operate. Every possible shortcut is made with all aspects of the plant construction. Someone is making a bucketful of money on the side with this operation, and it's not me, that's for bloody sure. OK then, you want to go back to Bula? When do you want to go… today, now?" Rojer queries with raised eyebrows.

"Yeah, I'll go pick up my things from my room. Then let's get the hell out of here to Bula. I'll get RJ to organise the charter. You might want to consider coming out with me, Rojer?" I suggest, as I exit the truck and begin to walk back to my room.

"Now, there's a can of screwed up worms I really don't want to have to consider just yet. On the other hand, you might be on the bloody money there," Rojer yells at me, gracefully spitting out another wad of black chewing tobacco slime.

We drive out of the PT Indolian car park slowly, towards the Bula main road again, talking generally about the multitude of concerns we both have with what is going on here. As we drive around the outer perimeter ring road of the construction site, two BCC security trucks have created a road block across the only road leading to Bula. Rojer immediately stops our truck, a long way back from the roadblock.

"Well now, no real big shock there, I guess?" he sneers sarcastically, withdrawing the pistol from the door holster, checks its load and then reinserts it back into the holster. Then he checks the box of bullets in the central armrest storage box. "What is a surprise for me, though, is all three of those pricks down there are armed with automatic assault rifles. Now, that's unusual around here." Rojer glances over at me and smiles. He seems to actually be enjoying this encounter for some unusual reason. "Looks like the Sasol camp is the go now then, heh? What do ya think, Kelly?"

I agree, coldly. I still just don't know how the hell we've got to this extreme point so quickly. Nothing at all pragmatic can possibly come out of this for BCC by them conducting themselves like this, or at least for their security guys to carry on like this. Nothing satisfactory for us either.

"Let's do it, then. Where is this track leading to the Sasol camp?" I inquire, assuming it's off in some obscure direction somewhere difficult to get to.

"Well, therein lies a small bloody issue for us. No big thing, nothing we can't deal with at the end of the day. Nevertheless, it is still a fucking problem. See the mongrel track off to the left of those pricks?" Rojer points to a small, cleared area, directly behind and slightly off to the side of the road block. A tall red post stands proud with a number of coloured ribbons attached, flapping in the breeze. "That, Kelly, is the beginning of the dead straight seismic shot line. It also serves as a transit track between us and Sasol. These bastards are making sure we don't have many options left open to us."

"What the bloody hell is a 'dead straight seismic shot line'?" I ask seriously.

Rojer explains how a major feature of initial oil and gas exploration is the seismic work, which requires seismic lines or what they call shot lines. They're narrow, bulldozed corridors used to transport and deploy geophysical survey testing equipment. The lines vary subject to the terrain, but they're commonly about 10–15 feet wide, sometimes wider. It traverses whatever is in front of it, in a straight line – forests, tundra, hilly lands or whatever else gets in the way, as he explains it. They run in straight lines for the entire length of the exploration permit area. Knowing this does absolutely nothing positive for my self-confidence.

I believe this single act by the BCC guards has upped the threat factor towards us tenfold, or maybe just towards me immeasurably. By my estimate, we now face a very serious risk of harm by these guys. I still cannot believe it's purely because I've uncovered evidence of some minor level corruption and noncompliance infractions. There is something else entirely going on here. Way beyond screwed-up contracts, kickbacks or heavy pollution from an inferior wastewater treatment plant.

"So Rojer, how much are we stuffed here? Do we have a master plan hanging around in your back pocket?" I ask uneasily, staring at the roadblock in front of us and the men with guns.

"Well, Kelly, it all depends on if you want to be the royal fucker, or the right royal fuckee? My guess is you're not the surrendering type, right?" Rojer says, smiling sickly at me again.

Yep, there's a plan lying in wait around here somewhere. "Correct. Not my thing to do that, if possible. So, tell me then, what's the deal?" I probe, full well thinking his plan is to simply barge his way right around the edge of the roadblock, all guns blazing in order to reach the Sasol seismic line.

"Screw 'em. Let's just quietly go back to camp, OK? To them, it'll look like we've run out of options and given up. At the back of the camp kitchen area though, there's a scrap of a track which leads to the rubbish dump. Right next to it is a grassed-over track most people don't know about. It'll take us past some light brush where the original oil wells were drilled around here years ago. From there, though, we might have to do a bit of old-fashioned cross-bloody-country bush-bashing our way through to the Sasol shot line. You up for it, Kelly?" Rojer asks, as he puts the truck into reverse, backing it around slowly.

"Yep, right now, I'm pretty much up for anything, I guess. Let's do whatever it is you think might work for us. I've gotta tell ya though, Rojer, I'd be way more comfortable if I have one of those things as well," I say, pointing to his gun in the door holster.

"Check under your seat," is all he says as he begins driving forward, back to camp.

Under my seat, I do indeed find a duplicate gun to what Rojer has in his fancy door holster. I pull it out, inspect the weapon and the load, then look across at Rojer with a query on my face.

"It's my spare. Thought it might come in handy," he utters, again blessing me with one of his sallow skinned smiles. I wonder how long it's been there. Was it under here during the fateful trip from Bula?

We leisurely drive into and around the back of the PT Indolian camp and past the kitchen, turning left to continue down a narrow-rutted track to the camp rubbish dump. Tree branches and heavy foliage scrape violently down both sides and under the truck. It doesn't feel or sound like any vehicle of our size has been along this way for a very long time. Rojer stops the truck, gets out and lifts a couple of old cut logs lying next to the track, drags them around to the back of the truck and drops them across the track in amongst the high weeds and foliage. Trying to create a very temporary barrier, I guess.

Whilst he's doing this, I call RJ to update her on the latest bizarre change in our circumstances. Like me, she's pretty troubled by how things have escalated, and so quickly, for no apparent reason, or at least no obvious motive to us. Yeah, we know there are various layers of corruption in play. On the other hand, though, I certainly didn't think it's enough at this stage to create the scenario we're currently facing.

She advises, "PT Indolian board members have authorised the activation of the Indolian private security team, who I believe are already in Ambon on their way to site. They will in turn notify the police and the local army commander. What happens from there, James, is anybody's guess. I'll still do some more heavy pushing and shoving with them to see how quickly we can get all of this moving. I'll also try and determine what options are available to us to balance this out again, although I'm not expecting there will be anything constructive, or prompt."

Rojer and I continue on our way, slowly bouncing and pitching through overgrown foliage to the rubbish dump, which is an interesting site all by itself. A massive hole has been bulldozed into the ground with mounds of rubbish underneath a variety of wire mesh covers in the hole. Some of the mounds are on fire, or at least smouldering now from earlier having been on fire.

"The mesh is to keep the critters out, especially those bloody monkeys, the little pricks. They get into the rubbish and have a hell of a party with it, dragging scraps around everywhere. The arseholes pinched one of the mesh covers once. We've never been able to find it again since," Rojer says, laughing, at the antics of the monkeys, I suppose.

"OK, Kelly, we're now going to deviate a tad to one of the original oil wells, so hang onto your hat," Rojer says, still laughing as we take off.

We drive, at speed, straight up and over the top of the steep rubbish tip dirt bank and down the backside onto a narrower track than the one we'd just been on. More ferocious scraping and scratching, bouncing and turbulent riding through masses of foliage, suddenly landing onto a reasonable sort of track, almost like a bloody road. I look over at Rojer, and he's laughing his head off again, seemingly enjoying this part of our little journey. I probably would too, if there wasn't such a deadly legacy attached to it.

"Gotta leave some wonderment in the box for ya, Kelly. The locals use this road here to milk a few old oilwells out this way, and from the natural oil seeps. Bit of a marvel, that one. The seeps discharge the light crude oil as it bubbles straight up from deep in the earth onto the ground surface around here. It's quite the sight, not the spectacle you might be imagining. Nonetheless, it's a scene you won't forget in a hurry." Rojer laughs as he speeds up the truck on the slightly smoother track.

We round a sharp bend, and right in front of us is an old car that looks like it's been cut down to just the windscreen and the driver's seat. Everything seems to be swathed in the thick black oil, including the ground all around the car. We slow down momentarily as we're about to pass. There's a number of four-gallon drums tied to this 'car' with no lids on them, all filled to overflowing with the soupy black crude oil.

"See those two locals over there?" Rojer asks, pointing to the two young guys covered in oil themselves. "Well, they're standing in the centre of an actual oil seepage pit itself, right in the midst of all that oil bubbling up with no pumps or pressure to assist. Can ya get your mind around that, Kelly? They're been doing it for years." Rojer stops the truck for me to have a closer look.

The men are up to their knees in thick black bubbling oil mud, totally surrounded by it. He's right, though – it's a scene I won't forget in a hurry. There's thick black oil everywhere, spread all over the place. It's a minor environmental catastrophe all by itself, probably well beyond reclamation.

"They do this daily, using the seepage pit like it's some sort of prehistoric service station. He's scooping up the thin surface crude over there with the pail, as it bubbles to the top, straight out of the ground. He then transfers it to their open top drums in the buggy there. They get about a dozen or so drums a day, a barrel or more of oil. Quite lucrative and innovative, don't you think?" Rojer drives off again slowly, tooting his horn and waving to the two guys standing in the thick black oil mud. They both wave back with their black arms dripping in oil.

"Yeah, I guess. A dozen or so of those drums, that's about what, 40 or 50 gallons a day, yeah? Or a barrel a day? In today's market, that's about US$ 60–70 a day per barrel, that right Rojer?

Bloody hell, that's around US$25,000 a year, cash. It has to be pretty good income for these guys?" I query, unsure of my maths on this subject.

"Yeah, something like it. Currently, light crude oil is about US$75 a barrel, so they're doing OK, considering the average local worker around here makes way less than that a week. So yeah, bloody hard work, although extremely beneficial. Mind you, it's way more beneficial when the price of oil goes through the damn roof to $100 plus a barrel." Rojer laughs, then speeds up the truck, still on the reasonably good track weaving around the various natural oil seeps. We round another bunch of low shrubby trees, and a similar scenario plays out with yet another group of locals. These are much older men though. At this site, there's some sort of low metal structure sticking out of the ground, which is where they're syphoning oil from.

"What's the deal here, Rojer? What the hell is that metal post sticking up out of the ground, the thing covered in oil?" I ask, staring at the short skeleton-like structure next to the guys with the buckets, who are once again standing in yet another environmentally unfriendly patch of black oil.

"That's all that is left of the very original oil wellhead. I think they call that piece the conductor pipe or conductor head. Buggered if I know, something like that. Drilled about 30–40 something years ago, I reckon. It's been long abandoned by the oil company that drilled it, so these guys at some stage, unbolted all of the heavy-duty steel wellhead structure and all of its associated piping and equipment, sold it off for scrap metal. Made a killing. Again, pretty innovative, don't ya think?" Rojer is clearly pleased with the conduct of the locals. I predict he has some sort of financial involvement in all this innovation and productivity. Good on him if he has. This is way beyond my corporate scope of interest.

"So then Kelly, you ready to fuck some things up around here, now? We'll soon get to the end of these locally maintained tracks, and then we'll have to bush bash a bit west across country towards the Sasol shot line. I've got no idea what it's likely to entail. However, by now, those cocksucking security guys will be beside themselves trying to find us. Nothing is going to be easy with any of this though, you got me?" Rojer demands, with his sour pallor facial expression.

"Yeah, well, no real choice in the matter now, Rojer, is there? Let's go 'fuck some things up', as you delicately put it, whatever that might involve." I'm nowhere near as enthused as I probably sound. Once again, I'm quite literally terrorising myself with fear. Only consolation, I have a gun now. I don't want one. However, I do have one just in case. As the old saying goes, better to have a gun and not need it than to need a gun and not have one.

God only knows why, but we hit the low undergrowth at an insanely fast pace. Instantly fully immersed, it's a rowdy encounter, even though the vegetation density is reasonably light initially. The terrain features, on the other hand, are actually harder to determine, although it's definitely not flat, that much I can tell. The high revving of the truck engine is pronounced in the hollowness of the thinner foliage, more so when we try to navigate the denser vegetation in four-wheel drive. As we continue amid the undergrowth, I can hear the sounds of branches and shrubs being crushed or snapping underneath and in front of us. The soundscape is actually quite dynamic, periodically changing as we navigate different types of vegetation and routes. Low-hanging branches and thick vegetation scrape against the roof, sides and under the truck, tearing at the panels, causing excruciating scratching sounds, a bit like the fingernails on a blackboard. I occasionally hear the sound of splashing water as the truck bounces and charges over wet, muddy patches, tires spinning intermittently, protesting whilst trying to get some sort of grip in the intensely slippery ground. We periodically stumble upon extremely rough surfaces, like a small creek bed that refuses to allow us to go any further in this direction. It takes us considerable time and some heavy winch work to manoeuvre ourselves out of this situation, losing a couple of valuable hours in the process to the point where it's now getting darker, making it more difficult to find our way around the dense wilderness any longer.

"Well, that's buggered things up a bit then. Not worth trying to continue any further now. We'll have to camp here overnight in this goddamned place."

We finally get ourselves untangled from the vines draped around the edges of the creek bed and the front end of the truck.

"You gonna be OK with this, Kelly? It always gets a little daunting, so you'll need to put your big boy pants on tonight. No doubt there'll be a few challenges with it. Nothing we can't handle, right?" Rojer asks, it sounds sarcastic to me.

"Yeah, no big deal. We good for a small fire way out here? Unlikely anybody will spot us this far into the bush, yeah? As in the BCC pricks, I mean?" I ask.

"Screw that, Kelly. Let's light up a bloody great big bastard. Help scare off any critters, keep us warm in the early morning chill and try to counteract the bugs from eating us alive overnight."

Attempting to set up any sort of a camp as the night quickly descends on us brings with it an unnerving feeling. The tree canopy overhead soon blocks out any of the light the moon might shed, as well as any starlight later in the night. The discord of intensifying wilderness noises cloaks us in a multitude of unfamiliar sounds, haunting calls of the nocturnal creatures and an unbelievable assemblage of bugs. Whilst collecting our wood for the fire, the rustling of unseen creatures comes to life amongst the murkier foliage. Darkness amplifies the feeling of isolation, magnifying every shadow, creating an atmosphere of unease, until the fire takes off, which is awhile, as much of the wood is still mostly damp regardless of it having been dead forever and a day. When Rojer says a big fire, bloody hell, he's talking the real deal… immense, starting it in the fractured top of a stump and root system of a huge fallen tree, aiding it with a bit of diesel from the truck. The outer perimeter visibility diminishes rapidly, leaving us to rely on the flickering glow of the massive crackling fire to help navigate our immediate surroundings.

Every movement we make is accompanied by an endless rustling of animal life in the undergrowth, heightening my senses and keeping me on edge periodically. I continually check the outer gloominess for any signs of danger or potential threats. The air is thick with humidity and smoke, clinging to our skin and saturating our clothes, welcoming swarms of insects in to attack us incessantly, testing our patience and resolve, well mine at least. As the night wears on, fatigue sets in for me, weighing heavy on my eyelids as I struggle to maintain vigilance against the encroaching wilderness. Time seems to stretch itself out, each hour dragging by as I sleep fitfully. Yet, amidst the uncertainty and adversity, there is a primal beauty to be found in the heart of the night-time jungle, a sense of awe and fear of the untamed wilderness and any lurking predators that might surround us.

Spending the night in here demands more than just physical resilience of me; it requires a deep reservoir of inner strength and willpower. It's a test of my character, I guess, an ordeal where fear and uncertainty must be confronted regardless, because no one knows we're here. During the sporadic moments when I stir, I look for the first light of a false dawn to break through the dense canopy. Finally, in time as it does so, the meagre light of daybreak pierces the blackness, casting long, thin silhouettes over the thick foliage floor. We slowly emerge from the darkness and early morning chill of the day, weary as buggery and bitten all to hell and back by insects.

With no food to nourish us, we begin our trek once again when we have enough daylight to assist us with our navigation. My biggest fear is that the multitude of daunting creaks and groans coming from the suspension and chassis will ultimately bring an early dead end to our journey, as the truck tries to absorb the impacts of the challenging territory. The poor old bloody engine revs excessively as Rojer tries to accelerate against the resistance from the thick vegetation. Loud grinding sounds come from the gearbox whilst we try to traverse the steeper, more irregular, rocky terrain.

This is just total bloody madness, I'm thinking.

Whatever cargo or equipment is in the back of the truck rattles and bangs, items shift and bounce around violently during our cross-country excursion. A stench of hot oil from the engine and gearbox overheating is now periodically becoming noticeable. We stumble over and into random obstacles along the way – rocky outcrops concealed by foliage and fallen tree trunks hidden in the lush undergrowth. The truck roars in agony above the thudding and bumping until we come to an abrupt, crashing halt. Rojer backs us up a little once again, then tries to find a way out and around whatever hindrance blocks our way this time. He coerces the truck on our way again, back over the scrubland towards what Rojer's compass tells us should be towards the seismic shot line. Not far now, he lies to me.

Climbing ever so slowly up what I figure is a modest elevation in the forest floor, Rojer assures me it will provide us with a clear view of the shot line from the top. His skills have got us this far, I guess, prompting me to cut him some slack and trust he is right. However, a minor correction is required in his calculations. We can indeed see a brief glimpse of the bulldozed shot line in the distance momentarily from the top of a small rise. Unfortunately, the minor correction part of the journey merges with us at this very point. As we crest this seemingly small rise, at a reasonably high revving pace, the other side of it – to our collective horror – presents as a sheer, incredibly steep, foliage covered rocky overhang. We encounter this at an unreasonable speed, full momentum by now, actually. Rojer reacts swiftly, just not fast enough to prevent us peaking and then rapidly entering into an express descent. The motion and weight of our truck carry us slowly over the precipice. An ominous feeling settles in my gut. I'm pretty bloody certain this isn't going to end well, for us – or the truck.

The initial descent feels a little like it's in slow motion, filled with disturbing sounds of breaking branches, crushing metal and shattering glass. The truck slowly rolls and bounces down the steep incline, creating a chaotic, destructive symphony along with the occasional roar of the engine and my mouth. A sudden violent impact tosses me around inside the cabin, regardless of having my seatbelt on. Rojer's fate is of little concern to me amid this mayhem. He's on his own as far as I'm bloody concerned. During brief moments of free fall between impacts, the periodic weightlessness adds to my terror. Desperately clinging to anything stable, I try unsuccessfully to anticipate and brace for each jarring collision. This painful descent has beaten the hell out of my earlier fear brought on by the threats from the BCC security guys. The outside view, from inside the bucking and lurching truck cabin, is a frenzied kaleidoscope of all manner of flying objects and breaking, airborne glass. Rapid changes in our orientation frequently blur the scene as we continue to tumble uncontrollably downward, our momentum ominously picking up pace. The realization of our dire situation hits me abruptly – we're right royally screwed, right here, right now. All of a sudden, we crash to a brutal stop in a painfully dead standstill. The truck on its side, pointing downhill on Rojer's side. He's moaning, louder now as my body gradually slides down to rest on top of him. At least he's alive still. There's got to be some sort of a bonus in that somewhere.

"You okay, Rojer?" I inquire cautiously, conducting my own self assessment of potential bodily or spiritual damage.

"Yeah, sort of. Well, then… that's all a wee bit untidy, isn't it? How're you holding up there, Kelly? Still in one piece?" Rojer responds, a strong hint of pain evident in his voice.

"Yeah, still sort of together, I guess. I haven't enjoyed this much excitement for years. I'm pretty bloody sure there's a lesson in here for us somewhere, just as I'm equally sure I don't know what it is… yet. I do know one thing, it involves pain. Probably lots of it," I reply, trying to slowly work out which parts of my body are generating that pain.

"Yeah, well, ya reckon you can get the fuck off me neck Kelly, before you choke me to death, ya prick?" Rojer gasps at me.

After a sustained period of overly painful exertion, grunting, groaning and moaning, accompanied with significant profanity, we somehow escape the battered cabin. Collapsing now, heavily battered and bruised, up against one of the boulders the mangled truck is now resting against. Having tested our physical elements, miraculously, we've both managed somehow to have endured our crash with no apparent major bones broken. Many cuts, bruises and abrasions all the same, accompanied by one possibly punctured or collapsed lung for Rojer to go with his black eye. I seem to have survived reasonably well, considering. Our next move is to take stock of whatever we're likely to want to be able to continue our luxury journey on foot. My backpack of personal items, mobile phones, satellite phone, water, first aid kit, a machete, a small axe. The two guns and ammunition are the key items. Rojer advises even though there is no food in the truck, he thinks we're only about 10 km from the Sasol camp where there will be food. How he determines this is anybody's guess. Who knows, or really cares, at this point in time. We eventually stagger off, painfully, slowly down amongst the much thicker undergrowth generally towards the shot line, both in excruciating agony.

It takes us a lot longer than anticipated to tentatively hack our way out of the denser vegetation in order to rest up near the shot line – more than three hot, muggy hours, which adds its toll on us, primarily because we're both so bruised and beaten up by our recent crash adventure. All our new ailments are vying for immediate care and attention whilst we lurch our way down and out of the sweltering tropical wilderness. Once we finally, gratefully, reach bushes close to the shot line, we collapse under the canopy of a tree, a juvenile Kapok tree, Rojer tells me. Yeah, whatever.

"So, Kelly, fine fucking mess you've got us into now, isn't it?" Rojer says, panting and wincing with pain at every movement.

"Why me, arsehole?" I'm indignant at his comment, not sure if he's taking the piss, or he's serious with it. I'm guessing he's earnest all the same. "I'm here just doing a pretty routine bloody audit, Hoag. You're the idiots who have allowed this rampant epidemic of corruption to flourish. Why the hell you guys haven't knocked these matters on the head that you already knew about is beyond me. Right there, is what's kicked all this debacle off, Hoag. Too many bloody red flags popping up all over the goddamned place like genital warts. I suspect too many for your greedy arse-licking bosses in Jakarta and Sydney to ignore. Seriously, whatever were you guys actually thinking was likely to happen by just letting all this fester under your noses?"

I'm already angry at the stupidity and ignorance these guys have displayed back at the site. "It had nowhere else to go, Hoag, except to raise all sorts of complications for everyone involved. Nowhere! You guys have well and truly screwed this whole thing up. Now I have to try and unscrew it! Why should that be my 'fine goddamned mess' to fix, hey?" I know, I'm getting a little agitated here now. Really, though?

"Listen Kelly, historically, all these types of shortfalls usually sort themselves out organically, you know what I mean? As we progressively move our way through the various phases of the job proper, we can ordinarily rectify any of the screwed-up complications as they periodically arise, except too bloody many have gotten away from us on this venture, and too early." Rojer tries to make a lame excuse for the poor Indolian compliance performance. His history lesson justification doesn't sit at all well with me.

"There are many types of history, Rojer – the type you read about, the type you dream about and the type you live and are actually part of. That's what we have here, and generally, it's the one that'll screw with you the most, every bloody day of the week," I reply.

We don't have time to continue our stimulating conversation, as we – or actually I – hear a truck coming down the shot line at a slow pace.

"That hasn't taken long, eh? Miraculously rescued," I say, laughing as I begin to agonisingly try and stand up to stumble out onto the shot line to flag it down.

"Stop. Get back down. Now! At the back of the foliage here. Hurry," Rojer orders softly, in near panic. "It's going too slow. I don't think it's the seismic guys, because they drive like bloody maniacs. I reckon it's those BCC security pricks."

I don't want to capitulate, although I do for whatever reason; awkwardly. We both lay down full length in the thick foliage under the back of the Kapok tree, now well hidden from anybody likely to be viewing from the shot line. "I doubt they'll be able to see the truck from down here, at least. I reckon it's pretty well covered by all the trees and crap we dragged down with us," he whispers.

It took a few minutes to regrettably realise, it actually is one of the BCC security trucks. There's a driver alone in the front and in the back utility tray are two guards standing up, armed with assault rifles. One is Boarke. He's searching for us with a pair of binoculars. I look across at Rojer to acknowledge his foresight on this matter, only his face is buried in the foliage. He looks in a lot of pain. Maybe the rib into his lung is giving him more grief than he's letting on. I'll have to keep an eye on him.

"You OK, Rojer?" I ask quietly, as we hear the BCC security truck slowly drive, rattle and squeak past us. We appear unobserved, for now anyway, it would seem. Rojer hasn't moved since we hid in amongst the foliage. "Hey Rojer, you OK, bloke?" I whisper again.

"No, not so good. I'm struggling to get my breath," he stutters painfully, trying to disguise a deep cough from the BCC guys hearing it. The cough increases after taking, or attempting to take, a deep breath. "I got a hell of a lot of chest pain and fuck-all breath," he says, coughing with difficulty.

I notice the colour of his skin is changing from his standard sickly yellow to an even worse looking pale colour, almost grey. This can't be good. I check his pulse to see how his heart is handling things. It's pounding away at too fast a rate. I don't actually know what this means, except if I combine it with the chest pain, shortness of breath and the now pale skin, I definitely know it can't be positive. I don't believe any of these symptoms are likely to be favourable for his longevity whilst we're here hiding in the grass, not without medical attention anyway.

I get out the satellite phone and try to call up RJ. For whatever reason, it takes an interminable amount of time for the phone to search for, find and then connect to a satellite. Once it connects, though, RJ answers surprisingly quickly. I update her on our little venture and its untimely and painful demise. I ask her to try to arrange for Sasol to maybe come to our rescue and to bring a medic to look at Rojer.

"I doubt that's likely to happen in the short term, James. I just spoke to Du Preez about 30 minutes ago to see if he'd heard from you. He advises they are tied up at the moment with a major incident of their own out in the bush somewhere. Seems a tree they'd been clearing for their seismic work has fallen on a couple of their workers, crushing them both. I get the feeling it's all hands on deck at the moment out there, trying to rescue these two guys and save their lives," RJ informs, with a heavy tone of voice.

"Righto, OK then I'll see what I can organise from this end. Gotta go. The BCC guys are coming back." I shut the call down abruptly as I duck down deeper into the foliage to watch the security truck turning around again further up on the shot line, ready to come back past us.

"No help coming from Sasol, Rojer. Regardless, I gotta get someone to have a look at your injuries. I'm going to hand ourselves into these BCC…" I don't get to finish.

"Don't you dare think about doing that you, dickhead. They ain't got those assault rifles to make it easier to find us. They've got them so that it's easier to kill us at long range, for fuck's sake. There isn't any giving up to these pricks, Kelly, just dying by them. Jesus Christ, what an idiot." I'm not sure if he's calling me that or himself. It hardly matters, I suppose. He's coughing up quite a lot of blood out of his mouth, suggesting to me his lung damage is far more severe than he's letting on.

The BCC truck stops about 50 metres down the road from us, which does absolutely nothing for my nervous system, because I'm assuming they've maybe spotted us or our truck up above us on the cliff. All three of the guards get out onto the track to take a pee. Boarke talks on the radio, whilst the other two turn to watch a huge seismic helicopter creeping slowly up over the top of the trees. It's massive. It has two sets of rotors, one above the other, a monster of a thing, and loud. It's struggling to lift a large cargo load on a long line. All three guards are now standing next to the truck to watch as the helicopter hovers, slowly lowering the huge load down into a semi-cleared area.

"Lazy pricks have left their rifles in the truck Kelly. Stupid dumb arses," Rojer groans painfully. "Now's your chance. Use both those guns and go take their truck off 'em. If they get in the way, then knock 'em off. Go on, fuck ya!" Rojer insists harshly, blood oozing from his mouth.

Bloody hell, I haven't done anything as stupid and reckless as this since my days back in Vietnam. Bugger it all the same, time to do something. I painfully and as quietly as possible, get up out of the foliage, both guns in my hands, as I soundlessly stagger out onto the side of the shot line and gradually make my way down towards the BCC truck. I have both guns pointing at them, my arse quivering, and my heart beating itself to bits, all of my pain points letting me know they are displeased. I probably don't have to make the effort to be all that quiet, as it turns out. The rotor noise and the downwash of the blades on the undergrowth under the huge helicopter cover my approach. None of the guys have noticed me by the time I reach the side of the truck.

Once there and I've convinced myself they can't hear me, I reach over into the tray and lift both of the assault rifles out carefully. I then bend into the open window of the cabin and take the driver's assault rifle from there as well as his radio, all while the guards seem to be utterly mesmerised by the huge helicopter readying to drop its load. As the load is released, the helicopter begins to lift up quickly and gradually manoeuvre away. It's almost as if the pilot can see what's about to happen and doesn't want any part of it. As the helicopter slowly departs, it thrashes up all the loose ground debris into a small wind-storm under it. The guards quickly turn back towards the truck to protect their faces from the airborne barrage, only to find me standing there with both guns pointing at them.

In this singular, most extraordinary moment of their awareness, all eyes widen with a blend of horror and disbelief. Colour literally drains from their dark faces, leaving a stunned, almost pale look of astonishment. A couple of them take a sharp breath which catches in their throat. The third guy, Boarke, he's quickly turning from shock to anger in a heartbeat. Muscles around his eyes tense up, creating furrows of deep angry lines to a sudden storm of emotion. I can tell he knows he's in deep trouble, the irrecoverable sort he doesn't want to be in, because it's basically terminal for his career at BCC. It's like watching a volcano slowly building up to a spectacular eruption, one I know I'm going to have to shut down quickly.

His eyebrows furrow into a dangerous kind of extreme anger and torment. He's desperately trying to grapple with his misfortune, jaw clenched, teeth grinding in response to this unexpected outcome. I know the feeling. It's subconscious adrenaline surging through his brain. Boarke is beyond angry now. I can tell from his explosive expression. He makes a reckless move for his rifle in the tray, quickly realising it isn't there. His next move is to dive around the back of the truck to attack me from there. I anticipated this, and as much as I don't really want to, he just leaves me with no choice. I shoot him in the shoulder, then – to hell with it – I shoot him again when he doesn't stop fast enough. When he finally drops to the ground screaming, I change my aim to the other two. The driver is bolting off as fast as his short legs will carry him, crashing around the low vegetation off to the side of the truck. The other guard just stands there, arms apprehensively raised in surrender. I put a warning shot over the top of the running driver to prompt him to stop. It misses him by a country mile, although you'd have thought I'd hit him by his reaction. He screams out and dives into a pile of dried foliage, before slowly standing back up again hesitantly. He's now regrettably wearing a heavily bleeding face and bloodied hands raised in the air. No gunshot wound, just dried foliage cuts and scratches.

I take the handcuffs off the driver's belt and cuff him and the other guard together using a hole in a fallen tree root on the side of the track. They'll be able to work their way out of this over the next few hours or so. They'll still be handcuffed together, regardless. Boarke, though, is screaming his guts out, not what I'm expecting from him by any means. I take his cuffs off his belt and handcuff his non-wounded side wrist to one of his ankles. It's a struggle for it to fit. I somehow manage to get it locked into place. It's just a bit tight.

Bugger him. I search their pockets and take out every possession. It's not as if there's anything of threat or value in them.

I drive their truck over to where Rojer is laying. He's trying desperately hard not to laugh too much. "Now look what you've screwed up, Kelly. Well done all the same." He laughs as he coughs up another mouthful of blood. I slowly help him to stand and put him in the tray of the truck. I hack off a bunch of fibrous foliage for him to lay on. Not much else I can do for now. At least he's flat, I guess. I put all three assault rifles into the tray with him, along with the rest of our small hoard of possessions and those of the BCC guys. The guards have a small pile of fruit, so I try to feed Rojer some. No go. He's just in too much pain to eat, so I give him some water instead.

I call RJ again and explain the situation. "Should have killed him," she says. "Best dead than to come after you later, all angry and vengeful. Anyway, it is what it is. What do you want to do now you have their truck? You going to Bula or continue to the Sasol camp?" RJ queries.

"Stuff it, RJ, I have to find someone to have a look at Rojer as soon as possible. He's bleeding out of his mouth pretty heavily, maybe from a lung puncture, so the least amount of movement is what is best at the moment, I think. The Sasol camp is the closest, so I guess it's the go. Can you get me picked up there, do you think? Do they have a fixed wing airstrip that you can get a charter in for me, or maybe a chopper? See what you can do. I'll call again once we get there," I say, as I hang up the phone.

I turn the truck around and slowly, gently drive towards the Sasol camp, trying to minimise the movement impact on Rojer. As we drive past the three handcuffed guards, I stop momentarily, to give them a last look, just to reassure myself they're still well and truly secure. I slowly drive off again, only to stop suddenly at the ear-splitting sound of automatic gunfire. Slamming on the brakes, I jump out of the truck, pointing my gun in every likely direction of where the shooting might have come from. I realise then that Rojer has the barrel of an assault rifle from in the back, pointing over the side of the tray. He's just shot Boarke – well no, he's obliterated him, actually.

"What the hell, Hoag? He was likely to bleed out and die of his wounds here, anyway. Was that necessary?" I snarl, as I angrily grab the rifle from him.

He slumps back down into the foliage in the tray with a smile on his sickly pale face. "Fuck him. He's dead now. He ain't ever going to come after us again, the prick. Let's get the hell outta here, Kelly, will ya? Come on, let's go?" Rojer says, choking on another mouthful of blood.

As it turns out, regrettably, Sasol's paramedic is still at the incident site when we arrive at their camp. I get the sense one of the victims has died, and the other is in a critical condition. Not good news for anybody. Mercifully, the South African camp cook Arnie Prost is also the backup medic for their seismic campaign, so he takes a look at a now very ailing pale grey Rojer.

"Yep, well, you definitely have a pneumothorax – a collapsed lung. Air has leaked into the space between your lung and chest wall, Rojer, no doubt probably caused by your vehicle rollover incident. My guess is a rib has penetrated your lung, or you may have some other sort of chest crush injury that is triggering it. The air pushes on the outside of your lung and makes it collapse. From what I can tell without an x-ray, you seem to have a complete lung collapse, which can be a life-threatening consequence," Arnie says as he injects Rojer with some pain relief medication, morphine with any luck, I'm hoping. He then pulls me aside momentarily.

"He doesn't look well, my friend. I suspect he has some other underlying health concerns as well, which are potentially going to complicate things for him… and maybe me. Anything you know about it that might guide me?" he inquires.

"Yeah, three or four things I'm aware of. He's nearly 70, smokes like a bloody open fire, uses that disgusting chewing tobacco, and he's got emphysema with a side serve of some breed of hepatitis. I'm sure there's a host of other life-defying issues running amok inside him. That's all I know of for sure, though," I reply.

"Righto, well, I'm going to have to treat him urgently. I don't know if you've come across things like this in the past, but I'm going to need your assistance, as I've never performed one of these by myself before." Arnie then explains how it will involve him inserting a hollow needle with a small flexible tube – a catheter – into Rojer's chest, between the air-filled space that's pressing on the collapsed lung, to remove the excess air. This apparently will relieve the pressure on his lung, allowing it to hopefully re-expand. The tube will have a one-way valve device that continuously removes air from the chest cavity until his lung can be more appropriately addressed in a hospital by a doctor.

"You good with that? Once we have this sorted, the nearest and best place to medivac him to will be to the Siloam hospital in Ambon. Makassar General is probably the best bet, only it's too far away, given his condition. It's further over in South Sulawesi."

"I'm good with it. Not sure Rojer will be too pleased to go to Ambon, though. He seems to think that's pretty much the epicentre of the evil universe for these latest conflicts. What are your thoughts?" I query, as we walk back to Rojer, laying on the first aid stretcher, moaning softly now in a drug induced pain-free zone.

"I don't know, I very much doubt it'd matter where you go just at the moment. It's still going to be problematic with the radicals, for now anyway. For my money, whichever one is closer is going to be the most beneficial for him given his severe condition. OK, let's get into this shall we? You ready?" he asks.

By the time Arnie nervously completes Rojer's medical procedure and the pressure is relieved off the lung, Rojer is slowly getting some colour back into his face. Granted, it's returning to his distinctive emphysema colouring, nevertheless, it's a far improvement from the deathly grey and pale tones that where beginning to take over earlier. We monitor him closely, especially for any progress in his breathing and his overall change in condition. He is now fully conscious again.

"We have to get you out of here to a hospital, Rojer. Doctors are going to need to have a much more serious look at you, take some x-rays maybe, things like that. You're not out of the woods yet. My guys have got a chopper on its way here to pick us up. They can take us to the one in Ambon."

"No way, Kelly, that is not going to goddamn happen. I'm not going anywhere near that hell hole, and you know why. I'll stay here for a day or so if I can, then I'll get Saleck to pick me up and take me back to his village to recover." Rojer is adamant.

Arnie is more adamant. "You're not staying here in your condition, rooinek. We've already endured one fatality today with the possibility of a second at that incident site. I know my boss is already stressed out about it and will not take the chance of you potentially being a third. Especially when there's a bloody crystal-clear opportunity for you to be quickly taken to a nearby facility where you can be treated pretty much straight away. Are you hearing me, bru? You are not freaking staying here!" He almost yells the last bit. I can see the agitation is building, and for good reason.

I regard the shocked look on Rojer's face. At the same time, I also hear the faint slapping sound of helicopter blades rotating through the thick air. I point my finger and eyes upwards; the other two have noticed it now as well.

Arnie looks up and listens. "I don't think that's ours. It's a very small unit, this one. Maybe yours? It's a different noise signature to our helicopters." He looks at me and shrugs.

"Decision time, Rojer. You can't stay here, and you have no means of getting to Saleck's village, which we wouldn't recommend if it were even possible somehow. Time to man up and make a mature choice here. Let's get you to Ambon to be looked after properly first thing, yeah? Then, if you want, put your cranky pants on and do whatever or go wherever you want, OK?" I say this whilst looking into Rojer's eyes. I already know he doesn't like being told what to do. I again point upwards as the sound of the approaching helicopter gets closer.

"I'm going in that helo, Rojer. You can come with me if you want. However, if you don't, you can't stay here. Not too many bloody options, bloke," I say, as I put my hand out to help him up, if he wishes. He just stares straight ahead, looking at nothing for the next minute or so, then slowly takes my hand.

Chapter 15

ONCE AGAIN, MY REVERY is disturbed by another knock on the bloody door. I'm too deep into… something, in some place called Bula, to be bothered responding to the knock. Of course, that's considered to be an open invitation to enter by Ray Tallis, as he barges right in. It looks like it's late afternoon outside of my window. Right where I'd like to bloody well be – outside my window.

"How are you feeling, James? It sounds like you're on the mend? Doc tells me you're unhappy about not being released? That probably rests on my shoulders, I'm not sorry to say," Ray shrugs those shoulders in a manner suggesting to me *'bad luck'*. "We still have some crazy people out there wanting to do you harm. As such, it's incumbent on me not to let that happen, James. Hence why we'll have to discuss with you about going into some sort of temporary protection," Ray states.

"Happy to do that every day of the week, Ray, and twice on Sundays, as long as it's with my family," I willingly propose.

"Not going to happen, James, no matter what. Your wife is currently being treated – medicated, actually – to try and help her and your daughter deal with their ordeal from the other morning. I doubt either of them will ever really recover 100% for a very long time. That is one hell of a shock to anybody's system, James, including yours. So, we're going to have to put some space between that distressing morning and you all getting back together again," Ray argues.

"Rubbish, Ray. The best person to help them with this is me, and you know it. I'm the husband and father, and unluckily, someone who's also been through that very same confrontation with them. So unless you have significant medical advice blocking our reunion, I'll be initiating legal action against you and the SA police force for interfering with that reunion," I reply coolly. There is a possibility Ray doesn't recognise the anger developing in my voice.

"Hey, good try, James. Go for it. Fill your boots trying to get that scenario initiated," Ray laughs quietly. "Because there is a very credible and immediate threat to the safety of you and possibly your family, we are obliged to temporarily delay the reunion until the threat is either neutralised or until the relevant protective security measures can be strengthened to ensure your safety."

"Well, that's what I plan to do Ray. I'm going to check myself out of here today, and for the time being, I'll be going back home. Then I'll kick the legal action into gear, so best you hang onto your own boots, Ray, because they might just get filled themselves. I want to be united with my family, end of story. Got that?" I say, trying to keep the intense irritation out of my voice.

"James, I want you to listen up here, OK, very carefully now, and please don't interrupt me. Whether you like it or not, in a situation where there's an immediate and credible threat to your life, we have the legal authority to take whatever emergency protective measures we deem necessary to protect you. Got it? Now, this may, if I should so choose, involve detaining you temporarily to ensure your safety, allowing us time to assess the threat further and to consider other security arrangements. One of those options may also include taking you into WitPro irrespective of you rejecting this option," Ray says, now standing at the end of my bed looking down at me with his best "I'm dead-set serious" look.

"Should you decide to make an arsehole of yourself and cause this to be a more complex situation than is necessary, we can then seek court orders to compel your cooperation. Particularly with regard to security measures, OK? You know, all I'd have to do is present the evidence of this credible threat and the necessity for protecting your life to a judge, and they'd sign off on it in the blink of an eye."

"Still makes no difference to my plans, Ray. I'm outta here this arvo no matter what."

"In extreme cases, James, which I consider this to be by the way, your refusal to enter into temporary protection might be viewed as a risk to public safety. We'd therefore argue the extraordinary measures including temporary custody are necessary to mitigate this particular risk." Ray actually seems to have a smirk on his face when saying this, throwing in the shrugged shoulders look to top off his little speech.

I'm sensing he's slowly escalating the levels of consequential retaliation he's prepared to apply, maybe even eager to utilise it, to shut down my noncompliance.

"Then however, should you continue to still make an arse of yourself further, James, while you're in protective custody, I can quite easily request our psychological health professionals to evaluate your state of mind and your rational decision-making capacity. If it is determined you are not capable of making rational decisions in the face of this very serious threat, psychological health authorities may in fact intervene to protect you specifically and the public in general. Do you want me to spell out what that actually means in big words, James? Have you got it yet? I'm not actually fucking around here; in case you hadn't noticed?"

Ouch, the king hit. I wasn't expecting that one to come at me, although I guess I should have. I don't want to give him any time to think it has an impact on me, although it does. "So tell me then, Ray, how on earth are you ever going to assess the threat further. We don't know for sure who is at the bottom of it or who is involved. With that lack of knowledge, how then are you going to consider other security related arrangements. What might they involve?" I ask, with a somewhat deflated voice now with the mental health threat hanging over me.

"We've been able to track the two Syrians coming through airport immigration on CCTV two days before they visited you, all false names and passports as expected. They're met by another person in the arrivals area, who we believe to be a local Middle Eastern crime colleague. We have now identified him as Ali Dawoud. Do you know him? Maybe heard that name mentioned?"

I shake my head no. "Not that I'm aware of."

"We're in the process of locating him. We'll bring him in if we can find him and have a bit of a chat. Additionally, this might interest you. Yesterday, a burnt-out F250 Ford truck was found in an old quarry on the other side of town, over near Houghton. You know where that is?"

I shake my head no again. I doubt it'd really matter even if I did.

"Anyway, there's a body in the driver's seat, burnt all to hell. Forensics are doing their thing as we speak. The truck apparently has a mangled front left mudguard and headlight. Might be what hit your tractor the other morning?" Ray sort of smiles at his remark. "So, as you can see James, we're not just sitting around waiting for something to fall in our lap. We are making headway. I'm hoping you now grasp why it's important for you to stay in our care until we can bed the last of this down?" he asks.

"Yeah, I suppose I get all that. What I don't get is why I can't at least talk to my wife and daughter on the phone? They must be frantic with worry about me. This has to happen, Ray, and I'm asking you to authorise it. Can you do it for me?" I ask, gradually conceding in my own mind that I'll be entering into one form of safeguard or another.

"Not my place to authorise, James. The only authority for it to happen comes from your wife. She's been adamant in her instructions to us that this is not to occur at the moment. Nothing more I can do about it. She has given us no reasoning for her decision. I can only assume Mrs Kelly has been so terrorised by the incident from the other morning that she has withdrawn into like a protective emotional cocoon for her and your daughter's sake. This happens sometimes, with extreme shock occasions. Give it some more time, James. Let it settle down by itself. Best if you don't push it," Ray says as he turns to leave the room.

"It will be best if you stay here for now. I'll have you transferred out to a secure location late this afternoon or early evening. You still have a guard on your door, in case you have thoughts of attempting to quietly abscond out of here. I'll get back to you later, hopefully with anything further on the F250."

The next week or so goes by in a flurry of nothingness. I'm quietly moved into a safe house at night, via a blacked-out van, down the south coast somewhere I think, at least somewhere I can smell the sea, in a secluded, semi-gated property they hint at. No neighbours, main roads, views, visitors, walks along the beach. No nothing. Security detail is professional at least, talkative and they sure can cook. Hard to work out if they're federal police or SA state police. They won't discuss such things. I'm thankfully not required to have a new identity, name, date of birth or any other personal details changed, as I'm advised my situation is a temporary security program only, unlike a full change of life WitPro, which requires all of those other protective measures. The focus for me evidently is to conceal my identity for the time being rather than creating an entirely new persona. They have let me know, politely, that they intend for me to be out of here as soon as possible. Whatever this actually means in reality is a bit vague to me, as no one can put a timeframe on when this is likely to be.

At the beginning of the second week Ray Tallis arrives, all dressed up in his finery, with my first guest as well, RJ. I am taken aback just a bit to see them… especially both together. The aspect of a joint social call adds an ominous overtone to their visit for me. My gut says watch out for Murphy and sons – or daughters.

"Greetings, James. How are they treating you here?" Ray asks, as he leads us into a private sitting room, already knowing full well how things are working out here.

"You have any update for me, Ray? Or do you dress up in your Sunday best for some other reason?" I ask, whilst observing RJ, who has said nothing as yet, nor has she made any meaningful eye contact.

"Yes, well, quite a few things have changed since you came out here, James. Not least of all, it appears our burnt-out F250 truck is indeed the vehicle that came to your farm in the early hours of the morning a few weeks ago, the same one which ploughed into your tractor on departure." Ray smiles at this clarification, another mystery solved.

"Also, the dead crispy driver, as it turns out, is in fact Ali Dawoud, according to our forensics people, anyway, and they are very good. We get the impression Ali might have been attempting to attach an incendiary device of some sort to a 10 L metal container of accelerant next to him. Presumably to burn up the truck once he departed. It's quite unclear what might have happened next. Our initial assumption is in some way he accidently set off the incendiary device, and the accelerant ignited, setting fire to Ali. The inside driver's side door handle is torn off, so it looks like Ali tried to exit the truck. However, it seems the door wouldn't open for whatever reason," Ray states.

"Or someone set it off for him and locked him in there to burn. That possible? Probable?" I ask Ray quietly. I look over at RJ, who still hasn't made direct eye contact with me. Something's not quite right there.

"Yes, we've also considered that option, although much of the forensic analyses disputes it. I won't go into the dreary technical details of it all. Nonetheless, it appears this scenario doesn't rate highly on their assessments. Suicide is a possibility, except it's rather a gruesome and painful way to go out by your own hand, don't you think?" Ray adds.

I nod at the thought. "So, am I to assume I can now go home, unhindered and unprotected? Is this what this little joint get together is about, to explain all this to me?" I question, slowly looking at both RJ and then Ray, presenting my best French shrug whilst waving my hand at both of them.

"Well, we'd rather another week or so with you here just to be sure. Nonetheless yes, I guess we seem to have closed out as many of the loose ends as we can for now. So I suppose it's up to you now to decide if you want to stay a little longer under protective custody with us or not. I'll leave that with you to ponder James. In the meantime, RJ has some other matters to discuss with you, so I'll leave you both for now. Give me a hoy outside if you want to discuss anything further with me," Ray says, as he walks out of the sitting room, gently closing the double glass doors.

"So then RJ, avoiding eye contact, no greeting on arrival, no supporting Ray's spiel. What in bloody hell is going on here, old girl?" I utter, not entirely unkindly, although with more than just a slight tinge of annoyance in my words.

"I'm actually here to take you home, James. That's the primary reason. We anticipated this to be the case, anyway. I've arranged for your house to be professionally cleaned of all things likely to physically remind you of that ugly morning. The non-visuals of it will no doubt be with you for a very long time."

"C'mon, RJ, give. No way you came all this way out to wherever the hell we are just to pick me up or to tell me that, have you? C'mon girl, what else?" I ask coldly, the ominous part of my earlier thoughts starting to now build an unpleasant picture in my mind's eye, likewise in my chest.

"Correct. So, on that other matter, I met with Carla a couple of days ago," RJ says quietly, almost inaudibly. She looks very apprehensive, suggesting to me this is not going to be a very comfortable conversation for her to give – or me either to receive more like it.

"You know I've not been allowed to talk to either of them since the morning of the incident, yeah? You do know that, RJ? So why has this been the case, eh? Can you maybe get off your well-dressed high horse to explain to me why, RJ? Because its knocked me for six, I can tell you." I throw this at her, almost angrily now, and I'm not in the mood to conceal it.

"It's been Carla's decision all the way, James. No one is allowed to communicate directly with her or Katerina, not just you, initially, anyway. It's for Carla's own good, psychologically. She's an absolute wreck, James, so is Katerina. Carla simply cannot reconcile herself to the level of violence they witnessed that morning. She's really struggling with it. Like, I'm talking really struggling, intrusive memories, leading to disturbing daily nightmares, detailed flashbacks all the time of the harrowing morning. She spends most of the day in tears. They now have a full-time doctor on-site to help deal with her emotional and health well-being. She has a massively increased heart rate, along with something called hypervigilance. I'm not entirely sure what that actually means, so please don't ask me to explain." RJ pauses a moment, I guess to see if I have any questions. I do, many, just not yet.

"I've also spoken to the doctor to see if there's anything we can do to help Carla or Katerina going forward. The doctor earlier suggested she may ultimately be required to go into some sort of a secure psychological health facility, James. That is how much she has deteriorated. She also suffers from an exaggerated distress response. You know what that means?"

I shake my head no. I'd probably be able to guess if I have to.

"Carla flinches or recoils involuntarily at almost anything that moves or makes a noise. Curtains, wind outside, overhead fans casting a flicker, lights coming on, doors opening or closing, things like that." RJ looks sad in the telling of this disorder that has developed.

I'm gutted. Clearly, I've been looking at this all the wrong way. I've been literally sleepwalking my way around it all. "Why has no one bought this to my attention then, RJ. Why have I been kept in the dark over all of this?" I challenge.

"Because there is no value in it for either of you. You're still suffering from your gunshot wound, and Carla was… well, she is enduring a completely different level of distress. She's pretty much isolated herself from everybody, including you. So no matter what you want or feel is the best thing for you or the family unit, it just isn't going to happen, James, regardless. So, we have to abide by

Carla's instructions, until they hopefully change, which they have not as yet."

"In your discussions, has Carla elaborated on anything else in our marriage that might be a problem, maybe something underlying that this incident triggered, something which might have persuaded her to have this reaction?" I'm still struggling with the seemingly conscious lack of communication from Carla. I can't help sense something else is the trigger for this.

"No, nothing else was mentioned. Quite the reverse, in fact. It's not about your marriage James. Apparently, the intensity of violence you displayed that morning is what has scared her. She is petrified of you. The doctor tells me the disturbing encounter has seriously tripped Carla over into almost a catatonic state. She is nearly comatose, almost having a nervous breakdown. They have both been on heavy medication ever since for chronic anxiety disorder. It's impacting her daily functioning, her quality of life, especially as she is pregnant. Do you appreciate what I'm trying to tell you here, James?" RJ says quietly.

I know she's trying to deliver an ugly message as delicately as possible. I'm just shattered all the same at what that message is. "Yes, I do – I understand what you're saying, only not why she is petrified of me, though. I was defending our home as best I knew how, trying to protect her and our daughter. I don't get it. I've never raised an angry word to her, ever, let alone a hand. I simply don't do the family violence thing, never have. It's just not me," I try to desperately explain.

"I know all this, James, I really do. What's more, I honestly believe you. Carla has tried to explain it to me, although I'm not sure I entirely comprehend it myself. I don't believe it's you *"per se"* she's afraid of. It's the violence lying dormant within you, I think, that's what she is concerned about, as it can obviously be triggered. I'm starting to believe we, as in myself and Castelle, are possibly responsible for this, and I'm devastated this might be the case." RJ took a breath; I can sense she's struggling with this potential outcome for her as well.

"We may have perhaps unwittingly reinvigorated this aggressiveness in you after it had probably been resting dormant inside you for all those years. The last two assignments have not at all been easy for you, I agree – or for any of us, actually. Nor have they been in any way what I'd consider 'normal' jobs, whatever the bloody hell that might represent in this ever-changing world," RJ says, hyphenating her fingers to emphasise normal, once again, uncharacteristically swearing.

"So where do we go from here, RJ? Sure, I know I can go back home now if I want. Nevertheless, what I really want is to be reunited with my family. From what I'm hearing from you on the other hand, is this may not be possible, at least not at the moment. Am I hearing this correctly? Is this what you're trying to tell me?" I ask, miserably.

"Basically, yes. Again though, there is much more to it I'm not able to adequately explain. What I'd like you to do first of all is talk with the clinical psychiatrist who is looking after them both. Her name is Doctor Gloria Whylie. She's very compassionate, as well as a very knowledgeable person on this topic. I can call her now if you're ready to discuss things with her?" RJ offers glumly.

"Wha… what! A clinical psychiatrist? They have a clinical psychiatrist in the WitPro house? That sounds unusual to me RJ, doesn't it? A bit of overkill?" I ask, suspiciously.

"No, not at the WitPro house, James. My understanding is Carla's condition deteriorated further this morning. Doctor Whylie called me on the way here to advise both Carla and Katerina have been sedated as a result of their extreme anxiety. They've been taken to that secure health clinic I mentioned earlier. I'd like you to talk to Doctor Whylie now, or maybe a bit later?" RJ prompts.

"Jesus bloody Christ on a stick, RJ, what the hell is happening here? Why didn't you tell me this straight up? How does this all turn around so fast… so badly?" I'm in a deep state of brutal shock, more so now. This is my family going through this!

"I know, it's devastating. They've both been deteriorating over the past week. The degree of stress they've both encountered is extreme. What's more is the Doctor doesn't know why.

Please talk to Doctor Whylie now will you? Let me call her for you?" RJ urges.

"Yeah, whatever," I respond, distressed, well beyond anything I've ever emotionally been through – in my life, which is big call I reckon, as I've got a pretty good, almost exhilarating, storybook of anguished occurrences to quote from. Totally disoriented, lost in my jumbled thoughts, for once I have absolutely no idea what to do next. I'm ordinarily pretty good at manoeuvring myself in, out or around situations on the fly, to think things out on my feet, not today.

"Hallo James, I'm Doctor Whylie. I want to emphasise from the beginning, conversing about distressing events like the violent home invasion again can be upsetting for you as well. It's important we both approach this with utmost compassion in mind. In reality, the impact of a violent home invasion can vary widely from person to person. It's crucial for you to recognise the complexity of the individual responses that Carla and Katerina are experiencing. Are you OK to proceed, James?" Doctor Whylie asks me quietly.

"To be honest, Doc, I have no idea if I'm ready to go with this or not. Let's give it a shot, anyway. I have to warn you, though, I'm probably distressed just as much because I've not been allowed to talk to them or see them. I'm in a very awful place right at this point in time," I say, feeling the tremors in my voice giving my anxiety away.

"I can believe it. As you suggest, let's move slowly with this. Admitting anybody to a high security psychological health clinic is a very critical step to take. It's one we have not taken lightly. Disappointingly, none of the treatment we have prescribed so far for either of them has given us the reactions we'd hoped for. I suspect Katerina is sadly feeding off her mother's extreme anxiety, as she doesn't know how to deal with the distressing morning by herself. Are you following, James?"

"Yes, please continue." I reply mournfully.

"Carla's immediate reactions after the incident have been quite predictable. It's what we'd have expected – things like shock, fear, disbelief, a sense of unreality to the actual episode itself. That unfortunate occurrence has led her to heightened levels of fear, anxiety and fatigue, making it difficult for either of them to feel safe, even in their secure witness protection surroundings. I believe Carla perhaps feels a little guilty or maybe even ashamed, she's questioning whether she should have done more or something differently during that distressing incident. Combine this with her now also suffering severe headaches, gastrointestinal distress along with other disquieting physical symptoms like hypervigilance which has also begun to arise in her. Katerina as well, due to the stress response. Do you understand what hypervigilance is, James?" Doctor Whylie queries.

"No not really." I have undeniably no idea what anything means at this very moment.

"OK, hypervigilance is really where we're at right now. It's a condition characterised by an overactive and overly sensitive nervous system. In this state of mind, Carla's sensory information processing is inaccurate. This leads to a heightened awareness and responsiveness to almost all stimuli in her environment. Her nervous system has become what we call "dysregulated", which refers to an imbalance or malfunction in the normal functioning of the system. Traumatic occurrences like the home invasion disrupt the regulation of her nervous system. Normally, it would release stress signals. I won't bore you with the medical technicalities of this, but these signals are in response to perceived perils or dangers. This is a natural defence mechanism designed to prepare the body to face challenges. In cases of chronic dysregulation, the system continuously and inappropriately releases stress signals, particularly in situations where there is no real threat. This leads to an ongoing state of heightened alertness, of sensitivity, which is not beneficial. Due to the chronic dysregulation, she is experiencing responses entirely disproportionate to the actual level of any danger in her environment. For example, a minor stressor might trigger an intense or even exaggerated reaction. Still with me, James?" Doctor Whylie checks on me.

"Yes, sort of, I think," I reply. No is actually the real answer.

"The violent home invasion was the trigger for the dysregulation of her nervous system. Experiencing this distress has disrupted the normal functioning of it, leading to persistent hypervigilance, which is where we currently are. The chronic release of the stress signals lead to constant responses, which are emotionally and physically exhausting for her. In summary, hypervigilance is a condition where the nervous system is stuck in this amplified state of an anxious mind. It continuously reacts to a wide range of stimuli as if they're real threats coming at her from every direction, when in fact there are none. That's what we're dealing with here, James. Both of them are categorically exhausted, beyond just nervous exhaustion. This is why they are now here under expert professional care, along with being sedated, for their own well-being. Do you have any questions about what I've just explained James?" Doctor Whylie enquires.

Do I have any bloody questions? Where the hell to start? After maybe a silent minute or so I reply. "Can I at least visit them?"

"Not at the moment. This facility has specific visitation policies, which doesn't encourage family involvement at the early stages of admission. I'll get you connected with her treatment team; you can consult with them to get a better grasp of the best way you can support Carla. This will include discussions about the possible impact of any visits by you on her healing process. You must appreciate James, Carla's wishes and comfort level in relation to family visitation must be respected. Typically, family visits are a big part of a gradual reintegration process, allowing them to reconnect with a support system while still receiving the necessary therapeutic care. Apart from that, visiting can be emotionally challenging for you all. So, it's essential for you to prepare yourself for a range of emotions or even rejections and to approach any visits with sympathy and compassion. Ultimately, the decision to allow you to visit will be based on their needs under the guidance of the treatment team. I know this is probably not what you want to hear, James, although we're desperately attempting to avert a full-blown cerebral breakdown with Carla."

Christ, those bloody pricks from BCC. I'm enraged, infuriated at their pointless and dangerous intervention into our lives and what has now occurred with Carla and Katerina. I thank Doctor Whylie and arrange to talk with her again tomorrow. Then I ask RJ to get me the hell out of here.

The long drive back home to the farm is initially in almost stony silence. I've got so many conflicting emotions grinding away inside, I can't tell the difference between my arse and my elbow anymore. I'm just so exhausted from the after-effects of the home invasion itself still and the subsequent medications. I do know though, that I've got to keep trying to push my way beyond all this, one way or another, for Carla and Katerina's sake.

"So, RJ, maybe it's time you gave me a bit of a head's up from your debrief with Ben? How did it all go?" I ask glumly. I don't really want to know such things at the moment, but with my mind in such turmoil over my family's situation, I might benefit from a moment or two of distraction.

"OK, but is now such a good time though? Do you think you're really ready for a chat about it at the moment? You seem pretty strung-out with all these other things on your mind, James. You sure you don't want to wait and do this later, after things settle down for you?"

"Nah, let's give it a go. I need to get my mind off these other issues. Hopefully, a diversion like this might do me the world of good." I reply optimistically, as I pick up a delicate waft of RJ's fragrant perfume drift around the car.

"Alrighty then, if you say so. Well, according to Ben, it seems everything was pretty much not going to plan from the start of the trip. For the first few hours or so, as Ben tells it, the minister was acting quite strange throughout, quite irritated and continually panicking over something. He was asking Ben all sorts of oddball questions, demanding he call Serge and tell him to meet them in Laayoune as soon as possible. The minister also kept talking angrily to the driver in Arabic periodically throughout the journey. It gave Ben the impression the minister and the driver were both very rattled about something. I think you knew about the call to Serge, didn't you?" she queries.

"Yeah, Serge told me about it when I called to alert him Ben was missing. What sort of oddball questions was the minister asking? Did he tell you?" I query.

"Not really. He didn't elaborate too much on it but evidently the minister kept asking him 'why did that happen' and 'why did you do that'? Except, when Ben asked him what he meant, that was when he demanded Ben call Serge. He couldn't get the minister to explain what he was referring to, except it seemed as if he was blaming Ben or the project team for something." RJ took a breath and hesitated for a second or two.

"All sounds very suss, doesn't it? What are your thoughts on it?" I question.

"As I've said previously, I was already of the belief the minister was deep into whatever exploitation was going on outside of the EEZ. My money was on it having already been in place long before the radar project commenced, and it had nothing to do with overfishing, more likely guns or drugs. He somehow screwed it up with whatever arrangements were in place, or maybe he betrayed whatever agreement he had in place with all the Muhammads out there, and it all turned to grief. Like maybe authorising those unofficial last-minute trials out past the EEZ limits, lighting up all those vessels huddled up out there?" she infers.

"Yeah, hence the rapid departure next morning, I guess? He was probably watching the radar when that collection of vessels out there dispersed once the radar latched onto them. Then the analyst, becoming alarmed about the EMP attack, doubtless sent him into a panic. He knew he was in trouble and possibly mistakenly thought by coercing Ben to go with him, he might be safe from whatever he feared," I suggest.

"Yes, possibly. Anyway, Ben said things changed then, just before they got to Dakhla. Which I think is what... about 4–5 hours away from Nouadhibou?"

"Yeah, around about that, the whole trip is a bit of a hike actually when you consider it's then another six or so hours to Laayoune. Rumour has it the minister is terrified of flying so he always chooses to go back and forth by road it seems."

"My understanding is Ben was becoming concerned and asked for a pit stop so the driver called it in to their security escort, who directed them into that unscheduled stop at the wayside 'hanout' shanty store. As Ben got out of their car, he sensed something was definitely not right, so he turned to go back and get his phone and bag out of the back seat. One of the security guys pushed him away from the car, which understandably alarmed Ben. By this stage the minister and his driver were also out of the other side of the car arguing heatedly with the security team. Ben was close to the 'hanout' and took a chance while this was happening, walked inside, then asked to use the owners' phone. Seems he had a wad of local money on him that inspired the store guy to give Ben his phone, this was when he called you, yes?"

"Bloody hard to forget that RJ, it's what started this whole thing off."

"So, my understanding from there is that while he was on the phone to you, one of the security guys who had been looking for him, stormed up behind and tried to snatch the phone away, miscalculating momentarily. It gave Ben enough time to end the call with you calmly, but with a few key words he said. He desperately wanted to scream for help from you but was reluctant at the time because he felt it might aggravate the situation, which at that point, he was wholly unsure of what the situation really was anyway." RJ takes a gasp as she slightly misjudges a sharp corner of the road, composes herself and starts again.

"The security guard dragged Ben back outside and pushed him into the backseat of their car. It sounds like it was all very hostile by then. The minister and the driver were already in the car, with a black bag or hood over the head of the driver. The phones and bags had been taken; Ben never saw them again. You sure you're OK to keep going with this James?" RJ asks nervously.

"Yeah, after all we've been through its interesting to connect some of the dots don't you think? Keep going."

"OK then. Before they left that 'hanout', Ben said he and the minister had putrid black hoods put over their heads as well, and their wrists zip tied. Evidently, the minister wasn't favourable to this treatment and began arguing fiercely with the security guys, trying to push back with this being done to him. They retaliated by attacking him, violently it seems, the minister that is. Quite a few heavy blows, like something hard hitting flesh and bone Ben said. He was terrified at this stage as you could imagine, especially as he couldn't see anything. Lots of thuds, grunts and groans, then silence. Ben suspected the minister had probably been beaten unconscious. They were then driven away, doing an about turn, driving off rapidly, he said it felt like it was about an hour afterwards they eventually stopped somewhere near the coast and he was transferred into a truck of some sort. My guess is this might have been at that old El Argoub resort where they found the security support car buried in the sand? Remember that?"

"Yeah, bloody hell, they didn't get far did they, any thoughts yet on why it all turned to shit, we're talking about a government minister here, no small thing when you think about it?"

"No idea. Apparently not long after that they parked near a beach, Ben could hear the waves crashing and the strong smell of the sea. He was hustled roughly into a boat, by himself and the boat operator, immediately covered with a tarp or something similar. The boat motored away from the beach calmly he said, it seems they bounced around for quite a while before they eventually stopped along-side another much bigger boat, which he was transferred to. After what he thought felt like at least a couple of days onboard there, he was moved to the wreck out in the bay at Nouadhibou." RJ took a deep breath and looked over at me momentarily.

"That was the end of things for him, he didn't see anybody, hear anything about the minister or the driver after that. In fact, he felt his kidnappers had no idea what he was talking about when he kept asking about the minister, not that the dialogue was all that easy with the Islamists not speaking much English and Ben not wanting them to know he spoke some Arabic."

"Well, I guess that kinda makes sense when we take into account what we had been told about those jihadi's buying and selling their captives. They probably had no idea about who or what the minister was, or the driver… or probably cared." I reply.

"Yes, all very messy isn't it?" RJ says quietly, seemingly in deep thought.

"I've just had a bizarre thought RJ. Remember those two treacherous looking hoers I mentioned who were out in the workshop with Samir? That was early the next morning, right after those unauthorised runs. You know what I'm thinking? I reckon they were sent there to deal with the minister, my guess is because of those runs capturing all the vessels partying it up just outside of the EEZ the night before. The minister had already left though, he had probably by then anticipated he was in deep shit of some sort. Samir had most likely informed them about the minister having left earlier, with Ben, which screwed up their assassination plans. Doubtless next on their hit list was me and Samir." I reflected on that small window in time, for a moment or two, on how lucky I was to have actually gone down to the workshop in the first place.

"I basically got away because I saw one of them with the machine pistol, while unfortunately Samir stayed, and got very dead, brutally, unexpectedly." The realisation of all this was like a gut punch to me, Samir was in all probability trying to talk those guys around, from doing whatever it was he thought they'd been sent to do. I was saddened for him, and his extended family who relied on him as the only bread winner. All because of the treacherous minister.

"My God, that makes perfect sense James, doesn't it? What a hell of a predicament that prick of a minister created." RJ says slowly, seemingly considering all of the various issues.

We fell into another period of thoughtful silence between us once again, broken as we eventually arrive at the front gate entrance to my property. I can't help but immediately notice our entrance sign is missing, my original hand carved wooden 'Kasbah' sign that I put up so many years ago. I query RJ about the missing sign, she just shrugs and quickly looks away, back to the road. I couldn't interpret what the shrug or the look was about, maybe she was unaware of the absent sign herself, I guess. She has nothing further to offer, other than to suggest maybe the police have taken it for some unknown reason. I don't believe it's likely to be the case although I'll follow it up with them anyway.

RJ steers us up the long winding gravel driveway to our house, with all the unique skills and detachment of a kamikaze pilot who by some means has miraculously survived his… her mission. Having been away so much recently and with so many other uninvited distractions interfering in our lives of late, I'd almost forgotten about the invigorating occurrence of autumn on the farm. The vast kaleidoscope of changing leaf colours from the many deciduous trees is awesome, varying shades of red, orange and yellow, it's like a hand-made embroidery of brilliant colours, dazzling. I wind my window down to better appreciate the beauty of the season, inhaling the brisk afternoon breeze stirring up the aroma of fallen leaves being gently blown around. A couple of kangaroos are munching away at the grass verge of the track, unfazed by our intrusion, along with 3 deer further down. Unlike the many rabbits now running frantically around in the dappled sunlight breaking out under the tree canopies. Viewing it out of the car window, the atmosphere is so serene it's almost like I'm seeing the place for the very first time. It appears so curiously different to me now, almost alien, as if it belongs to someone else.

"Remember the first time you came out here, a few years ago RJ?" I ask, looking across at this elegant, attractive woman driving me.

"Yes James I do. Been quite some water under the bridge since then hasn't there?"

"Yes, there has been. I think that old bridge is pretty much utterly rooted now sadly. It's hard to forget your pitch from back then… *get involved in some of our more interesting projects* you said, *still maintain the lifestyle you have here* I remember you saying something like that, wasn't it? Then there's also the stringer about *there'll be some travel, maybe a touch of danger, nothing like what you've under-*

gone previously, no war zones.' you said. I remember it well, all those encouraging lines you delivered back then. What bloody garbage RJ." I say as I burst out laughing.

RJ joined in, laughing raucously. "I know, I know. Can you accept I actually meant every word of it believe it or not? We have never, not ever, been exposed to any of our assignments escalating into what you have encountered in Indonesia, West Africa and what happened to the guys in Karachi. I shit you not James, I swear." RJ looks at me with what I assume she intends as a serious expression. "Cross my girl guide heart." She implores.

"Yeah well, whatever. You know, as I ultimately got involved with your team, l soon realised you're really only slightly different, better funded, organised and much more diverse brand of what I was part of in Vietnam, so many years ago." I say as I roll out of her car and limp, at a snail's pace, up the steps to the house veranda. Apprehensive as to what I'm likely to find once I go past that front door, how I'm likely to feel.

"I can't believe you think that of us James, we're nothing like what those guys were about, absolutely nothing – in any manner. Anyway, let's not talk about this at the moment, plenty of time for us to do it later. Right now, I have to know how you're feeling, are you OK to go inside? You're probably experiencing a pretty complex mix of psychological and physical emotions at this moment, about facing the scene again?" RJ asks warily, eyeing me intently.

"I have no idea actually RJ. I don't know how I feel about anything right at this very point in time. Let's just get it over with, shall we?" I say as she unlocks the house door for me and pushes it open, handing the keys back to me.

"I'll let you be alone in there for a bit James, with whatever thoughts come to the surface. I'll be in the garden. Call me if you want anything – maybe if you want to talk about it, or... I don't know, whatever?" RJ says quietly as she turns and clacks back down the wooden steps in her bright coloured high heels. Good luck in the garden with those heels on are my immediate thoughts.

I hesitate momentarily before I step inside. Still stunned and angry at the unexpected nature of the attack that morning. I feel claustrophobic the instant I walk into the now sanitised and antiseptic smelling kitchen, glancing down that dreadful passageway, also heavily decontaminated. I can still see all the blood and violence in my mind's eye, knowing instinctively, I can no longer live here… ever again. My anxiety at being back in here is immediate. Memories of the ordeal come flooding back in a miasma of bloodshed, noise and foul odours, all associated with the distressing encounter. I begin to feel vulnerable, physically and emotionally, becoming aware of a sensation of discomfort in the left side of the chest. It's like a worrisome pressure, squeezing my torso as I gasp for breath, I break out into a cold sweat. Thankfully, the pain only lasts for a minute or so, going away almost as quickly as it arrived. I'm feeling a little weak, light-headed, probably as a result of the distress of being back in this dreadful environment. I pour a glass of water and sit down to drink it greedily, thinking about what just happened to me. My concern I suppose, is I may be experiencing a mild heart attack, no big shock there, given what my body's been through over the past month or so – and my nervous system.

Then it comes back suddenly, ferociously. I'm shocked at the sudden onset of this chest pain again, rapidly becoming extremely distressed now as whatever it is, it's also ventured into my jaw, neck and back. The pain is like a burning or a clenched fist squashing my chest, then bit by bit it travels to both my arms. Breathing is suddenly more difficult; I begin to experience a sharp aching in my stomach. I know instantly, for sure, I'm definitely suffering some sort of heart issue, making me break into a cold sweat; skin now all clammy. A catastrophic feeling of impending doom invades my head as I desperately try to call out to RJ. Dizziness overcomes me, I try to stand up then instantly collapse down onto the hard wooden kitchen floor. My mind is undergoing intense fear and anguish about this immediate health crisis. Fever and nausea begins to crawl all over me, forcing me to vomit, right onto the floor in front of me. It feels like an extremely heavy weight has been placed on my chest and suddenly my entire body has just become so exhausted, so tired.

Laying on the floor, I reflect on the vulnerability of life and its fragility, the unpredictability of whatever this medical situation is I'm undergoing. Especially when alone, which makes it way more fearful. A renewed appreciation for life and a determination to overcome this challenge tries to force its way into my consciousness, as I reflect on the susceptibility of my own mortality. My inner life journey reminds me of another time in years gone by, where I had again contemplated the purpose of life and my place in it. During that particular instance, I was facing a potential end-of-life encounter from various gun-shot wounds in Vietnam. I remember thinking then, as I thought my life was ebbing away, 'so then, this is dying, it's not so bad is it?'

About the Author

KERRI REEKS WAS BORN in Adelaide in 1953 and spent his formative years in Broken Hill, Cockburn, and later Mount Gambier. At 18, he enlisted in the Royal Australian Army and qualified as a Sapper in the Corps of Engineers, training in combat engineering, earthmoving construction, minefield clearance, and demolition. Though fully trained, he did not serve in Vietnam.

Following his military service, Kerri carved out a diverse career — first as a multi-award-winning landscape gardener, then as the owner and operator of both a restaurant and a hotel. For over 35 years since, he has consulted in the global oil and gas industry, working across more than 60 countries. Along the way, he earned a Graduate Diploma and a Graduate Certificate in International Disaster Management.

His writing draws heavily on his international experiences and the many cultural intersections encountered throughout his travels. Castelle, his second novel, continues the journey of James 'Ned' Kelly, the central character introduced in his first book Cage of War, a story inspired by the Vietnam War.

Kerri now lives in the Adelaide Hills on a small acreage with his partner and their dog, Beau. When he's not consulting to the energy sector or working on his next novel, he finds joy in landscaping and nurturing his property.